UPGRADED

UPGRADED

EDITED BY
NEIL CLARKE

WYRM PUBLISHING

UPGRADED

Wyrm Publishing
www.wyrmpublishing.com

For more information, contact Wyrm Publishing:
wyrmpublishing@gmail.com

ISBN: 978-1-890464-30-1 (trade paperback)
ISBN: 978-1-890464-31-8 (ebook)

Second Printing

*For Arachne Jericho
& the doctors who rebuilt me.*

CONTENTS

CONTINUED

INTRODUCTION

NEIL CLARKE

I remember when I saw my first cyborg. It was 1974 and I was watching *The Six Million Dollar Man* on channel seven. I was riveted by the continuing story of Steve Austin and his bionic upgrades. It wasn't long before all the kids were running around in slow-motion saying "dit dit dit dit," and I was among them. We all dreamed that someday we'd become "Better . . . stronger . . . faster."

On the other side of the coin, TV has provided us with ample reasons to fear a cyborg future. Among the most popular, we have the Cybermen (*Doctor Who*), the Borg (*Star Trek*), and Darth Vader (*Star Wars*). We must avoid becoming "more machine than man" and resist being upgraded at all costs.

In the 80s, cyberpunks gave us another view of our cyborg future. There was power in having implants, but it was also dark, edgy and dangerous. Imagine a world where new skills or memories could be bought and downloaded or where you could visit with a friend in a virtual reality . . . but cyborgs, like the computers and networks of today, could be also compromised, used, and destroyed by hackers or our even own governments.

Media and literature have provided us a lot to think about. The cyborg has been used to thrill, frighten, inspire, and educate us about just what it is to be human. Since the term was first coined in 1960—by Manfred Clynes and Nathan S. Kline—the science has finally caught up with the theory. There are cyborgs among us, and in 2013, I became one of them.

The genesis of this anthology starts a few months earlier, in July 2012. I was attending a science fiction convention and suddenly felt ill. What I thought was food poisoning would, a few hours later, reveal itself to be a heart attack. Fortunately, we were less than two blocks away from the Lahey Clinic, a well-respected and excellent hospital in Burlington, MA. Many hours later, they would explain to me that I was one of the lucky ones and that I had survived a "widow maker." They had been able to place two stents in my heart, but it would be weeks before they knew the full extent of the damage. Back at home, months later, my cardiologist made his final assessment of the damage: it was considerable and I was immediately directed to the electro-cardiologist across the street for a consultation. He agreed. The blood flow in my heart was less than half of what it should be and that placed me in a high-risk group. Given my age, they advised that I get a defibrillator and in mid-January 2013, I did.

There isn't a day that goes by that I don't notice the box that sits between my ribs and skin. Its wires snake their way through an artery and into my heart, where they are screwed into place. In the event I should need it, that box will notice and send a potentially life-saving jolt of electricity into my heart. I download the data from that box—wirelessly—into another device that shares all the collected data with my doctor. I have a special card that I have to show to hospitals and airport security, and I have to avoid magnetic fields. There's even a speaker built into this thing. Let me tell you, when a warning tone starts playing from within your chest, it gets your attention. I've asked to get a USB port and headphone jack added, but that option is not available or a bit too forward-thinking. Guess I won't be a data mule anytime soon.

As I recovered from my surgery, I made a passing joke about being a cyborg editor. Did I pick the right field or what? It also occurred to me that while I had edited *Clarkesworld Magazine* for years, I had never edited an original anthology. Why not start with cyborgs? Shouldn't one of our own be editing that one? It was an idea that just wouldn't die and thanks to some wonderful people (many of them listed as honorary cyborgs in the appendix of this book) and the power of Kickstarter, I was given the chance. This book makes the best of a bad thing.

When I was a kid, I wondered what ability I'd get. Strength? Super-learning? Better eyesight? It never crossed my mind that my cyborg upgrade would be a failsafe system.

The cyborg future is now. We are among you.

Neil Clarke
May 2014

ALWAYS THE HARVEST
YOON HA LEE

Nissaea-of-the-Slant wasn't even looking for an eye implant in the mazeway lode when she came across the half-smashed ocular. It was worthless in any case, and she gritted her teeth at her bad luck. A hand was what she needed, and this was her last chance. The sputtering confounders, the only ones she'd been able to afford, would give out sooner or later, and then she wouldn't be able to hide her illegal implant-mining from the Watch.

She was about to try again to the left when she heard the sound. It was hard to make out. In the city above, she heard the echoes of a distant chant accompanied by drums, undoubtedly temple services. She must have been down here longer than she'd realized. And the damned drums made it harder for her to hear anything else. She straightened and looked around, ready to spring toward the nearest exit at the slightest indication of trouble.

It took only a moment a locate the source of the noise. Crumpled near one of the heaps of partially digested motherboards was a slight figure, smaller even than Nissaea herself. Nissaea's darkvision (a simple modification based on a sensor patch, not a full ocular replacement) didn't offer much discrimination. She didn't want to draw attention from the tunnels by switching on a brighter light source, just in case, but she was still dismayed at herself for not spotting the figure earlier.

I have to get out of here, Nissaea thought, edging away as quickly as she could without tripping over the wrack of discarded packaging, outcroppings, bent pipes. Just before her circle had cast her out for the circuit-infection that had disabled her hand, she'd heard persistent rumors of a murderer lurking in the mazeways. Not that murder was anything new, especially among the undercircles and those who had no circle at all, but the descriptions of the corpses had been particularly gory and Nissaea preferred not to take chances. She was halfway to the exit from the chamber to the lower mazeways when a new sound stopped her.

"Water," the figure said softly, in a voice not so much sexless as pure of timbre. It had lifted its head and was watching Nissaea with eyes of indeterminate color.

Nissaea could have kept on going, but the utter hopelessness in its eyes stopped her. The voice's owner expected her to abandon it. She remembered how the head of her former circle, Addit, had turned his back to her the moment she showed up with the infection. It hadn't even been worth pleading to buy part of a new hand on credit and pay the rest back later. She wasn't going to be like Addit. Well, not straightaway.

"How long have you been there?" she demanded in a fierce whisper.

It bowed its head, drew a shuddering breath. "Always," it said, a questioning lilt to its voice, then: "Always."

The answer made no sense, but she assumed that it was addled from being trapped down here who knew how long. All at once she made up her mind, and offered it her canteen. It looked at her, awaiting her nod before taking one measured sip, then a second one.

In the meantime, Nissaea took the opportunity to scrutinize the stranger. One of its eyes was artificial and almost seemed to glow faintly in facets, insectine. The other, human eye, set in a face quiltwork-patched together from alternating swatches of metal and skin, was sunken and fever-bright. An extravagant inlaid mark, like a captive prism, decorated one cheek. It was weirdly incongruous beneath the melancholy human eye. And then there were its hands: the left one, although a prosthetic, was very close to human in shape, except for the stubby pearlescent talons, which looked like they might retract. The right arm, worryingly thin, was of flesh, and led down to fingers with bitten nails. The stranger wore a shift too large for it, and no shoes, revealing too human feet with scarred soles.

"Drink," Nissaea said, realizing it wasn't going to take any more unless she said to.

It took three more sips, paused, then allowed itself one more. Nissaea found this polite parsimony oddly endearing. Then it said, "Thank you," and sank partway down with a whispered exhalation.

They were interrupted by a distorted sound from above: rough voices, some buzzing and scarcely human, and the thump of footsteps above the chamber, mediated through layers of honeycombed metal and nestled pipes. Nissaea couldn't quite make out what the speakers were saying, but she was betting that that was the guttural rhythm of the Watch's dialect. More to the point, if they were Watch and they could hear the reverberations under their feet, they might figure out there was an illegal dig here. She'd thought that this chamber was some distance from their usual patrol routes, but apparently not.

"Go," the stranger said. "You can't let them find you."

"I can't leave you here," Nissaea returned, although this was patently untrue. Still, she remembered how it had stung when Addit had discarded her, the moment when she'd gone from valued scavenger to unnecessary expense. She could do better than that, be better than that.

"I won't be able to keep up with you," it said.

"Are they after you?"

It looked confused by the question. "Why would they be after me?"

Hell with it. They shouldn't linger here any longer. "Come with me," she said insistently. When it didn't respond, she tugged hard on its human hand.

The stranger wasn't completely stupid. It didn't jerk away from her, or yank itself out of the mess of rough-edged debris, not that it looked like it had much strength for that sort of thing anyway. Instead, as carefully as it could, it worked itself loose from the entanglement of chiaroscuro wires. Its breath hitched when a sharp edge scraped across its ankle, although Nissaea couldn't help being glad that the segment was flesh, not something that would have made a louder noise.

At last it stood. The footsteps had paused abruptly. Nissaea heard snatches of words, as clear as hallucinations of water: *illegal, hollow, rats in the tunnels.* She cursed inwardly.

"This way," she breathed, glancing back once. She couldn't see anything; had it sunk back down? But she couldn't afford to wait any longer, either. She padded to the exit leading downward and plunged past. Dank air soughed through the darkness, smelling nauseatingly of metallic precipitates and mold.

The Watch was tapping, tapping, tapping. She could hear their scanners' thrum at the base of her skull. It wouldn't be long before they located her confounders and destroyed them.

Nissaea heard an intake of breath, and risked turning on the smallest of lights, a pin-flicker in her wrist. It was the only thing in her prosthetic that still functioned. "Don't lose sight of me in the mazeways," she said without slowing down. "Stay close. I won't have time to backtrack and search for you."

"Yes," the stranger said, very quietly.

The distinct sizzle-zap-pop of confounders being overloaded followed them into the mazeways. Nissaea's darkvision helped her less than she would have liked. Most well-equipped scavengers opted for wide-spectrum oculars for situations like this. However, Nissaea had spent many hours in the mazeways, and she knew them well. In the swollen shadows, she could see great wheels of uncertain diameter and unknown purpose, wrecked resonators, crystal displays roused to phantom splendor in this faintest of lights. The footing was unsure, and more than once she had to slow, as much as she hated any delay, to pick a safe route through the corrugated rubble.

Clanging noises tracked them through the mazeways, knotting and unknotting in unsettling bursts. Nissaea reminded herself more than once to breathe. If the Watch was close enough to hear her breathing, she'd already have a bullet in her back anyway. By this point she had forgotten about her impetuous decision to drag the stranger with her. If anything, she assumed it had gotten lost some time back.

Then she heard a shout, distant but angry. For once she lost her composure and bolted forward and to the right without having any clear plan for where to go next, panic translated into pure motion. Her foot caught hard on something hard and thin, a wire perhaps. She went down. Only the habits of survival kept her from crying out as she thumped down with appalling loudness against a shape made of sharp angles. Her palms were scraped raw, and her breath whooshed out between her teeth.

"I'm here," the stranger said in its soft, colorless voice. Nissaea was too busy fighting back sobs to answer, or even to be surprised at its presence. It didn't bother her with further attempts at conversation. Instead, it offered its hand, gently at first, then more insistently. Once she understood its intent—the pain was making her stupid—she accepted its help stumbling to her feet. A deep roar reverberated through the passages, and she flinched: they were getting awfully close.

Her shin throbbed abominably and a sticky warmth soaked her pant leg. She risked fumbling for a tube of skinseal, almost dropping it in her haste, and rolled up her pant leg to apply it as best she could in the dark. It didn't feel as though she'd quite covered the wound, but it would have to do.

Another roar. Footsteps and their echoes pattered through the mazeways like a drumroll. Nissaea wasn't one of the lucky people with an acoustic analyzer that, combined with an up-to-date map, would tell her exactly where the sounds were coming from. The mazeways changed hourly, little by little, and mapping them was a profession in itself.

"Where?" the stranger said. She realized it was asking the question for the second time.

"They won't gas us," Nissaea said, a hope she would normally have kept to herself, except the pain was still muddling her thoughts. The mazeways connected too many inhabited areas, or more accurately, too many areas inhabited by people who paid protection money to the Watch, or who had influence with the city's high circles. "But they haven't given up."

"I can still hear them," the stranger agreed, just as softly as before. "Point the way."

Nissaea squinted into the shadows. For a horrible moment she couldn't tell where they were. Then she found the passage she remembered and pointed. The stranger took her hand again and led her in.

Nissaea wasn't one of those people who was timelocked to the city's cycles. She spent the next interval in a haze, guiding them each time the stranger squeezed her hand. Ordinarily the power drain of her implants would have given her some indication of passing time, but she was having trouble monitoring her internals, and the few that had associated clocks had never been all that reliable.

She came out of her haze when they ran into the corpse. The stranger didn't seem to notice it, or didn't slow when they approached it, at any rate. In all fairness, Nissaea almost didn't notice it herself. There was no smell of blood, or shit, or decay, or any of the weary universals she associated with death. Instead, a wavering, almost aquatic fragrance permeated the air, as of certain preservatives.

The corpse had had its spine cracked backwards into a bridge-like arc, and was suspended by a spider-profusion of wires that led tautly to the chamber's walls and ceiling. Unfocused glass beads shone from the wires, held in place by barbed hooks. No evidence remained of whatever tools had been used to pound open the sternum and scrape out the organs, or extract the eyes—she could just barely see the trails that the optic nerves made down the corpse's face, arranged into butterfly curves. In the low light it was impossible to discern colors clearly, probably a blessing. Everything appeared in washed-pale blues and sullen whites and silhouette blacks. The murderer had done an especially conscientious job of draining the blood, to the point where it almost wasn't clear the corpse had ever possessed any.

"Are you hurt?" the stranger said, having finally noticed that Nissaea wasn't moving forward.

"So it's true about the murderer," Nissaea said.

Nissaea wasn't squeamish. She had seen her share of back-alley deaths, learning from an early age to hide when the Watch took out its need for hilarity on some vagabond. In particular, she'd learned enough to be distantly grateful that the guardsman who had taken her original hand, long ago, hadn't thought of something more inventive to do.

Nevertheless, the corpse bothered her, mainly because of the finicky thoroughness with which it had been arranged. It was almost possible to regard it as a sculpture, or a puzzle. Focus on the cleanness of the incisions, of the precisely placed punctures that the wires made in the body, and you could admire the murderer's skill; focus on the mathematical curve of the spine and the graceful angles of the limbs, and you had to wonder if the murderer had some aesthetic insight to convey.

"We should go," the stranger said, only a little questioning. "There's nothing useful left here."

"What if the murderer's down here looking for us too?" Nissaea said. There was an odd warning twinge in her leg, higher than the injury, and it worried her.

"Staying still won't help us," the stranger said dryly. "Please. Let's go."

Reluctantly, Nissaea looked away from the corpse, and they hobbled out of the chamber together. Her imagination insisted that the corpse was muttering at their backs, even if she couldn't hear anything, and even if the flow of air currents was dank and steady.

They proceeded more carefully after that, alert to every chance clatter and pin-drop trickle of sound. It seemed that the Watch had lost their trail, or lost interest, anyway, but Nissaea couldn't help flinching every time she heard something unexpected. To her mortification, her damaged hand went into convulsions just as they nudged their way onto a bridge of stiff swaying fibers, fingers spasming in rattling metallic syncopation. *Not now*, Nissaea begged the universe, although it was unlikely that it mattered at this point.

The stranger stopped, to her dismay. "This injury," it said, gaze going directly to the prosthetic. "An old one?"

She tried to shove past it, which the bridge was too narrow to permit if it was determined not to let her. "It's not important," she said through her teeth. After all, she thought wildly, a hand that alternated between being dead and going into spasms still beat being cut up like the corpse back there. "We're not far from the Cat-Eyed Gate. Let's keep going."

To her surprise, the stranger didn't argue this, although she could sense its unhappiness. Why it wanted to deal with diagnostics just this moment was beyond her, but since it wasn't pressing the point, neither would she.

At last the bridge was far behind them, and they reached the Cat-Eyed Gate. It had been mined out years ago, and nothing remained but the occasional chatoyant glimmer of green or blue or gold substrate.

"This is the gate?" the stranger asked.

By now Nissaea was panting softly. Her entire leg hurt now, hot raking fingers of pain that were even now reaching upward. "Yes," she said, or thought she said. She wasn't sure she had much of a voice left.

"Tell me where to take you," the stranger said.

She had the vague thought that this had started with her intent to help the stranger and not the other way around. She opened her mouth to protest, but nothing came out. It wasn't as though she had any allies left anyway. Then the pain clawed up again, toward groin and torso, and she collapsed into a vast constricting darkness.

When human explorers discovered the city, they thought it was another ruin from some earlier wave of colonization. It wasn't until settlers had abandoned the ship over a doctrinal schism that people discovered the city's peculiar properties.

The city, which the majority sect named Contemplating Orthodoxy, originally showed the blandest of faces to its settlers. It was a sphere orbiting a dismal sun, hollowed out by nonorthogonal passages and irregular chambers, like an apple cored by enthusiastic worms. The chambers were composed of corroded walls and beams of bent metal and unreliable floors. People assessed the structure, shored up what needed shoring up, built their own dwellings and factories from a combination of their own supplies and the city's excess material, and moved in.

Not long afterward, the walls changed. And the floors. And the ceilings. And the columns, and the bridges, and the doors, and the occasional couch. At first the phenomenon was confined to items made of the city's original material, but later everything was affected.

Contemplating Orthodoxy, it turned out, had what one of the early philosopher-poets called *mirror-nature*. When it was uninhabited, it lay quiescent. When humans crept into it, it reflected them according to its own kaleidoscope understanding.

The form the city's understanding took was, so to speak, spare parts for its inhabitants. From the walls grew tangled tendrils of wire, and the tendrils fused together into bones of strong composites, and the bones hinged together into hands, or feet, or hips sheathed in plastic or metal. There were eyes in every conceivable color, growing like fervent grapes from pillars, the sensors glittering pale and vigilant; there were infrared sensors and scanners and seismic analyzers.

Most people were convinced that this signaled that the city was going to eat them. The riots that followed involved smashing, hacking, and huddling in shelters ineffectually treated with everything from insecticide to surfactants in hopes of warding off the unsettling growths. But one surgeon hit upon the idea of harvesting an eye from the city and implanting it in his brother. According to some accounts, he pitied his brother for an eye maimed in an accident involving a staple gun. According to less flattering stories, he was driven by malicious curiosity. (Why the brother didn't resist or flee, they don't say.) Either way, the experiment was a success. The filaments that emerged from the back of the cybernetic eye successfully interfaced with human nerves, and, as a side-effect, gave the surgeon's brother the ability to see partway into the ultraviolet.

It didn't take long for other surgeons to begin offering this service, to say nothing of eager charlatans. After all, the riots had resulted in any number of injuries, and the regenerative tanks that the settlers had brought with them were running low on the necessary gels. People came around to the idea that ready-made spare parts and enhancements weren't such a bad thing, even if they came in outlandish colors. Scarcely any time passed before the outlandish colors became a motivation in themselves, and soon after that, the first Harvests were organized in earnest.

Nissaea dreamt for a long time of low-lidded octopuses floating through space so black it was red, or so red it was black; of stars the color of incisions, and a bird singing in a voice like a bone flute on the verge of breaking. When at last she struggled awake, she blinked crusted eyelids against light sere and pitiless, as though it were part of the dream itself. "Jeni?" she asked hoarsely, mistaking the shape in front of her for a circle-sister from years past. But of course Jeni had died in a Watch raid.

"This is a name?" said a voice she didn't recognize at first. "It's not one I know." A smooth hand, although not a soft one, pressed itself against her wrist, testing—perhaps for her pulse.

She flinched. Something about her wrist felt wrong, but she couldn't figure out what it was. Instead, she scrabbled uselessly among the blankets, scratchy but warmed by her own heat, for some weapon better than her fists—fist.

Fist. Her entire left hand was missing. It shocked her fully awake. She bolted out of the bed, blankets tangling her legs, and looked around, forcing herself to take in details that might help her escape. Walls that wound up to a cusp. No windows, although there were vents covered by lavender membranes, like fungus gills, that she might be able to tear through. The familiar whisk-whirr of the mass transit system somewhere beyond them. Flowers, of all things: not the cybernetic blossoms that the city produced, with their unwilting plastic petals and stamens shaped like upside-down catenary curves, but a dented steel can of genuine weeds, yellow-bright, with holes in the lopsided leaves. Next to the flowers was the exit she'd sought. The door was slightly ajar, and the stranger wasn't standing in her way toward it.

All this, and no sign of her hand. She fixed the stranger with a stare.

The stranger wasn't stupid. "It was infected," it said simply. "That wasn't just a cut you took. The nano-rot introduced by your wound was drawn to the faulty components in your hand. I removed it as a precaution."

Nissaea narrowed her eyes at it. In full light, its features possessed the same patchwork sense of balance she had noted before, human and machine parts alternating with each other as though they were being weighed against each other. "If you're a scrap surgeon," she said, "what were you doing abandoned like a slab of meat gone bad?" Surreptitiously, she tensed and untensed the muscles of her afflicted leg. The cut still throbbed distantly, but otherwise most of the pain was gone.

Even a half-competent surgeon was usually valued enough that some circle would retain them. "Scrap surgeon" was a derogatory term, but the stranger showed no sign of offense. "I was always there," it said in a voice tinged with sadness. It raised its chin, considered her, then shook its head.

Maybe its former circle had gotten rid of it because its mind wasn't all there. Still, she raised her wrist, steeling herself, and inspected the amputation. A very clean job, the bone sawed and the stump capped with a bright green-gold metal. She had a brief phantom sensation of locked fingers, but that was old news. "Thank you," she said. The truth was that she couldn't afford work this good.

"I would have harvested a prosthesis for you already," it added, "but I didn't want to leave you unattended in case the fever got worse."

Nissaea drew her breath in, not sure she had understood correctly. "I can't pay—"

"It's not a question of payment," it said. "I want—" Its voice became unexpectedly scratchy on *want*. "I want a roof."

"You mean sponsorship into a circle," Nissaea said after she parsed the archaic word. She made herself look at it straight-on. "This is terrible recompense, but I can't give you that. I'm not a circle-breaker, so the enforcers won't shoot me, but my circle revoked my membership. I don't have any connections."

Looking into the stranger's mismatched eyes told her only that its desire was real, but why wouldn't it be? Even scavengers like Nissaea, even fences and circuit-cutters belonged to circles. It was the order of things.

"You gave me water and helped me out of the dark," it said. "You didn't have to do either. It's not a circle's companionship I want. It's yours."

She gentled her voice. "I don't mean to be ungrateful. My name is Nissaea-of-the-Slant." She'd been withholding it all this time, since you didn't casually introduce your name-chant to a stranger, but it had probably saved her life and she didn't see any point in being coy. "What should I call you?"

"I never needed a name before," it said.

Did it come from one of the more esoteric circles where people called each other by numbers? There were a few of those. "Well, you could pick something you like?" she suggested.

"Muhad," it said after a moment. "I don't have a chant."

"Muhad," she said, being as careful with the name as she would with a delicate piece of jewelry. "Have I got it right?"

She was rewarded by Muhad's smile, a curve made beautiful rather than perfect by its asymmetry, one side of the mouth a nudge higher than the other. *Oh, do that again,* she thought in spite of herself.

"Of course it's right," Muhad said, shyly. It would have been flirtatious coming from anyone else. Its gaze went to Nissaea's stump. "I meant it, about a hand. You shouldn't go without one." It paused, suddenly uncertain. "Unless you wanted a different appendage?"

Pincers, tentacles, integrated guns . . . Nissaea had never been attracted to the more exotic options, which cost more anyway. "No," she said hastily. "Just a hand. If I can find a compatible one without having to raid a parts bank." Not that they'd have any luck doing that. They'd be safer picking a fight directly with the Watch.

"I can do that," Muhad said. "I know of a lode in the deep places, now that you are well enough to travel." It spoke as tranquilly as if it had made a simple statement of arithmetic, were it not for the shadow in its eyes.

"Then I'll need supplies," Nissaea said. "I'm out of confounders. I'm not going out without any." She didn't ask what Muhad meant by the "deep places," and didn't want to know until the last possible moment. There was no way such a harvest could be legal, even by the undercircles' codes. But she found that she cared less and less. She'd followed the codes and worked hard at her profession, only to be tossed out like scrap. At this point, she might as well look out for herself and the one person who had showed her kindness.

Few people gave Nissaea so much as a pitying look when she showed up with a missing hand, even the ones who recognized her. Instead, they ignored her pointedly. Muhad drew more attention, although Nissaea stood protectively near it at all times. She knew they couldn't linger. The local undercircles didn't keep formal registries the way the high circles did, but the stranger's presence would be marked, and sooner or later someone would be sent to investigate. Sideways Hano did attempt to draw Muhad into a discussion of heterodoxies in Chamberish theology when Nissaea was buying them grub fritters, but he did that to everyone, and after several rambling lectures, even he figured out that Muhad's polite bewilderment wasn't faked.

Getting together supplies didn't take long, mainly because Nissaea had been flat broke before and she was still flat broke now. But they obtained confounders and a few other basics because Muhad matter-of-factly volunteered to have the decorative inlay work on its face removed. The angry-looking scar left behind saddened Nissaea. Silently, she promised to make it up to Muhad.

One of the things that Nissaea insisted on was shoes for Muhad. They didn't fit very well. The soles were worn thin and the canvas looked all but translucent, and not in the aesthetic way either. Muhad didn't seem to mind, however.

Nissaea's nerves finally gave out when they slipped down into the mazeways. She asked about the lode: Would it be underwater? Flooded with acid? Require special breathing apparatus or hacked frequency keys? These were all things she should have asked before they went shopping, except for the fact that they couldn't afford specialized equipment anyway. Even when she'd been in good standing with Addit's circle, she'd only ever touched that kind of thing on loan, for particular assignments.

At last Muhad said, after a series of patient reassurances, "Nothing down there will harm you, Nissaea-of-the-Slant. I don't think there's even much to trip on."

Nissaea opened her mouth to protest, then caught Muhad's almost-smile and realized she was being teased.

They left for the lode during nighttime. The city's cycles were signaled along the major thoroughfares by clocklights that changed color from morning pink to noon gold to alluring evening blue. According to a past circle-sister, the color scheme mimicked that of the original planet's skies, something that reproductions of very old paintings and photographs suggested might have some basis in fact. Every few years one or another of the high circles petitioned to have the colors reprogrammed to match their livery (undercircles didn't bother with livery), and the rest of the high circles quashed the notion. Nissaea wouldn't have minded the variety, but she didn't get a say. Besides, tonight's dim blue glow was pretty enough.

The light faded behind them as they entered the mazeways beneath the statue called Embracing Birds. One of Nissaea's former circle-kin stood guard in the hollows by the gate, collecting the toll. He was a cadaverous man, each rib emphasized by a pitted metal stripe, and his leg was ribbon-thin all the way up to the joint at his hip. A clear covering exposed the organs of his torso, but Nissaea had seen stranger things than a man's inner workings.

"You know the toll," the man said in a voice like stone scraped thin. The toll would be higher now that she was an independent.

In answer, Nissaea made an abbreviated gesture of respect and pressed her palm twice against his, once for herself and once for Muhad. There was a tiny beep as the transaction went through. She raised her eyebrows at the man, wondering if he would make trouble for her.

She was lucky, or in any case, not unluckier than she already had been for the last few days. The man shook his head, although the gleam in his eye suggested that he was thinking of reporting her and Muhad. Well, she could deal with that later. She nodded to Muhad, and they slipped into the mazeways together.

The transition into the mazeways always caused Nissaea's breath to stutter in her lungs even after all these years. Great whippy tendrils of fiber and hungry iron-jawed mouths grew from the gate's throat, slick with the dew of anticipated carrion. They were careful to walk precisely down the middle of the passage, so as not to attract the tendrils' attention.

After years of being the one handling the navigation, Nissaea was dismayed to discover how rapidly she got lost following Muhad. If she hadn't known better, she would have suspected that the mazeways had reshuffled themselves like a cheater's hand of cards, except she'd never known them to do so with such haste. She paid attention to the scissored shadows, the malevolent gleam of fetal sensors, the grit beneath her feet the way she hadn't since she was a small child clinging to her sister's hand.

She couldn't help wondering if they would run into another corpse, whether one neatly cracked open like the last one, or smashed into stains. It took an effort to make herself breathe evenly instead of hyperventilating. But the only human reek was her own rank sweat. Even Muhad, perhaps because its modifications were more extensive than her own, smelled only of pale salt.

Between one passage (paint peeling away like butterflies in transition, the occasional white mass that *oozed* when you didn't look at it directly) and the next (a blast of acrid vapor from a hole in a pipe, rattling as of librarian lizards realphabetizing their movements), they arrived in a vast pulsing garden of hands. Nissaea had never seen anything like it before. She bet that even the high circles' harvesters hadn't seen anything like it in generations, either.

A braidweave splendor of limbs made up the walls. Even the floor pulsed with rhythmic lights. Nissaea was tempted to close her eyes and sink into the pattern, deeper, deeper, until nothing was left of song and synapse except a dross of decaying static. Instead, she was captivated by the limbs and, more importantly, the hands that sprouted from them.

They weren't all hands, although some were. Great gun muzzles with their barrels pointing obsessively at her heart; you'd need to replace the entire arm with a specialized rig to bear that kind of weight. The ever-popular tentacles, except Nissaea had never seen any with integrated syringes up close before; some kind of medical appendage, or perhaps intended for drug-fests? Claws in a variety of configurations and lengths, some jewel-tipped and some bladed. Of the most interest to Nissaea were the quotidian prostheses that resembled ordinary human hands if not for the exacting angles, the unsoft curves.

"Muhad," Nissaea said wonderingly, "you're *rich*." Aside from the matter of finding a reliable fence, and paying protection money, and organizing shipments, and—well. She was certain Muhad didn't have any of those things set up, or it wouldn't have been lying in the mazeways having given up all will to fight.

"It has nothing to do with wealth," Muhad said absently. "Nissaea-of-the-Slant, which one do you want?"

Tempting though it was to linger over the choices, Nissaea had already picked one out. She pointed to a slender hand of dull blue-silver, not a bad match for her born-hand, and—she hoped—not too greedy. It was, however, beautifully articulated and its knuckles were ringed by shimmering bands. "What do you think of that one?" she asked.

Muhad, apparently, had no problems walking right up to the wall of limbs. They stirred and several of them beeped disharmoniously, but nothing disastrous happened. Muhad tapped the hand's joints, squeezed it, ran its fingers over the sleek surfaces, frowned thoughtfully. "It will serve you well," it said. "Most of them would."

They set up the harvesting equipment. Simple enough: the small reinforced tank and its clear pink fluid, the selection of screwdrivers, the saws, the neural stimulators to ensure that the hand's internals didn't sputter dead during the transfer. Oddly, for all Muhad's deftness, it didn't seem to have any experience with the knifework of harvesting. Nissaea ended up doing most of it, although it was more soothing than she would have expected to have a companion while listening for the Watch, or carrion maws, or other mazeway hazards.

This will be my hand, she thought. A freshly harvested hand from the richest imaginable lode, a hand she had picked out herself. The luxury was inconceivable.

One by one they freed the connectors and the sensory hookups, and the fingers clenched slightly as Nissaea eased the hand from its former home. She weighed it in her born-hand for a second, marveling that its weight was so perfect: not too heavy, not too light.

"I don't know of a safe place for the operation," Nissaea said at last, her voice hushed.

"This is safe enough," Muhad said. "I hear no footsteps."

Nissaea listened again, just in case, but all she heard was the low thrum of the confounders and the occasional slithering friction of tubes crossing tubes. "We didn't purchase anesthetic," she said after a juddery pause. While she could survive a little pain, the moment of hookup could be agonizing.

"We won't need it," Muhad said. "We can use needles."

Acupuncture? Well, she knew it worked, and it wasn't improbable that a surgeon would know the techniques. Nissaea inhaled, then said, "What should I do?"

Muhad took her shoulder and steered her, not ungently, toward the center of the chamber. "Sit," it said. Nissaea sat. After a moment, she heard Muhad humming to itself, a sequence of notes at the threshold of melody. It picked up the snippers and moved among the hands, harvesting over a dozen fine wires. Each was cut to precisely the same length, with the tips sharply angled. The makeshift needles gleamed tooth-hungry in the partial dark.

"Rest your stump on your knee, tendons facing down," Muhad said then, and Nissaea complied. She admitted to curiosity: there were different schools of acupuncture in Contemplating Orthodoxy, and she had heard that the disruptions caused by the implants, or even by the city's very nature, had altered the map of meridians that the original settlers had brought with them.

One by one Muhad inserted the needles. It had a delicate touch, and if any of the needles penetrated far below the surface of her skin, Nissaea couldn't tell. Only partway through did she notice an almost pleasing numbness, and the fact that her arm was now locked in place.

"I'd tell you to relax, but—" Muhad said, not without irony. It stroked her unaffected arm once, twice. Then it brought the harvested hand out of the tank where it had spent so little time, toweled down the pink dripping fluid, and connected up wires and vessels with a briskness that would have been surprising if Nissaea had still been capable of surprise.

"I'm relaxing," Nissaea lied.

Muhad's sudden grin flashed at her. She smiled back reflexively. Muhad pressed some cluster of nerves without warning and slammed the hand into place. She cried out as the hand activated. It was like a white spiked star in the back of her brain, and then the pain dwindled and she opened and closed its fingers, giddy with relief. "Oh," she said articulately, and then, after she had a chance to stare dazedly at the fingers' delicately molded tips, the responsive joints, "Thank you."

It seemed as tongue-tied as she was. First it ducked its head as it removed all the needles. Then, hesitantly, it reached down, its own hand hovering over her newly attached one. It flinched away at the last second.

The absurdity of the situation struck Nissaea. Who knew how late into the night it was, and here they were surrounded by a garden of hands, with tools pitifully inadequate to harvest them all. She couldn't think of any sustainable way to derive benefit from the lode, never mind that it was Muhad's find and not hers. Even though she should have been calculating matters of profit and survival, all she could do was look into Muhad's eyes, suddenly petal-soft. Her pulse beat loudly in her ears as she brought her palm up to meet Muhad's. Its breath caught.

"Tell me," Nissaea said, meaning it, "what is it that you want?"

She didn't care that she still had no idea what offense would cause a scrap surgeon to be expelled from its home circle, or that it made no sense for Muhad to be going around like a vagabond when it had casual access to this kind of wealth. All she saw was the way it met her eyes, as though she were the only lamp in a world of shadows.

We could be found here tomorrow morning all carved up, she thought; but that didn't matter either.

Muhad's answer didn't come in words, which wasn't unexpected. It drew Nissaea down above it, pausing midway so they could arrange their limbs so they didn't gouge each other with elbows and knees. Nissaea had slept with circle-kin in years past, but it had been a lonely year since she had known another's embrace. Muhad's mouth was, if anything, hungrier than hers, and at the same time, she was aware of its hands reaching up to dig into her spine so hard it hurt, if pain ever felt this close to breathless joy. She knew she must be pressing the breath out of it, and her weight was stamping the pattern of its joins into her skin, metal and glass and plastic riveted to flesh, map begetting map.

Its lips parted wide as they each drew back from the kiss, and it breathed something that might have been her name. Nissaea resumed the kiss before it could say anything else. "Shh," she said, desperate and happy and incoherent with the desire not to know more than she knew right that moment, "don't, don't talk, don't." And then she began to undress it.

They slept afterward, or anyway she did. Her dreams were full of organs made of puzzle pieces, or puzzle pieces made of organs: here a tessellated liver, there a lung made of dodecahedral crystals.

Nissaea woke parched. Muhad had pillowed its head on her shoulder, and her arm had fallen asleep. For a long moment Nissaea admired its eyelashes, the long curving sweep of them, then eased its head to the floor.

She stretched, massaging the tingling arm, then padded over to their supplies and treated herself to a few careful sips of water. It was lukewarm, but tasted sweet.

Then she returned to Muhad's side. Its shift was a crumpled pile, its shoes on opposite sides of the chamber, and it was, unclothed, almost a work of art. Some warning whispered at her awareness, but she was too busy smiling at its slim curves—it was not quite angular enough to be a man, but too narrow to be an adult woman—to pay it heed at first.

Nissaea didn't have any illusions about her own beauty, although there had been advantages to being plain when she belonged to an undercircle. She did, however, appreciate beauty in others—who didn't?—and she looked admiringly at Muhad now that they weren't clutching each other in the heat of hunger. Whoever had done its modifications had cared very much about aesthetics, about gradations of color and nuances of luster. The diagnostic lights that wound around its torso, for instance, like twin subtle snakes.

She drew a hand across its skin and paused at its hip. Muhad sighed in its sleep, mouth curving up. Slowly, she walked her fingers down its thigh, then to the artificial joint at the knee, and all the way down to—

That was odd. Nissaea frowned at the two human feet. She didn't expect one to be artificial; Muhad hadn't been designed around that kind of petty symmetry. But something about the feet seemed wrong. She scooted over and peered at them.

Muhad's feet didn't match. She would have expected some deformity to be the issue, but the fact was that both were perfectly normal feet, just different from each other. One was significantly longer than the other, and the other had broader, stubbier toes, and a different skeletal structure. She hadn't noticed before because people looked at faces and sometimes hands, but feet?

Her heart went cold. She examined both feet more closely, not sure what she was looking for. Two scars caught her attention. The first ringed an ankle, so faint that she wouldn't have seen it if she hadn't been checking for something like it. She wasn't positive she'd find another on the other leg, but there it was, circling the calf about a third of the way up to the knee. It was pale, with a clumsy jagged mark, as though the surgeon had been careless with the stitches.

She crawled away, almost to the wall, then hugged her knees to her, willing herself to interpret the evidence. Instead, she started breathing to the clap-slither rhythm of the hands.

"Nissaea-of-the-Slant," Muhad said. Its eyes had opened, and it rolled over, then sat up. It had spoken her name like a prayer, but this time the prayer was a desperate one. "Are you hurting?"

"Not the way you think," Nissaea said. "Your feet, Muhad. What happened to your feet?"

I should leave, she thought, but she couldn't bear to, not yet.

"My born-feet were taken away from me," Muhad said, very steadily. Then, as if it were aware of the inadequacy of this explanation, it added, "It didn't hurt."

She knew she would regret asking this, especially since all she could see in her mind's eye was the corpse back-bent, splayed, sterile of smell. "Why would you replace human feet with human feet?" Especially since the last regenerative tanks had run out generations ago. You couldn't grow human parts that way anymore.

"Because it's always the harvest," Muhad said. "Because it's what we learned people do. Because it was what you were doing, Nissaea-of-the-Slant, when you came into the darkness. The harvest."

I'm missing something obvious. "Yes," she said, "but we're harvesting from the city. We don't—"

Except people had been turning up dead, they'd both seen it, and you could cut someone apart for anything you had the scalpel-skill to excise, like feet. Human feet.

Nausea rose up in Nissaea's throat, and she turned away before Muhad could see the revulsion in her eyes.

"People harvest the city," Muhad said, sounding terribly calm. "That's how we've been talking to each other all this time. You became more like us, so we thought you wanted us to become more like you."

"Become more like us what," Nissaea said inflectionlessly, remembering how she had lain with it.

"I wasn't born human," Muhad said softly, "and I didn't have eyes that you would recognize as eyes, or feet either. I had silicon thoughts and a piezoelectric heartbeat. They cut pieces of me out so that I could be given human implants the way that you were given city implants."

Nissaea stood up. It tensed, expecting her to strike it. *You are so beautiful,* she thought, grieving; thought, too, of the way it had cried out and shuddered beneath her. Its heart had sounded wholly human, afterward.

Her mind was working. "How long has this been going on?" she asked. She hadn't been able to distinguish Muhad from an ordinary human. Only the feet had given it away.

It told her. The city was very old, she had known that. She hadn't, however, realized just how old it was, or how alien.

Then she asked how many of its kindred there were, and it told her that, too.

Mirror-nature: something she'd heard about from a drunk woman once. The city that responded to its inhabitants by changing itself. In more ways than they'd realized, apparently.

"One more question," she said, still looking down at Muhad. "If the city—if your people—went through so much trouble to make you like this, why did they just abandon you in the mazeways afterward?"

Muhad shivered and made itself hold her gaze. "Humans abandon their own all the time," it said quietly. "If this isn't what you wanted us to understand about you, why do you do it so often?"

Nissaea bit her lip, hard. Then she knelt and laid her hands on Muhad's shoulders. In times past she would have thought only of warning someone, her undercircle if no one else, but now she didn't think it mattered. She was free of debts; what did she care who was harvesting whom? "Why do we do it indeed," she murmured, and kissed Muhad deeply. Its mouth was warmly yielding. "You've already cut my heart out anyway."

Around them, the maimed city's hands grabbed at each other and scratched cryptic shapes into the air as the two of them sank down in each other's arms once more, human and unhuman entwined.

A COLD HEART

TOBIAS S. BUCKELL

In the mining facility's automated sickbay she'd put her metal hand on your chest and said, "I'm sorry." The starry glinting fragments of ice and debris bounced around the portholes. Twinkling like stars, but shaken loose of their spots in the dark vacuum.

They shot her hand, but she had pushed the raiders right back off her claim. The asteroid was still bagged and tagged as her own to prospect. You never told her they were all dead now, mere bloodstains on the corridors of Ceres, but one imagines she suspects as much.

"I have a cold hand, but you have a cold heart," she had said. "I can't love a cold heart."

And it's true.

Strange place to part ways, but she's been thinking about it for a while. Susan knows her path.

"You'll keep hunting for your memories?" she asks. "That corporate data fence?"

You nod. "I'll have more time on my hands."

It's a strange thing to image a whole brain down to the quantum level. Crack a person apart and bolt stronger skeletal system into him. Refashion him into a machine, a weapon to be used for one's gain. Then burn the memories out. Use the lie of getting them back as a lure to make that human serve you. But stranger things had been done during the initial occupation of Earth.

Now you'll be having those back. You want to know who you were.

You want more than just the one they left you to whet your appetite.

Your first encounter with the *Xaymaca Pride*'s crew is an intense-looking engineer. Small scabs on her shaved head show she's sloppy with a blade, and there's irritation around the eye sockets, where a sad-looking metal eye has been welded into the skin somewhere in a cheap bodyshop.

"You're the mercenary," she says. "Pepper."

You're both hanging in the air inside the lock. The pressure differential slightly pushes at your ears. You crack your jaw, left, right, and the pressure ceases. The movement causes your dreadlocks to shift around you, tapping the side of your face.

"I'm not on a job," you tell her. "I don't work for anyone anymore."

But you used to. And there's a reputation. It's spread in front of you like a bow wave. Dopplering around, varying in intensity here and there.

Five years working with miners, stripping ore from asteroids enveloped in plastic bags and putting in sweat-work, and all anyone knows about is the old wetwork. Stuff that should have been left to the shadows. Secrets never meant for civilians.

But that shit didn't fly out in the tight tin cans floating around the outer solar system. Everyone had their noses in everyone else's business.

"The captain wants to see you before detach."

Probably having second thoughts, you think. Been hard to find a way to get out of the system, because the new rulers of the worlds here want you dead for past actions. You can skulk around the fringes, or even go back to Earth and hide in the packed masses and cities.

But to go interstellar: you eventually get noticed when you're one of the trickle of humanity leaving to the other forty-eight habitable worlds. Particularly if you're one of the few that's not a servant of the various alien species that are now the overlords of humanity.

The bridge crew all twist in place to get a good look at you when you float into the orb-shaped cockpit at the deep heart of the cylindrical starship. They're all lined up on one plane of the cockpit, the orb able to gimbal with the ship's orientation to orient them to the pressures of high acceleration.

Not common on an average container ship. Usually those were little more than a set of girders cargo could get slotted into with a living area on one end and engines on the other.

The captain hangs in the air, eyes drowned in shipboard internal information, but now he stirs and looks at you. His skin is brown, like yours. Like many of the crew's. From what you've heard, they all hail from the Caribbean. DeBrun has been smuggling people out of the solar system to points beyond for a whole year now.

"I'm John deBrun," he says. "You're Pepper."

You regard him neutrally.

DeBrun starts the conversation jovially. "In order to leave the solar system, I need anti-matter, Pepper. And no one makes it but the Satraps and they only sell to those they like. They own interstellar commerce, and most of the planets in the solar system. And according to the bastard aliens, you do not have interstellar travel privileges. I've let you aboard, to ask you a question, face to face."

You raise an eyebrow. It's a staged meeting. DeBrun is putting on a show for the bridge crew. "Yes?"

"Why should I smuggle you from here to Nova Terra's Orbital?"

A moment passes as you seem to consider that, letting deBrun's little moment stretch out. "It'll piss off the Satraps, and I'll wait long enough so that it's not obvious you're the ship that slipped me in."

DeBrun dramatically considers that, rubbing his chin. "How will you do that?"

"I'm going to steal something from a Satrap."

"Steal what?"

"My memories," you tell him.

DeBrun grins. "Okay. We'll take you."

"Just like that?"

"You know who we are, what we're planning to do?"

You nod. "An exodus. To find a new world, free of the Satrapy."

"Not to find," deBrun says. "We found it. We just need to get there again, with five ships. And having you distract the Satrap at our rally point . . . well, I like that. There are a lot of people hiding on that habitat, waiting to get loaded up while we fuel. The first people of a whole new world, a new society. You should join."

"The Satrap at your rally point has something I want."

"So I've heard. Okay. Jay, shut the locks, clear us out. Our last passenger is on board."

Jay and DeBrun could be brothers. Same smile. Though you're not sure. You don't look at people that much anymore. Not since Susan. You don't care anymore. You can explore the fleshy side of what remains of you after you get the memories back.

Because they will make you whole again.

The ship's cat adopts you. It hangs in the air just above the nape of your neck, and whenever the ship adjusts its flight patch claws dig into the nape of your neck.

Claws, it seems, are a benefit in zero gravity.

No matter how many times you toss the furball off down the corridor it finds its way back into your room.

How many wormholes between Earth and Nova Terra? You lose track of the stomach-lurching transits as the cylindrical ship burns its way upstream through the network.

You dream about the one memory you still have. The palm tree, sand in your toes.

It could have been a vacation, that beach. But the aquamarine colors just inside the reef feel like *home*. It's why, when you heard the shipboard accents you followed crew back to this ship and chose it. The oil-cooked johnny cakes, pate, curry, rice . . . muscle memory and habit leave you thinking you came from the islands.

You don't know them. But they are your people.

At Nova Terra, slipping out via an airlock and a liberated spacesuit, you look back at the pockmarked outer shell of the ship. It's nestled against the massive, goblet-shaped alien habitat orbiting Nova Terra's purplish atmosphere, itself circling the gas giant Medea. The few hundred free humans who live here call the glass and steel cup-shaped orbital Hope's End.

You're a long way from home now. Hundreds of wormholes away, each of them many lightyears of jumps. Each wormhole a transit point in a vast network that patch together the various worlds the Satrapy rules over.

Too far to stop now. You only were able to come one way. This wasn't a round-trip ticket. You'll have to figure out how to get back home later.

Once you have memories. Once you know exactly where that palm tree was, you'll have something to actually go back *for*.

The woman who sits at the table across from you a week later does so stiffly, and yet with such a sense of implied ownership that your back tenses. There's something puppet-like, and you know the strings are digital. Hardware buried into this one's neuro-cortex allow something else to ride shotgun.

Something.

She's in full thrall, eyes glinting with an alien intelligence behind them. The Satrap of Hope's End has noticed your arrival and walked one of his human ROVs out to have a chat. That it took it two days for it to notice you, when you've just been sitting out in the open all this time, demonstrates a level of amateurishness for its kind.

Then again, Hope's End is sort of the Satrapy's equivalent of a dead-end position. A small assignment on a small habitat in orbit. The real players live down the gravity well, on the juicy planets.

"I know who you are," the woman says. Around you free humans in gray paper suits stream to work in the distant crevices of the station. Life is hard on Hope's End, you can tell just by their posture. The guarded faces, the invisible heaviness on the shoulders.

You say nothing to the woman across from you.

"You are here without permission. Do you know you I could have you killed for that?"

"You could try that," you say. "The cost would be high."

"Oh, I imagine." She leans back, and flails an arm in what must be some far-off alien physical expression badly translated. There is a pit, a cavern, somewhere deep in the bowels of Hope's End. Somewhere with three quarter's gravity, and a dirt pit, and a massive recreation pool. And slopping around is a giant wormy trilobite of an alien. "I know a lot about you. More than you know about yourself."

Indeed.

The thing you need is that cavern's location.

Until you get that, everything is a dance. A game. A series of feints and jabs. Your life is the price of a single misstep.

But what do you have to lose? You don't know. Because you can't remember. It was taken from you. The Satrap owns everything you would lose by dying. You're already dead, you think.

"So why haven't you killed me?" you ask the Satrap.

"The *Xaymaca Pride*," it says. "They're sneaking people around my habitat. As if I wouldn't notice. And they're hoping to leave . . . for a new world."

"You believe deBrun's propaganda?" you ask. Because even you don't half believe it. The man is slightly messianic. He's probably going to lead them all to their deaths, so far from Earth. Alone among uncaring, hard aliens the likes of which haven't even bothered to make it to Earth.

The Satrapy is vast. Hundreds of wormhole junctions between each habitable world, and dozens and dozens of those linked up. And the Satraps hold the navigation routes to themselves. The few individual ships out there blunder around and retrace their steps and are lucky they're not shot down by the Satrapy's gun banks in the process.

"DeBrun destroyed his own ship upon return from the Fringes," the woman says. "He has memorized the location in his head."

"Ah. So you believe it is true." A ship. There were corporations on Earth that couldn't afford an interstellar ship. Not a small act, destroying one.

"Many people raised funds to create this . . . Black Starliner Corporation's fleet," the Satrap's thrall says. "I believe the world he found is real. Unspoiled and real. And I want it for myself." That last bit is lashed out. There is hunger in that statement, and a hint of frustration.

This Satrap is trapped up here, while its siblings cavort on the surface of Nova Terra. They have thousands of humans and aliens in thrall at their disposal, chipped with neurotech that let them create an army of servants they can remote control around with mere thought.

"I am stuck in this boring, metal cage. But I have great plans. Would you like to know how you got that scar above your left inner thigh? The jagged one, that is faded because you've had it since you were a teenager?"

You stop breathing for a second. Unconsciously you run a hand down and trace the zig-zag pattern with your thumb.

"You were climbing a fence. Barbed wire curled around the top, and you were trying to get over it into a field. You slipped. You were so scared, for a split second, as it ripped open your leg. The blood was so bright in the sun, and the ground tumbled up toward you as fell, in shock."

When you break the stare, you've lost a little battle of the wills. "So you do have them."

"I love collecting the strangest things," the Satrap said through the woman. Now that you are paying attention, you see that her hair is unwashed, and that there are sores above her clavicle. "I have two thousand humans, in thrall to me. Many other species as well. And I've used these eyes to pry, sneak, and attempt my way on board. I want John deBrun. I'm tired of watching these free humans skulk about."

"So go pick him up," you say.

"Oh, yes. I want to sink my tendrils into deBrun's fleshy little mind and suck those coordinates out. But he remains on that damn ship, with guards ever at the airlocks. I've learned he has protocols for an attack, and anything I can do leaves me too high a risk of him dying in a large attack. So I want *you* to bring me John deBrun. It is the sort of thing, I'm told, you are good at."

"And in exchange you give me my memories back?"

"You're every bit as sharp as your memories indicate you ever were," the woman says, and stands up.

"What if I refuse? What if I go after the memories myself?" you smile.

"You are alone, on a station, where only a few hold their own freedom. Every other eye in here is in thrall to me. Most of the time, they are free to engage in their petty lives, but the moment I desire, I could command them all to rip you from limb to limb with their bare hands. I considered it. But I think instead, we will both be happier if you bring John deBrun to level A7. Portal fourteen. My security forces will be waiting."

And there is your way in.

You wait in the shadows.

You've often been something that goes bump in the night.

The Satraps consider themselves gods to the species they rule over. But sometimes, gods want other gods killed. In theory their reasons are arcane and unknowable. But as far as you can tell they are the usual: jealousy. Covetousness. A desire for more power.

Sometimes gods want other gods to die, and you decided you didn't just want to go bump in the night and scare people. You decided you could aim higher than being just a human assassin. And when the Satrap of Mars decided it wanted the blue jewel of Earth, you let it sharpen you into a weapon the likes of which few wished to imagine.

All that gooey alien nanotechnology that burrowed through your pores, all that power . . .

Behold the giant slayer, you once thought, looking in the mirror.

You weren't supposed to live, but even jealous alien eyes from the dusty red ruin of Mars couldn't imagine the hells you would face to continue feeding your quest. It had no idea the depths of your anger. The strength of your resolve.

It didn't know you had such a cold, cold heart, and that it had helped make it so much colder. You were already steel, and artificial sinew. It only furthered a transformation that had begun long ago.

◆ ◆ ◆

The gun that John deBrun points at your head when he comes into his quarters is capable of doing much more than give you a headache. He's good. Knew you were in the room. Maybe considered flushing out this part of the ship, but instead comes in to talk.

He's keeping his distance though.

"You're here for the coordinates, aren't you?" he asks.

You nod. "I am."

You keep your hands in the air and sit down. You want John as comfortable as possible.

"If it's not me, someone else will come. They'll cut your head off and run it back to the Satrap. What I have in mind is a little different."

John shakes his head sadly. He lifts up his shirt to show several puckered scars. "You're not the first to try. We have systems in place to deal with this. Every possible variable. I have to assume that everyone is trying to stop me. Other humans, my own crew, people at Hope's End. I'm tougher than they realize."

"You'll want to do this my way," you say.

"And why is that?"

"Because it is happening, John. This right now is happening: I will take you to the Satrap. Because I have come too far, and done too many things, to not go there and get my memories back. Nothing else matters to me. Not you, your ships, your cause, the people in this habitat. There is nothing for me there. There is everything in the Satrap's den."

John shakes his head. "Do you know how much they've taken from us? You think your memories are the worst of it? Let me lay down some history on you: there's always been someone taking it away. They took it away from people like us when we were transported across an ocean. Taken away when aliens landed and ripped our countries away from us. Claimed our planets. There's a long, long list of things ripped away from people in history. You are not alone."

"Unlike them," you say, "what was taken from me is just within reach now."

"At a price," John says.

"Everything has a price," you say, moving toward him.

John blinks, surprised. He's been thinking we were having a dialogue, but you were waiting for the gun to dip slightly. For his attention to waver.

He's a good shot. Hits you right in the chest. A killing shot. One that would have stopped anyone else. The round penetrates, explodes. Shrapnel shreds the place a heart usually rests.

But that is just one small part. One bloodstream.

That faint hiccup of backup pumps dizzies you slightly as your blood pressure shifts and adapts. You cough blood, and grab John. You break his hand as you disarm him and knock him out.

For a while you sit next to him, the horrible feeling in your chest filling you with waves of pain.

Eventually that ebbs. You evaluate the damage, glyphs and messages ghosting across your eyeballs as your body, more alien machine than human, begins to process the damage and heal itself.

You won't be facing the Satrap in optimal fighting condition.

But you're so close. And if you delay, you invite the risk of the Satrap sending someone for John. That could be messy. And it won't give you the one thing you really want out of all this: an invitation into the Satrap's personal cavern, deep past its layers of defenses.

Hello there you slimy alien shit, you're thinking. *I've got a treat for you.*

Just come a little closer, and don't mind the big teeth behind this smile.

You snap the ammonia capsule apart under John's nose and he jerks awake. You're both in a loading bay near the rim of Hope's End. Water drips off in a corner, and the industrial grit on the walls is old and faded. A section of the habitat that has fallen into disuse.

"Don't do this. You should join us, Pepper. Leave all this behind. Start something fresh."

"That's not what's happening right now," you say. "The direction of this journey was set a long time ago." The door at the far end of the bay creaks open.

"You can't kill a Satrap," he says.

You lean next to him. "Your ships, they were never going to leave Hope's End. The Satrap here gave you enough fuel to bring those people here. But right now, you're being given dribs and drabs of antimatter. Enough to go back and from to Earth. But not enough to make it back where you want to go with a whole fleet, right?"

John is silent.

You laugh. "The creature strings you along, until it can get what it wants. And then every single person who came here, well, they'll truly understand the name the few hundred free humans scraping by here gave it. Won't they? Hope's End. Because even if you're free, you're not free of the Satrap's long arm. And you'll be the one who lured them here with tales of a free world."

John lets out a deep breath, and slumps forward.

"But listen to me. Work with me, and I'll help you get what you need. Do you understand?"

"Neither of us will walk away alive from this," John says. "We are both dead men. We're talking, but we are dead men."

The empty-eyed vassals of the Satrap encircle you, a watchful, coordinated crowd that sighs happily as their eyes confirm that you have indeed delivered John deBrun.

"I want my memories, now," you say, holding tight to John.

"Come with us."

Somewhere deep inside, hope stirs. Anticipation builds.

Caution, you warn.

You're both herded deep into Hope's End by ten humans in thrall to the Satrap. Away from the green commons, below the corridors, below the subways and utility pipes, out of storage, and into the core ballast in the heart of the structure. The shadows are everywhere, and fluids drip slowly in the reduced gravity.

Muck oozes from grates, and biological mists hang in the air, thick on the lungs.

The Satrap's subterranean cavern is dim, and the wormy trilobite itself slouched in a dust pit at the center. The long tendrils around its maw socketed into machines, and from those machines, controlled anyone unfortunate enough to be in thrall.

A curious adaptation. You imagine the Satrap evolved somewhere deep underground, where it could lie in weight and plunge its neuro-tendrils into a prey's spine. And then what? It could use predators to grab prey, without harm to itself? Use prey as lures, dangling around that eager, gaping mouth.

"Finally," all ten voices around you say in unison.

John is shoved to the floor in front of you, and you move into the next section of your plan. You reach up to your back and use carbon-fibre fingernails to rip into the scars on your back.

This hurts.

But pain doesn't last forever. Not the pain of your skin ripping apart, or your fingers pulling. The pain of grabbing the handle just underneath as you pull the modified machete of your shoulder blade with a wet tearing and hiss.

Memory strata reforms the blade's handle to fit your grasp, and the black edge of the blade sucks the light into it. The molecular surface is hydrophobic, the viscera and blood on it slide off and splash to the floor.

The Satrap's thralls move toward you, but you put the edge of the short blade against the back of John's skull. "Don't."

As one, they all pull back.

You could have killed John with your bare hands, you don't need the sword. This is part statement. Theater to help the Satrap realize that you're far more dangerous than it has realized. Because, if it can get away with it, the Satrap will have both its prize and keep your memories.

And that isn't going to be happening.

"Give me my memories," you tell it.

"Let me have my new world," it replies in ten voices.

Ten. That's all it has surrounding you.

But you want those memories, so the standoff continues. You broadcast your implacability. You will not be moving until you are given those memories. And first.

"Tell it half the coordinates," you order John. You push the edge of the machete against his neck. Let's dangle the prize a little, you think.

"No," John says firmly.

"John," You kneel next to him. And you whisper, "it will die with those coordinates in its head. Trust me. Don't hold it to just yourself now, let it go. Let go of the burden. Let me help you. And then this will be all over."

But you notice something in his response.

He has been sharing the burden. Someone else knows the coordinates. Who? His first mate. Jay. There was a bond there, you remember.

John stumbles to his feet. "If you want the coordinates, you'll have to rip them out of my head yourself," he says to the Satrap.

And why would he do that?

His body is warm, near feverish. A Satrap wouldn't notice. Not a Satrap that had people under thrall to it with sores on their skin. But you notice.

You're not the only player in this game. John has a different plan. A plan to protect the coordinates. A plan to give his people time to grab what they need: fuel. He's got a bomb in him. Hidden, like your machete.

Well done, Mr. deBrun, you think.

Something moves from in the shadows. A large man with shaggy hair, seven and a half feet tall, muscle and fat and pistoned machine all stitched together like an art show gone wrong. A glimpse of what you could have been, if you'd been designed for strength and strength alone.

In the palm of his oversized hand, a brick that leaked superconducting fluid. ShinnCo logo on the outside and all. The last time you saw it . . . the last time you saw it, you'd woken up in a room and a man in a suit had sat with it in his lap. He'd explained to you that you were in that box. Everything that had once been you, at least. And now they owned it. And by extension, you.

"A copy of your memories," the Satrap says. "You'll hand deBrun over. I know you. I have tasted your memories. Partaken of you."

"You know who I was, know who I *am*," you say. "That was the me before, I'm the me after they took all that, sliced me apart, rebuilt me, and deployed me."

You grab John's head, and before anyone in the cavern can twitch, you slice his head off and hold it up into the air. John's body slumps forward, blood fountaining out over the rock at your feet.

"How long before the dying neurons are inaccessible in here?" you shout.

Everything in the room is flailing, responding to the movements of the Satrap's tendrils as they shake in anger.

You ignore all that. "Give me. My memories."

The Satrap calms. "You are too impertinent," the mouths around you chorus. "I am near immortal. I know the region the man was in. I will continue hunting for that world, and I will eventually have it. But you . . . "

The large man crushes the memory box. Hyperdense storage crumples easily under the carbon fiber fingers and steaming coolant bursts from between his knuckles.

Fragments drop to the ground.

You stare at them, lips tight.

"Ah," the Satrap sighs all around you. "Now those memories only live inside me. They are, once again, unique within flesh. So . . . if you kneel and behave from now on, I'll tell you all about your life. Every time you complete a task, you will return and bow before me right here, and I will tell you about your life. I will give you your past back. Just hand me the head, and kneel."

"You actually believe that I will hand you this head, and take a knee?" you ask.

"I do. From here, those are your only two choices. So the question is . . . "

You throw the head aside and hold the machete in both hands firmly.

As expected, half the men and women in thrall scrabble for the head. There's a twinge of regret. Maybe John would have been able to hide in his ship if you hadn't shown up. Maybe he would have been able to sneak enough fuel to his ragged fleet to make for that hidden world.

But you doubt it.

And here you are.

Killing the puppets who are in thrall to the Satrap is a thankless task. They are human. Many of them would not have asked for this life. They are people from the home world who fell on hard times, and were given a promise of future wealth in exchange for service. If they live long enough. Others were prepaid: a line of credit, a burst of wealth for a year, and then thrall. Others are criminals, or harvested from debtor's prison. Prisoners of war left over from various conflicts.

The Satrapy is "civilized." So it says. It doesn't raid for subjects. They have to, nominally, be beings that have lost their rights. Or agreed to lose them.

Doesn't mean most can't see what thralldom is.

But you kill anyway. Their blood, sliding down the hydrophobic blade to drench your sleeves. The three nearest, beheaded quickly and cleanly. There's no reason to make them suffer.

You walk through a mist of their jugular blood settling ever so slowly to the ground in the lower gravity. The Satrap, realizing what's happening, pulls humans around itself. One of them holds deBrun's head in their arms covetously.

The big guy is the artillery.

He advances, legs thudding, even here. Dust stirs. You walk calmly at him. He swings, a mass-driver, extinction-level powered punch that grazes you. Because what you have is speed. Mechanical tendons that trigger and snap you deep into his reach.

Just the whiff of his punch catches you in the ribs, though. They all crack, and alloys underneath are bent out of shape.

Warning glyphs cascade down your field of sight.

You ignore it all to bury your blade deep into the giant's right eye socket, then yank up.

Even as the body falls to the ground, you're facing the Satrap once more.

"I've already called my brothers and sisters down on the ground to come for you," it says through the remaining puppets. "You are dead."

"People keep telling me that," you say.

And maybe they're right.

The puppets come at you in a wedge. All seven. It's trying to overwhelm you.

You use the machete to cut through the jungle of flesh, leaving arms and limbs on the ground. And when you stand in front of the Satrap, it wriggles back away from you in fear.

"Let me tell you a memory," it begs through speakers, using the machines now that it has been shorn of biological toy things.

"It's too late," you tell it. "I'm dead."

You drive the machete deep. And then you keep pushing until you have to use your fingers to rip it apart.

There's a sense throughout the habitat that something major has shifted. Free humans are bunched together in corners, and others are dazed and wandering around. The rumor is that the Satrap has suddenly disappeared, or died. But what if it comes back? What happens when other Satraps arrive?

You find the docks and a row of deBrun's crew with guns guarding the lock. They stare at you, and you realize you are still covered in blood and carrying a machete. Everyone on the station has given you a wide, wide berth.

"If you wanted to steal fuel, now's the time," you tell them. "The Satrap's not going to be able to stop you. Everyone out there doesn't know what to do."

There are some other alien races sprinkled in throughout the station. But they seem to have locked themselves away, sensing something has gone wrong. Smart.

"Who did the captain leave in charge, if he died?" you ask. They don't answer, but take you back into the ship, and the first mate comes up.

"You're in charge?" you ask.

"Yes," he nods. "I'm John."

You frown. "He called you Jay on the bridge, when I came out."

The first mate smiles sadly. "John deBrun. The junior John deBrun. Jay because we don't need two Johns on the bridge. Though . . . I guess that won't happen anymore."

"He gave you the coordinates, in case he was taken."

John's son nods. "You were taken with him, by the Satrap? You were there?"

You pause for a moment, trying to find words that suddenly flee you. You change direction. "You have three hours to steal as much fuel as you can before forces from the planet below arrive. We should both be long gone by then. Understand?"

"Three hours isn't long enough."

You shrug. "Take what time you have been given."

"You don't understand, we're taking on extra people. People we didn't plan to take on. That adds to the mass we need to spin up. We have the other ships docking hard, and we're taking refugees from Hope's End. People, who if they stay, will be back in thrall at the end of those few hours. We won't have enough fuel to get where we need to go. Maybe, three quarters of the way?"

And out there in space, you were either there or not. There was no part way. No one was getting out on foot to push a ship. Those are cold calculations. They come with the job of captain. Air. Food. Water. Carbon filters. Fuel.

"Sounds like you need to shut your locks soon," you say. "Or you risk throwing away your father's sacrifice."

"I will not leave them," John says calmly. "He may have been able to. You may. But I will not. We are human beings. We should not leave other human beings behind."

"Then you'd better hope your men hurry on the fuel siphoning."

You have no use for goodbyes. You leave him in his cockpit. But you stand in the corridor by yourself in the quiet. Your legs buckle slightly. A wound? Overtired muscles sizzling from the performance earlier? You lean against the wall and take a deep breath.

When you let go, you stare at the bloody handprint.

You lost it all. So close, and you lost it all.

And now what? What are you?

You'll never have those memories. They aren't you anymore. You are you. What you have right now, is you. What you do next, will be you. What will that be?

A cold heart and a bloody hand. That's what you've been. What you are.

You turn and go back into the cockpit.

"Is the planet real?" you ask. And look John's son for any hint, any sign of a lie. You can see pulse, heat, and micro-expressions. Things that help you fight, spot the move. And now, spot intent.

"It's real."

"There is another way," you say.

"And what is that?"

"Take me with you. Get as much fuel as you can, but leave early. Even if it means we only get halfway to where you are going. I killed the Satrap, and everything protecting him. And it wasn't the first. When we run out of fuel, we'll dock and I'll rip more fuel out of their alien hands for you. For you. Understand? I can train more like me. When your fleet passes through, those that stand against us will rue it. I will do this because there is a debt here, understand?"

John looks warily at you. "You were with my father. He didn't kill the Satrap?"

"There is a debt," you repeat.

"He helped you?"

"Give me weapons. The non-humans on the station, they enjoy a position of power. They have avoided mostly being in thrall, as we are the new species for that. So even though we have time, they will figure out what we are doing and act against us. You'll want me out there, buying you time."

John nods, and reaches out a hand to shake.

You don't take it. You can't take it. Not with his father's blood still on it.

"Weapons," you repeat. "Before your men start dying unnecessarily."

Cycled through the locks, deBrun's men behind you, you walk past the stream of frightened people heading for the ship.

You stand in the large docking bays and survey the battlefield.

This is who you are. This is who you will be. This is who you choose.

A cold heart and bloody hands.

When this is over, when you help deliver them to their new world and repay your debt, you can go home to Earth. Stalk for clues to your past. See if you wander until you find that palm tree on the island you remember.

But for now, you are right here.

Right now.

Waiting for the fight to come to you.

THE SARCOPHAGUS
ROBERT REED

The object was gray and smooth to the eye and the eye's first glance gave no clue about its size or mass or its true importance. The second look, a much more careful examination, proved nothing except that almost nothing about the object's appearance had changed. One very simple sphere was reflecting the light of a million suns. The likely assumption was that the eye had found something close and quite small. Old instincts judged its speed; the object crossed its diameter twice every second. That made for a very slow walk between the stars. Even the laziest eye could follow its passage, and the lazy hand had ample time to reach up, fashioning a bowl of fingers that would catch what was making its gentle plunge.

But no hand remained, certainly none that would ever work, and the eye was not much of eye either. Death had severely degraded its imagination, and worse, slowed its capacity to recognize even obvious mistakes.

Something huge and quite ancient was approaching. The object only seemed to be dumbly simple. The reality was that this was a machine woven out of complications, baffling and enigmatic to every eye. That gray hull was smoother than any polish, and as it grew closer, the eye noticed fierce little lights rising from hull and crisscrossing its face. Between here and there, the vacuum was filled with brilliant sparks and whispery veils. Each glow had its flavor. Every glimmer excited the basic elements of the universe. That eager light held telltale blue-shiftings, and once its old talents were awakened, the eye began to understand how utterly wrong it had been, believing in small sluggish things as insignificant as a child's ball.

The machine was fifty thousand kilometers in diameter.

Bigger than most worlds, ten seconds would carry this marvel across one million kilometers. That meant it was moving at one-third the sacred speed of light, and what's more, that eye wasn't too stupid or too dead to ignore what would surely happen next.

Slashing its way through the galaxy, the Great Ship refused to be slowed and only grudgingly allowed itself to maneuver. Space was a cool vacuum mixed with quite a lot more than vacuum. Gas and dust waited in the darkness. There were

41

also lumps of stone and iron, and little comets and giant comets, and countless sunless worlds, most of them dead but the living worlds still numbering in the millions. The captains had methodically laid out the safest profitable course. But to hold that course meant firing the giant engines, and even a tiny course correction meant a long burn many years ago. There were always obstacles that couldn't be avoided. Collisions were inevitable, and every impact had to be absorbed. The hull was deep pure hyperfiber, able to endure horrific abuse, but no machine, not even this machine, would survive forever. Without smart help, the hull would eventually erode away, and the soft body beneath would shatter, and how could anyone measure such a loss?

Fortunes were lashed to this wonder.

Monetary fortunes, and the egos of captains and crew, plus the rich long lives of passengers numbering in the hundreds of billions.

The Great Ship had no choice but plunge onwards. That's why the captains ordered gigantic mechanical eyes built on the bow, mapping every hazard; and that's why an arsenal of lasers and shaped nukes and other superior weapons had been pressed into an endless, unwinnable war. Comets and lost moons had to be found early and properly shattered. Then the rubble was chiseled to dust and the dust was boiled into gases that quickly mixed with the native interstellar fog. Brilliant, brilliantly stubborn engineers had devised elaborate means to harvest what was useful from the fog. Each tiny fragment of matter was given an EM charge, enough charge to obey magnetic fluxes, and what was valuable and what had no particular value was gathered up in these electric nets, gently guided into traps and fuel tanks.

But not every inbound object could be stopped. Every war had lost battles. Sometimes an asteroid would slip past. Jolting impacts proved spectacular, without doubt. But casualties were few, bearable and few, the damage limited to the hull. Specialists quickly patched every hole. And because any successful voyage can become more successful, the captains deep beneath the hull made plans, acting on some very old questions:

"What if something we happen to want happens to be ahead of us?

"What if we spot a small, enticing treasure?

"What are our options to save that treasure, and what are the costs, and how do we pay those costs, and what lives do we risk?"

For two trillion seconds, the Great Ship had been plunging through the populated heart of the Way of Milk.

That day, one muscular pulse of microwave light was sent ahead, as a scout.

And what returned was a tiny bright echo.

Something peculiar was lurking out there.

AIs aimed city-sized mirrors, and they aimed their curiosity. An otherwise ordinary lump of iron and frost was found spinning around its long axis. No broadcasts rose from the asteroid's surface or from its interior. There were no heat signatures, no warnings of slumbering, helpless life. The asteroid had an old face, eroded to rubble save for the largest crater—a deep hole riding that narrow equator. The echo came from a slender gray shape tucked at the crater's bottom. The oddity was gray and otherwise too faint to resolve, and the crater soon turned out of view. But more telescopes were brought to bear, watching the little world spinning, and eventually the crater and its slight mystery swept back into view.

Diagnostic lasers pounded their target with blunt, calibrated fury.

Woven diamond and its various alloys would have boiled along the edges, creating a angry mist of carbon. Polished metals and metametals should have surrendered a stew of elements, each throwing up signals and clean interpretations. But the returning data were simple, simple, simple. Most of the heat was absorbed without effect. The only signatures came from the iron and nickel dust that had presumably gathered on the object's surface. Hyperfiber was the best answer. What the object was was hyperfiber, which was always high-tech artificial, and until more thorough tests were run, that was the only conclusion worth holding.

An army of AIs helped design the next phase.

Standing on that crater lip, a human witness would have seen stars overhead, but no Great Ship. The Ship was still too distant for small eyes. Then brilliance would arrive, coherent light scorching the crater's bowl until the iron was red-hot and soft. A second pulse, aimed like a scalpel, vaporized the metal substrates, resulting in an asymmetric blast, and the mysterious object was thrown high, beginning a good hard spin as the lasers quit.

A mysterious, slightly warm object rotated around its own long axis.

Then the asteroid's faint gravity reclaimed it, letting it settle on the sloppy iron.

Mirrors watched everything while talking to one another, piecing together a definitive image of something still thousands of seconds in the future.

An old protocol was triggered.

More lasers were brought on line, aimed and calibrated but holding their fire, waiting for the prize to vanish.

And with that, the doomed little world began its final day.

The crew was between jobs, physically and mentally. Hundreds of Remoras working with machines and reactors had just finished pouring a large patch on the hull. But while others shepherded the curing, his crew was committed to something smaller and much quicker, and in the end, far more important than a big patch job. Orleans was taking a group of youngsters to an undisclosed location. The old Remora intended to give them a tour of one of the Ship's oldest patches, letting them learn from the successes and glaring failures of people who died long ago.

The Remoras rode inside a big, nearly empty skimmer. Each of them was genetically human. Each one was also a lifesuit of hyperfiber with a single diamond plate over what passed for a face. Each suit held a tiny reactor feeding the machinery as well as an array of recycling systems that fed what wasn't quite human anymore. Fourteen youngsters were onboard. But of course calling anyone a "youngster" was a tease. The baby in the group was three hundred standard years old, while the oldest student was over a thousand. But being a Remora—a honorable, trustworthy Remora—involved skills that were mastered slowly, like the layers patiently building an enduring reef. And living like any Remora, exposed to the universe, was a hazardous, often too-brief species of life.

Three thousand years. That was a milestone largely regarded as worthy of celebration.

Ten thousand years. If a Remora could care for the Great Ship that long . . . well, that was one way to define a good, noble existence.

When death came, it did so suddenly, usually without generous warnings. Some dense chunk of asteroid slipped past the lasers and bombs. An old power plant went sideways, and the skimmer blew. Or maybe the Remora became careless, and his or her lifesuit body failed in some spectacular fashion.

Despite endless hazards, a respectable few Remoras reached twenty thousand years.

A portion of those old-timers were destined for forty thousand birthdays.

But Orleans was one of the exceptional few. Like every other Remora, he was born on the Great Ship. But that was eighty thousand years ago. Orleans was one of the final survivors of those very early generations.

As such, he had to be be famous.

And he had to be notorious.

Perhaps no other creature in existence, Remora or otherwise, had Orleans' spectacular capacity to measure threat and opportunity, while his reservoirs of luck seemed to defy all calculation.

There were times when the people worshipped Orleans for his good fortune as well as his wealth of practical knowledge, and they would repeat every good story about the long odds that their friend had defeated or tricked or at least endured.

But this was not one of those times.

Youngsters in this generation had suffered horrible losses. More comets than usual had slipped past defense systems, impacting on brave smart and very unlucky Remoras. Worse still, early this year an alien reactor detonated unexpectedly, and the blast was in the hundred megaton range. Thousands of their peers had been vaporized. That's why these fourteen youngsters felt abused by the Creation. They were entitled. And that is why they had embraced some very narrow, exceptionally rigid beliefs, including one simple, well-polished belief was that the oldest Remora was a coward in his heart. How else could Orleans have survived for so long? And with that faith in hand, they were free to look at him as if he were nothing but a contemptible piece of worn-out man.

The youngsters liked to glare at Orleans, snarling on private channels. As if he couldn't read their baby faces.

And Orleans rather enjoyed these harsh thoughts. It made him a better teacher by making more determined students, each one of these half-born children hungry to prove the old man's flaws in front of her peers.

"I know where you're taking us," one child began.

Gleem was her name.

Orleans looked at the ugly, almost-human face. "You know where, do you?"

"Yes. And I'm warning you. I know the trick."

Gleem had a bright gray human face and two white eyes, a crooked nose that couldn't decide where to grow, and a shiny black-lipped mouth full of black teeth. Being three hundred years and few months old, she was the babies' baby. According to a calendar full of arbitrary timemarks, she was also the last of her generation, and as sometimes happened with the lastborn, she was something of a prodigy—an expert with machines of every species and every useful job.

The girl had a two-and-a-half meter tall lifesuit for a shell.

For a skin.

Every Remora lived inside a lifesuit. Each lifesuit was built at the instant of conception, and that suit was theirs until a final moment of existence, usually on the leading edge of plasmatic fire.

"I know exactly what you're planning," she said.

Orleans laughed at his student.

The black-lipped mouth sneered.

And he laughed louder, on the public channel. Very little that was human showed in Orleans current face. He had six eyes evenly spread around the edges, and down low was a complicated nose full of delicately folded skin, looking like a flower blossom decorating the region where a chin might be set. The skull inside the helmet had been reassembled in novel ways, while his current mouth was in the middle of his inspired face—a large and wet and very good mouth designed for laughing.

Every mouth Orleans grew could enjoy a good joke.

"So you know," he said. "And I thought I had such a fine surprise waiting."

"It's the Rudger fissure, that's where the patch is. And you built that patch when you were our age."

"A full crew built it, and I happened to be there, yeah, except others were in charge of the operation. But you're right, I did some of the work."

"You made mistakes," she said.

"We all did that," he agreed.

"But we won't fix the mistakes, because you never let us."

"I don't let anyone do anything. Haven't you heard?"

The other youngsters were listening. But like people anywhere, they felt obliged to look elsewhere, pretending indifference.

"You'll take us to some corner of that patch, and we'll have to mark each little blunder," she said.

Orleans let everybody consider his silence. Then with a sturdy, careful voice, he said, "Your name. Gleem."

"What about it?"

"I've been meaning to ask. I knew another woman named Gleem. Did you steal the sound from her?"

The black mouth wasn't bad at laughing, but scoffing was its specialty. "That's a simple question to answer. Look at the records."

"Except I wanted to ask you," he said. "Which is not so simple, apparently."

Others laughed at that.

Gleem tightened her sneer. And then very quietly, she said, "It was my mother's mother's mother's name."

Orleans knew that, or he didn't. What mattered was to hear her explain a little bit about her simple, unfinished self.

"It's just a name," she said.

Orleans broke into a hard, long laugh.

"What do you mean?" the youngster demanded. "What's so funny, old man?"

One of her peers called out a warning. "He's got a lesson for us."

Which Orleans intended to impart on everyone, probably right away. But before his good-at-laughing mouth could offer another word, an encrypted transmission arrived. It came from a location that in eighty thousand years had never once spoken to Orleans, even by accident. He listened to the transmission. He listened, and the others watched him saying nothing, every young eye narrowed with thought. And then feeling bored, they began to chat among themselves while he continued to absorb orders and suggestions from high machine-minds that were too smart to be wrong and far too smart to appreciate what it was that they had discovered.

That one eye used to be alive, fully and utterly alive, and the body and mind attached to the eye were healthy, possessed by the certainty that nothing would ever go seriously wrong. Yet in the middle of a routine moment, everything went wrong. Other eyes and minds were close by. Everybody was riding a fine ship, rockets opened to full throttle, pushing colonists to some world far too distant to be seen. Then there was no one else. The others were missing. What happened to them? And where did the ship go? And why was this single creature tumbling through the blackness, screaming hard with a mouth barely born?

He was scared, far too scared to think along proper lines. And he spun wildly, and then he managed to quit weeping but couldn't stop tumbling, stars sweeping past his lidless gaze.

What had gone so horribly wrong?

Life on the starship had always been busy and pleasant, free of discord and blessed with moments of small joy. Then a critical machine on the bow demanded attention. It was decided that one of the crew had to dress in a lifesuit and step into the cold black. There was a song from the bridge, a rousing plea for one brave volunteer, and nobody answered. Then the leaders examined the rosters, identifying the most deserving, least important crewmen. That was when he sang back at them. That's when he volunteered, and it was the last time in his life that he would hear others singing about their own happiness and considerable relief.

Inside the airlock, ten lifesuits stood at attention. Because he was small, he claimed the largest, thickest suit for himself. Feeling big was the only reason. Then he passed through the airlock and into space. The work itself was quite routine. Nothing went wrong and nothing felt wrong. One navigation system needed close attention, and there was a menu to follow, and he did the job perfectly if a little slowly. His suit and his body were tethered to the outside of the starship, nearly finished with the job, and then the ship was gone. Some huge soundless event tore him loose, gave him new momentum, and that terrific jolt turned his body into living water and scared grit.

Modern life could endure almost any abuse, short of plasmatic fire. His bioceramic mind fell into a state deeper than sleep but far, far removed from Death. Then his water and organelles and phages found one another, and they found energy and heat, reconstituting a body that allowed him to become aware again, spinning and screaming, weeping and then not weeping.

How much time had passed?

He asked the suit.

The big lifesuit had counted five days.

But what happened to the ship and colonists and the rest of the crew?

It was a critical matter, but the suit had no opinion. And no interest. It was a minimally conscious machine, somewhat damaged by the abrupt fury. Maybe the ship's engines exploded. Or a black comet gutted its body. Speculation was pointless. Circumstances were critical. But the suit was still able to hear a close strong radio signal, and there were no signals. The vacuum was silent. Nobody was calling to the suit or to its ungrateful passenger.

The passenger wailed until exhausted.

Detecting hunger, the suit fed him and infused his fluids with fresh oxygen.

The simplest lifesuit could purify water and air, and it could synthesize food, and when necessary, generate pleasant sounds and odors. This particular lifesuit also possessed two fully-fueled reactors and several banks of unfinished machinery. Unfinished machines could be organized in any direction necessary. The suit had been designed to serve this starship and another fifty ships in the future. And to the limits of its cognitive powers, this suit could help its passenger survive.

The starship was no more. There would be no rescue or even a sorrowful greeting from the black of space. An undeserving life had been delivered to this one creature, and it came for no good reason, and now his suffering would stretch into an eternity.

That passenger proved to be an obsessive, half-mad beast. Each conscious moment was suffused with thoughts about those last moments of normal life. In excruciating detail, he replayed routine events where nothing went wrong, where he did what was expected of him, and every memory left him aching with guilt. Perhaps the engines failed. But if he hadn't been brave enough or pliable enough to march out onto the hull, he would have remained inside, and maybe he would have seen the malfunction and saved the ship. Or an impact killed everyone. But if he had volunteered with the first call, and if he had worn a smaller, less massive suit, the vagaries of those tiny motions and masses would have shifted the ship's trajectory a cell's width. In another ten million kilometers, that faint change would have shifted the ship hundreds of meters, and everybody would have been saved, and he would have been the unknown hero.

Enticing stories want to be told. But of all the possibilities, what was most likely, and what was most wonderful, was any variation killed him along with everybody else, leaving him beyond doubt and every misery.

"Kill me," he told the suit.

Not understanding, the suit continued its important work.

So the passenger tried to murder himself. But the lifesuit was designed to care for almost any level of damage. There were multiple ways to force its passenger to breathe and find nutrition as well as adequate energy to repair what pathetic little damages that the creature could inflict on a body that couldn't be touched.

Ages passed.

Immortal beings can bear horrible things, and misery found its natural, bearable state. But with the ages and small measures of cleverness, the suit did manage one small decency: Wasted heat had to be bled off the reactors, and the suit did so in an uneven fashion, the wild spinning body slowing and then stopping entirely.

Eventually the passenger went through space with his one eye forward.

Still screaming, still weeping, but never quite as much as before.

Orleans offered telemetry and images, and then he let the fourteen children weave their own conclusions.

"The object, the artifact, is eight meters long, two wide," he told them, opening the full files for examination. "Hyperfiber on the outside, and that's all we know. This is the AIs' best guess of its shape, its density, and this is its velocity right now, and this is how much the prize needs to slow to survive its impact with the Ship. Which is coming in just a little while. There's no way around that ending."

Orleans realized that his voice was too excited, and so he paused. He didn't want hopes escaping too soon.

"That's a biological shape," said one boy, and another, and the oldest girl. But Gleem was first to point out, "It's a high-grav configuration, but I'm not seeing this beast in any of our libraries . . . "

"How old is it?" someone asked.

Orleans had no idea.

But for fun, he said, "One billion years, and a day."

Nobody believed that. But all of the children, or even Orleans, could not stop playing with enormous numbers.

"So how do we manage this landing?" another boy asked. "Because they want to save the artifact, right?"

"I'm an idiot," their teacher said. "You tell me how."

A debate was launched. Fifty opinions came from every mouth. Except for Gleem. She walked to the front of the skimmer, silently making calculations, answering an entirely different problem.

And Orleans remained behind everyone, watching.

Thirteen students devised one utterly workable scheme. The artifact was built from hyperfiber, but descending at one-third the speed of light, even the finest grade of fiber would shatter. The Great Ship refused to slow, so the target needed to find quite a lot of velocity and find it quickly. Thankfully the asteroid was a tough, useful blessing. One hundred billion tons of iron could be melted, and that melt could be vaporized in controlled bursts, banks of lasers working with surgical grace and surgical conviction, delivering just enough thrust with just enough stability to launch the artifact away from the Great Ship. And then with luck, the inevitable collision might not spoil the object's value for engineers and historians.

The girl took no part in the discussion. She stood apart. She was a baby barely able to control the mutations of her own flesh, dressed in a suit nearly identical to everyone else's suit. In a cabin full of chatter and hand gestures, she ordered the skimmer's wall to become clear. The Ship's slick gray hull raced beneath them, and nobody else noticed. Then her hyperfiber arm lifted, bent at first and then straight, and one finger was pointed at the wrong place and then the right place. The correction was made instantly, without anyone's help.

One of the boys asked Gleem, "What are you doing?"

She didn't answer. Really, if he didn't appreciate what her arm meant, then he was too ignorant to survive long as a Remora.

The oldest girl said, "Oh, that's where it's going to crash."

Everyone but Gleem turned towards Orleans.

"Of course it is," said the baby, laughing at all of them. "Don't you see? The old coward already has us making a nice safe spiral around the crash site!"

The epiphany was tiny. Nothing about any recent day was better or worse, certainly not special, and the passenger couldn't recall so much as one novel thought inside the boredom. He ate and breathed and wept and begged for death, and his dreams were ordinary or they were forgotten. And then he was awake again, hungry enough to endure the simple salted paste—the easiest food that could be made by machinery that was shepherding its energy. He ate until the immortal stomachs stopped complaining, and he drank sweetened water, and he evacuated his bowels twice before realizing that he hadn't screamed or sobbed once, much less complained about this unyielding hell of existence.

Why wasn't he shrieking in agony?

The question posed itself, and the same voice tried to give a worthy answer.

"Because you have come to terms with your fate."

But no, that wasn't the case. What he realized at last—what he should have appreciated from the first moment inside this tomb—was that he had resources beyond count. The lifesuit was tough but idiotic. But the body inside the suit was infused with phages and nanotools and genetic materials, modern as well as ancient. Every emergency pathway was a finger. The mechanisms that could rebuild a body might be fooled by that same body. Apply willpower to these armies of cells and their modern scaffolding, and quite a lot might be accomplished.

The day passed quietly.

And the next twenty days too.

Then another question was posed. This time the suit spoke, with a voice that could never sound concerned or particularly curious.

"What are doing now?" asked the lifesuit.

"I am doing nothing," the passenger said.

"But you are," it maintained. "You have slowed your circulation, and the acidity in your blood is a mistake."

"Maybe you should stop me," he said.

"When you harm yourself, I will."

But these matters of hearts and blood were only practice. They were the exploratory fumblings of a child. What he wanted would take eons, if it ever came. But that was the better fate than wild misery.

Every waking moment was spent in furious concentration.

And in his dreams, the passenger was blood moving where it wished, and little bones breaking where they needed to break, and single cells mutated in their deep genetics, producing wonderful little cancers, happy as could be, that were born eager to remake their world.

The dead eye saw familiar stars but no tumbling gray ball. The asteroid stood between the eye and the Great Ship.

The day ended with a hard jolt that shook worse by the moment. The eye and body rose up out of the slag. There were moments when any wrong impact would send it tumbling wildly into space. Every other velocity was the wrong velocity. But instead of being lost, the ancient lifesuit rose straight out of the crater, hovering for a long moment before beginning a slow, patient fall back into the quiet, grim pool of red iron.

No warning was offered.

One moment, the illusion of timeless cold space held sway. Then the blue light slashed into the asteroid, devastating the far hemisphere. That entire world was accelerated, heaved into the lifesuit. Like a hand, the crater swept up what it had already held for untold ages. The dead eye remained pointed upwards, outwards. The universe was stripped its stars. Nothing existed but violet plasmas infused with a mist of iron, every atom carrying away a billion years of aimless drifting.

The acceleration diminished for a moment. And then it returned, doubling and doubling again.

Hyperfiber fought to endure.

At various junctures, where the stresses were the worst, little fissures opened up, threatening to spread.

The suit nearly shattered.

At a thousand points, it wanted to surrender.

But the lasers throttled back, and wielding more data, the lasers' aim grew surer, and the dead eye and the rest of the artifact settled into their new, very much unexpected existence.

The youngsters wished they were closer, but there was a coward among them. They wanted to see the flash of the impact, which they did see, but through remote eyes, mechanical, indifferent to fear and caution. But Orleans insisted on distance, and at the end, when everything was a little exciting and a little fun, the old Remora was distracted, busily talking to others still farther away than they were.

He talked about nothing important.

Equipment lists.

Favorite foods.

Gossip about the cowardly humans living under their boots.

Too late, the children realized that Orleans was using code—strings of words and subjects and probably the pauses between—sounds and nonsounds informing others about quite a lot more than the ugliness of an old rich woman.

Five seconds after the impact, the AIs in charge heard a broadcast from Orleans. A big stern voice said, "The sky's too hot. There's too much debris falling. I'm taking the babies on to Rudgers."

On every screen, their skimmer began racing for the old patch and its new, boring lessons.

But the babies and their teacher as well as the real skimmer were flying straight to that point where something very old had fallen from the stars.

The suit had never quit calculating the passage of time.

Certain days and moments were important beyond every other. There was that instant when the suit was born, and long years later, there was the instant when it and passenger were stripped from the starship. There was the day when the passenger stopped weeping. And after that, there was that first moment when a new bone formed inside the immortal body, and the suit asked about this odd structure, and the passenger offered words that, in retrospect, had no bearing on what was true.

"I am entertaining myself, with myself," the passenger claimed.

Eventually quite a lot more than bones appeared. Tissues changed color, changed density. What looked random slowly revealed planning, and the details and scope of the changes impressed those little parts of the machine could feel. The passenger's eye changed its shape and nature, becoming far more sensitive to dim light and starlight and the faint reflection of the face inside the diamond faceplate.

Too late by a long while, the lifesuit answered that old question: What are you doing with yourself?

Armed with an insight, it woke the passenger instantly, roughly. "You are trying to kill yourself," it said.

"I cannot kill myself," he replied.

"No, but there are emergency metabolisms. If you generate the right one, and if you subvert my means of overriding what you're trying to accomplish—"

"I could do that," he said. "I considered doing that, yes."

"But you haven't," the suit said.

"Nor will I," said the happy passenger. "Unlikely as it seems, I've come to enjoy this existence. Life in its purest form. Nothing but the body and soul striving for some never-to-be-achieved perfection."

"Good," was a worthy offering. So the suit said the word many times.

"Yes," the passenger agreed, every time.

Then a feeling that wasn't guilt and wasn't sadness took hold of the machine. And with the same voice as always, except slower, it said to the passenger, "I have news that concerns you."

"What news?"

"The reactors on which we depend . . . "

"Yes?"

"One has failed. Three hundred thousand days ago, it ceased to work, and I have maintained both of us with the other reactor."

It was the passenger's moment to say, "Good."

Then he thought harder, and with a pensive sound, he asked, "How is our other reactor doing?"

"Poorly," said the suit.

Silence.

"But it will last for this day," the suit offered. "And for another day, and perhaps another million days. It is impossible for me to judge such things."

"You are lucky," said the shapeshifting passenger.

"I have known some good fortune, yes."

"Who hasn't?" he asked, and then he began to laugh—a bright wild laugh, as if he were trying to fill Existence with his joy.

◆ ◆ ◆

Atoms were elegant in design, reliable of mood and simple by any fair measure, while the visible universe, taken in its entirety, looked like a single thing that did not vary from end to end.

But between atoms and the universe lay the unmeasured, the unknown.

Hidden fissures and incursions lurked inside every asteroid, and just as critical, distant AIs could never anticipate where the wild iron was heroically strong. Laser light was absorbed as predicted and a clean plume of million degree fire blossomed, and the old asteroid flung off most of its mass, gaining velocity. But not quite enough velocity. And when there was no place for error, the blistered core shattered where it shouldn't and remained together where it shouldn't, and that little world began to wobble one way and then the next.

Too late, the AIs stopped firing.

The shriveled asteroid rolled and fell to pieces, room-sized gobs of liquid iron and tacky red iron tumbling inside whirlwinds of plasma.

A single wisp of hyperfiber appeared for an instant, then vanished.

Which was horrible, and good. Debris began crashing across a larger sliver of the hull than anticipated. The old Remora had kept his crew at a cowardly distance, ensuring their survival, and that's why they were alive to hear him explaining how that was not best, all things considered. "But one big mess does make our job easier," he added.

And then he fell silent.

Obvious words, obvious questions. Nothing seemed worth saying. Even Gleem kept her human mouth silent. Their skimmer was weaving camouflage, and then the iron rain slackened and they began a sprint between the small, newborn craters. Tiny fragments kept falling far ahead of them, each impact marked by a blue flash and the idea of thunder, if not the roar. But every eye was fixed on the ancient creature still standing at the back of the cabin, apparently doing nothing.

Orleans rather enjoyed the moment and that fine, rich energy that came from deep curiosity.

"This is inevitable," he began.

A final blue flash washed over them, and then the skies cleared.

"Little starships die every day, die and break open," he said. "Souls get scattered across deep space, and some of the souls are immortal, in a fashion. If a lucky immortal wears escape pods and lifesuits, the soul can survive the disaster. In a fashion. Of course some pods and a few suits are rescued soon enough. But most of them are lost forever, and cheap suits usually fail after a century or ten thousand years, and those don't matter so much to us. What matters are souls who can live and live and live. Those are the ones facing an eternity, and some sliver of them will survive, and a few retain their sanity, or they find a new sanity, and in some fashion, each of them remakes himself in small ways, or otherwise.

"Call them our brothers.

"The heavens are littered with Remoras. They don't have voices that we can hear. They drift in darkness, invisible up until that moment when they find themselves helpless before the Great Ship. And we kill them. Most of them. If there's a big lifepod ahead of us, of course it gets shattered with shaped nukes. Little suits, naked to space, are incinerated, or they're left to poke a hole that other Remoras have to fill. We can't save what we don't see until it's too late. We can't grieve for what we'll never know. But there are instances, and I won't tell you how many, like today. An old lifesuit is pinned to a mass substantial enough and tough enough to be thrown ahead of us, given just enough momentum to save what might, might, might still be alive.

"For the next little while, let's assume we have a Remora."

Trajectory models were in agreement. Orleans pointed a confident finger at their destination, and the skimmer began to brake.

"Our sibling came in too fast. Probably. But we won't know until you go out there and look. Take the medical kits. Take hope if you want, although it won't help, and carry cutting tools, yes. When we come to a stop, you'll have maybe three minutes to measure our sibling's health, and if he's dead, we have to decide if he was a genuine Remora. Because if he was . . . "

Orleans paused.

Everyone knew the rest of it. But Gleem felt it her duty to shout out, "Only Remoras put Remoras into the grave."

"What will you do if he is, was one of us?" another youngster asked.

"Stand where I am and keep fooling every captain," Orleans said. "Making camouflage is too much work to do anything else. This job is yours. All yours."

The second reactor was failing.

Every day was probably the last day.

The reactor's death would result in the passenger's death, fast at first and then very slow. He knew his flesh would seize up for lack of calories, and then it would freeze. A sequence of increasingly deep comas would claim his mind, allowing life to persist a little longer. But even the most minimal existence needed energy. Even the slightest flame flickered out after ten million years of darkness. That was why the oldest Remora tore apart his mouth and skull, using that flesh to manipulate his one eye, making a broad disk black as ink and more sensitive than ever.

Greedy pigments absorbed every photon, or nearly so.

The weakest starlight was visible, but that light also wobbled a few electrons that weren't seen, that would push back into a mind, precipitating some good lazy thought that would be enjoyed and then forgotten.

It was a strange, desperate plan, and when he was awake, he was full of doubt. He seriously reconsidered his plan.

But before he could make himself blind, the reactor failed, and the suit died without a final word, and with his flesh freezing, the passenger fell into an imperfect, eternal half-death.

Dust struck, and the lifesuit and corpse began to spin again.

Slow memories wandered through him, bumping into one another. But sometimes he drifted close to a sun, and if that eye stared at the glare, the old mind woke long enough to remember its circumstances and an immeasurable past.

Full life returned just twice.

The first rebirth came when he crashed into the iron world. Cloaked in radiant energy, the Remora enjoyed several minutes of consciousness, ending with feeling grateful to find himself at the bottom of a bowl, the great eye pointing upwards, not down.

And then after a very long darkness, he saw the simple gray ball that wasn't simple, and then laser light and plasmas were wrapped around him, dragging the mind back into a frantic, disjointed life, and as the world around him fell to pieces, and as the Great Ship rose too fast, his final thought was a premonition.

He was about to be rescued.

Regardless what happened next, he was saved.

A newborn crater stretched before them, shallow but wide. In its center, where the Ship's hull was shiny gray after the impact, lay a chunk of what looked like trash hyperfiber, dark and broken into at least three unequal portions.

The skimmer stopped beside the prize and hovered.

Fourteen youngsters grabbed gear and jumped free. As he had promised, Orleans was busy weaving a fine believable picture of things that were not happening, but he also read everything that others read on the sensors. The ancient prize lay in three pieces. Two fragments were full of flesh dead long before the crash. But the dust showed complications, shifting metabolisms and invented forms familiar to any Remora. The third fragment had served as the head, presumably wearing some intricate structure erased by this catastrophic change of momentum. A bioceramic brain was nestled inside the goo—a robustly-built model matching nothing in the database—and it might well have been alive at the end. But there was an end. The crash had shattered the old mind in a thousand places, and there was no sign of thought or a soul sleeping deeply, and every memory had slipped into Nothingness.

The fourteen of them stopped their work, just for a moment.

Then Orleans called to them. Not quietly, but with a smooth patient voice, he said, "Put all of the body onboard. Another crew's bringing scrap hyperfiber. They'll build a likely mess here. For the captains' sake. To fool everyone else."

Each piece of the body, shell and dust and drip, was pulled out of the crater, secured inside the cargo hold.

Finished, the youngsters came back inside the cabin.

Orleans told the skimmer to move again.

Until halfway to the Rudger fissure, nobody spoke. Then Gleem approached the silent old man, her two eyes watching his six.

"You've done this kind of thing before," she guessed.

"I've done every kind of thing before," he said.

"Have any of these falling souls lived?" she asked.

Orleans closed every eye, and his young mouth sighed.

"Tell me. Am I right?"

He waited.

"Because if you did, then they could still be living among us now. Remoras from the beginnings of space flight."

Nothing needed to be said.

"Why won't you tell me?" she asked. "Tell me that I'm right!"

That's when one of the other youngsters—a middle-aged boy who rarely spoke and only with a soft voice—stepped close to her. Using both arms, he tried to knock Gleem off her feet, which was almost impossible. It was a gesture, a show of theater. And then on the public channel, with a booming voice, said, "He isn't telling us because it's a secret!"

"Of course it's a secret," she said.

"Shut up," the boy said.

"Why? I want to know."

Then the boy said, "He won't tell because you aren't. None of us are."

"We're not what?"

"Like him!" the boy screamed, pounding her helmet with both of his hyperfiber hands. "Not yet and maybe never. We're not Remoras, and of course he doesn't trust you with secrets, and this is an awful day, a very sad day, and can't you understand that . . . ?"

OIL OF ANGELS
CHEN QIUFAN, TRANSLATED BY KEN LIU

As soon as Doctor Qing's hands pressed against my naked back and slid downwards, my skin felt as though it had grown wings. I knew then that all my efforts had been worth it.

This massage clinic was located near Di'anmen, the Gate of Earthly Peace, along the ancient Hundred Flowers *hutong*. The clinic had no sign and took no walk-ins. New clients had to be recommended by existing clients and call a special phone number to make an appointment. The initial waiting period ranged from a week to a month, depending on how busy the clinic was and the doctors' moods.

After checking my ID and appointment number, the receptionist brought me upstairs to a small waiting room decorated in a minimalist Scandinavian style rarely seen in Beijing. The cream-colored wallpaper and furniture appeared faded in the city's corrosive, dirty air, but the owners didn't seem to care. A faint fragrance permeated the air without the pungency of artificial scents. It smelled familiar, but I couldn't place it. I struggled to recall it, forcing myself to scan the bad sectors of my memory over and over, until a sweet-looking girl came to tell me that the aromatherapy room was ready for me.

This new room suggested the dim inside of a silkworm cocoon: purple light, filtered through layers of silk, cast moiré patterns against the wall like ripples in a pound. I felt lost in this tiny room no more than a few feet on a side.

As I came out of the bath, I found Doctor Qing silently waiting for me. She was an ordinary, middle-aged woman, not too tall, dressed in a light-colored uniform. Pointing to the massage table, she said, in an authoritative tone exactly like a real doctor's, "Undress and lie on the table. Face down. Arms at your sides."

But I was already nude.

She was blind and couldn't see my body, and this made me feel less awkward. I climbed onto the bed, carefully settling my face into the hole. Below me, I saw a lotus-shaped ceramic candleholder. Air heated by the tiny flame wafted up to me, carrying the familiar scent.

"That's neroli oil. It helps you relax. Calms you," Doctor Qing said as if she knew what I was thinking.

"Doctor, there's something on my mind . . . " I struggled to bring up my problem. A hand lightly pressed against the back of my head, where my MAD was installed.

"Stop thinking. Your mind will never tell the truth. But your body never lies."

Warm oil dripped against the center of my back. Her palms then spread the oil around in a circular motion. My consciousness seemed to follow the same motion, swirling slowly, drifting, like a leaf caught in an eddy.

"I'm using only carrier oil, made from sweet almond extract, suitable for a wide variety of skins." Doctor Qing's voice seemed to come from outer space, from light years away. "Since this is your first time, I can't use any essential oils. I have to get to know your reactions first. Of course, I'm not just talking about your body . . . "

Before I could react, her hands shifted direction and dashed from my back to my sides like two slippery fish. An indescribable pleasure bloomed against my body like the layers of a lotus flower. I had never imagined that one woman could set another woman's body on fire so quickly. I felt aroused.

Even more incredibly, as she continued to manipulate my body, the thoughts that had confused and bothered me floated up into consciousness like bubbles, and then burst and disappeared, one after another. What remained of my reason tried to figure out just how the therapy worked, but suddenly, I cried out.

A surge of dark emotion wrapped around my hip like a python. My womb felt squeezed, distorted, even though it was empty. Terror oozed from my skin, making me clammy and cold. I heard someone sobbing like a lost child. I searched for the source of the sound, which seemed so close at one moment and so far away the next.

The python disappeared, taking away the terror and discomfort. I woke up. Doctor Qing's hands left my waist.

"I think that's enough for today." She seemed to want to say more but stopped herself. "You should rest."

Doctor Qing left the room. It was a long while before I recovered enough to turn over. I was trembling, panting, like I had just emerged from a nightmare or a passionate bout of sex.

My face felt wet and cold. I was the one who had cried, the disconsolate child.

And I could no longer avoid that word, the source of all my questions, the word that filled my mind.

Mother.

My mother left me when I was four, leaving me with my grandparents. I never saw my father. He had died before I was born, and how he died was always a mystery to me.

When I was eleven, my mother returned, and took me from my small town to Beijing, where order had finally been restored. She had married a man with money and power, and she paid for me to go to an expensive private school, bought me the best of everything. But from then on, I refused to call her *mom*.

After I began college, I moved out of my mother's home. I worked extra jobs and didn't sleep more than five hours a night so that I would not have to spend another cent of that man's money. I didn't hate my stepfather. He was a nice man, and until my grandparents died, he would often send money to them in my mother's name. I just didn't want my mother to get the mistaken impression that I *needed* her.

Whenever anyone commented that I was like my mother, I would stare at them until they realized that it was a gaffe and apologized.

But they were right.

From the little I remembered, she never showed love, or even care, the way other mothers did. She was always demanding, nervous, moody. Sometimes she would scream, swear at me, and demand I leave the table for doing nothing more than scraping the spoon against the bowl too loudly. When she felt down, she would not speak to me for days. Her home always felt like an ice cellar.

I tried to understand how my stepfather could love her, especially when she hit him. He always told me: *Your mother hasn't had it easy.*

I thought: *No one in the world has had it easy.*

We were all born in the years after the Catastrophe, and she had been born during it.

Good thing that we have the MAD.

The Memory Assistant Device was invented back in my grandmother's time. Initially, it was meant to help the victims of mental trauma after the Catastrophe. Then the government sponsored it, and it became a part of every infant's standard medical care, like immunizations. The earliest MAD models required wired connections, but by my mother's generation, wireless was the norm.

Of course, not just anybody had the right to access and control memories— even their own—only experienced memory doctors had such authority. This meant that you had to explain your problems to them.

I wasn't good at talking about my feelings. This was a trait my mother and I shared, I admit.

I remember a young doctor and myself facing off for half an hour. I answered his questions with silence until he threatened me: "I won't sign the authorization form unless you give me a reason."

I knew that he really did want to help me—otherwise he wouldn't have bothered asking. I hesitated, and then said, "Abuse."

He glanced at me and wrote something down in his notebook. I thought: *I'm so not good at lying.*

In the end, I accepted his proposal: since eliminating all memories having to do with the abuse would have left me with nothing, leaching the emotions from those memories would work much better.

"Every memory would seem like a scene from a TV show," the doctor said. "And you've turned the volume way, way down."

I suddenly found him attractive.

We dated for a while, until he—like the others—left me because he could stand me no more. Most of the time we were together, I said nothing. Like other men, he tried to please me in various ways: trying to figure out why I was feeling low, plying me with good food, surprise presents, trips, music, sex, but nothing was particularly effective. Instead, I grew contemptuous of his apparent stupidity and excessive solicitousness and responded with manipulative gestures, such as suddenly cutting off all contact with him. When I imagined him almost driven to madness by my antics, my mood lifted—even I couldn't explain why.

"You're sick," he finally said.

"You should have known that already," I retorted.

"But those memories have already been tuned!"

"What you erased was only the shadow."

After the procedure, I could recall the time my mother and I spent together without becoming emotional, but my own life had become a bad copy of a flawed original. An irresistible force compelled me in her direction, to start down some fated path, towards self-destruction. I tried everything: psychotherapy, yoga, mystical Buddhism, vegetarianism, anti-depression medication, family systems therapy . . . nothing worked.

I felt myself connected to my mother in some way that surpassed time and space. Or maybe it was what he said: epigenetic memory.

The theory holds that stress from childhoods spent under the care of irresponsible, cold, short-tempered parents could increase the amount of DNA methylation experienced by children. Many important genes responsible for neural communications, brain development and functioning would then not express normally, resulting in difficulties for these children in perceiving and expressing love, substituting fear and desperation in its place.

Worst of all, such damage is heritable.

As I grew older, my friends got married and became parents, but I felt myself pulled away from this well-trodden path. I knew what that force was: I was afraid that I might become another nightmarish mother; I was afraid that my children would be like me. I might die, but the curse would be passed on, generation after generation.

My mother contacted me through my friends. She was sick, and wanted to see me.

I told her I didn't want to see her.

After a period of silence, I received another message. *If you change your mind, you can find me here.*

I looked at the address. Resisting it was like resisting gravity.

◆ ◆ ◆

"I'm using Angelica oil this time. It can reduce tension and relieve stress-induced migraines and anxiety." Doctor Qing's voice drifted down to me from above. "But remember not to expose yourself to too much sun afterwards. Some of the components are light-sensitive."

I mumbled an acknowledgment, too focused on the feeling of her hands roaming about my neck and head. This was my fourth time here. Now that Doctor Qing and I knew each other better, there was a kind of doctor-patient trust between us. She was professional, experienced, and able to intuit meaning from my body's slightest responses. I hadn't told her about my mother yet; the right opportunity hadn't arisen.

Lulled by that grassy, slightly acrid scent, I again sank into semi-consciousness. My body floated, drifting along the ground. I couldn't control the speed, altitude, or direction. Like a passenger on a rollercoaster, all I could do was to allow myself to be carried along the rails.

My vision became dim and fuzzy, and it was impossible for me to say what I truly saw. But the emotional flavor of everything was sharpened. I felt anxiety and anger coming from all around me, resonating with me, as though I was in the middle of a crowd swarming like a hive of bees.

A stone fell into the water; fiery light flickered; sorrow, like the muddy ground after spring rain, held me in place. I felt death approach me, step by step, and I had no way to escape, my consciousness imprisoned in such a tiny space that all that was left was desperation.

I saw a little girl squatting in the only sphere of light in the endless darkness. She seemed to be drawing something.

In spite of her blurred features, I was absolutely certain that she was my mother.

Of course, in dreams we often know for certain who a particular person is, even when we do not see her clearly, but it was odd to dream about your mother as a little girl.

I tried to touch her, but I couldn't move at all. The sphere of light shrank and moved further away.

I tried to scream, but no sound came out.

She disappeared in the darkness.

"Perhaps I shouldn't pry." Doctor Qing's voice pulled me back into the real world. "You must love your mother very much."

"What makes you say that?" My voice rasped with resentment.

"You cried out for her."

I said nothing.

"Aromatherapy works on the body and the mind at the same time. Some people react to essential oils in unpredictable ways. Feelings repressed for many years could suddenly resurface."

"—I haven't seen her in nearly five years," I blurted out.

"Would you like to talk about it? It can help with your therapy."

I took a deep breath, exhaled, and the flame in the lotus candleholder flickered. She couldn't see me, and I couldn't see her. This made me feel safe enough to talk.

My lack of reservation surprised even myself. This was the first time I had ever told anyone of the history between my mother and me. I told her of my childhood, my mother's odd moods, my stepfather, and my many boyfriends. Finally, I brought up my experience with MAD.

"You really went through with it?"

"But it didn't work. I changed the past, but I couldn't change the present." I mentioned the strange dream I had just had. "Maybe I even made it worse."

Doctor Qing seemed to be deep in thought and didn't answer me right away. When she spoke again, her tone sounded unnatural.

"Have you ever thought . . . it might not be your mother's fault? The dreams—they might not belong to you either."

"What are you trying to say?"

"Before I became a masseuse, I was involved in scientific research. A dangerous project I was working on blinded me, and then I was laid off. I was just glad that I survived."

"What kind of research, exactly?"

"I don't know. They erased all my memories of it."

"Oh." In fact, I had heard many other stories like hers. The state would sometimes erase the memories of some individuals because they violated the law or because they knew too much. Afterwards, their social status inevitably declined. "But what does this have to do with my dream?"

"After I lost my old job as a researcher, I tried to make a living in many different ways. But because of my blindness, I couldn't last in any of them very long. In the end, I sort of stumbled into this profession. Sometimes, I wonder if it was all arranged ahead of time." Her tone was casual, amused. She also didn't really answer my question.

"Arranged? By who?"

"The person who saved me, who laid me off, and maybe even . . . who blinded me in the first place." She sounded so calm, as though she were only discussing some essential oil. "Even though my memory had been erased, some aspects of my training remained with me. My intuition and logical approach have served me well in this new profession, too. For example, I've noticed that some of my clients react to certain essential oils in an unusual manner. They're like jewelry boxes that are opened by different keys; yet, once open, they all held the same jewels."

"You mean—" I held my breath.

"Yes. You're all dreaming the same dream. I can't say it with one hundred percent certainty, but based on the descriptions, you've all experienced the same scene. All of you saw your parents as children. It's . . . odd."

My heart beat faster, as though suddenly free of the bounds of gravity.

"Why are you telling me this?"

"I like you. You remind me of my daughter. After the accident, she never let me near her again. Sometimes, I think maybe there's a way to correct all these errors. I don't believe in fate or any kind of supernatural force. I believe in rationality and logic.

"I believe it's almost time to reveal the answer to the riddle. I can help you, and you can also help me—assuming you want to."

" . . . how do I help you?"

"Go see your mother."

She lay in the special care unit, looking even thinner and older than the version of her I had imagined. Her eyes struggled to hold me, but her gaze kept on slipping away as though my body had been covered by light-deflecting grease.

The doctor told me that she was suffering from ataxia, cause unknown. They needed to do more tests, but something was probably wrong with her cerebellum.

In front of her bed, I stood with my arms crossed, staring at her coldly. Even the most impatient nurse would appear more like a daughter to her than I. I tried to push away the hateful thought, but it refused to obey and leapt into my consciousness, unbidden:

You deserve this.

"Come, come closer." Her lips quivered violently.

I shook my head, sighed, and walked to the head of her bed, getting as close to her as I could tolerate. I detected a strong medicinal odor, but under that was another scent that I hadn't encountered in a long time. In a flash, it was as if a tunnel through space and time had opened up and brought me back to my distant childhood.

It was the smell of my mother.

"I'm going to die soon . . . "

"No, you won't."

"I know you hate me."

"No." My voice grew fainter. "I . . . don't."

She appeared to want to laugh, but the muscles on her face spasmed and twisted even more violently. The sides of her face throbbed as though they were about to take off into air.

"You're indeed my flesh and blood . . . when I was young, I also . . . hated my mother."

"Grandma? Why? She was so good to you!"

"Not your Grandma. She was only my stepmother. I'm talking about my real mother. She died . . . when I was a teenager."

"What was she like?" I tried to imagine the grandmother I had never seen.

"Pretty, like you. Bad-tempered, like me." She finally managed a smile. "They called her a hero not only because she had survived, and not only because she was among the first to be implanted with a MAD . . . When she had decided to have a child, the world had already started to collapse. Your grandfather had lost all hope and wanted to abort the baby. But she insisted on having me . . . "

"Why did she want a child so much?"

"I couldn't understand it, either, not until I was pregnant with you. Then I understood that feeling. Though the Catastrophe had been over by then, every day, I lived in fear, wondering whether it was the right thing to do to bring you into this mess of a world. What little sleep I got was filled with nightmares. Everyone tried to talk me out of it, but, in the end, I made the same decision she had."

I understood what my mother wanted to say but didn't.

"My father didn't want me. Am I right?"

My mother's eyes began to wander, as though she couldn't find anything on which to fix her gaze. She looked outside the window.

"Your father was a good man. But . . . he had seen so much that terrorized him . . . " Like me, she wasn't any good at lying.

"Maybe he was right," I said, keeping my voice cold.

"No! You don't understand!" My mother's voice was hot, searing. "Every time I see you, it's like I see the past that had been wiped away from me and your father. You're the proof that we were *alive*. I've never regretted that decision."

I felt like crying.

We fell silent together. In the surviving pieces of this family history was a heart-breaking story. Much of it wasn't motivated by love, but survival. Doctor Qing was right: I understood my mother too little. She had been molded by too many stories that had been forgotten, that had been erased, but I blamed everything on her, as though she had become the way she was by an act of conscious will. I felt apologetic.

The smell in the room became intolerable; I needed fresh air.

"Rest well. I'll come see you again." I got up and gently patted the back of her hand. But she grabbed me and held on. In my memory, my mother had never touched me except to hit me.

"I had a dream . . . It was so dark, so frightening. I dreamt that I was a child again . . . " Her breath was shallow, fast, her gaze anxious and without focus. Her dry, thin fingers refused to let go.

We shared the same dream. This was far more frightening than the dream itself.

"It's only a dream," I said gently, trying to comfort her. I combed through her thinning, gray hair.

"So dark . . . so dark . . . " My mother muttered, as though she had turned into the little girl in the dream.

I thought, *Maybe it's possible for me to become a good mother.*

The blindfold was very tight, and I couldn't see anything. My hand rested on Doctor Qing's shoulder. As a blind woman, she was skilled at leading another.

I took each step with care, as though walking into the depth of the night sky. When deprived of sight, your ears and nose became especially sensitive. I could hear tiny teeth grinding in invisible corners; I could detect the stench of rotting garbage, mixed with the sweet, rusty scent of metal, and the remnants of the complex compounds in essential oils lingering on Doctor Qing.

She thought I was the one they had been seeking.

"Who are *they*?" I asked.

"The less you know, the better," she said.

After a long journey during which we passed several cramped, tight corners, the air smelled fresh again. We had arrived.

"Sorry, but we can't take off the blindfold just yet." The man's voice was flat, without a trace of regional accent.

I nodded, indicating that it was all right.

"I need to thank you. You're without a doubt the best subject. But I hope you understand that the experiment is not without risks. If you want to back out, there's still enough time."

I shook my head. "I just want to know: why me?" I meant not only for this experiment, but also the rest of my life.

He laughed. The sound was open, frank.

"Remember your dream? It's not a dream at all, but the remnants of memory. It came not from your mother, but your grandmother."

"How is that possible? You're telling me that memory can be inherited?"

"I concede that this is a bit hard to believe . . . " He paused, as though pondering how to explain.

It was that damned epigenetic memory again. At least I wasn't completely ignorant anymore.

Diet, the environment, and drugs can all cause DNA to methylate, affecting genetic expression. While the DNA sequences are not altered, these methylation results can be inherited. Moreover, certain traumatic events, such as childhood neglect, abuse, surviving a massacre, drug abuse, or mental breakdown, can also affect epigenetics. In other words, the experiences of our most recent generations of ancestors can leave wounds in our DNA in the form of methylation patterns. Even if those experiences have long been forgotten, and the bodies that had experienced them long gone, the scars, passed on through bloodlines, become part of our lives.

Take my mother: she inherited not only my grandmother's beautiful features, but also her apathy, irritability, and nervousness. These features then influenced the next generation—me. It was like a row of collapsing dominoes without end.

"You're not the only victim." Doctor Qing placed her hand on my shoulder: warm, strong, comforting, the way I imagined how a mother's touch would feel. "Many have experienced similar dreams . . . "

"That means . . . " I tried to understand what this implied. "Their ancestors all shared the same experience, like . . . the Catastrophe?"

The truth was so obvious.

"The timing works out," the man said. "But no one knows exactly what happened. All the official records describe the Catastrophe vaguely as nothing more than a natural disaster."

"And everyone who lived through it had their memories erased by MAD, just like my grandmother." My body began to tremble uncontrollably.

"Memories imbued with too much pain cannot be erased. They are etched into our DNA through methylation, and are passed onto the next generation. This is why we need you."

"But I don't remember anything . . . "

"Not you, but your body." As Doctor Qing spoke, I seemed to smell the neroli oil again, soothing my sorrow. "Remember what I told you the other day? A certain essential oil is like a key, and can unlock the box of your memories. The chemical ingredients in the oil can demethylate specific DNA sequences, freeing the fragments of memory."

I recalled the first time I saw her. It wasn't a comfortable experience.

"We want to collect as many of these broken bits of memory as possible and decipher their meaning," the man said. "With them, we can piece together the truth about the Catastrophe, and stop the scars of history from extending into the future. You will become a hero."

The corners of my lips twitched, but I said nothing. I knew I was no hero.

Memory is like an onion. The different sensory input sources correspond to different layers. Visual memories are the outermost layer: easiest to trigger, and easiest to be erased. When I used MAD to weaken the memories of my mother, the process stirred up all the pieces of the past. Like a long montage, I was forced to relive through everything, and only then could the emotional content, buried deep within, be stripped away. That sinful pleasure felt like scratching a wound into a numbed arm.

I looked forward to the sensation of those painful memories, inherited from my grandmother, exploding into joyful fireworks in my mind.

I lay down. A harness secured my neck and head, and a mask was put over my face. I smelled a familiar, grassy fragrance: White Angelica, the oil of angels. The demethylation compound was about to be injected into my brain.

The countdown began in my ear: five, four, three . . .

Something shattered in my brain.

I was wrong. The fragments of memory did not manifest visually, but rather were like an epic recited by a blind bard. I experienced condensed emotions, feelings, but no concrete scenes. The long passage of time and the multiple generations in between meant that the original memories had become blurred, twisted, broken, and were now mixed with the real memories of my mother and me, as well as the official explanations and propaganda about the Catastrophe. History rewrote memory, and memory recreated history. I could no longer tell what was real and what was not. Judged by emotional impact, they were equally effective.

But they were wrong, too. The dream they had been so interested in wasn't a real memory. It was more accurate to call it a side effect of the Catastrophe, a psychological wound suffered during pregnancy, extreme anxiety at the possibility of losing a child. Even though my grandmother had no idea back then what her unborn daughter would look like, like all parents, she had imagined a person and projected her fears onto it.

Those fears were then etched in my mother's genome, and, like family lore, passed on from generation to generation.

They were the jewels my mother and I had hidden inside the dark box. Now that the box had been forcefully opened up, they lay exposed to bright sunlight.

Like a castle made of sand, they fell apart in the strong wind.

It was MAD. The released fragments of memory were rapidly indexed, recorded, and then erased by MAD. I understood their intent. No matter who was affected, this was the safest path. Powerful, detailed, unbearably painful memories flowed towards the future like time itself, dissolving the past.

A pang of fear seized me. The dream was perhaps the only thing in the world that connected my mother to me, the only thing that surpassed blood and familial ties, the only constant that didn't change.

And it was now gone.

I was going to forget everything. That was how history healed itself.

. . . three, two, one, say cheese!

In the picture, my mother looked as serious and rigid as ever, only the corner of her mouth lifting slightly. I was holding little Nuo, who had just turned one. Both of us had wide grins.

"Mom, look at you! You never smile." I scolded her half-heartedly. After a long regimen of medicine and physical therapy, my mother was recovering well. But sometimes, her facial muscles still didn't entirely obey her will.

"I *was* smiling. You think I was crying?" she argued.

"Look at Nuo. Now *that's* a smile." I played with the baby. Her lips opened in a toothless grin as she cooed.

"She's like you. When you were little, you were just this way. Like you had no care in the world."

"You must be remembering it wrong. I didn't like to smile when I was little."

"I gave birth to you! You think I wouldn't remember that?"

My mother had changed. Her odd moods and ill temper had disappeared so completely that I questioned my memory. I could only attribute it to the demethylation treatments. She had become optimistic, cheerful, outgoing. If it weren't for her bad legs, she would be holding Nuo twenty-four hours a day.

Maybe she wasn't a good mother, but she is *a good grandmother.*

I was incredibly busy. While caring for Nuo, I also studied every topic related to caring for a newborn: diet, physical exercise, early mental stimulation. Every evening, I massaged her whole body with a special type of baby oil. The doctor told me that touch was one of the most important sources of sensory input for the baby's neural development, and it was also a way to bring her and me closer.

She would not have an opportunity to erase me from her memory. The MAD had been abolished. I belonged to the last generation who would have such implants. After my death, perhaps they would build a museum to commemorate pathetic creatures like me whose skulls had been outfitted with a metal box.

The official explanation for the Catastrophe also changed. It now became harder to understand, more ambiguous. But in folklore, there were dozens of competing versions of the Catastrophe, all vivid and sensational. Sometimes, I felt as if I knew something, but then I couldn't remember any of it. That was fine. Too many things had changed. Peopled needed time to adjust.

I hummed a lullaby, trying to get Nuo to sleep. Her breathing became even and slow. I kissed her forehead. The milky aroma mixed with the fragrance of rose smelled angelic.

From time to time, she twitched, as though dreaming of something. If I held out my finger, she would clutch it tightly.

I wanted to know if I was in her dream.

Whatever she dreamed, as long as it belonged only to her and wasn't a repeat of someone else's dream, even her mother's, I imagined it was the sweetest dream possible.

WHAT I'VE SEEN WITH YOUR EYES
BY JASON K. CHAPMAN

"So, Ms. Wei," Detective Perez said. "Your brother was killed by a Yeti. With a knife."

Lisa Wei glanced around the 983rd Precinct. It was a dozen desks and a five-foot-square cage crammed into an old bodega. Only five of the desks were occupied, though. That made the room feel spacious. She shifted in the cracked, plastic chair next to Perez's desk, reaching down to slide her purse and the old gym bag underneath it. On the walls, signs and a scrolling marquee insisted that ForGen Motors had proudly sponsored the 983rd.

"That's what I saw," Lisa said. "A pale blue one—the Yeti, not the knife—with a unicorn horn."

The detective nodded, but didn't note anything on his tablet. Instead, he stared at her face. "Would you please remove your sunglasses," he said.

She hesitated. The man had city written all over him—no ads on his clean, crisp clothes; no desperate sideways glances at the trash can. He hadn't stood in a crowded alley at midnight waiting for the hash houses to close so he could kick and claw his way to a choice spot at the dumpster buffet. He hadn't smiled and pretended not to notice as his older brother wiped the grime from a misshapen cupcake he'd scored from behind the bakery on his fourteenth birthday.

No. He just wanted to see the poor little exurb girl's eyes and say, "There, but for a steady paycheck, an education, and parents who could afford to give a flying fuck, go I." She took the glasses off and stared at him defiantly.

To his credit, he didn't even twitch. Most city people at least showed *some* kind of reaction when they saw the glittery gold C# logo of Captain Sharp's GhotiBurgers staring at them.

"GhotiBurgers," he said. He pronounced it "goaty."

"Fish," Lisa said.

"Not really." The detective got a sour look on his face. "They grow that stuff in a vat." He shrugged and pointed to the wall. "That poster in the middle, below the ForGen sign. What's it say?"

She barely glanced at it. "It's a Captain Sharp's ad," she said. "GhotiNuggets are half off this week with a large soda."

"So your eyes are net-connected."

"Of course," Lisa said. "That's how FedMed works. Why? What do you see there?"

Perez glanced up at the sign. "Some cologne that's supposed to make me rich and beautiful."

"City ads, then."

"How so?"

"No one tries to sell beauty to exurbs," she said. "We can't relate."

It had been decades since the suburban experiment finally failed and people flocked back into the cities. They built, rebuilt, managed, and mangled, tearing down everything to set up their livable, loveable urban paradises, where the old dreams of picket fences and split-level ranches were reborn as the new ideals of sidewalk cafés and gleaming high-rises.

But the rubble had to fall somewhere.

These remade cities were ringed with rocky, exurban shoals, where the displaced and dispossessed fetched up to mingle with the shipwrecked souls who didn't quite have what it took to make it all the way onto the island.

"I live in the Ex," Perez said.

Lisa laughed. "No, you don't."

He gave her a pair of cross streets as if showing her a medal.

"That's ex-Ex," she said. "What do they call it? Transitional?"

"Not when I was growing up," he said.

Lisa studied his face. Maybe he was lying. Maybe not. It didn't matter. Whatever Ex-cred he might claim, he was an urbie, now.

Lisa was just seven years old when she learned about growing up. She huddled on her bed, an old sofa cushion shoved in the corner of a one-room apartment. She still had her own eyes then, but they were nearly useless. She clutched her old cracked-glass tablet to her chest, crying in frustration because she couldn't read anymore.

Eddie came home from whatever teenage brothers did to keep the rent paid and the two of them fed. He crossed the tiny apartment in a dozen quick steps and sat down next to her, holding her close.

"What's the matter, Little One?" he said.

She leaned against him. "I couldn't read," she said. "No matter how big I made the letters."

"Isn't the audio working?"

"It's not the same," she said. "Not like when you read to me. Or Mama."

Eddie took a deep, shuddery breath and let it out slowly. His heart thumped loudly in Lisa's ear. "I told you," he said. "I don't think Mama's coming home."

"I know." Lisa wiped away a tear that was running across the bridge of her nose. "It's because I can't see."

Eddie kissed her on the top of the head. "She was never very strong," he said.

She managed a tiny smile. She knew this game. "Not like us, right?"

"Toughest pair in the Ex," he said.

"Cuz we can do anything."

"With nothing."

"And like it!" they finished together.

Lisa showed Detective Perez a half smile. "Only urbies get to grow up," she said.

"If you say so." Perez grabbed his stylus and scrawled a quick note on the tablet. "Were you blind from birth?"

"Does it matter?"

Perez gave her a heavy sigh. He tapped his tablet. "Let's start with the easy stuff. This is strictly for statistical purposes and has nothing to do with the investigation. Okay?"

"Why not?"

"Race?"

"Call me ish."

"Excuse me?"

"I'm told my father was Chinese-ish. I had a grandmother who was Korean-ish and a grandfather who was a black-ish Irish man. You tell me."

"What do you identify as?"

"Is there a box for 'mutt'?"

The detective gave her another sigh and turned the tablet face down. He frowned at the bright blue ForGen logo on the back of it before casually covering it up with his hand. "The recorder's off," he said.

"I never knew it was on."

"Ms. Wei, do you know why we're here?"

"Sure," Lisa said. "So the police can say they tried to solve my brother's murder."

"They said that a week ago." He leaned closer and lowered his voice. "I'm with the NetCrimes division. Actually, for this and twelve other precincts, I *am* the NetCrimes division."

She leaned forward, too, matching his conspiratorial tone. "I'm pretty sure the knife didn't have Wi-Fi."

"I'm investigating your brother, Eddie Wei."

Lisa sat back and carefully kept her face blank. She'd suspected something like that when the detective had asked her to come in to the station. She stayed silent.

"Someone hacked your eye feed," Perez went on. "They used the ad stream to map the thing you saw over the killer's real appearance. That's pretty sophisticated stuff."

"I know that."

"It's not the kind of thing you do for a simple robbery."

"Simple." She sneered at him. "Thanks for your sympathy."

He gave her another of those heavy sighs and turned the tablet back over. "Have you ever heard the nickname 'Easyway'?"

"As in Eddie Zen Wei?"

"You tell me."

"I live in the Ex," she said. "There is no easy way."

"That's a 'no,' then?"

"Yes," she said. "That's a 'no.' So who's this Easyway person?"

"Just a name," he said. "Eddie worked part-time at an electronics store for a while. That right?"

"Before it closed down," Lisa said. "No more city stores in the Ex. And no exurbs working in the city stores, either."

"So he was good with computers, then?"

Lisa was nine when Eddie took her to Xavier Park, three blocks from their apartment. It wasn't a real park, like they had in the city, just an empty lot the neighborhood had adopted and named. Whatever plans the owner had had for it fell through before Lisa was born. It was just another frayed spot in the city's ragged collar.

He took her to the middle of the lot and put on these funny glasses. Wires trailed from the earpiece to a box he held in one hand.

"You don't wear glasses," she said. "They look dumb."

He leaned down, looking directly into her brand-new eyes. She'd only had them a month and still wasn't used to how bright and clear everything was. He said, "These are magic glasses. They let me see what you see."

"GhotiBurgers!"

He smiled. "Those, too," he said. "But mostly, I wanted to see this."

"See what?"

"Look up there."

Across the street stood a five-story building with a fire escape that only reached down to the third floor. Ugly plaster scars pocked the front, exposing the building's brick bones. Something flashed above the roof. At first, Lisa thought it was a bird, but it was too big. It flew right at them.

The winged horse swooped over the roof and dived down over the street. Its coat was brilliant white and iridescent rainbows raced across its rippling muscles. Its broad wings spread out, grabbing the air as it tilted back, seeming to hover for a moment before setting down just a few feet away.

Lisa stared at it, afraid to look away. It needed her to see it, needed her to believe. She watched it fold its wings over its back and bow to her. It was just steps away. She *had* to touch it.

"No, no," Eddie said, holding her hand tightly. "It's magic. If you touch it, it'll disappear."

"But it's so beautiful."

The horse bowed more deeply this time, one front hoof extended, the other knee touching the ground. Then it spread its great wings and flew away. Lisa watched until it disappeared in the distance.

"Was it real?" she said.

Eddie led her over to where the horse had stood. "Did it look real?"

"Captain Sharp looks real."

"But Captain Sharp doesn't leave hoof prints," he said, pointing to deep, half-moon indentations in the dirt. "Or feathers."

She took the white feather from him. It was longer than her hand and tiny little rainbows ran along its edge as she tilted it in the sunlight.

"It's not all ugly out there, Little One," Eddie said. "I just wanted you to know that."

"Ms. Wei?"

Lisa found Detective Perez staring at her. "What? Oh. I was seven when everything finally went dark. Nine when I got the new eyes."

"Most people spend five years on the waiting list."

"I guess I got lucky," Lisa said.

"Maybe so," Perez said, smiling, "but I asked if your brother was good with computers."

She shrugged. "I never saw him beat one."

His mouth squeezed into a tight little line as he looked away, shaking his head. After a moment, he looked back at her. "I'd like to think you're cooperating with this investigation."

"Go ahead."

"What?"

"Go ahead and think that," she said. "Nothing's stopping you."

"Don't you want to know the truth?"

"You don't want the truth," she said. "You want Eddie to be a criminal. That way his death moves out of the 'murder' column and into the 'incidental criminal activity' column and your mayor gets to keep his crime stats pretty."

He watched her silently for a while. Finally, he said, "Is that a pigeon feather?"

She hadn't realized she'd been toying with the long white feather that dangled from a thin braid on the left side of her hair. "Why pigeon?" she asked.

"It's just what it looks like."

"Why not dove?"

"It's a dove feather, then?"

"They're basically white pigeons, with blue rings around their eyes. Quite pretty, really."

"I've never seen a dove."

"You've never *noticed* a dove," Lisa said. "There's a difference."

"What's your point?"

"That you might be an exurb after all." She smiled, then. It was a genuine smile. "It's not all ugly out there, Detective Perez."

On Lisa's fourteenth birthday, Eddie took her over to the bazaar on 343rd Avenue. It was the neighborhood's mall, not that Lisa had ever seen a real mall. This one was a riot of ramshackle carts and makeshift booths filling the street that stretched for two blocks. Smoke leaked from the trunk of the burned-out sedan where Yakky Yamato cooked his famous barbecued rat skewers just a few feet away from a filthy Captain Sharp's food cart. The smell mingled with the scent of desperation as people sold or bartered whatever they could scrounge. Lisa kept her gaze on the street as she always did at the bazaar. The side of one crumbling building bore a fifty-foot-tall ad space. She didn't know what it looked like to normal eyes, but to hers, the enormous figure of Captain Sharp always seemed menacing.

Eddie led her to a rickety old booth and bought her an extravagant treat: Five chunks of pineapple on a toothpick. The empty black-and-white welfare can stared brazenly up from the trash next to the booth. Canned fruit was rare. It was mostly all lost or stolen before the trucks reached the Ex. Eddie handed the man nearly a week's rent.

"It's your birthday," Eddie said when she tried to stop him. "We can splurge."

"It won't be tomorrow," Lisa said, "and we'll still need to eat."

He cupped her chin in his hand and kissed her on the forehead. "I did some work for some guys," he said. "We're okay."

"I worry, Eddie. All the time."

"I know, Little One. But not today." He turned her head and tilted it up toward the monstrous Captain Sharp, but he wasn't there.

In ten-foot glittering letters, the sign read, "Happy Birthday Lisa." Beneath that, a unicorn grew as it seemed to run toward them. Sparks shot from its horn and the letters exploded into a shower of confetti, leaving a quiet sunset beach. Waves rolled gently onto the shore, retreating before they could wash away the "Love, Eddie" someone had scrawled in the wet sand.

Tears on her cheeks, Lisa smiled, softly touching the feather in her hair. "It's beautiful," she said.

"What do you think it means?" Detective Perez said.

"What's that?"

"The phrase 'Uri sent him a bunny tail.' "

"That's what the Yeti said, right before . . . "

"I've read the report. I'm asking you what you think it means."

Lisa looked over at the Captain Sharp's ad that only she could see. *Ghoti-Nuggets. Half off.* "I feel sorry for the bunny."

"The killer almost certainly wore a mask," he said. He held up his hands to keep her from responding. "The *real* killer. The one you couldn't see behind the Yeti pixels."

"If you say so."

"It could have muffled his voice."

"I suppose."

"I ran it through a speech processor," Perez said, "looking for variations."

"You must be good with computers," she said. "Is that the easy way?"

He smiled, then. "You're very clever."

"Maybe I should be a detective."

"Anyway, it came up with some alternatives."

"There are always alternatives. Someone famous said that."

"How about this? 'You're the end of the money trail.' "

"Or 'furry end of the monkey jail,' " she said. "This is fun."

"Mine makes more sense."

"Unless you've actually been in a monkey jail."

"Let's suppose your brother really was this 'Easyway' character."

"You said it was just a name."

"It is," Perez said. He leaned toward her as he spoke. "It's the name of the go-to hacker for a lot of local criminals. Rumor has it he can go anywhere the net goes. Make it do whatever he wants it to."

"Sounds smart," she said. "Wouldn't a guy like that be rich?"

"You'd think so."

"My brother? Rich?"

"He'd be good at hiding things, too."

"Search our apartment," she said. "It won't take long. You probably have closets that are bigger."

"We already have," Perez said. "And no, I don't."

"That brings us back to the monkey jail."

"Did your brother have a place he liked to go? A getaway, maybe?"

Eddie had only been dead a week when Lisa answered the door to find Yusef standing there looking uncomfortable in his torn khakis and a t-shirt that might once have been white. Lisa was never sure if Yusef owned the building or just worked there as the super. All she knew was that he fixed what he could, which wasn't much, and showed up at the door when the rent was due.

"It's paid already," Lisa said.

"No, no," Yusef said. His fingers looked like they were trying to knot his hands together and he wouldn't look her in the eye. "I just heard about . . . anyway, I wanted to say I'm sorry."

"Thank you," Lisa said.

She waited for him to say something else, but he didn't. He didn't leave, either.

"What is it?" she asked.

"I just wanted to make sure—I know this is a bad time, but . . . "

"It's okay, Yusef."

"The basement," he said. "I kind of really need the extra welfare chits and I wanted to make—with what happened and everything—we're still good with that, right?"

Lisa had no idea what the man was talking about, but she knew her brother. "Any deals you had with Eddie stand," she said.

"Thank you!" He finally looked her right in the C-sharps. "If you need anything, just tell me. And I'm so sorry. He was a good man."

"There's one thing," she said.

"Of course."

"Would you happen to have an extra basement key?"

She barely waited for the man to leave before heading downstairs with Yusef's own key in her hand. She crept down the chipped concrete steps to the basement door. Beyond it, she found a maze of pipes and rooms. It smelled damp and rotten. Overhead, light strips barely made dents in the gloom. If it hadn't been for the glowing unicorn, she never would have found the room.

It seemed to be playing on a loop, trotting from the entrance and through the twists and turns. She knew it was there for her eyes alone. It led her to a door with a cheerful sign on it that read, "Hi, Lisa. Press here and here." Arrows pointed to the spots she was supposed to press. When she touched them, the door popped open.

Inside, the tiny room was crammed with computers and displays. Cables hung like vines in an electronic jungle. One screen lit up and flashed her name along with the words "It's your ninth birthday."

She tapped out "Pegasus" on the screen and was rewarded with a letter from her brother. It told her that he loved her and he hoped she never had to read it, but if she did, she should always remember to look for the beauty in the world and know that he would always watch over her. It told her where to find a battered, blue gym bag and about the thousands of dollars in cash it held. It told her about the very real passports in the names of Eddie and Lisa Sharp and about the matching chip cards for the well-protected bank account with two hundred thousand more.

Finally, the letter warned her to never, ever look behind the Yeti.

"You're a lousy witness," Detective Perez said.

Lisa shrugged. "I told you everything I saw."

"That's what makes it lousy. You can be perfectly honest and still not give me a thing. You know, the investigating officer subpoenaed your 48-hour witness buffer. All FedMed eyes have one. It confirms exactly what you say you saw."

"Too bad," Lisa said.

"What's that?"

"That it's the only thing you've seen through my eyes." She gently brushed the edge of the feather in her hair. "You've been hunting pigeons, Detective. Maybe you should be looking for doves."

He looked down, pausing to rub a dark smudge from the palm of his hand. "I can't imagine they'd stay white for very long around here."

"Try to."

"What? Imagine it?"

"Yes," Lisa said. "Imagine something so achingly beautiful that it makes everything else fade into the blurred edges of a vignette."

He laughed. "And then what?"

"And then hold on to it." Lisa leaned her arm on the edge of the desk, not quite reaching for the detective's hand. "Hold on tight. Imagine it's the mast you tie yourself to when the storm hits, or the lamp that swallows the shadows where the bad things live. Imagine it's your shield. Your shelter. Your talisman."

He looked at her, and for a moment it seemed as if he might reach across those few inches of desk between their hands, but he sat back suddenly, as if afraid of what might happen if he touched her. He folded his hands in his lap, instead. "I'll try that sometime."

"No, you won't," Lisa said. "You'll just keep doing what you do, climbing your ladder and hoping like hell you don't get washed out onto the rocks by the wave of urbies crashing into your neighborhood."

"You're not the only one who's had it rough," Perez said.

"That's what I've been trying to say, Detective. Maybe there is no easy way." She took her arm off the desk, eyeing the space that had grown between them. "Maybe there never was."

"Oh, there is."

"And maybe," Lisa went on, edging forward in her seat, "it's not as easy as you think."

He smiled, then, but it was a tiny thing, without much joy in it. "They might still come after you, you know."

Lisa stood up, retrieving her purse and the battered gym bag. She slipped her hand into her jacket pocket, pressing the button on Eddie's magic box, and winked at the detective. "I'll keep a sharp eye out."

Perez stood up, too, but made no move to stop her. "As a cooperating witness, you'd be protected."

She looked back at the Captain Sharp ad and smiled. Her brother stared out from the poster. "I'll be fine," she said.

Perez carefully turned his tablet face down before shoving his hands into his pockets. "I have more questions, Ms. Sharp."

Lisa stopped and turned slowly toward the detective, clutching the gym bag's handles a little more tightly. The man still hadn't moved to stop her from leaving. "Don't let the eyes fool you, Detective. My name is Wei."

"My mistake," Perez said, glancing at the blue bag in her hand.

"You know, I think you're very clever, too, Detective Perez."

The detective shook his head. "I'm afraid my Lieutenant won't."

"Why's that?"

He shrugged. "I still have no idea who Easyway is."

She spoke slowly, wary of a trap. "So you don't think it was my brother anymore?"

He looked pointedly at the tablet on his desk and its brave, blue ForGen logo. "Nothing in the record points to it," he said.

"Then I'm free?"

"You are." He smiled. This time there was a warmth to it that reminded Lisa a little of her brother's smile.

"You seemed so determined a while ago," Lisa said.

He nodded slowly, mouth pinched together. After a moment, he said, "That's before you gave me what I needed, instead of what I was looking for."

"What's that?"

"Something to think about," he said. He looked over at the poster as if he, too, could see Eddie's picture. "Something that isn't ugly."

NO PLACE TO DREAM, BUT A PLACE TO DIE

ELIZABETH BEAR

"Dig, dig; and if I come to ledges, blast."
—Edna St. Vincent Millay, "Intention to Escape from Him"

You say there's ghosts in the mine, and there are. I should know, on account of I'm one of 'em.

We come and go under you, behind you, in the darkness down deep tunnels, chasing that rich half-meter seam that plunges to the bottom of the world, twisting this way and that, wandering off into the endless heavy depths. You turn in the dark when you hear us, glance over your shoulders, never see much of anything. In these mines, with our machine-augmented ears, you can hear somebody moving a long way off.

It gets hot, that far down, close to the churning molten dynamo at the core of this world with no name, just a serial number. In the old days, back on Earth, they cooled and ventilated the mines with air blown over ice. These days, they just cool the miners. We huddle in our carapaces. We pack in our own oxy, our own H_2O. It's hot and toxic and tight down here, but we slip through like roaches in the walls of the world.

You cut our communications lines when you find them, so we hide them better—in among the environmental feeds is good. We tap off your nipples when your backs are turned—bleed water to fork into oxy to breathe, hydrogen to burn. We check our feeds at the same time. No blackleg is going to keep me from talking to my kids, even if it's been almost two years local since I saw them. A lot of our feeds are voice and text only—primitive, but when you're on the bottom of a hole on a poisonous planet in a different solar system, well. We take what we can get.

It's not like you Company miners have it so much better.

Sometimes, we like to sneak up close enough to hear you talking. What you say about us is one-half fear, one-half romance, one-half pity. If that's too many halves, well, that suits me like my carapace. I am made of too many halves, and so are you. Half worker, half parent, half lover, half machine. It all goes together awkwardly to make a human being.

Some of you leave us food, supplies, power cells at dead-drops, and we leave you shadow currency and ore in return. We always pay, because if we didn't, you wouldn't smuggle us in sandwiches, noodle bowls, jerky—and we pay you ten times what the supplies would be worth on the surface. So that's a profit for those that take the risk bringing it in, even given what the Company store charges you. Beef costs next to nothing to grow, once the initial outlay of tanks and nutrients is covered—those little cells just keep on dividing and dividing and dividing as long as you keep the nutrients coming. It's highway robbery what they sell it for on these backwater mining worlds.

Debt's a way of keeping people under control. So I don't grudge you anything you can do to pay down what you doubtless owe the Company. After two local years, I'd do just about anything to get out of my own debt to the Syndicates and go home. My kids are growing up without me . . . though they're well-housed and well-fed and well-educated, which is more than I could have done for them by staying upstairs.

Everybody downstairs is here because we owe. And they have ways of making sure that no matter what we do, we owe more and more.

We ghosts don't dare leave downstairs very often, because we have to be smuggled each way—which is dangerous and uncomfortable and expensive. I came in disguised as an ore extractor. That was cramped, even after the mods they do to cut us down for the carapaces and the narrow tunnels. I had to build that extractor into my carapace while protected by nothing but a skinsuit, and nearly died when a filter jammed. First-degree burns all over my hands and if I still had feet I'd have had them there, too. That memory's enough to keep me down here until I'm ready to leave for good.

It's not too hard, staying down. We get the food off you, and piggyback for air and water and fuel. And you lot . . . you don't dare come after us, even your guards. In the mines we can feel you moving a long way off. We have better wetware than you do, though both of us sold ourselves to get it.

Yours comes from the Company store. Ours comes from the Syndicates. And when I say better, well—that's theoretical. Quality assurance is not the illegal economy's strong point, if you know what I mean, and it seems like one out of five of everything they send us is defective somehow.

So your job is safer—at least theoretically. Ours (theoretically) pays better. But neither one of us can ever earn enough to quit. We kid ourselves before we sign—we'll be disciplined. We'll be careful. We won't make those mistakes everybody else makes, because we're better than them.

Human psychology is the biggest confidence game of all.

But even more than that, you don't come after us because the Company doesn't like you having weapons. There would be no end of trouble with the insurers.

And we, on the other hand—we are *very* well armed.

I'm working a side tunnel in the far reaches, sketchy as hell and twice as isolated, when you stumble across my . . . well, I can't really call it a claim, can I, when I'm jumping it? I know you're a Company miner the instant I catch sight of you, because you have the running lights all up and down your carapace. Ghost miners don't run with lights—not visible-spectrum lights, anyway. And what an archaism that is, that we're still talking about the electromagnetic spectrum in terms of physiological imitations that haven't mattered in five hundred home-years. I heard you coming, of course—metal clicks on stone, grates over tracks. This far down, there are no elevators—we move in our carapaces, feeling the rock with fingertips made of titanium alloys, ceramics, carbyne laced with dynamic returns. It works better than flesh; pinpoint sensitivity.

And best of all, it cannot burn.

So I heard you coming. And I'm still surprised to see you. You're off the beaten path, even for us. I'm down in a side tunnel we dug in particular, working to set up the refiners—dangerous and nasty, but we're not hauling ore upstairs when we can haul metal, given the value per kilogram of each. So nobody who knows they're here and doesn't have to should want to come down, and none of your folks should be this deep in ghost territory. And yet, here I am with my claws locked around the release bolt of a damned jammed pressure relief valve, and here you come: blundering along, lit up in sixteen different wavelengths, using your floods to find your way instead of picking through the dark on ambient thermal as one of us would.

In my gray unlit carapace, I let go of the valve, hunker down into the rocks and pretend you can see right through me. I don't feel like shooting anybody today.

Wonder of wonders, it works. It also turns out to be a great big mistake, but if I could see the future, I wouldn't be out here on this fucking serial number growing old in a roach shell, now would I?

You pass over the tunnel ceiling with a click of grippers on stone. Your carapace flows with the motion of the body bonded to it. I wonder if you, like me, left anybody behind. Or if you, like me, got left behind by somebody.

If you miss the warm contact of flesh to flesh. If you make do with simstim, like so many of us. If you look forward to a day when you can buy your way out of the carapace and maybe feel that touch again. If maybe, like me, you figure that you're better off with simstim.

Programmed lovers never let you down.

I have plenty of time to wonder. You pick your way slowly, carefully. It occurs to me that you're sneaking. You can't miss the refiner beyond me, though, once you come around the corner. And then I figure you'll do one of several things.

The most likely is to slip back the way you came, and pretend you never saw any of this, and count yourself lucky you didn't find ten armed ghosts looking for a little sport. Some of my colleagues aren't the nicest.

But that's not what happens. You get to about where I guessed you would spot the refiner I just finished building and loading—it chugs away contentedly, turning ore into bright metal and toxic sludge—and you stop. Through the dark, I see your antennae twitching, sensors processing. I pull myself closer to the rocks. I'm armed—of course I'm armed—but where's the point in picking a fight if I don't have to? Too many risks.

I want to get back to my kids, one of these years. That's why I'm out here in nowhereland working these refiners alone. Bigger dangers, sure, but no split of the credits—and bigger margins, too. And you know, if I'm here alone, nobody else is going to disappoint me.

It's a risk, I admit. But it's a calculated risk.

Starting a shooting match with an unknown quantity? There's nothing calculated about *that* risk at all.

And you're alone, and I figure you're here by accident. Lost, malfunctioning, caught a funky nav trail or something. I hope you find a way out. I've never known it to happen personally, but there's tales of hauntings, of miners who got lost down here in all these kliks and kliks and kliks of corridors and oxy-starved or just never found a way out.

I don't know what I'm going to do if you go for the refiner. The Syndicates would charge me for it. And I can't afford that kind of debt. I don't want to bring my weapons live—you'll notice that for sure. Especially if I try for an IR lock—but even chambering a round makes a sound that carries, down here in the close spaces and thick gas.

So I wait.

You suspect I'm here. I can tell because your lights dim, your floods die, and you go passive input only. Antennae still twitching, you in turn press close to the rock.

Well, this is entertaining. I hope we're not going to be here all day. Night. Whatever the hell this is.

I have to clamp down on the urge to jump out from behind my rock and yell BOO! Shit, that's tempting.

So tempting that I'm still wrestling with it when the refiner whose pressure release I hadn't finished unclogging . . . explodes.

Remember what I said about the twenty percent rate of defectives?

I guess you and me, we got lucky.

The carapaces take the worst of it. And the fact that both of us are huddled behind rocks, ridiculously hiding from one another, means that the worst of what they soak up is something both carapaces can survive. The atmosphere burns—it does that down here sometimes, something to do with toxic volatiles—but not methane because nothing on this planet except for us has ever been alive—and the fire sweeps over and between us in a wall of blue and violet and sickly green.

Yep, working alone, nobody else is going to disappoint me. I have to do all the disappointing for myself.

Guess it's lucky I'm so good at it.

I lose external sensors about then. Which is just as well, because I've already watched my whole world burn the one time. Though this iteration is both prettier and more dramatic, well. I don't have a lot of stomach for the instant replay.

Something's tugging at my carapace. At my manipulators, to be precise. A fritz of static; a shiver of IR. I can see, sort of; the carapace is repairing itself. Just the way it's supposed to. At first I think, *Pity about living through; this is going to be one hell of a hangover.* Then I think, *Don't you dare die. Myah and Koral are counting on you.*

They'd be better off without me. The Syndicates have a pretty good insurance policy. They call it, "We take care of our own." I die, and Myah and Koral wind up in a top-ranked creche, being raised alongside the kids of the Syndicates seniors.

It's so comforting that I almost want to shake off the tugging. But as I swim back up to myself, I realize that it's a little more complicated than that. Because the truth is: I die, and they wind up in debt to the Syndicates in their own names. And saddled with a family loyalty to the next generation, too.

That's upsetting. Because given the situation, I'm not quite sure I can manage to live.

I take a moment to assess. Systems reporting surface damage, scouring, burned sensors. Repairs underway. One of my primary manipulators is spot-welded to the rock by a melted chunk of refiner—or maybe a big old blob of what the refiner was refining. That's going to be a problem.

Inside the carapace, though, my wetware indicates the meat is more or less okay. Bruised up, trickling some fluids from places they're not normally supposed to flow. But functional, and not losing anything critical critically fast. I dial up my hydration, and focus on what's tugging me.

It's you. Specifically, you're trying to drill the rock around my fixed manipulator away without breaching my carapace, or me. You're scorched, but don't seem hurt, and your running lights are back on. They illuminate a lot of billowing dust and smoke, mostly. Your diamond-tipped bit is making short work of the stone, too. I think I'm impressed.

"What are you doing?" I ask.

"Not leaving you here to die," you answer. "Do me a favor and don't explode or electrocute me, Ghost."

Well, that wasn't what I was expecting. "The refiner overpressurized," I said. "My fault."

There's a shrug in your voice as you continue drilling. "Accidents happen."

"If your colleagues are going to come looking, you should head back." I don't want to be found here by them, pinned down. And what the hell is a blackleg doing chiseling me out, anyway?

I realize I said that last out loud when you grab my manipulator and twist, cracking the last thin column of stone. I look at it, then at you. Your sensors reflect my carapace with a resounding blankness of expression. But that's what I'm giving you.

"Tunnel's collapsed," you reply conversationally. "And nobody's going to be looking for me. I'm jumping indenture."

Oh. Well, that explains what you were doing out here in the ass-end of nowhere. One mystery solved!

I wish I felt more cheerful about it.

After a long pause, you let go of my manipulator.

"I'm Chi," you say. Dryly, you add, "I guess it's a pleasure."

You extend a manipulator. I reply with my ruined one, still bonded to a lump of stone. We tap claws tentatively, making sure no metal touches metal to avoid any potential spark. I probably burned off the volatiles by blowing up the refiner—great planning!—but you never know.

"I'm Kely," I say. "I'm really sorry to meet you."

Then it's quiet and dark and hot, and we separate to explore the limits of our de facto prison. The tunnel was about two meters at its widest, and half a meter tall. It's irregular, and the segment we're sealed into is about two meters long—so we don't get far. Not very big, in other words, though it takes us some poking about and shifting piles of rocks to determine where the cave-in is. In the course of our conversation, I learn that, apparently, I was under some rubble before you shoveled me off.

Thanks, Chi. Next time I'm hiding from somebody who's not actually a threat, remind me to finish servicing the equipment first.

By the time we run out of tunnel, we've fallen into conversation. We've realized that nobody is coming to look for us—the Syndicates don't expect to hear from me any time soon, and you snuck off at the end of a shift-set, after punchout. It's your weekend.

We're limited to the consumables we have on board. I suggest drilling out. You point out that neither one of us is packing enough hydrogen to run our fuel cells long enough to make that happen. And if the cooling in our carapaces quits, we'll cook.

That seems like a bad death.

The bad news is that we'll oxy-starve before anybody notices us missing. The good news is that if we sit still, we'll run out of oxy before we do hydrogen. Suffocation is a better death than broiling in our shells like old Earth lobsters—and it's even a better death than thirst.

In the bottom of a mine, you harvest your mercies young and tender if you want to get any.

We settle in, side by side, to contemplate our options. I find myself worrying more about your hypothetical plans for the increasingly hypothetical future, somehow. I know I'm avoiding thinking about dying down here when I ask, "What were you going to do for a body if you got out?"

It seems like a fair question: the carapaces aren't well adapted for life outside the mines. And they take a lot of us off to prep us—all those nerve trunks that used to run nonessential systems like legs and so forth, they're used for other stuff after we're rebuilt.

"I have a cache," you say, after a pause. Apparently you've decided that if you're dying, it doesn't matter if you admit to smuggling. "It'd be enough to buy out my contract, but then there would be questions about where it came from."

"Ah," I say. "You know the Company will chase you down."

"Not if they think I vanished in the deep mine," you answer. "They'd just blame your folks."

I snort. "Well, turns out they'd be right."

"Stop it," you say.

"What?"

"Stop it. Stop blaming yourself."

"Because it's my fault we're stuck here?"

"Or it's my fault because I distracted you. Or it's the Syndicates' fault for shipping you a faulty refiner." Your mandibles clack. "What good is blame?"

That brings me up short. *It's everything,* I want to say. But I know that's because I don't want to stop blaming somebody I haven't seen in four home-years, close to a year and a half, local.

"I'm taking responsibility." Gently, I thump my paralyzed manipulator on the tunnel floor, wondering if, if I chip loose the stone, I'll be able to use it at all. "That's all."

"If you say so." I can hear the shrug in your voice. "Fine. You're forgiven. Let's talk about how we get out."

We don't. But you don't want to hear that.

"If we drill, we die," I say.

"We die if we don't, too. Was there anything behind the refiners?"

"The tunnel ended after about a hundred meters. It was just a branch."

"So it's back the way I came."

There's a whine—the familiar sound of a drill. I drag my carapace over scattered bits of not-yet-assembled refiners (and the exploded one) to get a look at what you're doing. The tunnel out is closed with a big slab of rock, and I realize that you're not trying to drill through it, or drill it to pieces. You're going *around*.

"The tunnel was wider on this side," you explain. "And the rock is fractured. Maybe it won't go too far back."

It does.

Finally, wearied, you cling to the rocks. I don't need to read your exhaust to know your consumables are running dangerously low. Power barely humming, you lower your carapace to the tunnel floor and ask, "You got something to live for?"

I don't mean to tell you—I've heard it all—but I must be tired too because it just comes out bald. "I'm a single parent."

You stop, shocked. I'm used to this. Tired of it, but accustomed. What will come next is a flurry of questions—why I have no creche, no family network, no partners. Who would be so irresponsible as to bring a child into the world alone. Questions I save my breath to deflect. I had partners. I thought two were enough. But one died, and the other one turned out to have been sticking around for something other than a relationship with me, or with the kids.

So what are you going to do?

Whatever you need to to take care of the kids. And to grow a thicker skin, and move on.

Whatever you have to do.

But you don't ask. You just crouch there, humming. So I fill in the silence, because the pressure of the answers I called up in anticipation has to be released.

If only I'd had the sense to do that with the refiner.

"I had partners. I don't anymore. And before you ask why I didn't surrender my kids to a creche—they're *my* kids. They're my only family." *They're all I have left of Oam.* "I'm going to trust somebody else to raise them?"

"Who's raising them while you're—" You make a cursory wiggle of your manipulators. *Here. Downstairs. Dying at the bottom of a gravity well.*

Touché. "They're in school."

"Ah," you say.

But you don't make it sound like an insult, somehow.

"Wait," I say, seventy-two minutes later. Because I just thought of something.

The dust has settled. We've been lying in silence, watching the remaining minutes of our lives tick by on various wetware monitors. Having used up your consumables digging, Chi, you're going to die before I do. And though I hardly know you, I'm just not ready for that.

I don't want to die alone. Why is it better to have company?

The dust of the explosion and your digging has settled. And that's what ticks the idea over in my brain. Because it's settled over the scattered remains of the refiners—the casings, the bits, the burr grinders, the things I don't know what they are but I know how to plug them in to make slag and ingots come out of the other end, the power cells—and it's settled over the visible edge of the big block of collapsed tunnel ceiling that's trapping us.

And there, by that edge . . . there's a ripple.

Not a big one. But a sharp one, a defined edge. Something that shows the path of a current. Air, if you can call it that—okay, atmosphere—is moving through that blockage.

I reach out and touch your carapace with my ruined manipulator. I draw your attention to it. You look, but you don't comment. I wonder if that's because you don't dare hope, or because you're too new to the mines to understand what it signifies.

I say, "Where air can go, we can go."

Okay, that's a lie. But we all need a good encouraging lie every once in a while.

"You were right, Kely," you say. "We don't have the juice to drill our way ou—"

Your sensors focus, then, on my non-ruined manipulator. And on the refiner power cell I'm holding high for your examination.

Well, we dig. We're still hurting for oxy, but the power cells mean that the suits can move for us rather than the other way around, so we use less of it. And I manage to browbeat you into letting me transfer some of my H2O over to your carapace. Even if I do have to play the "don't make me die alone" card to get you to agree.

I think the fact that authentically, one of us has to prop and brace the slab for the other to dig without being crushed to death makes the difference. You might nobly sacrifice yourself for me. Especially since I notice you didn't answer your own question about having anything to live for. But you're not willing to kill us both in order to refuse sharing resources.

And then, I'm a little dubious about going down into that hole with nothing holding up the tons of rock except your locked-out hydraulics.

"You have to trust me," you say, and sure that's problematic for a lot of reasons. Not the least of them all the ones why I'm down in this hole in the first place.

But I don't just have to trust you. I have to trust all those fuckers who engineered your shell, and all the ones who built it.

But hell, it's your life too. And what choice have we got?

It's not good. It's none of it good. The space I'm digging in is just as big as I am—the flat cross-section of my carapace, and no taller—and I can feel that slab shifting over me, groaning against your locked manipulators. I scrabble with my fused claw, using it to push the drilled chips of rock out behind me, and then kick it back with my legs like a burrowing scarab. If anyone had ever asked me how I wanted to die, this would have been down the list somewhere under drowning in caterpillars.

I know there's a level where we're lying to ourselves, where this is just a way to get it over with faster. To run through our resources so it's done that much quicker.

Right now, under this big slab of rock in the hot dark—right now, I'm okay with that.

And I'm okay with it—my carapace scraping rock, hoping I won't throw a spark and boom something else, worming through the crawlspace like a roach—right up until the moment when my forward manipulator breaks out into air.

Well, atmosphere. Space, anyway.

Gently, gently, I back out of the hole. I face you, expressionless shell reflected in your expressionless shell in turn. "We're through," I tell you. Before you can crank at me to get back in there.

Then I say, "You go first."

Dust shifts from under your manipulator.

You say, "Not happening."

"The longer we sit here arguing, the more unstable the tunnel gets."

I think if you weren't busy holding up the rock, you'd fold your manipulators and stamp one insectile leg. It's a pity you have the goddamn I Win card: "I let you give me your water."

Emotional blackmail. What can I say? It works.

"Shit," I say, and go back in as fast as I can, because your huff outhuffs my huff, and I'm already figuring that out.

When I get to the other side, I snake my manipulators back in, and I brace the big slab best I can from the wrong end. "Chi," I yell back to you. "Do it! Run!"

Or bellycrawl as fast as your six legs can scrape you through, anyway.

You almost make it. I can feel the big fucking rock teetering. And I can only grip it with one manipulator, because the other's still fused to a chunk of chipped-out ore. So I think of all the big slabs I've seen jammed on rocks no bigger than my fist, and I do that—jam the rock into the crevice and hope. Hope the wedge will hold. Hope you make it through. Hope I can keep the whole fucking slab from falling on my head when I try to pull loose again, and hope for that matter that I *can* pull loose.

Well, it nearly works. The things slips, and teeters, but it doesn't crunch you. It wedges on my claw, and the ridged middle of your carapace. You're caught like a turtle in a nutcracker, whereas I'm more like the stop in a door.

"Pop your hand," you say then, after assessing the situation. "Get out and leave me."

"Maybe," I answer. Actually, I'm thinking, I *could* pop the hand. It's wedged too hard to be going anywhere—I'm not leaving with it either way. So with or without you, I'm going to leave it behind, like a lizard's tail in a hawk's mouth. Except if I let go of the other side the slab before you're out, the whole damn planet might come down on you and pop your carapace like the shell of a particularly tasty crab.

"Hey," you say. "Data." You touch a manipulator to my intake, and there's not much I can do to stop it. My claws are busy.

You dump, and what you dump in me is money. Or as good as—coordinates, access codes, account numbers, balances. Your offworld cache.

Chi, damn. You're a pretty good smuggler. There's enough in there to cover . . . anything. New bodies, sure. And a nice long retirement, for that matter.

"Go," you say. "You've got no reason to help me now."

If I were a better person, I wouldn't be tempted. But I am. For two, maybe three long seconds.

Then I say, "You're just going to have to trust me."

And I pop the claw at the shoulder—sacrificing a little more meat-me, what can it hurt now?—then wedge my carapace where my other manipulator was—jamming myself under the rock with you, even though you push at me with both damned claws, because *that's* helping—then grab the severed end in the now-freed manipulator and jam it against the tunnel floor. I trigger a full extension and it springs taut, like a jack.

Dust sifting on every side of us, metal and stone grinding, groaning—it gets the slab up, oh, a whole three centimeters.

Enough to send you sliding backwards when suddenly you're pushing at my shell and not braced. I snag your claw in my one remaining one and scoot backwards as fast as my dented, frayed, scrabbling legs can carry me.

We fetch up against the far wall, beyond the rock slide, just as my detached, improvised arm-jack fails. The big slab crumps the tunnel shut with a whumpf like a soft explosion. For a moment I'm sure that that impact is going to bring the tunnel down on us one more time.

It doesn't. I'd planned to laugh if it happened. Can't get rid of an unused laugh any other way, so when we don't die, I have to dry-fire it. You click your claws at me, but after a minute, you start laughing too. You're on your back, legs waving in the air like an overturned sow bug.

Eventually, we stop. And then, after a while, it occurs to me that our problems aren't over—because we still have to get upstairs, either past the Company or past the Syndicates. Without letting them know we're not dead in the cave-in, because we'd both really rather they didn't come looking.

I figure I'll ask. You seem to have good ideas sometimes. "So how the hell do we get out of the mine?"

You roll over onto your treads and shake rock dust off your manipulators. "I'm confident," you say, "that—between the two of us—we'll think of something."

MARRIED

HELENA BELL

The last part of himself my husband will lose to his ghost will be his teeth. There will be a graying out, a glint of silver as the calcium is absorbed, repurposed. A few may be pushed out to fall onto his pillow like pale, rotten splinters. The process will take days or only hours depending on the molecular compatibility between the human and Sentin. My husband has excellent compatibility, they tell me. We are so lucky.

When my husband and his ghost sleep, I lift the corners of his mouth and peer inside him with a dim flashlight. Incisor, cuspid, molar. I count the line of them and wonder at what age each came in. I think of his older brothers tying one end of a string around one of his baby teeth, the other to a brick to be thrown from a second floor balcony. I think of the first apple he ever tried to eat, of pulling back to find a tiny bump of white against the red skin. Sometimes I count his teeth twice, itching to run my finger along his gums to feel for the metal threads racing through his body. The doctors tell me we have decades left, but they have been wrong before.

My husband's ghost began as a silver fist clenched at the center of his spleen. A team of technicians placed it there, a tangle of wires and other bits which they claimed would absorb and reconstitute his damaged tissue. Sentin is not self-aware, they said; it is not alive in the usual sense. It can neither feel nor understand, merely mimic the thing which came before. When it senses potential failure, it stretches its roots like a weed, eliminating the weak and buttressing the strong.

We each held the ball of putty in our hands, pulling and stretching it to see if we could break it. We marveled at how it snapped back to its original, perfect shape each time.

"It is not yet FDA approved," the surgeon warned. "But we've had remarkable success thus far."

Lungs, heart, liver: these are still my husband's. The saphenous vein in his left leg, his kidneys, arteries, left hand, and his lips: these things are the ghost's. There is nothing in the body which does not eventually fail, and thus the Sentin reaches out, settles in the crevices of age, and seeks to change it.

In the morning, my husband's ghost showers and dresses. He cooks four eggs: sometimes scrambled, sometimes fried. He undersalts. He reads the paper on his computer while I scrub the dishes in the sink. We compare schedules. He has meetings all day but should be home in time for dinner. I have three operations scheduled: all wisdom teeth extractions. I should be home in time to cook dinner.

"Good," he says. "I'll see you then."

He kisses me with his ghost mouth. I let him.

In the evening, my husband's ghost looks at me through my husband's eyes, and speaks to me with my husband's tongue. When I close my eyes, they are resolved into a singular wave function. He doesn't like it when I listen to him with my head down, or turned to the side. He wants me to watch him, to see his ghost lips move while he tells me about a timing error regarding the statute of limitations.

"The client is fucked," he says.

"SOL!"

"What?"

"Shit out of luck. Statue of Limitations. They have the same acronym. I thought it was amusing."

"Oh," he says.

My husband never found me funny. Neither has the ghost. Something they have in common.

At night, the ghost rests with my husband's right arm dangling over the side of the bed, fingers barely brushing the floor. His other hand folds into mine and though this is his ghost hand, cold and hard and pulsing with electricity, I cling to it because I do not know how to let go. Our therapist says this is a good sign; we must tread in our familiar forms of intimacy. I simply do not know how to sleep any way else. Sometimes fumbling in the dark, there is a brushing, an unbuckling, and I pretend the metal in his kiss is not the ghost, but a metaphor for desire. I breathe on him, pant until his lips are the same temperature of my skin and after we have been drawn out, mixed together and poured back into our bodies, I pull away from him, shivering and awake.

Other nights he wraps his arm around me and talks into my hair. When did I feel loved today? Did I feel appreciated? We talk, and we argue. He hates the movie I made him watch last week. He loves that I made him watch it twice just so we could discuss it.

My husband's ghost is very clean. He scrubs the glass tile in the bathroom and runs a metal finger beneath the lip of the drain to catch any hairs or epithelials. My husband is coming out of himself in drips and pieces, and once I thought if only I could collect them all, I could be happy again. I could stitch his body anew from its fractions and leave. But there is so little of him to keep: hair, nails, a crescent of skin and blood snagged by the gleaming metal of a cheese grater. I dream of cutting him open, peeling away his skin and removing his organs as the Sentin races to fill the divots I have made. Other nights I dream that after I leave with my knitted husband, my husband's ghost rebuilds me in its own image: silver hair, hard skin and the glimmer of binary in my eyes.

Not all Sentin patients are as lucky as we have been, they tell us. Others have been suffocated in their beds because something grew where it should not: a hand wedged in the larynx, a thousand alveoli reborn as toenails. A medical student in New Orleans cut open his cadaver and found a stomach full of glistening metal ears. My husband and his ghost share a unique molecular compatibility. They move into and through each other. The ghost never takes more than is needed to maintain proper function. A perfect symbiosis culminating in my husband's disappearance.

When I realize I am pregnant, I do not tell them. I do not wish to give birth to a ghost child who will grow ghost teeth, whose hair will be silver and cold and will resist the care of my hands. I have no lessons for ghosts, no wisdom to impart on the dating of ghost boys.

I beg my husband's physician to refer me to a Sentin specialist in another city. The night before the appointment, I count my husband's teeth three times. I tap on the enamel with my fingertips, an act I have done so many times, I do not worry about waking him. I almost do not notice the fluttering of his lashes, or the way his chest constricts with a suppressed cough. When I release his lips, they fall back too quickly and he turns over on his side. I whisper an apology, but he says nothing.

The specialist shares a building with three other medical practices, yet the waiting room is completely empty when I arrive. A nurse stares at me as the specialist ushers me down the hall to her office.

"Slow day?" I ask, and the specialist shakes her head.

"Slow year. It's an interesting problem," she says. "Some think there won't be a need for medical schools within one or two generations, but that's nonsense."

She draws my blood and pulls two gray hairs from the root. Her hands never stop moving as she talks about studies and research she has read, about how excited she is for the future. "They think Sentin is the answer to a thousand problems, rather than the catalyst for a thousand new types of failures. It's a very exciting time."

When she finally asks about the progress of my condition, I tell her about counting my husband's teeth at night, of insisting that he walk without shoes or socks through the house so he will remember the feel of wood and linoleum against his bare feet.

"But what of your own? Is the Sentin adapting according to prescribed rates? Do you experience any difficulty breathing? Sleeping? Any changes in appetite? In some cases patients feel a craving for batteries, silver coins, even Christmas tree tinsel when it's in season."

"I'm still human," I tell her.

She sighs. "If you're having trouble adjusting, or anxiety, I can recommend a support group. Denial will only undermine compatibility."

"I don't need a support group. I'm pregnant."

She stares out at me with cold, gray eyes and I wonder if she's a ghost too, transitioning to better understand and study. "Congratulations," she says. "And you're concerned about how the Sentin may interfere with fetal development?"

"I'm concerned the fetus *is* Sentin."

She opens the file on her lap. Pinned to the inside is the faxed sheet from my husband's physician. I can make out only two works upside down: Wife: Uncannyism.

"Oh," she says. "That's not as interesting."

She tosses the folder aside, stuffs the blood samples and the hair she took into a biohazard bag, and hands me my purse.

"The baby?" I ask.

"Is fine. Sentin can mimic reproductive organs, but not their functions. Men eventually go sterile, women experience early onset menopause. It's why we don't currently recommend the procedure to anyone under the age of 35. That will change one day, but for now . . . " she suggests a few websites and medical journals, but her mouth is a tight line. She has other appointments, other patients. She thanks me for coming in and congratulates me a second and third time.

I call my husband from the car.

We name her Chandler, a family name on his side. By her fourth birthday, my husband is a frayed patchwork of flesh. We learn that he sinks immediately to the bottom of a pool should he fall in. When we visit the ocean, I am careful to keep him on the side away from the waves though he assures me he could walk along the bottom collecting scotch bonnets and limpets. He promises me a lettered olive, whole, for which I have been searching. I almost tell him to dive in after it, to scour the sea for the skeletons of mollusks, and to only come back to me when he has completed his quest. It would take years, I think. Years enough for me to forget. When he comes back to me, a silver ghost on a silver charger, his banner flying, I will have forgotten his brown eyes, his dark hair. I will know him by the tasks I set: peel a lemon in one long strip, hit the smoke detector in just the right spot with the broom, kiss me *just so* on the back of my neck. Make me laugh; make me cry. String the unstringable bow.

Chandler is not the only one in her Kindergarten class with a ghost for a parent. Matching compatibility has improved: there are fewer fatalities and more elective procedures. Within a few years, they believe that ordinary transplants will be the exception rather than the rule. Chandler introduces us to her friend Tom and then Mr. and Mrs. Tom's Parents. His mother's skin gleams like pale moonlight and I hear the inexplicable *clink* of her fingers as she ruffles my daughter's hair. I pull Chandler against me as my husband's ghost grasps her hand in both of his and shakes it up and down.

"A pleasure," the ghost says, "a pleasure."

Mr. Tom's Dad and I sip apple juice and watch as my husband and his wife discuss the difficulties of metal detectors. She insists that he look into the ID program and proudly pulls hers from her wallet.

"Within a century," I say. "We could all be like that."

Tom's Dad nods. His skin is almost as pale as his wife's, though his cheeks flush when he speaks. "They're beautiful, aren't they?"

Some nights I wander the house alone and barefooted, later counting the long hairs which tangle between my toes. To my daughter, my husband and her father are the same being and she is too young for me to contradict her. One vacation, she learns how to knock a hammer *just so* into the tip of a Queen Conch, to break the vacuum between shell and snail, to pull its meat gasping into the sun. She sits on the side of the boat and giggles as her father ties ropes and life preservers around his middle.

"The ocean is so deep here," he says. "It would take me ages to walk back."

The guide doesn't think I notice, but he glances from me to the ghost, to Chandler and back again.

"She takes after her father," I say.

He reaches as if to touch her skin, to examine its texture, but instead leans far over the side of the boat, splashing the knife in the water. He hands the shell to my daughter and joins me under the boat's canopy.

"It would take a long, long time," he says, "to climb out of one of the blue holes."

"Assuming you didn't get crushed first," I say.

"Pressure is the same all around. It's air spaces you need to worry about. You hold your breath, dive down. It hurts. You learn to balance, it doesn't hurt anymore."

"You should write fortune cookies."

He shrugs. "It's just science."

At the airport my husband is pulled to the side. They pass the wand over his arms and legs, over his head. The security guard asks if my husband would mind waiting.

"No problem," the ghost says.

Chandler and I wait on the other side. There are a dozen men now, a few women. They each take turns with the wand. They run their hands up his arms and legs. They touch his hair, his face.

I tell Chandler to tie her shoes. Then to retie them.

"Are they doing it just to be safe?" Chandler asks.

"They're just curious," I tell her.

"It'll be better," she says. "When one day we're all the same."

I hold her hand in mine. Tan against pale. "Maybe," I say.

Chandler is fifteen when they find the tumor. It curls against her heart like a question. The doctors say they can remove it, but surgery has risks that other options do not. I tell them no, as the ghost says yes. The doctor leaves us and we stare at each other across the white linoleum.

"You would risk letting her die over something so small," he says.

We decide to let her make her own decision and follow the doctors into her room. They explain the risks, the potential complications of various procedures. When she asks about Sentin, they tell her the procedure is irreversible, and there are always unanswered questions: her ability to have children, the shifting compatibility of a developing body.

The ghost and I wait. I know he expects me to attempt to sway her, to tell her that she will be stepping into a shell which believes she is something other than herself. He expects me to call on her sympathy and describe how I will walk barefoot through her room, brushing her hair from the floor, how I will see each loss as the punctuation to betrayal.

The knowing hurts as much as the waiting hurts. As our daughter considers her future, the ghost grips his seat in his gray hands. He rocks back and forth and I find myself rocking too. Back and forth, and the white floor between our chairs is a horizon disappearing and reappearing beyond the crest of a wave.

"What do you think?" my daughter says.

My husband opens his mouth to speak, his gray lips stretching across gray teeth. Last night I heard a faint pop as the last of his molars fell out upon his pillow. It was warm against my skin, and so small in my hand I forgot how it was ever alive.

COME FROM AWAY
MADELINE ASHBY

"*Get up,*" her boss said, in her bones. "*Hwa. Go. Go Jung-hwa. Stop generating so much delta pattern and wake up.*"

"Top of the morning to you, too." Hwa rolled over. This whole constant contact thing between her and the chief of urban tactics had to stop. So what if her new employer had bought a whole city. There had to be limits. Boundaries. *Boundaries,* that was the right word. That was the word that came up all the time in the United Sex Workers of Canada handbook. She missed working for them. They had *boundaries.* You could be a bodyguard without signing on for a bunch of other crap, like Daniel Síofra rousing you from a sound sleep just because he felt like it, on a morning when your stomach felt like the Great Wave off Kanagawa and your mind was just the poor dumb bastard trapped in the rowboat beneath it.

Oh, Christ, she was so hung over.

"*You're not at home,*" Síofra said.

"No. I'm at my teacher's."

"*. . . Excuse me?*"

"My tae kwon do teacher's. We got to drinking. Toasting absent friends." Toasting her dead brother. Toasting his trophies. They'd even broken out the screech, sometime around one in the morning. Jesus wept.

"*You are aware that today is a school day?*"

"I'm aware."

"*And you're aware that you are now employed to watch out for one Joel Lynch, heir to the CEO position at Lynch, the company which just purchased this entire city, including the secondary school he attends?*"

"Yup. That's a big 10-4."

"*And that he's been getting death threats?*"

"From beyond the Singularity. Real Terminator shit. It's clear as fucking mud."

A long-suffering sigh vibrated through her bones from somewhere across the city. Probably the crystalline perfection of Tower Five, as far as possible from the rust and grime of Tower One. Hwa tried to imagine her boss hidden behind walls of glass and maps, directing the city with a twitch of his long fingers. A crossing signal here. A seemingly random outburst of music there. She imagined him plucking it like an instrument until it sang with activity.

"*I have a present for you.*"

"Is it a bacon roll? Because I could do with a bacon roll, right about now."

" . . . *I don't even know what that is.*"

"It's a thing for people who don't have nanites doing repair work on their livers every time they toast absent friends."

" . . . *How did you know I have those?*"

Hwa smiled despite her headache. "Just a hunch. When do I get my present?"

A knock sounded at the door. Hwa picked her way across the living room and peered through the peephole. A courier in yellow stood in the hallway, looking terrified to touch the buzzer. "*Now,*" her boss said.

"I hate these things," Hwa said.

"*They're the latest model. And perfect for someone without other augments.*"

"They're . . . " Hwa wiggled her fingers in front of her new specs. As she did, the device scanned the scars on her knuckles and filed them away in some silvery somewhere that was probably just a data-barge rusting off the coast of one former Eastern bloc nation or another. DAMAGED, the glasses said, and pointed helpful blinking arrows at her fingers and wrists and shins and feet and anywhere else she looked. DAMAGED. Like she didn't know that much already.

"They're loud," she said, finally.

"*They're the quietest on the market.*" Síofra actually sounded a little hurt. Like he'd gone to the trouble of picking out something great and fucked it up instead. Which was exactly what had happened.

"Don't worry. I'll get used to it." Hwa scanned the main entrance. The specs told her where every little camera and microphone was. They lit up snitch yellow on the map. She could pick out the angry kids (red halos), the sad ones (blue), the baselines (green), and the ones who were making out with each other (grinding columns of deep purple).

"*We should have gotten them for you sooner. But for someone like you, someone who's lived for so long without . . .* "

"Without any augments," Hwa said. "Without any help."

"*Most of these devices are designed to work alongside other services, other technologies. But you're different.*"

If by "different," he meant "poor," then he was onto something. It wasn't that Hwa had some moral or aesthetic commitment to living free of augmentation. The programmable tissues that spontaneously healed her classmates after hockey practice would have been much appreciated where her liver was concerned. But Sunny had never found money for that kind of thing. At least, not when it came to Hwa. Hwa was a bad investment. The lasers that were supposed to fix the stain running down her face had only made things worse. So why throw good money after bad?

"The good thing is, now I can see what you see."

Hwa snorted. "You know I'll be shutting these off when I'm in the girls' locker room, right?"

"Could you say that a little louder, please? I'm not sure the PTA heard you."

"Oh, come on," Hwa said. "You're not worried about the PTA. You work for Lynch, and Lynch pays the wages. They'd offer you a two-fer on the Lindgren twins, if they could."

She directed her gaze to a pair of blonde girls wearing varsity volleyball jackets over their uniforms. They reclined against the opposite wall, chests out, knees up, all shiny hair and white teeth and laughter. They were everybody's number one fantasy. If you didn't want to fuck them, you wanted to be them. Hwa didn't need a subscription to any one vision of reality or another to see that much.

"Not interested."

"Liar."

"Can we not discuss this, please? We're being recorded, you know. For quality assurance purposes."

Hwa examined the floor. Her tights had a run in them down her good leg. She inspected the damage idly, twisting her leg this way and that, but her specs had nothing to say about it.

"Much better."

"Did you like high school?" What a stupid question. Hwa had no idea why she'd asked that. Where was Joel, anyway? It was getting late.

"I don't know," Síofra said. *"I doubt I hated it as much as you do."*

"Yeah, well, I still can't believe I let you con me into coming back to this place."

"Better late than never. We were lucky to find a candidate for this position who lacked both a diploma and a prison record."

"Yeah, that's some luck, all right."

Across town, Síofra laughed. Hwa felt it as a tickle across her skull that skittered all the way to the base of her spine as sure as if someone had run a finger down there. She twitched against the wall.

"Hwa?"

Hwa opened her eyes to see Joel standing in front of her, blazer laid neatly across one arm, school tie in a tight little knot she couldn't help but want to mess up. Christ, he was even wearing the Krakens logo tie pin. *The tie pin.* Like he didn't already look enough like the skinniest little Tory ever.

Right then and there, Hwa decided she had to get the boy in some trouble before the trouble found him, first.

"Hwa? Are you okay?"

The warning bell rang. Hwa shoved herself off the wall and teetered only a little. "I'm fine," she said. "Let's get to physics."

"Were you talking to Daniel?"

"Yeah." She raised her voice slightly so her boss would be sure to hear it. "But he should be *working,* and we should be, uh . . . *learning,* I guess."

Joel blinked, as though he were not truly listening. Then he nodded to himself, fished in his bag, and pulled out a pouch of electrolytes. Orange flavored. Or so she assumed. There was a cartoon of a smiling orange on it, which was holding a glass of orange juice. Which sort of made it the Orange Jesus, holding out its blood and offering salvation of the breakfast beverage variety. Joel grinned and wiggled Orange Jesus in her face. It was the first time she'd ever seen him really smile. He put the pouch in her hand. "Daniel says you should drink this. For your hangover."

There was a basic problem on the desk when they got to class. At least, Joel said it was pretty basic: "It's Moore's Law," he said. "About exponential growth in computational ability. Didn't you cover exponents in Grade 8 algebra?"

Hwa tried to remember Grade 8. She'd turned fourteen that year, and had a general memory of fourteen sucking worse than the other years for some reason. Oh, yeah: because her mother wouldn't shut up about how *her* first single had gone *platinum,* when *she* was fourteen. And then she'd talk about pink champagne and parties and music producers and how to fend them off, always making certain to end her stories with something like, "Not that you'll ever have that problem, Hwa-jeon."

Hwa-jeon. It was a dessert in Korea. When she was little, Hwa thought her nickname being a dessert meant she was sweet and special, a nice treat at the end of a nice person's day. Then she asked Sunny to make it for her.

<<Why would I want to eat those? They're all rice flour and sugar. You know I can't eat things like that. Why would you ask me to spend money on something I can't eat?>> Her mother had taken one look at Hwa's face and rolled her eyes. <<Besides. I don't have edible flowers, much less purple ones. How can I make it look like your face, without big purple flower petals?>>

"Hwa?"

"Huh?" Hwa blinked at Mr. Branch, who was peering at her with his head cocked. In the specs, his emotions didn't register like the students' did. Maybe the faculty all had theirs screened out. Not exactly sporting. "What? Sorry. Were you talking to me?"

"Yes. I was asking you where your homework was. I was calling the roll for missed assignments. five hundred words on one problem you'd like science to solve?"

Hwa frowned. "What?"

"Your homework—"

"You *call the roll* for missed assignments?"

"We went over this during the syllabus review yesterday," Mr. Branch said. "When assignment are not sent to me by the start of class hours, I will call for them in case they've been forgotten."

Hwa arched her left eyebrow. "In case they've been forgotten," she said, slowly and deliberately. She turned her face to a little the right, just so he'd be sure to see the stain. Just like that, his lip twitched. A little ugly went a long way, with beautiful people. "Don't you think that'll make your students feel bad? Like, ashamed of themselves?" She plucked at her tartan tie. "I mean, we wear uniforms and everything, but this isn't a Catholic school. Shame isn't really a teaching tool."

A collective *Hmm* that went through the class, as though they hadn't really considered that side of things, before. Which they probably hadn't. But you couldn't grow up with Sunny as your mother and not start seeing opportunities for emotional manipulation for exactly what they were. In the specs, Hwa watched the baseline green ripple into contemplative orange.

Mr. Branch's mouth thinned. "Things have changed, since you dropped out three years ago."

The rest of the class *Oooh*'d. The orange turned back to green. Beside her, Joel winced. He shot her a look that begged her not to take this any further. He was worried—the aura around him was a thin bruise blue. She winked at him. Anybody who thought she was hurt by comments about having dropped out didn't really know her. The day she turned her back on this place was one of her favorite memories, and thinking about it never failed to make her feel better. She leaned back in her seat and looked at Mr. Branch. She crossed her hands over her stomach, like she'd just finished a big meal and was ready to relax.

"You're right," she said. "I'm sorry. I'm sure they gave you a whole seminar on the new rules, once you were come from away."

Nothing happened. Branch appeared to be processing what she'd said. She'd said it in slang deliberately, so he'd have to spend time working it out in front of the whole class. Because while he was her teacher, he was also being an asshole, and if there was anything she'd learned in three years of bodyguarding it was how to deal with assholes. You had to puncture them like the inflamed little sphincters they were and watch while all the pus drained out until they were just shriveled little rings of nothing special. Words were good for this. Like subtly reminding an entire classroom that Branch was a stranger, not a rigger, not even from the mainland but from Away, from Vancouver or wherever clear on the other side of the country.

"Just get me the assignment," Branch said. He started calling off more names.

"You can have mine," Joel whispered to her. "I wrote two."

Of course he did. "Why would you do twice the homework?"

"I'd already written one, on faster-than-light travel," Joel said, "but then I pinged him about it, just to show off, and he shot me down. Said he wasn't taking any science fiction questions in science class. Real problems only."

"So what'd you write about, instead?"

"How the ITER failed, in France."

Hwa nodded. "That'd be good for science to figure out."

"Science *has* figured it out." A smirk tugged at the edges of Joel's lips. He lowered his voice still further. "That's why we're building another one."

Hwa turned to him. "We?"

"The company," he said. "We're building another experimental thermonuclear reactor, right here. Underwater."

"Underwater." Hwa pointed at the floor. "Under *this* water?"

Joel nodded. "Under the city."

Hwa drew breath. "What the hell kind of James Bond villain bullshit—"

"*You promised your father you wouldn't discuss this outside the family, Joel,*" Síofra said. "*Hwa signed a non-disclosure agreement, but you shouldn't make it difficult for her to adhere to it.*"

"You're building a fucking *sun* under this town, and *I'm* the one you're worried—"

"Miss Go!"

Hwa's head snapped up. Branch did not look happy. Shit.

"Since you and Mr. Lynch have so many things to discuss, perhaps you'd like to discuss them in the hall. Eight bins of fetal pigs were just delivered for Miss Jarvis' biology class, and they're not getting any colder sitting out in mailroom. I'd like you to bring them from downstairs to the science lounge, and load them in the refrigerator."

"Can we have the elevator pass?" Joel asked.

Branch smiled. "No."

Hwa shrugged. She stood. "Come on."

"But—"

"It'll be good for your arms. Let's go."

"So, are you guys gonna disconnect the whole rig and fire everybody, or just wait until your science experiment explodes and kills us all?"

"It won't explode." Joel grunted, lost control of his one bin, and set it down on the floor. "Why wouldn't they give us a dolly or a hand-truck or something we could use to lift these things?" He flexed his fingers. "My hands hurt."

They were barely out of the mailroom off the main entrance. They'd been walking for all of two minutes, and hadn't even cleared the lobby, yet. Even if the death threats against Joel were totally bogus, and Hwa was inclined to believe they were, she'd be damned if she didn't whip him into shape. The kid could barely lift twenty pounds.

"That's because you're using your hands and not your arms. And that's because you got no arms."

Joel flapped his arms at his sides.

"No. I mean, you got no *arms*." Hwa squatted to put her two bins down and straightened up. Her spine popped as she rose to her full height. She'd been slacking off on her vinyasas, and that was clearly a mistake. She stepped close to Joel and flexed her right arm. "Feel that."

Joel poked her arm. His eyes widened. "Is that your *bicep*?"

"It's discipline, and years of training. That's what it is."

Sheepish, Joel shuffled back to his bin and tried to lift it in a single mighty move. Hwa winced as his back sloped forward. He was trying to carry the thing on his non-existent belly, like a fetus. Which was ironic, given the contents of the bin.

"Okay, lesson one," Hwa said. "Put that thing down."

"We have to get back to class."

"Oh, please. Fuck that guy. Seriously. Besides, this is physics too. Sort of. The physics of not fucking up your lumbar region."

"I think that's kinesiology."

"Whatever. Put that down. No, really, put it down. Now, watch me. See how my back is planked? It's a straight line, from the back of my head to the bottom of my spine. See?"

Joel cocked his head. "Okay."

"Now, I squat down like I'm doing a clean lift. Because that's basically what this is, is a clean lift. I'll show you one later, in the weight room. And I lift *from the knees—*"

"*THIS IS A LOCKDOWN. ALL STUDENTS MUST REPORT TO CLASS-ROOMS IMMEDIATELY.*"

"Is it a drill?" Joel asked.

"Probably. I'll check." Hwa's gaze slid slowly over a series of icons in the far right of her vision. One of them was an exclamation point. It was blinking. She focused on it and blinked three times. An alert swarmed up in her vision: *THIS IS A LOCKDOWN. ALL STUDENTS MUST REPORT TO CLASSROOMS IMMEDIATELY.*

"No shit, Sherlock," she muttered.

"Is it a drill?" Joel asked.

"*THIS IS A LOCKDOWN. ALL STUDENTS MUST REPORT TO CLASS-ROOMS IMMEDIATELY. DOORS WILL BE LOCKING IN SIXTY SECONDS.*"

Which one was the goddamn security icon? Why weren't these things more intuitive? She blinked out of the alerts menu and roved her gaze over the others. There it was. A badge. Security. She blinked three times.

"*FIFTY SECONDS.*"

There, in her left eye, was a juddering video feed of a man in a long coat. He was carrying a shotgun. He was on the edge of the atrium at the end of the lobby. Any minute now, he could change direction and cross the atrium, where he would see them. They were boxed in.

"*THIRTY SECONDS.*"

"Is it a drill?"

Hwa focused on Joel. "No," she said. "It's not."

"*TEN SECONDS.*"

Joel bolted back to the mailroom. He pounded on the door. He tried the knob. It was locked. The blinds were down. Hwa began stacking bins. If they couldn't find shelter, she would have to make one. Maybe if she stacked the bins outside the mailroom, they would just look like another delivery that hadn't been processed yet. Or maybe fetal pig bodies were especially good at absorbing hollow-points.

"Sorry, piggies," she murmured. "Joel!"

"They won't let us in!"

"Not so loud!" Hwa gestured for him to hunker down beside her in the shadow of the bins. He came over and crouched. "Here's what we're gonna do," she said, and belatedly realized that phrasing something that way meant she actually had to have a plan.

"What?"

Hwa watched the shooter in her left eye. He was moving in the other direction. Good. "We have to be really quiet," she whispered.

"Okay."

Hwa tried to remember what the school security briefing had said about lockdowns. She'd gone through lockdown drills before dropping out, but being on the other side of all that procedure was different. In the security tab, she found a subheading marked "Evacuations and Drills," and blinked at it. It unfolded across her right eye, and as she read, her heart sank.

"All the doors are locked, now. The whole school is sealed. Main doors, fire exits, everything. It's all remote; the cops are the only ones who can open it back up."

"Daniel could open it back up," Joel said. He focused elsewhere and whispered. "Daniel? Are you there? Daniel?"

Static.

"All the communications are being jammed," Hwa said. "That's part of it. In case there's a bomb. Or in case there's a hack in the system or the augments. Or a toxin. It's a total quarantine, until the cops come in. Nothing goes in or out. No people, no information, not even the air. Nothing."

There was a terrible silence. The silence of scared kids hiding behind locked doors. The silence of fans that have stopped spinning. Dead air, closed mouths, and empty halls. Hwa had never known the school to be so quiet. It sounded like everyone was already dead.

"We're alone," Joel said, finally.

"Yeah."

"So what do we do?"

Hwa looked again the shooter. He was far on the other side of the atrium. "We move. Now. Quietly." Hwa pointed to the left of the atrium. "We need to get to the elevator on that side. I'll force the doors open. We can use the elevator shaft to get into the ducts. Then we use the ducts to climb into the lighting booth above the auditorium."

Joel looked at her as though she had just relayed all that information in Korean. Given the situation, maybe she had. "You're crazy."

"The lighting booth is the safest place in school, Joel. It's why everybody goes there to make out. There's only one way in or out, and it's a ladder that pulls up behind you."

He didn't look any more confident.

"Joel. Come on. Your dad hired me for a reason, right?"

He nodded.

"This is that reason."

His lips firmed and he nodded again. "Okay."

Hwa poked her head out first. The shooter was peering down another hallway. This was the perfect time to move. She gestured behind herself. "Go. Now."

Joel skittered around from behind her and started running. She chased from behind, keeping herself in line behind him. Their new shoes squeaked across the floor; it was recently waxed and Joel wiped out and yelped. In her left eye, the shooter's head came up and she saw him raise his gun—

—heard the dry pops of fire—

—felt her right arm open up—

—skidded to the nearest bathroom. It was the girls' room; there was only one door and it didn't lock. Hwa pushed Joel toward the back stall and locked the door behind them.

"I thought we were going to the elevator!"

Hwa held up her arm. It was as though a mouth had yawned open across her flesh. Yellow globules of fat dangled from underneath her ragged skin. "Plan's changed."

Joel went even paler than usual. "Oh, no."

"Yeah, karma's a bitch," Hwa said. "Shouldn't have showed it off to you."

"We have to apply pressure." Joel grabbed her arm and held it. His hands shook. He seemed entirely too focused on his hands. "Wait. I have a better idea." He put Hwa's hand over her wound and held it there. "Hold on."

Hwa watched him hop off the toilet and open the stall door. "No, don't!"

He darted out and she heard a rough scraping sound and a few grunts. Finally there was a terrible screech, and he came back into the stall with a maxi pad in each hand. "I got the extra absorbent kind."

Hwa forced her grimace into a grin. "Nice work."

Joel removed the tie pin from his tie, loosened the tie, and pulled it off without un-knotting it. He tore open the packaging around one pad and frowned at the wad of antibacterial memory foam in his hand. "That's it? That's the best they can do?"

"Hey, those were miracle Space Age fibers, back in the day."

"Wow. No wonder you're so pissed off, all the time."

Joel wrapped the pad over Hwa's wound. Then she helped him slide his tie up her arm. He tightened the loop around the pad and then wrapped the rest of the tie's length around her arm and tucked the end into the wrap.

"Can you still move your fingers?" he asked.

Hwa flexed them. "Yeah. Thanks. You're kind of a genius."

Joel shrugged. "I know. That's what my test scores say."

"Seriously?"

"Pretty much. I have a certificate and everything."

She licked her lips. The wound in her arm was now more of a dull, throbbing ache. She could work with that. But only so much. "Well, you got any genius ideas for getting us back into that elevator? I can't force the doors with this arm."

Joel pulled the tie pin from his pocket. "Actually? I do."

The elevator had two access mechanisms: a standard chip-reader, and an old-fashioned turnkey system for when the power went out. Hwa stood guard as Joel worked the pin into the elevator's key slot.

"This always looks easier, in the dramas," Joel said.

"Don't force it," Hwa said. "Just feel around gently until you feel something push back. You know, like a clit."

Joel rolled his eyes, but didn't blush. Hwa coughed a laugh. Maybe she wasn't doing so great at not getting hurt, but as for teaching Joel some valuable life lessons, she was batting a thousand.

The doors chimed open. They fell inside, and Hwa slapped the "door close" button. Then she looked up at the ceiling of the elevator. There was all kinds of shit up there, wedged up between the lights and the plastic panels that were supposed to protect them. Pencils, rubber bands, dead flies both organic and robotic, even a pink assignment sheet with the word "GULLIBLE" written across it in green marker.

"Bunch of savages in this town," Hwa said. "Jump up there and take down one of those panels."

Joel reached up and jumped. It took him a couple of tries, but the panel fell open and showered him with dead flies and paperclips. "Now what?"

Hwa told him how to turn the lights off and gain access to the ceiling panel that would pop open the trapdoor on top of the elevator. She had to kneel down and let him stand on her knee to do it, but he had good hands and worked fast. Soon he had the trapdoor open, and after he climbed up through it, he helped her get up there, too.

"Hold on. Let me get into blueprint mode, here." Hwa found the blueprint icon in her vision. The school being a publicly funded building, it had to release all its plans. So she could see where all the shafts and ducts went. It took her a moment to orient herself, but the light booth was unmistakable. And as she suspected, it had a major HVAC duct sitting right up on top of it. With the stage lights, the auditorium got awfully hot during performances. The only way to control the temperature was to force the air one way or another. And the only way to do that without impeding anyone's view of the stage was to stick a big fan on top of the light booth.

Hopefully the quarantine would last long enough that none of the fans would be spinning while they were in the ducts.

She pointed at the spiny ladder leading up the shaft. "Okay. Let's go."

Climbing ladders and crawling through ducts with one arm was excruciating. There was no other word for it. Hwa smeared blood everywhere she went. The ducts were smaller and tighter than she'd expected, and the only thing that greased their way through the aluminum tunnels was anxious, frustrated sweat. It felt like being born, if your mother was an unfeeling machine with a pussy made of steel who didn't really care if you lived or died.

That was a fairly accurate description of Sunny, actually. Hwa would have to remember that for later. If there was a "later."

Finally they made it to the light booth. The fan was still off. Hwa checked her watch. This was a long time for the cops not to enter the building. What were they waiting for?

"Let's get through before it starts up again," Joel said.

"Yeah." Hwa wriggled around until her feet faced the fan. "Turn around so your back is to mine, okay? I need you to brace me, so my kicks have more force."

"Okay." He turned around. Through his shirt, she could feel how hot and damp he was. But he didn't seem frightened. He was doing well with this whole thing. "You're doing pretty well with this whole thing."

"I have an anti-anxiety implant," Joel said. "It's perched right on my amygdala. It's sort of like a pacemaker, for my emotions. I don't feel high highs or low lows. I'm right in the middle, all the time. Dad had it put in right when my voice started to change."

Hwa kicked twice. The fan squealed the second time, but didn't budge. "No shit?"

"No shit."

No wonder he hadn't blushed at her clit joke. "That must really fuck up your sex life."

"I'm fifteen," Joel said. "I don't have a sex life."

Hwa focused all her surprise into her legs and kicked again. "*Fifteen?* You're a senior! You're graduating this year!"

She felt him shrug against her shoulders. "Like I said. I'm a genius."

"Wow." She kicked right at the center of the fan. It dented around her feet. Now they were getting somewhere. She could see a rim of light around the panel. "So, that means I'm, what, seven years older than you?"

"I don't know how old you are," Joel said. "Does it matter?"

Hwa kicked hard. The fan fell in, and a couple of little kicks at its edges with her heels popped it the rest of the way. "Nope," Hwa said. And she pushed herself through.

The first thing they looked for was food. The light booth had an impressive array of snacks. All of it was the high-calorie contraband that the school had outlawed in the year of its founding: bright pouches and boxes of crisps and chocolate (a whole box of the cherry brandy kind), seaweed crackers, "cheddar" popcorn, "kettle" popcorn, and bottle after bottle of energy drinks. Hwa mainlined the first one like it was the blood of Christ.

Tossing the empty bottle into a bin, she took stock. The light booth's equipment was still all tarped over; no one had come in to use it since the summer. She plunked herself into one of the chairs and pulled the other one out for Joel.

"What's going on, out there?"

"Let's see."

Hwa opened the security tab again. More feeds had come online. The shooter was on the second floor, now. He was in the foreign language pod. He was standing outside Madame Clouzot's class—Hwa recognized the French flag across the door—and firing at it.

"It's not good."

Just as she was about to explain, the bell sounded. First period was over. Second period was about to start. Christ, where were the cops? A fidgety tension lit up her limbs. Joel was right. No one was coming. They were alone. Maybe the cops had some other assessment of the situation. Maybe they knew something she didn't. Like maybe this dude had chemical weapons, or there was a bomb somewhere, or he'd rigged himself to blow up. Maybe he wasn't the run-of-the-mill batshit shooter, after all. Maybe he was a terrorist.

Maybe he was the one trying to kill Joel.

"Fuck this," Hwa whispered. She stood up and started digging in the supply racks. Most of it was just extra wire and batteries, along with folders of gels and green wafers of chip for re-programming light and sound on the fly. There was an old red toolbox that looked promising, but it had a big fat padlock on it and Hwa had no time.

"What are you looking for?"

"The emergency ladder."

Hwa fished a box-cutter out of one bin. That could come in handy. She tried stuffing it down her skirt, but that didn't work so well. She dug out a tool belt, cinched it over her waist, and stuck the cutter in there, along with a couple of flat-head screwdrivers and a heavy flashlight. There was a drill, but it was a small battery-powered job without much force. She needed something bigger. Like a nail gun.

Fortunately, she knew exactly where to get one of those.

"What are you doing?" Joel asked.

Hwa's hands lit on the emergency ladder. It was lightweight yellow nylon. Joel would have no trouble hauling it up after her.

"Going to shop class."

The problem was the silence. That terrible, awful silence that had turned the whole school into an echo chamber. In order to bust open the door to the woodshop, Hwa would need to use a fire extinguisher. The sound of it clanging on the door would draw the shooter in no time. So she needed something to cover the sound.

"That's why you need to start a fire," Joel said. "That way the alarm goes off, right?"

Hwa winced. The school fire alarm was among her least favorite sounds in the world. The last time she'd heard it, the Old Rig was on fire. And her brother was in flames.

"Yeah," she said. "But it might open up all the doors, too. I don't know what the procedure is for a lockdown versus a fire. I *think* fire ranks above lockdown, but we might just throw the system for a loop and get nothing. The specs don't say anything about it."

Joel plucked out a bunch of the gels from the lighting cabinet. On their black envelopes was an orange sticker with a campfire on it. "WARNING: EXTREMELY FLAMMABLE," it read. Then he held up a black glass tube with an electrical cord dangling from it.

"What's that?"

"It's a black light. Probably the last incandescent bulb in this whole town."

"So it's hot."

"It's *very* hot. It has to absorb most of the visible light spectrum, and it's spectacularly inefficient. That makes it good for checking for lint on a red velvet curtain. So here it is." He knelt down and plugged in the light. Then he started unfolding the black envelopes.

"Hey! What are you doing?"

"I'm starting a fire," Joel said. "In a small space like this, the smoke detectors will notice in no time."

"I can do that myself, in a bathroom or something!"

"You only have one arm," Joel said. "You'll be slow."

The fire caught almost immediately. Joel quickly fed it more gels. A weird metallic smell arose from them. Smoke started to rise. Joel backed away. He reached for a bottle of water from the tub of snacks.

"Do we hug, or something?" he asked.

The fire leapt up about three feet.

"I don't think we have time to take our relationship that far," she said. The alarm sounded. It was a shrill keening sound, as though the whole building were shrieking in agony at being burned. Then the sprinklers came on. Together they stared up at the water. It tasted of ocean.

"Great," Hwa said. "Just great."

"I'll get the ladder."

They left the fire burning and opened the exit. Joel secured the ladder to a set of hooks hanging off the threshold. Hwa watched the ladder fall into the darkness around the nearest catwalk. If she fell, she would die. Period.

Joel's head stuck out above her. "Are you going to kill him?"

Hwa had not really considered this as a possibility. The shooter had a gun. If she were lucky, she would have a nailgun. It wasn't exactly a fair fight. "Maybe."

Joel nodded. "Well, if you do, I'm sure my dad's attorneys will defend you in court. They're very good. They got him out of a whole criminal negligence thing with an oil spill, before I was born. So you probably won't do any time."

Hwa winced. "That's a real comfort, Joel."

He held up both thumbs. "Good luck."

"You too. Lock that door, and turn off all the lights when I'm gone."

Going down a nylon ladder with one arm and a heavy tool belt wasn't easy, but it was a lot easier than the ducts. Her arm was oozing, but she felt okay. Sitting still and focusing on it would have just made the pain worse. Her feet found empty air, and she looked down. The catwalk was another two feet down. Holding the ladder with her wounded arm she quickly changed her left hand's grip on the ladder to something more like a one-armed chin-up. Then she slowly let herself dangle down off the ladder, and dropped onto the catwalk. It was slick and she slipped, gripping the railing with her whole body and getting an eyeful of auditorium. One of the screwdrivers dived out of the tool belt and glittered as it fell into the deep dark far below.

Righting herself, Hwa looked up at Joel. She gave him a thumbs-up, and he gave her one, too. Then he started pulling up the ladder.

Twisting on the flashlight and sticking it between her wounded arm and her body, Hwa navigated across the catwalk and down a set of stairs to the backstage area. Right near the outdoor exit (locked) was a fire extinguisher. Hwa lifted it off its housing and carried it to the interior exit that led to the drama department (also locked). She lifted the fire extinguisher and bashed at the lever on the door.

Behind the door, she heard screaming.

"It's just me!" Hwa bashed at the lever. After two more tries, it fell out with a clunk. She opened the door, and a stage sword jabbed her in the belly. "Ow! Fuck!"

"A rat! A rat!" Mrs. Cressey said. She was holding on to two crying girls. She smiled. Hwa thought she had maybe gone a little crazy. "Dead for a ducat! Dead!"

"What the hell is a ducat?" She had to yell to make herself heard above the sprinklers and the alarm. Hwa pushed the stage sword away and gave the huge boy holding it a hard stare. "One side, Zorro. I've got bigger fish to fry."

He backed off, and she pushed into the classroom. All the other students were staring at her. They were freshmen. They looked so small and formless. Like little tadpoles. She had never felt old, before. Not until this moment. She was still young, and she knew that, intellectually. But staring at these kids with their jeweled eyelashes and chipped nail polish and their knees all hugged to their chests, she felt like some ancient thing that had crawled up out of a very deep and ugly pit.

"I'm sorry about the door!" She pointed behind herself. "All of you will be safer if you go up into the catwalks! Get to higher ground!"

The students looked at each other. Then they looked at their teacher. Slowly, they got to their feet. Hwa threaded herself through them, and started bashing on the door to the hall with a fire extinguisher. As she did, other students started streaming out of the room. She watched as the last one left, and then kicked open the door and got out into the hall.

The hall was a loop that made up the vocational pod. Mr. McGarry's shop was around the bend. This time, she paused and looked through the window first before raising the fire extinguisher to the lever. No one was inside. Once the door was open, she dashed in and put the fire extinguisher down. The entire wall to her left was a pegboard of tools. The red chalk outlines for each tool's shape were all bleeding down under the sprinklers' onslaught. But the tools themselves were still in place and ready to be used. Including the big gas-powered nail gun, complete with its backpack of fuel.

Hwa wiggled her fingers. They were mostly numb. "Come to Mama."

Threading her injured arm made the wound open up again, and she wished she'd taken that other pad from Joel. Hissing, she managed to peel back the padding and spray some industrial adhesive on the wound. It stung mightily and she howled in shock. She suddenly felt a lot more awake and alive. Endorphins were a wonderful drug.

She checked her specs. The shooter was back on the main floor, now. The same floor as she was. He'd gone up and around and down, covering the whole school. Looking for something. Or someone. She had to get him before he found the open door to the drama department. Before he found the other students. Before he found Joel.

Hwa checked the fuel gauge on the tank. It was in the green. She added a couple of cartridges of nails to the tool belt. Then she wiped the specs dry with a chamois from Mr. McGarry's desk. In the security tab, she changed the video feed to a basic semi-transparent map in the lower left of her vision: the shooter was now just a red dot on a set of lines, and she was the blue one. It would be easier to see what was in front of her, this way.

Easier to aim.

She took a few deep yogic breaths to center herself. It wasn't easy with a heavy pack on, but it was necessary. In (two, three, four), hold (two, three, four), out (two, three, four). And again. The pain dissipated. So did the endorphins. There was only her—a calm person accustomed to hurting other people—and him—an imbalanced student who probably came here with a death wish. They were probably equally frustrated by the fact that the cops hadn't shown up. One way or another, they would have to have to end it themselves.

Hwa entered the hall. She moved past the doors. In other classrooms, there were kids pressed up against the windows. She felt them watching as she walked to the main hall. There, way on the other side of the school, was the shooter.

Behind her, something splashed.

Hwa whirled. At first, she couldn't see it. But in the rain created by the sprinklers was a . . . shape. A human shape outlined in water trickling off its surface. Only, she could see straight through it. Without the water it would have been completely invisible. She ripped off the specs.

It shifted. Glittered. Like a poltergeist caught in the act. *De-realization.* That was the medical word for it. That moment when everything around you seemed impossible. The moment before you had a seizure.

"Oh, Jesus."

All her calm vanished. She was cold and wet and wounded and alone. And she was about to seize for the first time in three years. It made sense: she'd barely eaten anything, meaning there was a dramatic change in her blood sugar, and she was under physical and emotional stress. Her brain had handled all of these challenges just fine until now, and now the sparkling aura in her vision was warning her to sit down and hold on before she hurt herself.

"Master control room," she said aloud. "Master control room."

She pictured the bank of buttons. Big and bright and perfectly fitted to her fingers. Imagined punching them. That satisfying click. The way each button lit up as she locked a series of doors behind her, locked herself away—

Behind her, the shotgun sounded. She turned. The shooter was running at her. Her icy fingers fumbled on the nail gun. She lifted it. It shook in her grasp. She pulled the trigger. Nothing happened. Oh, Christ, the safety, shit—

"*Hwa, get down!*"

Síofra. In her bones. Finally. She fell to the floor. So did the shooter. The sprinklers stopped. The siren died. Her ears rang. Her hands kept shaking. Something peeled away from the shooter's scalp. A skein of skin, with hair attached. Beneath it was a skullcap. Light danced across the shooter's skin. It slowed down, ceased, and he went limp.

"*He's inoperative, now, Hwa. He can't hurt you. I'm coming. Stay there.*"

She tried to say something. But then there were people in Lynch uniforms, and they had bright yellow towels of absorbent foam, and they were picking her up under her arms and dragging her to the nearest wall and taking her backpack off and unbuckling the tool belt. They were saying how sorry they were. How glad they were that she was okay.

"You passed with flying colors," they kept saying.

Síofra skidded out into the hall. He nearly wiped out on the wet surface. But he just kept running until he got to her end of the hall. The others scattered and lined up against the opposite wall, chins up, shoulders back. Waiting for orders.

"Hwa?" He snapped his fingers. "Are you in shock?"

"Yippee-ki-yay, motherfucker."

He laughed. He started dabbling her face with a towel. "Look at you. You're all wet. We didn't know the sprinklers would go off. We'll change the crash protocol before the next drill."

Hwa tried hard to make her lips shape the word. "Drill?"

"Yes."

She had lost so much blood. She realized that now, distantly, and without anxiety. She wasn't even angry. That was how she knew. "For . . . the school?"

"No. For you. To see how you would protect Joel." His lips thinned. He looked away. "I asked Mr. Lynch not to go through with it. But he wanted to test you, and I . . . I knew you would pass." He smiled like his mouth hurt. "That's why we didn't use real rounds."

She really was pretty far gone, now. She couldn't even come up with something clever to say. Why was she so hot? Why was she sweating so hard? She'd barely run at all. "Can blanks do this?"

Daniel peeled back the tie, and the pad, and looked down. Blood covered his fingers instantly. Hwa felt sticky all down her right side. She'd thought it was the sprinklers. But it was hot. It was blood. The hallway tipped over on its side.

Her boss was screaming.

"*I NEED A MEDIC!*"

"Hwa!"

Suddenly Joel was there. He was saying something to her. She didn't know what it was. Her ears were still ringing. *Go away,* she wanted to say. *Go. Go now. There's someone here who's trying to kill you. A ghost. The invisible man. And he's been following us this whole time.*

Then they were lifting her on something. A stretcher. And Hwa saw where Síofra had gone. He was shaking the skullcap by the collar of his long black coat. Shaking him and slamming him against the lockers and yelling in his face about how *you fucking idiot you had one job one fucking job and she's bleeding out just look just look JUST FUCKING LOOK WHAT YOU DID TO HER—*

"H . . . Hey." Hwa held out her hand. It fell. She had to concentrate to bring it back up. Imagined all her muscles working like the girders on a causeway. Imagined all the tendons in her hand working her fingers into a fist. Close. Open. Close. Open. Síofra dropped the skullcap and reached out. He held her hand in both of his. It felt almost obscenely warm. And strangely damp. Sweaty. The sprinklers. The towel. Had to be.

"What is it?"

"You can . . . "

"Yes?" He bent down closer. Like before, she directed her voice at the little purple dot below his ear.

"You can take this job and shove it."

NEGATIVE SPACE
AMANDA FORREST

With light-speed flickering of self, Lan forgot the color blue. She stared at the sidewalk between her feet and couldn't remember the hues of the sky. A breath, and she looked heavenward to learn them again—azure, cyan, indigo.

She played these sorts of games while she walked. Lan knew how to forget. Next, she changed blue to red, and remembered a sky full of blood. She knew how to remember, too.

She stepped onto the remnants of the Strip. Vegas, undone. A shatter-glass pyramid clawed the sky, jagged edges in a rusting skeleton. Rows of dead palms lined the main avenue—from a block away, she'd heard their fronds rattling in the wind. In front of a dry fountain, a sign had been hammered into the earth: *This water is property of the MGM Grand. Thieves are subject to fines and incarceration.* The letters had faded, their color sapped by years under the desert sun. A handful of bicycle taxis ferried diehard gamblers with private water supplies between hole-in-the-wall slot parlors.

She swiped the sweat from her forehead and checked the time. Noon. Just two hours until Alexis would return to their squat, an abandoned condo in the north-side ghost 'burb. When she found Lan missing—captured, she'd assume— she'd move on, head back east where the rain still fell and companies still hired.

At least, that's what Lan hoped. It's what she was counting on.

She just needed the guy to show up with the assembler cartridges. Her mind-melded nanocore was nearly complete. Just a few more assemblers to finish the storage for the really heavy-duty apps.

Soon Lan would erase her beginnings, scrub them. Rebuild herself with memories that didn't leave her feeling like half a person. She was a lacework being, full of holes, negative space where her Vietnamese self should have been. It hurt, a bone-deep ache, to remember her homeland. And her memories made her a target. Her and Alexis both. She was tired of running. Tired of hearing Alexis cry behind a closed door. Alexis didn't deserve this. She wasn't even Lan's real mother.

Once she was ready to wipe her memory, she'd be useless to the corporate thugs. They'd leave Alexis alone after that. And the information—the memories— they wanted would be gone.

♦ ♦ ♦

Negative space: On the sidewalks of Hanoi, women burned household trash, bit by bit, in old coffee cans. There was a zoo near Lan's home. At night the monkeys screeched in their cages. Vendors sold reused bottles of UV-sterilized lake water.

Negative space: Lan's father took her to Ha Long Bay on the weekends, to row with the fishermen between mist-shrouded islands. Water greener than jade. They floated through caverns on tidal currents, emerged in secret lagoons ringed by limestone and jungle.

Behind her, the slap of bare feet on sidewalk. Lan turned. Her hands were shaking—nerves. She shoved them into her pockets. The guy was about her age, a year or two older at most. Seventeen. Shirtless, with dirt-crusted denim sucked to his hips and legs like it had been sprayed on. He glanced back the way he'd come, and she saw the circuitry fused to the base of his skull.

Classic external-interface datahead. Post-plague augmentations. He'd probably spent all his cash on augs, and now couldn't afford to buy connected space on a private shard. Stuck selling off assemblers that he didn't have the skill to manipulate.

"Hey," she said.

He shaded his eyes and squinted at her. Lan crouched down in the shade cast by the fountain's low wall. She swung her backpack off her shoulder. The datahead sat, leaned his bare back against the concrete.

"You still want them?" he asked. Mood beads, aglow like dying coals, followed the ink-black lines of a dragon tattoo on his arm. They flared a lecherous red when he looked her up and down. She shuffled backward and tried not to grimace. She couldn't afford to be picky.

Two weeks ago, north of San Diego, someone had jacked the drive systems of Alexis' bus and ran it into the closest building. She's scrambled away in time to see, from a vantage down the street, the thugs descend. A man and a woman, the same pair that had kicked down the door to their Seattle studio and trip-wired the apartment in Boise. Lan couldn't put Alexis at risk any longer.

She met the datahead's eyes. "You've got two cartridges, right?"

The LED glow on his arm faded. He scratched at his neck. "Yeah. Selling for one-fifty each."

Lan emptied her backpack onto the sidewalk. A water bottle clanged against the concrete. She picked up her modeling clay and stuffed it back inside, then snagged a roll of bills.

"They're virgin, right? I don't want anything that's already encoded. Too slow to reconfigure."

He glanced at the skin-fused graphene circuits—standard installations, nothing like the latticework hidden deeper in her brain—that curled over the back of her neck, up into her hair and around her ears. "Looks like you've got the gear to do whatever coding you want."

"And if I had nothing to do all day but sit on my thumbs and—"

He wasn't looking at her anymore. Something, or someone, over her shoulder held his interest. The cartridges lay in his loose-cupped hand, and he jiggled them absently like he was trying to keep her attention. The lines on his dragon went incandescent—panic—when Lan started to turn her head, and he snapped his gaze back to her eyes. Lan tensed. A trap. Time to go.

Lan exploded into motion. She seized her pack straps, both in one hand, swiped the datahead's cartridges with the other. Leapt to her feet and spun. The woman, the same one from Seattle, Boise, the bus accident, stood in the center of the street. Across the asphalt, a door opened. The man came at a jog.

Lan shoved the cartridges into her pocket, slung her pack over a shoulder, and ran. Her legs were tired from trekking in from the suburbs. Still, sidewalk fell beneath her strides, the slap, slap, slap of tennis shoes on concrete. She heard the man's heavy gait behind her, closing. Bicycles stopped, riders staring. Gamblers leaned out from the shade of their wagons to look.

Her legs failed. Lan stumbled, recovered, tripped again and barely got a foot in front of her falling body. She glanced back and saw the man just yards behind, the woman on his tail. Lan's thoughts plunged, desperate, into her integrated circuitry and her app-building studio. She snared code modules, stuffed in library functions, pulled images, sounds, vids from the public shard, constructed a slapdash memory of a footrace she'd never run. She loaded the program into her nanocore, gave the order to execute, and, in an instant, remembered the endorphin thrill of sprinting for the finish, seconds ahead of the pack.

The wind blew harder on her face, her feet fell faster, and she heard her pursuers lag behind. But the burst fizzled. She couldn't comprehend the weakness in her legs, not with the fast-forward high of the race so fresh in her memory. *It's my own creation*, Lan remembered. For a moment, her memories stood in juxtaposition. She'd won a race. She'd never been on a track in her life. Then the false memory collapsed, falling under the weight of years of recollections that contradicted it.

Lan stumbled and smacked the sidewalk. She hadn't considered context. In order for a new memory to survive, it had to have stronger support than any contradicting information.

Hands latched her upper arms, lifted her from the ground. She kicked and tossed her head. Her heels connected, produced a couple grunts, but the clamps on her arms tightened.

The man spoke calmly in her ear, as if it took no effort to hold her. "You're going to hurt yourself."

Lan craned her neck, intent on spitting at him. Her muscles cramped. The woman perched on the curb, waving the cyclists and passengers onward. A public shardcast came over Lan's wireless, whispered in her circuitry. The spectators—absent integrated hardware, probably because they feared another plague—raised hands to cup their earbuds.

"Police business. Please keep moving. Excuse the disturbance."

Traffic resumed. Those morons! Lan couldn't believe it. Did they not understand why the sharding happened in the first place? Networks flayed open by sell-sword crypto-savants? Servers murdered, collateral damage in the Sino-Ascendant infowars? The most basic truism of the public shard, of the global internet's last gasp, was that nothing was secure. The woman on the curb could impersonate the president if she wanted.

"What's your deal?" Lan asked.

The man chuckled. "You mean, how do we get away with nabbing kids off the street? Don't play dumb. It was just a matter of time before we caught you."

"Screw you," Lan said. She kicked again.

The woman got in Lan's face. "Come off it, princess. We've got you on attempted shard infiltration. Fingered you last week when you were trying to insert a node into Hanoi's private domain. Too bad you couldn't just let daddy go, huh? Made you easy to follow."

"Bull," Lan said. "Public's got all the info I want. Private shards are glorified photo albums. I don't care about what such and such family did on their vacation."

"Yes, I'm sure that the Vietnamese government fills their private cloud with baby pictures and tourist shots. And that the server logs are lying about your connection attempts."

"It's—"

"Go ahead. Keep making a scene. When the cops notice we'll pass along our information on your hacking attempts. They'll connect you to Ms. Langstrom— or whatever alias your Alexis uses now—and scoop her up, too."

Lan closed her mouth. The woman smiled.

Negative space: Her father worked in a basement beneath downtown Hanoi, a warren of gray cubicle walls. Once, he took her deeper, down to the air-conditioned rooms where the LEDs on the stacks of machinery looked like lights in a city skyline. Her father's coworkers always stepped aside to let him pass. One told her to be proud—her father was a savant.

Negative space: A blond woman stood in the doorway. Lan's aunt set the bent end of her ladle's handle over the rim of the cauldron of phở and beckoned the woman inside. The stranger's name was Alexis. She'd been working with Lan's father on a data-scraping contract. A strange job, conducted in the jungle rather than beneath Hanoi. Something had gone wrong, and Alexis wanted to know if Lan could come with her.

Negative space: She spent a week watching TV in Alexis's hotel room. Her father hadn't returned. Alexis said there were still people searching the jungle, and that he must still be alive because they hadn't found anything. No dead body is what she meant, even though she didn't say it. Alexis suggested that Lan might want to leave for a while. With her. To America. Just until her father could be found.

Her captors left Lan alone in the room, sitting in an overstuffed chair. A wall of glass looked over the ruined city, across the desert to the sharp rise of red rock cliffs. An air conditioner hummed, probably using hundreds of dollars of kilowatts an hour.

Lan kept her eyes from the suburb where she and Alexis had been hiding. Soon, Alexis would leave. She'd be safer without Lan. Wouldn't have to run to keep Lan from the hands of the companies that wanted her abilities.

Negative space: The cab driver wove through Hanoi's afternoon traffic, veering into the oncoming lanes, shouldering bikes aside, scraping mirrors on exhaust-stained brickwork. Alexis spoke into a headset, arranging to have immigration paperwork delivered to her suite downtown. She argued. Clenched her jaw.

Negative space: Lan and Alexis walked the length of the pier to their ship. A man at the end of a jetty sold braces of flapping pigeons to hungry dockworkers. Nearby, a girl—mid-teens, data-geared—reclined against a piling. Her lids fluttered over eyes that rolled left to right. Fingers scuttled over dirty silk pants. Her throat moved, subvocal mumblings. Virus-bait. Fallen to the data plague that had spread just after Lan's father disappeared. The girl might stay alive if someone forced food and drink down her.

Negative space: Alexis joined her at the railing. Vietnam disappeared beneath the curve of the horizon. Farther down the deck someone mentioned a news blitz on the Sino-Ascendant conflict. The Chinese were flooding the net with infobombs. Data had stopped flowing—a worldwide denial of service. Markets were plummeting. Alexis chewed her thumb and pulled Lan to the ship's bow where the wind lifted their hair and played across their skin.

Negative space: Alexis said she'd do what she could for Lan's aunt, send money and literature for battered women. Lan just nodded, knowing her aunt would ignore the help, and turned her eyes back to the sea. They hadn't spoken of Lan's father in days because there was no need. He was gone. It was then that she decided to learn how to forget. To really forget.

The man and woman stalked into the room, taking seats that partially blocked Lan's view of the desert.

She locked eyes with the woman. "So here we are. The end of the chase. I still won't work for you."

"Your mom—Is that what you call her? Or is it just Alexis? Anyway, our company expended a lot of resources getting you out of Vietnam. She owes us a large debt."

Lan covered her surprise. She'd thought Alexis had used her own funds to bring Lan across the ocean. "You paid for my immigration. Big deal. You still don't own my nanocore. I have a right to my childhood."

"Is that what you think?" the woman said. "That Alexis keeps you running so that you can have a normal childhood?" The woman rolled her eyes. "How many other kids spend their lives hiding in abandoned apartments? You're smart enough to know that's a lie."

Lan folded her arms over her chest. She imagined a lump of clay in her hand, twisting it, breaking it. The visualization kept her calm.

"Did Alexis tell you what we wanted you to do?" the woman asked.

"I'm my father's daughter. You probably think that he taught me things that your captive geniuses can't figure out. Except I was six years old and just a year into primary school." Lan shook her head. "You people are crazy."

"It's not just what he taught you. It's your genetics. We're sure that you've got the ability to lay down the protocols that could bring the shards back into a single, secure network. Safe from data plagues."

Lan liked to think that her father had died fighting the plague. But sometimes, she worried that it was the other way around, that her father had released the first virtual microbes and then disappeared, running from his guilt. Sometimes that worry stuffed her chest and it got hard to breathe. Then she fled to the corners of her mind and practiced her source code manipulations, practiced forgetting.

"I'd rather beg on the street corner than build another plague breeding ground."

The woman draped one leg over the other. "But that's the thing—even if you don't help, another global network is inevitable. People are starting to forget the reason for the sharding. The US government just shut down a messenger app that linked with the pub shard. Think of all those kids that ran out and got augmented after the sharding made us feel safe. Think of the families trying to rebuild the savings they lost in the infowar crash. Humanity needs an unbreakable security solution."

And the company who provided the solution would have a monopoly. Lan shrugged. "It's not my problem."

"We have documentation proving that Alexis defaulted on her debt. Given the details of our arrangement, we can assure that she'll spend time in prison."

"And if you lock her up, you lose all your leverage. I'll have zero motivation to help you."

The woman's mouth made a hard line. Lan reached into her pocket and palmed the assembler cartridges she'd swiped from the datahead. Pretending to scratch an itch at her hairline, she snapped them home. At a quick mental command, the assemblers fled the container and filled the reservoir beneath her skull. There, they received their assembly instructions, then tunneled beneath her brain casing, deep into gray matter.

Lan began to code. She concentrated, working out contingencies and conditionals to account for her new circumstances. Soon, she'd forget everything about her father. She'd be useless to these people.

"We're an upstanding corporation. We'd rather not deviate from the legal guidelines of the countries in which we work. But . . . "

"But Alexis doesn't have to be arrested to disappear. Just like my daddy, right?"

The woman uncrossed her legs and set her hands on her knees. She leaned forward. The man stood and traversed the floor, stopping next to Lan's chair. He placed a hand on the upholstery near her shoulder, showed a set of rings that could do a lot of damage in a punch.

The woman spoke. "Imagine what you will about Alexis. As for your dad, I do have some interesting information. Unfortunately the documents are on a private shard. There's no connected node here and no DNA scanner that I could use to authenticate."

Lan sighed. "Nice try. All I have to do to see those documents is heal the Internet, right?"

The man removed his hand and stalked to the window. "Let's just pull the mom in, Sherri. We're not getting anywhere."

Lan's heart stuttered. She needed to work faster. She started shoving pre-canned subroutines into her apps. A few more minutes, and she'd be ready to execute.

The woman nodded. "There's a pharma kit in the bedroom. We ought to be able to pull Alexis' next destination if we get her semi-conscious and run through the scene library. Her brain will light up for images that share context with their travel plans. Whether she wants it to or not."

Context. Lan's confidence plummeted. Context. Just like the footrace memory. She could replace the Vietnamese recollections, but she'd never get rid of the other hints that pointed back to her beginning. It would take days, weeks, maybe a lifetime, of planning to remove enough dependencies that the new memories would stick. And anyway, these people weren't just after her memories of her father—they wanted her capabilities.

Wipe it. Reset. Memzero.

Restarting at nothing, it would take years for her to learn enough to even begin to manipulate software.

It took less than a second to compose the app, and she paused, thoughts poised over the command to execute.

The end of her identity. No more Vietnam, no more worry about Alexis, no more running. But no more memories of birthday parties either, no more late-night dancing to weird music, laughing at Alexis's clumsy attempts. What if Lan didn't have to lose herself forever?

She accessed the public shard and started pulling up the wikis she might use to breadcrumb the way back to herself. Lan worked fast, overclocking the process she used to pull the data, maxing her bandwidth.

"Get the pharma," the woman said.

Lan's throat clamped down. Just a few minutes left—Lan could never flag enough sites to describe herself.

It was time to let the negative space go. She'd planned it all along, but now that the moment had come, there didn't seem nearly enough time to say goodbye.

She'd lose the weekends spent rowing with her father in Ha Long Bay but keep the lasagna that Alexis always burned. So long to the taste of her aunt's *phở*. On summer weekends, Alexis used to push Lan on the swing for hours. That would stay.

Alexis. Always on the run, always protecting the child she'd first met as a six-year-old stranger. Lan could never repay the debt of gratitude. She realized, then, that the best way to thank her was to free her. Lan needed to make sure she could never find Alexis again.

She wiped the wiki changes and started again.

The trail began in Hanoi. Lan pinned a map reference, a satellite shot of her first home. She linked a photo of a woman burning trash on her apartment stoop. Piece by piece, Lan wove together references to her Vietnamese youth. Occasionally, she left memory dumps disguised as image or audio files, real mappings that could be loaded directly. Other times, the wiki article would have to be enough to rebuild a sense of self. When she was finished, she tacked a single command onto her reset app, one that would etch the first URL in the forefront of her mind with a stern directive to wait until she was free from captivity to open it.

The woman was talking. "IV drip stand is in the closet. I want to get the location on Alexis before we have to chase her across the country."

Lan took a breath and loaded her program into working memory. She said goodbye to herself and let it fly across her core.

The girl opened her eyes. A woman sat in front of her, looking somehow angry, and a series of letters that the girl couldn't really understand flashed in the upper corner of her vision. The girl cocked her head to the side.

"Your eyes are blue," the girl said. Her brows were raised, eyes wide. "Azure. Cyan. Indigo. I knew those once."

FUSION

GREG MELLOR

Glen walks down onto the bright sand. The tide is receding but he can still see waves pounding on the reef in the distance. Above the spray the sky is streaked with long white clouds. The backpack digs into his shoulders and he adjusts the straps and steps onto a rocky plateau fanning out from the headland. Colorful anemones shrink from his shadow as he leaps over pools left from the tide. Strange hermit crabs retreat into shells. There is a silver patina blending with the ancient rock layers that he hasn't noticed before. It's almost geometric in its structure but he doesn't stop to ponder such mysteries.

The plateau soon narrows down to a thin land bridge stretching out to the horizon. He sets off at a fast pace, striding from stone to stone. The faint mechanical tick in his breathing provides a comforting tempo. When he estimates he is halfway across he pauses to take a drink from his canteen. Out here the ocean is flat and mirror-like. The wind surges in humid gusts and the glare is intense and he curses out loud for forgetting his hat. Sweat beads on his forehead. The alloy skin on his right hand expands and flexes with the heat.

There's a ledge here on one side of the land bridge where the rock is flaky and dry and the washed up seaweed smells of decay. A man is sitting on the ledge facing away from Glen. He's dressed in tattered rags and his arms are tanned like leather. His hair is gray and long and windblown.

You don't have much time, boy, the stranger says without turning around.

Glen realises that the tide has changed. Clouds are rushing in from the north. Shading his eyes he glances east along the path ahead. The horizon is murky above the land bridge and he can't see much at all except for the tales in his mind's eye of lands across the water. He turns and looks west along the path he has traveled. The headland is a small brown lump blending into white beaches either side. He remembers a time on those vast sands when a whale washed up to shore. Its hide was covered in blotches and barnacles but there had been no sign of abnormal growths. Some living things, he knew, were still fully natural. He had waited for hours by the leviathan's side, small and safe beneath that ancient eye, listening to the waning hammer blows of its heart. When he returned the next day the beach was empty and he felt that something had been irretrievably lost from the world.

He looks now at the stranger's back, wondering if the man is indeed full flesh like the whale. Then the stranger turns as if sensing Glen's unspoken question. His face is alloy and reflects the sky. Terrifying mutated eyes bulge out on stalks.

Be careful what you wish for, the stranger says.

Glen quickly shoulders his pack and runs east and doesn't look back. A cross wind threatens to slow his progress and with it comes sand and leaves from some place along the coast. He soldiers on, head down against the stinging particles, boots scraping against the rocks. The sky darkens with the onrush of the late storm pushed south from the tropics. Waves begin to pound the land bridge and shower him in curtains of water streaked with fading rainbows from the last light of the sun.

He stumbles in the gray, clothes sodden and water curling off his chin and alloy hand, which feels warmer than the other. Lightning strobes across the sky and he sees the corpse he had tripped over. Hollow eyes in a grinning skull. Legs bent beneath its body with one ankle snagged under a rock. Alloy ribs exposed where sea denizens had stripped the full flesh away.

He sings a song from the nomad camps. It's an old song that is part lament, part celebration of the transformation of flesh. It blocks out the shriek of the wind and the crash of the waves. It doesn't block the memories.

See, Lizzy says.

She holds up a fish Glen just caught in the shoals. The creature is struggling for air, its mouth opening and closing stupidly. Glen watches in disbelief as she guts the thing with her morphing hooks that substitute for fingers. She eats the flesh.

He shrieks in disgust. Stop. You can't eat it. Tell her, Mum. I was going to throw it back in . . . Lizzy!

Mum sits on the sand with her legs tucked up against her chest and her hair shining bronze. She says nothing and continues to scratch at the metallic lumps protruding out of her cheeks like small tusks.

You were always holier than thou, Lizzy says between mouthfuls of raw fish.

We have to preserve nature.

Not anymore.

Tell her, Mum. Please.

Mum sighs. Leave your sister alone, Glen. We have to eat.

Lizzy sneers. Yeah, leave me alone, holy boy. Think you're gonna find the angels across the water one day? Well no one from round here ever made it. What makes you think you're any different?

Sounds of the storm filter back in. He sprints now, as much from the past as the surging elements. His lips tremble with cold and fear. Before he knows it the ground changes and he's running up a slope covered with wild tussock grass and broken gum trees. He reaches out and grips a shattered tree trunk. The ocean behind him covers the land bridge in large swells. Waves break at odd angles and surge up to his feet. He kicks against the ground and crawls higher until he finds the shelter of a tree. The sky howls and darkens under the full force of the cyclone and he hugs the tree with all his remaining strength and wonders if the very earth will be uprooted and flung into the sky.

By evening the storm twists away as quickly as it came, leaving the sound of the waves and the faint tick of his cooling alloy and the voices of the dead still stirring in his head.

At some point during the night he sleeps.

In the morning the sky is a blanket of gray clouds with red underbellies. Sunshine slants through in patches as if hesitant to bring warmth. The ocean to the west is a dull gray expanse carved with white tops. The ground he is on forms a wide promontory rising to misty heights to the east. There are things shining up there but he can't tell whether it's water falling off rocky outcrops or something else. Ice?

The rations in his pack are soaked and spoilt. He pulls out the rope and the knife and bandages and spare clothes and lays them out on the grass to dry. He quickly stifles the idea of going back to the shore to catch a fish and instead finds some wild berries and fills his canteen from a freshwater pool that appears to have formed during the storm.

Afterwards he packs and continues up the hillside. Sunlight casts the mist aglow and lifts his spirits as he walks. The incline steepens but the ground is solid and his legs are strong. Alloy not flesh. And still no sign of mutation even after fifteen winters. He wonders at that. His Mum blessed him for it. His sister hated him for it. The thought dampens his good mood and by evening he's tired and hungry. He makes a fire on a small ledge from twigs and eats more of the berries. The remains of old camps litter the ledge and he speculates as to how many pilgrims have ventured here in search of answers. Then he remembers the stranger with the eyes and he holds his hands closer to the fire and wonders if there really are answers to be found at all.

The embers dwindle in the small hours and mist cocoons his location. In the gray predawn the air currents shift to create a gap above. Stars glitter through. From this vantage point he can see a black expanse rising in the east like a void that fills him with dread. It's as if something had wedged a blade into the earth, taller than the mountains of his dreams.

The mist coils back over and try as he may he can't unravel the knots tightening his gut.

He lies awake until morning.

His eyes are gritty and his mind is full of tainted memories. He hikes until the mist clears to reveal a plateau littered with rocks. There is a broad cliff with wispy waterfalls at the end of the plateau. At the top of the cliff, the land slopes back into crumpled terrain covered by a sprawling favella. There are green pastures and animals in pens on the outskirts of the town and mirrored dishes that reflect harsh sunlight and create spots across his vision. Above the favella the land steepens to the ominous blade peak he had seen during the night.

He sees movement out along the plateau. A pack of wild dogs is chasing a girl dressed in black. She carries a bow and quiver of arrows slung over her back. She clubs one of the dogs across the snout with her bow but another one manages to get in close and mauls her ankle.

Glen races forward and waves his arms and claps his hands.

Hoy!

The pack turns as one. They sniff the air and growl and bare yellow fangs. Glen pulls out the knife. Every instinct tells him to run but he holds steady as the dogs lope toward him. The first one is taken clean but its momentum snaps the knife from his grip. He rolls to one side as the second dog clamps its jaws onto his alloy arm. Up this close Glen can see that most of the animal's fur has transformed to metallic spikes. He kicks the dog hard with as much power as he can muster. Once. Twice. The thing falls dead without a sound, its head and ribs crushed.

He spins around ready for another attack but the girl takes down the three remaining dogs with arrows. He watches through the silky lens of adrenalin as she limps up to him. She's older by a good three winters, has an air of confidence he hasn't got in this strange country. Her hair is dark and plaited and her face is hawkish and her legs are long beneath the black leather. She is by far the most beautiful thing he has ever seen.

Thank you, friend, she says. What's your name?

Glen.

I'm Rose.

He's not sure what to say at the way her pale eyes rummage into his soul as if seeking some immediate truth.

Better get that wound checked, she says.

He realises his shirt is all torn. The alloy along his forearm is punctured and oozing blood laced with black.

Ditto, he says pointing to her torn trousers where her natural ankle is raw and bleeding freely. The rest of her alluring white calf is exposed but unscathed.

He looks away.

She laughs. Come on, we should leave. There are worse things up here than mad dogs and lost boys. She winks at him.

Glen retrieves his knife and Rose retrieves her arrows.

He points at the strange looking peak.. What kind of mountain is that?

It's not a mountain.

She leads him to the foot of the cliff where a manmade staircase takes them up around the waterfalls. About half way up they find a cave. The roar of the water is like a balm and stops his thoughts from spinning. He fills their canteens while Rose cleans the bites on her ankle. She lets him apply a bandage. He's self conscious with her closeness and the way her soft skin glows in the faint light. He shies away when she reaches to his wounded arm.

What's the matter?

Nothing.

She grabs his sleeve and yanks it up and gasps. You're a healer, she says, brushing her palm across the unblemished alloy.

He shrugs and pulls his sleeve down. If that's what you call it, he says. Some days it feels lighter and stronger than flesh. Sometimes it feels like a phantom limb and it makes me think I might become a ghost that was once human. Maybe that's what the angels are. Fully cybernetic. No need to eat or drink. No need to claw every day to survive.

Her look is serious. You wouldn't be the first to think like that.

He shrugs again.

What about your legs? You smashed that dog pretty hard.

I was born with them. They feel different to the new parts. He taps the alloy beneath his trousers, knowing now he would never have made it across the land bridge with natural legs.

She holds his hand. You should consider yourself lucky.

Why? I hate knowing this plague in my veins kills everyone around me sooner or later.

I'm sorry, she says. We've all lost family.

Now he feels bad.

There's no need to look so gloomy, she says and stands tentatively on her ankle. Come with me.

They pack their gear and he follows her out of the cave and on up the stairs to the top of the cliff. After a short march across grassy knolls below the favella, they come to a narrow ledge jutting over open sky. Rose crawls out onto the ledge and waves for Glen to follow. He approaches cautiously and peers over the ledge. Wind billows up from two kilometers of open air and thumps into his lungs and he whoops out loud. Rose smiles and he notices the telltale sign of emerging mutation along her neckline. A pattern of veins like a tattoo scrolling from her ear lobe to her shoulder and down along the top of her chest and beneath the drawstrings of her leather top. He knows she has noticed him. She points to the scenery far below. There are green fields laced with silver. Farmsteads and lanes crisscross the landscape. The ocean curves away to the west and south.

My home was down there, she says. All these lands were once beneath the ocean they used to call the Pacific.

The name sounds strange to Glen. He follows her gaze to his left along the southern face of the blade peak. She was right; it's not a mountain at all but a wedge of land rammed upwards with incredible force. Whatever caused it is out of sight on the eastern face, but Glen can see its impossibly long shadow angling across the farmlands. He works it through in his head, begins to picture something long and straight-edged jutting out of the earth at a shallow angle.

The mutations are worse the closer you get to it, Rose says.

So you don't know what it is?

No, she says. There's so much knowledge lost. Some people call it the splinter. I heard an angel once call it the star bridge before he died. Others just call it home.

He feels suddenly nauseated and rolls on his back and closes his eyes. The sun is pale and strangely distant and doesn't warm his skin.

The favella is surprisingly clean. A patchwork quilt of shanties and corrugated sheets and steel salvaged from the industrial epoch. There is technology here. Shining solar dishes provide power to the township and a dam and pipes capture the rainwater off the peak. There's an orchard with fruit trees and a stockyard with some cattle and sheep. A modest trade of breads and leather and pottery exists. Glen meets new friends and is welcomed as one of their own, but before long he knows this is a ghost town. The mutations are mostly advanced and horrific, though there are a few like him and Rose who have yet to manifest abnormalities.

On the sunny days he forages with her along the highlands where the wild fruits and grains are threaded with delicate traces of silver. He moves into her shanty and accumulates things that might be useful for the journey ahead including a spike hammer and a tent and a thick woolen jacket. Despite the desire to keep moving forward he still finds himself settling into a disturbingly comfortable routine. Rose calls him a real homemaker, but he shrugs it off until one day in the middle of his sixteenth winter, as they lay talking before the open fire, she takes his hand and presses it to her breast. He stirs and is suddenly forgetful of the world. From then on the days turn into weeks in the warmth of their shanty as storms churn down the coast that used to be called Queensland.

The alloy spreads across Glen's skin during the winter. His left arm is transformed and his spine feels supple and stronger. The mechanical rhythm in his breathing seems to smooth out considerably and he wonders whether it's the thin air or something else going on inside.

On a chill day when the rain drums on the corrugated roof and forms copper-colored stains in the mud, he makes his way to the evangelist. Much of the township's solar power feeds to the hut and when Glen steps inside he has to hold his sleeve to his nose. The hut is filled with the pungent smell of weeping sores and metallic growths covering the evangelist's chubby limbs. Bundles of cables form a throne of sorts, connecting monitors on the evangelist's limbs to stacked boxes that work some old magic of computation. Tubes full of blood and other fluids lead into pumps and devices that whir softly in the background. Shelves around the hut are covered with charts and baroque mechanical devices and instruments.

The evangelist's breath wheezes in and out through a mask. There are broken cities to the south, he says between the click of his respirator. Sydney. Melbourne.

Glen had heard the legends. Is that where the equipment comes from?

Some of it. But that's not the real reason why you're here, is it?

No, Glen says glancing at the throne of cables. Is there a cure?

Ah, the evangelist says. I've been trying for years to figure that one out. But I've since come to the conclusion that it's the wrong question.

What do you mean?

There is no cure. I'll give you that for free. Besides, a cure would assume we are dealing with a disease.

Glen frowns, now uneasy with the conversation.

The evangelist smiles and coughs up phlegm. Oh, come now, there's no need to be coy. I think you already knew it or at least suspected the truth is not always so simple. I'll never be an angel but that won't stop me trying to control the spread of this wondrous thing in my veins. Then I'll be like you.

Glen chooses his next words carefully. You know about my abilities?

You've done well to hide it this long but that doesn't stop the rumour mongers. Your secret is safe with me but at some point . . .

What's the price?

The evangelist clasps his sweaty hands together. Cables move as he moves. The pumps stir more fluids. A sample of your blood, he says.

Glen turns and walks to the door. Before I leave. I'll give you some before I leave.

The evangelist points to some equipment on a bench. Take those. You'll need them. But then again, maybe you won't.

Glen picks up a breathing apparatus and goggles. There's also a small instrument on a wrist band. He turns it over in his hands. The technology seems crude and angular against the sleek lines of his alloy skin.

What is it?

An altimeter.

At the onset of spring when the orchard trees are in blossom, Glen sees an angel fall from the sky. It bounces once before his unbelieving eyes and impales on a concrete fence post. Shining silver wings twist and snap. Slick natural innards dangle out of its body cavity onto the mud. Its slender alloy limbs twitch once then hang limp. Its face is sprayed with blood and the jaw is crushed up close to vacant cybernetic eyes.

Onlookers crowd around within minutes. One man heavily burdened with metallic tumors steps up cautiously and rubs his hands in the angel's blood.

The crowd turns manic and shuffles forward to touch the angel. Glen is caught up in the frenzy and a woman with gleaming horns rupturing from her head grabs him and pushes him towards the angel. He resists and slips in the mud and is soon forgotten as more people arrive at the scene.

Then the sound of children running down the street causes everyone to stop and turn their heads. The young ones were kept hidden during the long winter with their shining hooves and tails and extra limbs. Now they shuffle towards the dead angel, ushered by teary-eyed parents.

Young faces smeared.

Red palm prints everywhere.

A kindergarten crime scene watched over by adults babbling in an old language that doesn't belong in this epoch.

Prayer.

Glen runs to the orchard and pukes under a gnarled plum tree.

Glen hugs Rose once. The growths on her neck look like bronze mushrooms in the early summer light. The sun rises over the blade peak, stoking the fire he has held in check these long months. He adjusts his extra large backpack and his utility belt.

I'm sorry, he says.

Why?

I . . . I'm not sure. It feels like I'm letting you down.

She laughs in the same way she had on the day they met. You'd be letting me down if you stay. Letting all the others down. Everyone wants to know the mystery but very few have the means.

Haven't you tried? He doesn't know why he never asked her.

Ha, me? No, I know my limits. She points to the blade peak. I've only ever reached the summit. That's not very far, he says.

It was far enough for me.

I'll come back.

She kisses him on the lips. No you won't, she says, and walks down to the favella and doesn't look back.

It takes him a day to reach the summit. His breath curls out in long plumes. The sky is blue and cloudless and the view on the other side makes him fall to one knee. It had been a shadow haunting his dreams these months but now the splinter juts from the earth below and angles up to the sky like a glossy black crystal stretching out forever. Layers of storm detritus crust its lower lengths and ice fields mottle the higher reaches. Further still the ice fades to black. The structure is about a kilometer wide with an angled peak. But the length? The length is incalculable. Fifty kilometers? More.

The voice of the evangelist stirs in his memory. It should collapse under its own weight.

I don't know what that means, was all Glen could say at the time.

He clambers down off the blade peak where the earth is broken and dotted with treacherous crevices, but he finds his way safely onto the northern slope of the splinter. There are tracts of land here where the detritus is compacted hard. The going is slow but the ground seems stable enough. Some sparse trees have seeded in tangled groves to provide crude shelter along the way.

He dons the oxygen mask and goggles and extra layers of clothing when he reaches the ice fields that creak and crack under his boots. He worries constantly about avalanches taking him under tonnes of ice and over the edge to the four-kilometer drop below.

When he sleeps, he dreams of fallen angels and praying humans.

In the cold mornings when he wakes, he knows the temperature would kill anyone else. There's very little natural skin left. Some patches on his stomach and chest beneath the woollen layers. He feels his numb face and wonders if frostbite has set in. He looks at his reflection in his palm and doesn't recognize the person looking back. His eyes are like the angel, more machine than man. Even his hair is bronze like Mum's used to be.

He survives on melted ice. The rations are long gone but he doesn't feel hungry. Things stir and rearrange in his belly and days go by where he is gripped with pain and cannot walk far at all. The ice gets thicker. Great fields of white. All sense of time and purpose drown in the glare. Memories lay dormant in some recess of his mind. He can't even remember the names of the dead but he still feels their ghosts. There are strange sounds in the air and he turns occasionally to see if anyone is following.

He hikes for days yet the splinter is at such a shallow angle that the altimeter on his wrist only reads thirty kilometers. The ice thins out to black. He has avoided the splinter's surface this far, but now there's no choice. The remaining length is pure black for as far as the eye can see. He takes a tentative step forward. The surface reminds him of the deep water beyond the reef and he half expects to fall through. As his confidence grows, he walks around in circles and stamps his feet. Satisfied, he kneels down and presses his face to the cold black. There's some kind of faint resonance within the structure that tingles his alloy skin. He wonders why he is not surprised.

Something causes him to glance back at his campsite. He had carved a hollow on the leeward side of an ice knoll. There's no sleeping bag or tent or equipment. He can't remember when he left them behind. The fact that he also left his jacket and boots and clothes somewhere on the trail is only remotely disturbing. And once he realizes he is no longer using the breathing apparatus, he doesn't much care about anything at all.

◆ ◆ ◆

Beyond fifty kilometers altitude, it's all about the curvature of the world. He ventures closer to the northern edge of the splinter to watch the sun shed dappled light over the Pacific. He wonders why people don't name things anymore. Weather patterns evolve like an artist's canvas. A cyclone unfurls along the coast trailing great white spirals of cloud.

Up here the air is warmer and calm and breathless, and he sees the beauty of the earth with his newfound eyes. There is a sense of longing at leaving the brown lands below. Some part of him is convinced he is fully cybernetic now. At what point did the cutover occur? Did it take his brain during the night only for him to wake with phantom thoughts indistinguishable from a real human mind?

Lizzy told him on the day the tumors took her face that she knew the plague had reached her brain but it didn't feel any different. She still liked the texture of sand between her toes. She still hated the taste of oysters and the color orange. She still wanted to strive with all her remaining breath to live and love and be with the people that meant the most to her.

Including you, little brother. Including you.

He sits on the edge with his feet dangling and unfastens the altimeter from his wrist and throws it out into open air. Days come and go against the permanence of the splinter sloping higher into impenetrable night. The feeling that he is now leaving everything cuts deep into his soul. Or the illusion of one that now resides in his computational brain that makes its own altitude calculations and swiftly scrutinizes his body and the surrounding environment.

You have your wings.

The voice drifts in from the middle distance. Somehow Glen knows the speed of sound varies with air density and temperature gradients and his brain accommodates. The angel flies beneath his vantage point, curving in a long lazy arc like an eagle he had seen once rising on thermals. Before Glen knows it, the angel lands next to him in a crouched position with wings folded over its back. The close proximity of another being after so long is alarming, and all Glen can do is stare in awe at the angel's bronze skin adorned with gray alloys like swirling tribal tattoos.

I suppose you could call them that, Glen says after a long silence. His emergent wings are small by comparison and move awkwardly, as if mimicking the majesty of the angel.

I've been waiting for someone to venture this far, the angel says.

Glen laughs at the stupidity of it all. How's that possible? I'm a dumb kid with stunted wings on a quest that never ends.

The angel laughs. Exactly!

Glen waves his hands absently. Whatever.

The angel laughs again and points to the Earth. It's everywhere, you know.

Glen sees the shining patterns radiating out from the splinter across the ground, like the veins along Rose's neck and the threads in the highland fruit and the patina on the rocks on the shore of his old home.

I know, Glen says.

It's touching the carbon in all living things, the angel says. And in the layers of the land that were once alive. It's mimicking all the forms hidden in the story book of our genes.

Glen wonders at all the manifestations in all the people he has encountered. The science is still new to me, he says, but I have seen the different forms emerge.

The angel seems nonchalant. It's searching the code of life.

Well it's not doing a very good job, is it?

The angel gives Glen a mysterious look and stands up and holds out its hand. Think of it more as evolution. Let me take you a little further.

There's no point, Glen says. He thinks back to the man on the land bridge. Even out here after all these months he feels much the same, lost before he has even started.

The angel arches an eyebrow. If you haven't noticed there are not many folk up here.

Glen slams his fist down on the hard surface of the splinter. It gives off a dull clang and he looks at his hand and sees the alloy is now disappearing beneath layers of tough black coating.

Did we create this? Is it from the industrial epoch?

Hardly.

Then where does it come from?

Let's go.

Why don't you just go on up there yourself?

The angel gives a grim smile. I would if I could. I still have flesh on the inside.

Glen reaches out and lets the angel pull him up to his feet. I don't think I can go much further, he says.

Oh, I think you can.

The curve of blue sky bleeds away into layers of umber and saffron. Sunrise is only minutes away. Glen turns to wave goodbye to the angel but remembers that it was days ago somewhere down in the deeper layers of the atmosphere. There's no sign of anything except the ever-present splinter beneath his feet and the patchwork of stars above and the odd meteor trail. His body is accommodating the colder temperature here. His skin is ultra hard and pure black, like the splinter. Wings are a mix of copper and tough alloys with delicate mirrored surfaces. Memories are still human, though he wonders at that.

The other splinters poke out across the horizon like needles. Most are embedded in the Earth at the same obtuse angle. Others are skewed at more severe inclines. One lays broken to the south, sheered into two pieces lying on the edge of the Australian coast like the pillars of some lost city. All the impact zones are filled with spreading geometries as the cybernetic life form continues to blend with nature. He can see many things with his far sight. He knows now that knowledge is never lost, just hidden in the world. He knows that the sentience of the splinters has tapped into the universal forms in the gene pool. Eyes. Wings. Legs. Spine. He knows that it is seeking perfection of form. Long and perfect as it is in its own symmetry. Maybe they arrived here on purpose. Maybe by mistake. A swarm caught up in the gravitational well.

He strides along the splinter until it narrows to a tip where the air thins out completely into vacuum. There is no room to walk here, so he crawls then wraps his arms around the end of the splinter and holds on tight.

He's more afraid than ever.

Which is ridiculous really.

After all this time.

He feels connections through his skin with the resonant patterns of the splinters, an emergent language as old as the stars themselves. There are others up here, in orbit way above his location. On clear nights he thinks he can see some on the moon.

What to do, he says to himself. There is no sound here, but there are signals if you listen close enough. There is no flesh now, but there is soul in the machinery if you delve deep enough. There is no end to the quest, but there are new shores if you look hard enough.

And there it is.

An answer!

Or part of one.

Life is a series of new shores blending from one to another. The fusion of genetic forms within forms. The fusion of biological layers upon layers spanning immense periods of time. And here was yet another layer wrapping around the globe. Cybernetic fusing with flesh.

There is nothing else for it. He stands up and balances precariously on the tip of the splinter. Ultralight wings spread out and soak up the energies of the sun now rising like a beacon.

Time to fly.

TAKING THE GHOST

A.C. WISE

"Still with me?"

Mac coughed and pushed at the face leaning over his, inches distant. The man didn't move.

"Still." It came out as a wheeze. Mac rolled onto his side, trying to put enough air into his lungs to ask where. He remembered smoke, cannon fire, crawling, trying to reach the prince. Motion. Someone carrying him? After that, a wash of red-black pain and the smell of something burning.

Another cough wracked him. He clutched aching ribs and let the pain shake him. It took a moment for mind to catch up to body. Only one arm wrapped his mid-section. The other . . . He could still feel it. Fuck, but he could feel it. Except . . .

"Shit!" He jerked back, but there was nowhere to go. His back collided with a hard edge of wood, heels scrabbling against dusty planks.

He stared. Visual input and physical sensation refused to mesh. Mac's arm folded around his body, holding the pain. And his arm ended at the shoulder, a charred stump smelling faintly of smoke.

"Cauterized it for you while you were out." The face leaning into his drew back. "Not the ideal setting." The man gestured to the wagon bed, boxy wood, bolted the back of an ancient truck cab, more rust than metal. "But I figured I'd better do it sooner'n not. Didn't want you to bleed out. You're welcome, by the way."

Gray dominated the man's dreads, but his skin showed barely any wrinkles. He rose from his crouch. His left leg was metal; the joints whined as he jumped from the truck bed, raising dust where he landed. He opened the truck door, but paused leaning to peer at Mac. Light glinted off green glass, jammed through the flesh of his brow, and burrowed into his cheek, obscuring his right eye. A mass of scars surrounded the glass, shiny and old.

"Name's Zeb." The man stuck out his hand; Mac cautiously peeled his left hand from his pained ribs and accepted it. Zeb's palm was calloused and rough, his skin warm.

"We got a ways to go yet. Best you rest up. You've been through a lot."

Mac tried again to ask where—where he was, where they were going. The prince. What had happened to her? His head ached, his mouth too dry to form the first word. As if reading his thoughts, Zeb leaned into the truck's cab and tossed a leather canteen into the truck bed.

"Try to sleep," he said as he closed the door.

Mac slumped back. The engine coughed to life. Vibrations shuddering up through the wood sent a fresh wave of pain through his body. He reached for the canteen with his right arm. Nothing. He fought rising bile, squeezing his eyes closed. He forced himself to take a breath before fumbling the canteen's cap off with his left hand and taking a pull of the warm, dusty water.

The truck lurched forward with a bang, spitting more dust and exhaust. Mac bit down on a scream. The next jolt of the truck did him in; unconsciousness mercifully shielded him from further pain.

Mac woke to the thump of the truck's tailgate lowering. He squinted, bleary. His head floated—hollow and fever-hot; his mouth tasted of red dirt and blood. An old man nudged a canteen within Mac's reach. Zeb. Yes, the old man was Zeb. Mac managed to sit up without vomiting, breathing shallow until dizziness passed.

Beyond Zeb's shoulder, a wall of junk cast its shadow over the truck—twisted metal, fused plastic, shattered chunks of concrete and stone, all studded with winking glass and topped in razor wire. One of the way station junkyards scattered along the trade routes between cities. But which one? Mac's knowledge of geography ended at the city walls. He'd been too young when they moved to remember anything but the city, and he'd never cared to learn anything beyond what the prince had deigned to tell him. Even then, he'd barely listened, more interested in her lips than the words falling from them.

Pain lanced Mac's right arm. He clapped a hand to it, and his fingers passed right through, touching his side.

"My arm." The memory of his right arm hung limp against his side. He couldn't move it. It was just there, heavy, shoulder itching.

"Yup. War's a bitch." Zeb scratched his nose. "Don't worry, we'll find something to replace it."

He held out a hand. Mac inched forward, not trusting his body, his weight. The indignity of Zeb hauling him from the truck, holding him up with an arm around his shoulders, was outweighed by the horror of the man's fingers touching an arm that wasn't there. Mac's stomach cramped and he brought up bile, spitting it onto the dust.

"Leave me." Mac wiped his lips, eyes closed. The city, the prince, everything was gone; all Mac wanted to do was lie down, let the sun bake his flesh from his bones—those that remained.

"Look, you wanna die out here that's your business." Zeb's strength, surprising for his age, kept Mac upright even though his knees wanted to buckle and crash him to the ground. "I saved your life, but if you don't want to extend me even the slightest bit of gratitude for my efforts, so be it."

Zeb released him. By some cruel trick of gravity, Mac didn't fall. He raised his head. Nothing but dust, as far as he could see, and the shadows of buzzards staining the red. The color brought the smell of burning and blood to clog nose and mouth. He brought up hands to claw the scent away. No . . . Only one hand. He bucked, his body trembling rebellion against his conviction to die.

"Wait!" At Mac's croak, Zeb paused, light winking from the green glass covering his eye. "I'm sorry."

Zeb grunted; he waited for Mac to catch up.

The wall gleamed in the late apricot light. All his will concentrated on not collapsing, Mac dragged himself to the way station door where Zeb waited. Two double-wide trailers, hollowed out and laid on their ends, had been soldered with hooks to fit a bar attached to a keypad with a red, blinking light. Zeb tapped in a code.

The light turned amber, then green; the bar rose. The double-wide trailers swung open, and the junkyard opened to them.

"Don't get much trade these days. Still, got a few bits around as might be useful. Build up more in my spare time. Gotta keep busy." The door swung shut. The encircling walls layered shadows thick between the piles of junk, and the air seemed colder.

"You're all alone?" Mac asked, trying focus on something other than panic and pain.

Zeb shrugged. "Most days. Sit before you fall down."

He pointed to an oil drum, sawed in half to make one of a pair of seats next to an ash-filled fire pit. Mac lowered himself, careful not to over-balance.

"Palace guard?" Zeb spoke over the rattle as he hauled open the drawer of a battered filing cabinet standing beside the nearest junk pile. If there was order in the chaos, Mac couldn't see it.

"Not anymore." Mac's throat tightened. "I . . . I tried to save the prince. She refused to leave the palace."

Mac shook his head. The ache filling the hollow space behind his eyes colored like a bruise. The prince's eyes, the stubborn set of her jaw. She'd never believed in her own mortality. She'd built the wall her father had spoken of all her life, filling her head with it until it became her dream, and she believed it would never fall. And because the wall had filled her world, she'd never thought to look to the people inside it for signs of danger.

Mac's throat worked, aching as he tried to swallow the salt-taste of memory. He'd believed in the prince's vision, stopped his ears when his sisters and brother had called the prince's regime unfair, pressed literature into his hands, invited him to their meetings, held in secret places far from the palace's prying eyes.

He told himself their lives weren't his. They'd always had their own world, their own shared language and memories. Mac was the intruder, the latecomer, blooming his mother's belly, and breaking into their established, closed world.

But they were family. And he'd offered no bribes, done nothing to stay the hangman's noose. For what? The prince's softening waist, the seed planted in her belly she wouldn't even confirm was his, the child growing inside the body she didn't believe in, preferring to see herself as incorruptible, immortal, inhuman?

Zeb slammed the drawer, and opened the door of a scarred, wooden object that might once have been a wardrobe. Mac caught a glimpse of limbs, stripped of skin, only metallic bones—gold, silver, and copper—hanging from hooks. His gaze went to Zeb's own mechanical leg. It bent the wrong direction. The discrepancy, one flesh knee facing forward, one metal knee bending back, gave the old man an odd, rolling gait, but it didn't slow him down.

"Ha!" Zeb emerged from the cabinet with an arm. He squinted, holding the appendage in front of him, assessing Mac. "This looks just your size."

Zeb shut the cabinet door, but it bounced open again. Something tumbled out, rolling to a stop against Mac's foot, a skull—emptied of eyes, lips, nose, mouth—everything but the silvered teeth and servo-powered jaws.

Mac kicked it away, the trembling he'd only just gotten under control threatening to start up again. He'd seen a trader come to the city once with a golden arm, wanting to sell armor to the prince. When Mac had asked, the prince told him the limbs were common during the war, before the wall. She'd waved further questions away, impatient.

The thought of metal joined to his flesh left cold sweat slicking his skin. Mac's head buzzed. Zeb's lips moved, but Mac couldn't hear him. The only thing was the roar of blood in his ears, the high-pitched ringing in the wake of the cannon that had taken his arm.

The world tilted out from under him, taking with it the smell of charred flesh, and a hand that no longer existed—phantom fingers scrabbling over marble, reaching for the prince sprawled upon the palace steps, braids spread around her head, the medals covering her uniform winking with reflected flame.

"That should do you." Zeb's face leaned into his again.

"Liana?" The name slipped, unbidden, from Mac's lips. He could clearly see Zeb leaning over him, but it was his sister's eyes, so like their mother's, peering anxiously at him. It was her hand touching his fevered brow.

Mac tried to push him away, but again, his hand didn't move. His whole body refused motion, sleep-drugged, blood thick with whatever Zeb had given him to keep him under.

"Li, I'm sick."

Zeb frowned. "It'll wear off soon."

Doubled behind Zeb, Liana hushed him. She took Mac's right hand, the missing one, humming a lullaby he remembered from when he was a child. Mac swallowed, his throat raw. He tried to close his eyes, but they were already closed. Had Zeb poisoned him? Why couldn't he think straight?

"Li?"

But, no. Li was dead. Trin had spit on him, and called him a traitor. Cal had refused to look at him. Only Liana, who had their mother's eyes, looked at him square on, and whispered *why*?

Why? The crows echoed the call: why, why, why—opening their rusty beaks, shaking their midnight wings, fixing Mac with eyes the color of dried blood. *Why*. And below the crows, three bodies swung from the prince's gibbet, turning slow.

Mac's ragged throat opened, repeating the question through lips that felt bruised and swollen. "Why?"

Zeb cleared his throat, looking away. Mac blinked. Liana no longer stood behind him.

Pain edged in as the confusion cleared. Mac struggled to focus. "Why are you helping me?"

"Soldiers gotta watch each other's backs." Zeb shrugged, still not looking at Mac. "Can you sit up?"

Mac reached out with his right hand, deliberate this time. It didn't move, not even the phantom sensation of motion. Mac rolled his head to look. Metal joined his burned shoulder, the slick scent of oil replacing charred flesh. It was dim enough, the sun having set, Mac could only just make out the pipe—mimicking bone—and the greased joints, mimicking ball sockets, trailing from his shoulder.

"What did you do?" Mac tasted rust and blood at the back of his throat; his voice grated accordingly.

"It'll take a bit of getting used to."

"The fuck?" Mac's tongue stuck thick to the roof of his mouth.

"That gratitude again." Zeb brought his gaze back to Mac's, expression sour. Something lay tucked beneath it, something Mac couldn't quite read.

Mac focused on the metal arm again, willed his fingers to move. The silvered joints, just visible by the plum-colored light, disobeyed. Weight dragged his shoulder, pinning him to the ground.

"Some of it's rust. Most of it's dead weight. We'll get you a ghost, and you'll be right as rain in no time."

"Ghost?" Mac jerked, but the space over Zeb's shoulder remained empty.

"I'll get you something to eat, help you regain your strength. Hang on."

Mac heard Zeb rattling around, but couldn't turn his head far enough to follow his motion. The whine of Zeb's wrong-facing knee gave away his return. The old man crouched, oddly bent, his good leg stuck straight out to accommodate the backward one. He helped Mac sit, propping him against one of the dented filing cabinets. Mac's right side listed under the weight of the metal arm.

Zeb handed him a tin plate, sloppy with beans and chunks of pork that were mostly fat. Mac's stomach grumbled, surprising him. When was the last time he ate? Balancing the plate awkwardly on his legs, he gripped the spoon on his left hand and shoveled food into his mouth. Zeb watched him, wary.

When he was done, he handed Zeb the plate. "Thanks."

His head felt clearer, he felt stronger, but his right-hand fingers remained dead-spider curled, palm open to the sky. With his left hand, Mac touched the metal. Desert cool. He traced the length of the arm. Fingers, wrist, elbow—and there. He stopped. Ridged flesh met his fingers and Mac pulled away.

"I need a new shirt."

Zeb nodded. He rose, rummaged again and returned with a shirt, clean but not new. "It belonged to . . . Never mind." Zeb helped Mac pull the shirt over the dead weight of his right arm.

"How . . . does this work?" Mac tilted his head, indicated the metal limb.

"You need a ghost."

"What are you talking about?" His chest tightened. The word *why* crow-cawed in his head.

"A ghost. To power your arm." Zeb pointed. "Didn't anybody ever lose a limb in the city?"

Mac blinked, comprehension lagging. Zeb's good eye twitched. He dug in his pocket.

"Tech won't work without something to drive it. Metal's metal. Life? That's something else." Zeb held up a round of metal surrounding dark red glass, like a lens. "Was gonna do it while you were under, but you woke up sooner'n I expected."

"What is it?"

"Lets you see ghosts. Useful in the desert. You can trap 'em for trade, or just avoid the ones who wanna eat your flesh."

Mac's head snapped up, looking for any sign Zeb was kidding. The old man shrugged. "Some ghosts are hungrier than others."

Mac licked his lips. Zeb's good eye showed sympathy; the other, blanked by green glass, was unreadable.

"It'll hurt like fuck, but it's the quickest way."

Zeb flipped the lens, showing the back tipped with wicked prongs. Ghosts. Would he see Liana again? Mac nodded on an out breath. Lightning quick, like a blow, like a slap, Zeb drove his hand into Mac's face. The metal prongs dug deep, biting skin. Mac yelled, clapped a hand over glass and metal, fingers scrabbling.

Only his hand didn't move.

Zeb touched something on the lens' rim. A click, and the prongs bit deeper, minute tips burying themselves in Mac's flesh so the lens stayed in place when Zeb lowered his hand. Stunned, Mac raised his left hand. His fingers met blood slickness, weeping from his cheek.

"Here." Zeb handed him a rag. Mac gingerly wiped the blood away. "Come on."

Zeb got an arm around Mac, dragging him to his feet. Mac leaned, too drained to protest. Zeb's wrong-bending knee whined with each step; he led Mac to the double-wide trailer doors and opened them to the desert dust and stars.

Mac sucked in a breath. Through his left eye, everything looked normal. Through his right, pomegranate tinted and aching from the new lens, he *saw*. The desert was full of ghosts.

"How do I tell the hungry ones?" Mac stood in the open doorway of the junk-yard. Another few days rest, and he could stand on his own now. More of Zeb's powder to kill the pain didn't hurt either, but he still felt unsteady, unmoored.

"They're usually faster." Zeb pointed to where a dart of color streaked over a rise in the ground. It didn't come, but Mac imagined the squeal of a rat or lizard, caught unaware and devoured whole. "Avoid those ones. The rest'll leave you alone."

The ghosts looked nothing like the shade of Liana he'd seen over Zeb's shoulder. She'd been fever-born, then. Still, she was out there somewhere, wasn't she? Cal and Trin, too. And the prince. Mac scanned, as if he might catch sight of something familiar, something to set one twist of light apart from the rest.

Most ghosts simply floated, like thermal currents, drifting above the desert floor, curls of plum-colored and dark pomegranate energy, visible only through his right eye.

"You get used to it." Zeb's spoon scraped over the last of their meal, what Mac assumed was burnt squirrel, but was afraid to ask.

"So how do I catch one?"

"Gotta find something they want."

"Like what?" Mac turned. Zeb rose and rooted in the nearest pile of junk.

"Something like this." Zeb held up a doll—bald, its fired-clay skin cracked, one eye missing, the other rolled back unsettlingly in its skull. From the black hole of the missing eye, a stream of ants threaded down the doll's cheek, indignant at having their home disturbed. The idea of catching the ghost of a little girl who would covet a doll like that turned Mac's stomach.

"I'll find something." Mac picked a different pile, nudging it with his toe, shifting bottles, broken pottery, foul-smelling sacks with splitting sides.

"Suit yourself. Try that drawer there." Zeb tossed the doll aside and pointed. "Once you find something, you gotta season it with something else a ghost would want. Strong tastes work best—whiskey, if you can get it, spices. Gotta be careful, though. Stronger tastes draw stronger ghosts—older ones, angrier ones who need more help to remember flavor. I have some salt. That usually does the trick."

Mac opened the drawer Zeb had indicated, running the fingers of his left hand over a jumble of buttons, spoons, hand-held mirrors, combs and other trinkets. He tried to think of something Liana or the prince might want. An intricately carved wooden flute caught his eye, but the moment he picked it up, Zeb was there, snatching it out of his hand.

"Not that." Startled, Mac opened his mouth. Zeb pressed his lips into a thin line, and tucked the flute into his pocket.

"It belonged to my son," he muttered, turning away before Mac could say anything. Mac watched the old man's back for a moment, the slump of his shoulders, before returning his attention to the drawer.

He picked out a tarnished brass star. Military insignia, but old. From before the city closed, before the prince built the wall. One of the few things Mac could ask the prince about without wouldn't earning an impatient wave of her hand, was military history. Mac swallowed, his throat tight.

"That's a good one." Zeb peered over Mac's shoulder. "Might catch a soldier."

The old man's sorrow had been carefully tucked away. Mac nodded, not trusting his voice. He closed his left hand around the star, metal warming against his palm.

Zeb removed a twist of cloth from his pocket. "Come on."

Outside, Zeb crouched and held out his hand. After a moment of reluctance, Mac handed over the star. Zeb set it in the dust, and sketched a circle around it. He sprinkled salt from the cloth.

"When the ghost comes, just plunge your hand right in. Nature should do the rest."

"I can't move my hand."

Zeb snorted. "You got two, don't ya?"

Mac's cheeks warmed. He crouched and closed his left eye, concentrating on his breath and heartbeat, trying to keep them under control. Would he know the prince, if she came to him? His siblings? Nerves made Mac's stomach flutter. He gripped the dead arm with the living and held it over the circle.

Swirls of purple and red drew closer, sniffing around the edge of the circle. Mac forced himself not to close his right eye, too. His pulse jumped.

"There." Zeb pointed. The glow over the star brightened.

Mac's fingers wouldn't let go. Panic locked him in place. He shook his head, trying to back away, but his legs wouldn't move either.

With a grunt, Zeb grabbed Mac's wrist and plunged the metal hand into the circle. Dust scattered. Mac tried to pull away, but Zeb kept his hand in place.

"'s for your own good." A muscle in Zeb's jaw twitched. "Let it go too long, and the flesh around the metal starts to necrotize. Fore you know it, your whole damned right side will be rotten."

An arc like lightning raced up Mac's arm, through metal and bone, the joined flesh searing all over again. He bit down on a scream, teeth clenched, lips peeled back with the effort. He breathed rapidly through his nose. Metal fingers scrabbled in the dust. They snapped closed on the brass star like a trap, crushing it.

"What do I do?" Mac strained to move the metal hand.

"Relax. You'll get the hang of it eventually. Sometimes it takes a while for the ghost to settle. For the moment, your hand has a mind of its own."

A fresh wave of panic drew beads of sweat to Mac's skin. The thing in his arm was hungry, mindless, wild. Even if he could draw the prince, or Liana, it wouldn't be them.

Loss slammed him all at once. A deep sound of grief hauled itself from Mac's chest. He tasted salt, his whole body shaking, save for the metal hand, still locked around the star and pinned to the ground.

"Here." Something touched his shoulder and Mac looked up through tear-blurred eyes. Zeb held out a flask. "Won't kill the pain, but it'll help some."

Mac took the flask with his left hand, fingers trembling. Light from the setting sun caught Zeb's glass, turning the green gold. In his other eye, damp, Mac saw a mirror for his own pain—dulled by time, but there nonetheless, not healed, never healed, just scabbed over. Zeb nodded and turned, leaving Mac to his hurting, full up with his own.

After roughly an hour, and half the bitter contents of Zeb's flask, one of the new metallic fingers uncurled. The sun had set, stars bruising the dark. Salt crusted Mac's cheeks, clumsily wiped away. His chest ached, everything inside him raw and hollow. But had no more tears, and he could breathe.

He stared at the metal hand. It was as though a larger hand wrapped his from the outside, exerting constant pressure. Rills of power ran up to his shoulder and back down again. But with enough concentration, the idea of motion translated along those lines of power.

Another half hour or so and he convinced all the fingers to uncurl. Mac plucked up the crushed star, fighting the image of metal closing on flesh, mangling skin and bone. He didn't dare ask the hand to do anything else, just let it trail at his side, shivering with the presence of the ghost.

Mac slipped the star in his pocket, dragging his weary body back inside. Behind him, the junkyard doors swung closed. Exhausted, he stretched out where he was, pillowing his head on his metallic arm. Minute vibrations made the polished joints shiver and hum. At least if his arm was pinned under his head, it couldn't do anything unexpected.

"Help them."

Mac jerked upright. Had he dozed? Starlight lit the junk piles, along with a thin sliver of unclouded moon.

"Zeb?"

Nothing stirred, no sign of Zeb. The voice he'd heard had been distinctly female. Rusty, yes, but female.

"Hello?"

No answer, then, faint, the rustle of midnight wings and a beak parting. "Help them."

Mac scrambled to his feet, spinning a circle. He looked through his left eye, then his right. Nothing. His flesh puckered.

He raised his metallic hand to his ear, cupping his palm to trap sound. A murmuring, like the rush of wind. "Go home."

He jerked away from his hand. The metal arm remained bent, winking in the starlight.

"Li?" He breathed the name, heart pounding.

His fingers wanted to move, and he hadn't asked them for motion. His first instinct was to fight. The metal ached cold, all through the false bones to the real beneath his flesh.

He brought the hand back to his ear, uncertain whether it was his idea. The back of his neck prickled. Again the whisper, the almost familiar buzz.

"Go home."

"What are you talking about?"

"Help them. Help you."

Mac pushed on the arm with his left hand, forcing it back to his side. The metal was cold. He listened, heart beating too hard. He breathed out. Following on the heels of his breath, a distinct and separate sound, a sigh.

"The ghosts that make the tech run . . . " Mac licked his lips, letting the question hang. Weariness pressed out from inside his skull; his eyes, dust dry, ached from lack of sleep. Zeb scraped beans from a black pot balanced over the fire. He passed a tin plate to Mac, and Mac accepted it in his metal hand, spilling nothing. The delicate operation of spoon to mouth, he left to his flesh hand.

Zeb chewed, meeting Mac's gaze with the eye not hidden behind green glass. Mac forced himself to ask the question.

"Are we haunted?" He tilted his head, indicating Zeb's wrong-way leg.

"You been hearing things?" Zeb straightened, fingers tightening on his spoon.

Mac started, almost dumping his plate, nothing to do with his metal hand.

"Pay no mind." Zeb leaned forward, the intensity of his gaze unsettling. "Get yourself in trouble thinking on things like that."

"But the ghosts can't want this, if we have to trap them, and . . . "

"We're living, they're dead." Zeb banged his plate down, raising dust. "Can't trust a ghost. They want what they want. Our job is not to give it to 'em."

"But . . . "

"Listen, boy. There's more than one way to be hungry. You start paying attention to those voices, you get better and better at hearing 'em. Pretty soon, you get muddled, forget which ideas are your own." Zeb's left hand made a fist. The way he clenched it made a livid, pink scar stand out against his dark skin. Mac had never noticed it before, but it ran all around the base of Zeb's thumb, disappearing into his palm.

"Put it out of your head." Zeb pushed himself up. His rolling walk carried him away, closing the conversation.

Mac kicked dust over the fire, appetite lost. Outside, he followed the curved junk wall until he could see the city. A haze still hung over it, evidence of where the palace had burned.

Go home.

Mac started. He glanced at the arm, laying still against his right side. He raised it cautiously, listening. Nothing.

He glanced back over his shoulder. A pounding sound from within the junkyard spoke of Zeb, hard at work. He took a deep breath, forcing himself to relax. Zeb had been kind to him, saved his life. Mac owed him. Zeb had been out here on his own a long time; he knew a thing or two about survival. Mac made his way back inside, intent on finding Zeb and seeing if he could be of any help.

They'd spent the day hauling, moving, shifting, sorting. Mac's body ached. Between the work and the fact that he was still healing, he was weary to the bone, but he couldn't sleep. Questions nagged. The ghost in his hand, if it really was Liana, she wouldn't want to hurt him, would she? Help them. She could only mean Cal and Trin. He could still set things right.

But what if Zeb was right? What if the ghost in his hand was trying to trick him, do him harm? But perhaps that was no more than Mac deserved. He rested his forehead on the metal arm, propped against his knee, closing his eyes.

The fingers cooled his brow. They were Liana's fingers. Her voice, a lullaby. "Hush. Rest."

Soothing. Mac let doubt go. It was easier to believe, to listen the wordless melody. His sister would take care of him. She would forgive him. Everything would be okay; they would be a family again.

Mac jerked awake, heart drumming wild. Shadows piled thick through the junkyard. Even though the night was cool, sweat stuck Mac's shirt to his skin. He threw back the rough blanket and rose, though he didn't remember crawling into bed.

"Help them."

Mac glanced at his hand. A hint of plum-red light rippled over its surface before fading.

"Li?"

A sigh swirled around him. He strained after it.

"Go home. Go home. Help them."

Mac closed his eyes. It only made things worse, calling Liana's image sharply to mind. Her eyes, fixed on his, lips shaping their question, hands bound, then turning to look over her shoulder as she climbed the gallows' steps just before the hood slipped over her head. His eyes snapped open.

Go home.

The refrain pounded in time with his pulse. A fresh wave of loss formed a lump in his throat. Mac moved quick, afraid if he allowed a moment's thought, he'd lose his nerve.

He found an old carry sack not too damaged by mold. As quietly as he could, he eased open the door of Zeb's cabinet. Metal limbs gleamed in the starlight. He took what he hoped Zeb wouldn't miss—a kneecap, a thumb, a third finger, a left foot. More. The sack hung heavy down his back as he slipped it over his shoulder.

As he eased the cabinet door closed, something caught his eye—a photograph tucked into the door's frame. The young man had Zeb's eyes.

Mac's heart kicked. He almost dropped the sack. But Zeb had lost family, too. Surely he would understand. Mac closed the door.

He patted his pockets. The only thing they contained was the crushed brass star. A poor trade, but maybe Zeb could use it again. With one last glance over his shoulder, Mac set out for the city.

The empty water skin banged Mac's hip. His legs ached and the sack of metal body parts bruised the small of his back. At least the ghost arm carried its weight, no longer dragging Mac's shoulder.

When he let his mind wander, it whispered to him, words snatched by a wind he couldn't feel, sliding just beyond his hearing. Sometimes, the ghost sighed. Just once it babbled, a near shout—*yeshomehelpthemhelpyou*, and its fingers drummed Mac's thigh which such ferocity he nearly dropped the pack and ran. When the ghost shouted, it didn't sound like Liana at all.

But when it sighed . . .

Mac ignored the salt-sting of sweat in his eyes and his growing thirst. He was closer to the city than the junkyard. More sense in going forward than back.

A breeze carried smoke from the city. Mac crested a rise in the sand, and all at once the city was there, spread below him. The wall had been breached, a section shattered and spilling out onto the desert floor. Mac closed his left eye. All around the base of the wall, hungry ghosts swarmed. He hefted his pack and half slid, half ran down the hill.

Merciful shade greeted him as he clambered over a broken section of wall. A beggar huddled next to the rubble, casting Mac a suspicious look from one rheumy eye. Mac tightened his grip on his pack, glad he no longer wore the ruins of his uniform.

People moved quickly, shoulders hunched and clothing pulled close against their bodies. By contrast, others strode, wearing weapons openly—brash knives at their waists, rifles slung across their backs. Were these Cal, Trin, and Liana's compatriots? The ones they'd given their lives for rather than naming? Or had some other faction risen up, taken advantage of the chaos to seize power?

Mac ducked his head, hurrying toward the palace. In the courtyard, he paused. It was almost empty, the clock tower's hands stilled. The fountain still ran, and he knelt, scooping water with his left hand, not caring that it tasted faintly of moss. No crows roosted on the gibbet arm, but Mac felt the weight of their stares anyway.

Why.

The smoke he'd seen from a distance centered over the palace. Mac tugged his shirt over his nose and mouth. He circled, watching for those watching him. There were none. He was only another shadow, another ghost left in the wake of the revolution.

He ignored the obvious entrances to the palace. Mac stopped when he found a spot where the bars were wrenched away from one of the windows rising halfway above the stones. He lay on his belly, peering into the dark, then pushed the carry sack ahead of him and wormed in after. His stomach dropped for the instant he had to trust the ghost hand to hold his weight, but the fingers didn't betray him. He eased to the cell floor.

Iron loops embedded in the walls were still threaded with broken chains. A pile of straw filled one corner, and a bucket occupied another. Mac forced himself to look. Forced himself to breathe, drawing in the old scents of shit and blood. He didn't need to close his left eye to conjure Liana's ghost in those chains, dark eyes holding hurt, fear, confusion. He didn't need to close it to see Trin spit at him, or Cal look away.

A single ghost clung to the wall above the pile of straw, stripped of identity. Mac reached out his good hand. The ghost didn't stir. He let it fall.

"Help them."

He should have died here with Trin and Cal and Liana. He should have died on the palace steps, sheltering the prince's body.

The carry sack weighed on Mac's shoulder. He shrugged the straps higher.

The palace may have been looted, but the prison hadn't been touched. Confiscated prisoner goods still filled the drawers in the guard room, and the guard's shelves still groaned with food.

Mac helped himself to garlic, aged cooking wine, and flaked chili peppers. He hoped it would be enough. In the common room, his metal fingers forced the safe and they did not protest. They ripped out drawers; trinkets clattered to the floor.

"Help them." Mac's left eye blurred. He swiped at it with his good hand.

"Are you really Liana?" He knew it was futile to ask.

He chose a leather bracelet and a hairpin from the scattered mess on the floor. If he tried, he could imagine Cal and Trin wearing these things. Yes, these were their possessions. Must be. Taken from them before they were tortured and hanged. He would use the items to call their ghosts, to carry them out of the dark.

Mac took everything he'd gathered to the prince's torture chamber and dumped them on the floor along with the contents of the pack stolen from Zeb. Blades there were aplenty, and means to light a fire.

Mac cleaned the knife in the flame and transferred it to his right hand. The metal fingers closed, steady and sure. He had no doubt the hand knew what to do. Rolling up the left leg of his trousers, Mac braced himself on a surface already darkened with old blood. He closed both eyes, and let the metal arm do its work.

If he screamed, the excited babble of his arm drowned it out. The flat of the blade cauterized the wound. Mac forced himself to open his eyes. With his flesh hand, Mac jammed the kneecap stolen from Zeb against the burnt-closed wound. Prongs bit deep, and this time he did scream. A faint click and the kneecap locked in place. Red-dark thumped behind his eyes. Mac leaned over, vomited a thin stream of bile. His stomach cramped.

He pushed himself away from the table. His left leg seized, the knee unbending and dead. He crashed to the ground, fresh pain spiking, and a sob tore from his throat. Ghost hand and flesh hand clawed the floor. Mac dragged himself to the scattered trinkets. He used the knife to scratch a circle on the floor, laid the hairpin in it, and sprinkled dried chili flakes over top.

The plum-crush glow came. Mac forced his knee into the circle. Pain arced through him. His body jerked, head slamming the stones and lips foaming. He let the ghost ride him. Welcomed the agony. Bit down on his lip until he tasted blood, and whispered Trin's name.

Stores stolen from the guard's kitchen sustained him through recovery. Dreams came and went, fever hot. Through his good eye, he saw Trin's ghost, mocking him. She peeled her lips back, snarling. When he reached for her, she crouched, releasing a stream of hot piss. He woke up, struggling to back away from the yellow threading its way to him across the floor. Liana came and smoothed his hair, sang to him. It hurt, yes, but he was doing the right thing.

His thumb and middle finger went easier, and just as hard. Mac screamed. He bled. He wept, still a coward, no matter what he did to atone. Crows flapped rusty wings, chorusing *why*, over and over again. Two ghost voices babbled in his ear, overlapping.

"Help them."

"I am." Mac's voice scraped raw, tasting like iron and salt.

"More," the voice said.

Mac poured cooking wine and garlic, and plunged finger and thumb into the essence of two more ghosts. Maybe one was Cal.

His body sang. It fizzed. His skin rebelled, and he doubled over, sick. His left thumb and middle finger pinched his cheeks, tugged at his lip, pulled his hair. He slapped them away with his right hand, and gave himself a black eye.

A ragged sound filled the room. Only the ache in his throat told Mac the laughter was his, and not the ghosts'. Tears leaked from his swelling eye.

"More," a voice exhorted.

His foot, and a key that could have belonged to the prince. These were her dungeons, after all.

Cloves and black pepper. Fresh ginger. Sharp cheese.

Days blurred. Mac's left eye crusted shut. Ghosts swarmed around him, voices buzzing in his jaw. Numb. He couldn't tell which parts of his body were his anymore. He shook, fever and chills warring. He curled into a ball of misery, exhausted, and slept. Liana held his hand.

He had no idea how much time passed. Starved thin, chest heaving, body whining with unaccustomed joints and babbling with the voices of ghosts, Mac crawled from the prison.

He wanted to rest. To sleep. But there were other cities, other horizons. Other ghosts. Clanking, rattling, bruised and crusted in blood he staggered to the wall, the clatter of wings following him.

He stepped over the ruins and onto the desert sand. Dust streaked him. He walked, half metal, half haunted. Behind him, a rusted beak parted for a single caw.

"Why?"

Mac didn't turn; he answered with rust of his own, a single word.

"More."

HONEYCOMB GIRLS

ERIN CASHIER

Those were the days Geo couldn't walk through the market without stepping on someone else's shoe. If money wasn't tied to waist it was zipped, and anything dropped—paper, panks, crumbs—zipped too. Geo sold junk there: stripped wires, sharp green-squares, transistors like pills. "Someone junk, someone treasure!" Geo call. Men come over to see what Geo had, comb over findings, and Geo with stick, ready to slap at zippers. Stand all day, stand half night, then walk home to hard mat shared on second floor. Kick junk man out, eat food, sleep, till day begin again.

Geo hunt for junk at old places when junk run low. Sometimes old posters hidden from rain. Posters show things that not there. Happy men, metal cages. Men touching screens. Men smiling. Like said, old posters. No smiles now.

And sometimes, girls. Some cut out, but see where shape was left. Cut here, tear there. Reach out and feel where maybe curve had been. Hold nothing in hand. Imagine, if no one watching. Geo knew girls. There, but not there, like the sun. Never touch the sun, and never touch the girls, neither.

Jon yell, "Junk, junk!" Geo with stick, watching men come by. Man comes to table. Leans over. Clothing new. Business man? Tinker man? Jon's boy watches man's back. Makes sure no one else steal his money before Geo can.

Geo sees glint in man's eye. He like something he see. Geo step forward. Geo like what *Geo* see. "You like?"

Man's head bows. "No, no, nothing."

Geo knows glint. Geo *knows* lie.

Man scans table, sniffs. "There's nothing here. None of this is worth anything to me."

Geo grunts.

"I'm an artist. I can maybe use this." Man picks up three metal bits.

Geo grunts again, waits. Watches man's hand reach for first thing he like. *Glint-thing.*

"And maybe this too. How much?"

Geo point to first pile. "Four panks." Geo look at man clothing, hair, naked chin. Points to hand. "That, too expensive for you. Put down."

"But—"

Geo hold up zip-stick. "Too pricey! Put down!"

Man's eyes narrow. Geo offend him. He think he can afford all junk here, all table, all tent. But he do what Geo say, sets glint-thing down. Geo pick it up: round, metal, cold. Geo ask for most expensive thing Geo can think of. "Worth one night."

Man's eyes widen. Anger blaze. But he cannot steal from Geo here. Whole tent junk men watching. Under table, Jon step on Geo's shoe.

Man lean over table, snatch ball from hand. "Done."

Geo blinks.

"Go to the third tower two days from now. I'll let them know you're coming." Holds up metal thing from pocket. Light flashes. Geo is blind.

When sight come back, man gone. Geo works, goes back home, lays on mat. Feels junk man's fear. Should Geo have bargained harder?

Honeycomb Tower Three in middle of city. Girls inside. Men too. Depend on hive how many. Some hive ten to girl. Others, four, five. More money, less men.

Geo never known hive man before. Or girl. Satisfy self with other men, hand. Now Geo hand makes empty fist. Geo wonder if strange man lie.

Two days pass. Dawn. Geo travel, stand, watch Tower Three door. Men come out, men go in. No junk men.

Geo gets in line. Other men snicker. Geo ignore them, enters small room. Door close. Alone. Expect to be turn away. Another bright flash.

"You're approved for one night, contractually obligated—" Person behind door has high voice, like dancer in the Genghi zone. Geo hears words. Doesn't listen. At the end of them, Geo nod.

"Please take the elevator." Door opens in front of Geo. Geo step in.

Moving! Geo hold onto walls. Door opens again, Geo jumps out, crouches. Carpet here. Hall of doors. New. No smells. No, smell of no smells. Geo creeps down hall, until a door opens. Geo looks inside.

Four men. One familiar from market. Market man seems pleased. Other men not. Geo braces. "Hello there!" Market man say.

"Hello," Geo say back. Formal greeting. Feels official. Old.

The other men circle, angry. Geo see cats circle rat before. Like this.

"When's the last time he bathed?" tall one asks.

"Does he even know how?" asks short one.

"He's a man of the world," man Geo knows say, and hits Geo's shoulder. Geo tenses for second blow. "If he doesn't know how, he'll learn soon enough, you know our Sukilee."

Last man with crossed arms, looks Geo up and down. "God, did you even do an STD check on him?"

"Not yet. He's not up till tomorrow."

"What?" Crossed arms man whirl. "You're trading me my day?"

"No. I traded him your day."

"That's not—"

"You're behind on rent."

"I'll borrow money! I can pay you back—"

Man Geo knows shakes head. "Too late."

"But!" Crossed arm man looks at Geo with hate. Then look at tall and short.
Tall shrugs. "This is a bad idea."

Short shakes head. "You keep smoking quay, and we'll kick you out, too."

"As long as my money's good, no one's kicking me out," Tall says.

"As long as you have money," man Geo knows points out.

Geo wonders if this is fight. So many words. Room is strange, strange no
smells, strange mad men. Where is girl?

Crossed arm man leaves room. Maybe go get money. Man Geo knows say,
"You're day four now. They'll get you your STD screening." Points to other
two. One and Two. Tall and short. "You can sleep in my bed tonight, since I
won't be needing it." Man—Day Three—points to bed.

"You'll want to burn it tomorrow, then," says Day One.

"Maybe so. But tonight I'll be with Sukilee." Day Three walks to closed door.
Knocks twice. Door slides open, he enters. Door closes, before Geo can peek in.

Geo look at room. So much space. Each man own bed. Little doors on
wall. Reach for one.

"Hey! You're not moving in." Day One slaps Geo's hands. Geo makes fist.
Day One does not. Geo let go.

"Come over here. We need some blood." Day Two tap on table. Pick up
wire. Geo go over, he grab hand. Spread out fingers. Jabs Geo.

Geo makes fist again. Looks at room. Lets go.

Bed too soft. Day One, Two talk. Ignore Geo.

Night comes. Day Three has turn. Geo crawls over to hear. Thick door. No
words. Grunts, groans. Geo's hand finds self. Thicken, spit-hand-rub, bite-lip,
blood-salt. Behind door Day Three yells. Geo gushes, groans.

Day One calls from bed, "You're a rube."

Geo crawls back to bed. Wipe hand on sheet. Insult for sure. But why care?
Tomorrow Geo's turn.

Geo up with morning. One, Two, snore. Day Three come out. Door close
quick behind.

"Now?"

Day Three shake head. "Soon. Wait."

Geo waits. Day slow. Others sleep, leave, return. Play game. Stare at screen.
Stare at paper.

Endless food from box. So much space. If Geo lived in hive, might never leave. Only too quiet. No junk yells here.

Geo paces. Watches door.

"Remember, she's a shared investment." Day Two talks. Geo pretend to listen. "Don't hurt her. Don't be rough with her. You hear me?"

"If you break her, we'll break you." Day One says. His day after Geo. Understand concern.

Stand outside the door, nod. Look to Day Three. "Just do what she tells you," he says.

Evening comes. Door slide open. Geo goes in.

Smells sweet. Window to right. Whole wall of room gone. Just air, city, below. Geo stares out. Amazed. Frightened.

"Hello new man." Face rises from sheets, bed to left. Face oval, pale like moon.

"Hello."

Covered but her face. Room has tables, chairs. Walk to table. Put down what Geo have brought. Fistful of grass. Hard to find in city. Saw man on old poster, giving to girl. And small jar of lube. Helps with men. Girls? Who know.

Girl rises out of sheets, comes over to table beside Geo. Arms like Geo's. Legs hidden by clothes. Chest like inverted shallow bowls. Geo breathes, stands. Warned not to break her. Is girl like glass?

Her hand stirs blades of grass. She opens jar, smells, wrinkles nose.

"Who are you?" she asks.

"Day Four."

Laughing sound. Sweet.

"Go bathe. And then, we'll see."

Geo stands, still. Bathe?

"Oh, come now." She grabs Geo's wrist. Geo's other hand makes fist, lets it go.

Outside, rain burn. Bathing standing in filtered rain. Girl rough with Geo, scraping, scrubbing. Like no man Geo with before. Outside, when rain comes, Geo hide, not stand in it.

When done, emerge. Geo naked. Girl in wet clothes. Nipples poke out.

"Dry yourself off." She throws fabric at Geo. So soft, like petting cat. Geo dries. She appraises. Girl sold things in past, Geo can tell.

"Come here," girl say, walking to other room. Sinks into massive bed. Geo follows, like kitten. "Don't you know what this is for?" she says, reaching out. Touches Geo.

"With junk man."

She shake her head, pulls Geo down.

No edges. Soft. All the posters torn with rough brick behind. Geo never knew.

◆ ◆ ◆

"How did you get here?" she ask. Geo beside her, tired. But this night only night. Can't sleep yet.

"Day Three."

"Hmmm?"

"Day Three want something. I sell."

"Oh. Oh!" She turns over. "Do you have more? Of whatever it was?"

Shake head.

"Can you get more?"

"Not sure." Just solid metal ball. "Can look—"

"Do. Even if you can't sell it to him, it might be worth something, to someone else."

Geo nod. She is wise. Her hand touches Geo. Moves. Geo moves with her.

The next day Geo with her again. Then girl points to door. "Time to go," she say. Her voice like chime. Geo stands, looks at girl.

"You're my favorite," she says. Smiles wide.

Door opens. Geo leaves.

Day One, Day Two, wait outside. Door to hallway open. But Day Three has glasses ready. Four. Hands out, all drink. Liquid burns like rain.

"Now you're a Honeycomb Man!" Day Three says. He smiles. Day Two takes back glass. Points to hall.

Geo walk away from tower. Day is day, like night never was. Man runs out, clutches at Geo's pants. Geo kicks him. He cowers. "How did you do it? How did you make so much money?" Old Day Four crawls after Geo. Geo ignores. "I'm her favorite! Her favorite!" he say.

Geo shakes head. Not anymore.

Junk table still there. Other junk men squint eyes. Ask later, Geo say. Ask. Eat food, ask. Sleep now, shoo, still ask.

Walk back to mat. "Look like Genghi dancer?" Jon ask. Rain comes down. Step together inside forgotten door.

"No. Yes. Different." Geo can't explain. Soft. Voice. Bones.

Jon laugh. Voice deep, strong.

"Worried for you. Hive men—" Jon whistles, shakes head. Geo looks at Jon. Others? Jealousy. But Jon's eyes, sadness, fear.

"Here now. Be in me." Geo turns towards door. Jon waits, then hands on waist. Storm thunderclap above. Geo wish Geo not left jar behind, but not long.

Go from junk place to junk place. Right of junk man, look at junk in back of tents. Junk men watch for glint. Geo controls Geo's eyes. Two metal balls, price too high, walk away. But three of them, Geo buy.

Go to Towers. Sit by door. Waiting.

◆ ◆ ◆

Day Three come out. Hair parted, greased. Clothes, so new. Sees Geo. Eyes squint.

Geo holds out hand. Metal clicks metal.

"Ah! You have come to do more business!" Now eyes glow. Hand reaches. "Three more nights?"

Pull back. "Two nights." Push two balls forward. Keep back third.

Day Three smile. Teeth like hungry cat. "And?"

"Panks for this one."

"Oh? Sukilee not good enough for you? Or, you want to spend money—join a bigger hive, get more nights out of the deal?"

No. Easy food. Clothing. No-filter water. Space to sleep. Geo open mouth. No words come out. No way to explain. Finally Geo say, "Family."

Day Three tilts head. "Really?"

"Junk men."

Day Three pats Geo's back. "Fine then. Done."

"Which day?" Geo ask.

"Still Day Four." Take third ball from hand. "I'll have your panks for you then, too, all right?"

Geo nods.

"Look at you. You're a regular businessman!"

No. Geo is junk man. Hates businessmen.

Geo goes up day early. Prick hand again.

Wait.

Day One, Two, work, so they say. Both stare at screens. Doesn't look like work to Geo.

"What's wrong with you?" Day Two say.

Geo shrugs. "Nice junk."

"This isn't junk—it's loss prevention data from the west-wall factory."

Geo sighs.

Day One frowns. Hands junk over.

"Careful, he'll just break it," Day Two warn.

Geo stares at screen. Things move across it. Seen them before, on posters. Like life. Like look through hole in wall. Like look out Sukilee's window.

"Where?" Geo asks, points at small people.

Day Two makes noise. "Don't touch the screen."

"It isn't anywhere. It's old. Taped," Day One explain.

Tape rare. Tape nice junk. Geo turn over loss prevention data. Looks for tape on junk. Don't find.

Soon Geo room of Sukilee again. "You're back!"

Geo touch Geo's chest. "Am favorite. Of course."

She laughs. Starts bath.

It is same-different from last time. Her hands move Geo's over strange places. Soft, rich, warm. Soon Geo collapses, spent.

Sukilee crawls out of bed, over to bottom of window. Sits naked, perched. Geo follows.

"Tell me what it's like out there."

What can Geo say? Told not to break her. "Hard." Press hand to glass, look down. Her shoulders, smooth. Never been caught out in rain before.

"Are there other girls like me? Outside?"

"Men like girls, sometimes." Dancers. Long hair. Full lips. "Not all like you, though."

"The toilet told me I'm pregnant." Sukilee looks up. "Do you even know what that means?"

"No."

"Me either, really." Stands up. Takes Geo's hand. Leads back to bed.

Every third ball, keep panks instead. Geo shows full bag to Day Three. Day Three pleased.

"What are?" Geo ask, shaking bag. Five balls inside. Four nights, many panks.

"What what? Oh! What—" Day Three take bag Geo holds. Zipper! Geo tense, relax.

Day Three pulls out one ball. Still black, metal, cold. "Have you ever seen a man take a blow to the head?"

Geo nods.

"So you know that's where people get their controls from, right? Too big a blow to the head, and you can't remember where you came from, where you're going, how to talk or see. That's your brains inside."

Geo sighs. Seen brains too. Do not tell this to Day Three.

"These—these are like small minds. From the old world, before the Big Burn." Puts orb up to head. Day Three hits against skull. Laughs.

"They remember?" Geo looks at balls.

Day Three nods. "And much more."

Geo grunts. All look same to Geo.

Geo exhaust supplies from known junk men. Go further, finish these. Soon have one night left. Could spend panks, but—Jon use panks. For food, for space. What better, Sukilee, or Jon? Girl soft, but Jon is junk man.

"This last night." Geo tell Sukilee when door close behind.

"Really?" She sits up. "Am I going somewhere?"

"Not you. Me." Look to window. Geo can see whole junk-world beyond city edge from Tower. All there to scavenge.

"Oh." Sinks back down.

Geo sits. Girl's belly round. Like dying junk man—only she healthy. So strange. "Want leave?" Geo say.

"Of course I do." She looks up at Geo. "It's lonely here. And I'd like to meet another girl. I want to know what's happening to me." Puts hand on overfull belly. "I don't understand."

Don't know unsafe food. Don't know burning rain. Geo imagine her outside. Torn apart by men. Like rats on dying cat. Geo pets her hair. "Better here."

"But—"

Shake head. "Sorry. Better. Not much. Better."

"The others won't tell me about their outsides. Only you."

"Junk man, good man. Hive men, eh." Geo waves hand in air, leans over, spits.

Morning comes. Geo exits. Sukilee wave good-bye.

"Well, I'm sorry it's come to this," Day Three say.

"Time done." Geo shrugs.

"If you happen to find anymore—"

Geo shakes head. Walks out. Won't cling to any legs.

Months later, Geo with Jon. Whole room on top of building. Room as big as tower room. Two other junk men here besides.

On clear day, Geo climb to roof. Look out at Tower.

Jon follows. "What better there?"

Geo smiles at him. "Food."

Jon snorts. "Buy better food." Jon takes hand, pulls Geo's chin. "Tower done. Stay here."

Geo wonders what Day it is. Shakes head. Being junk man better than hive man.

But panks run low. Need find more junk.

Easy junk nearby all gone. Good junk far, dangerous.

People live in junk. City life hard, junk life harder. Sometimes walk in junk, floor break. Fall onto metal spear below. Geo seen that. Took shoes. Dead man need no shoes. Rain too much? Eat through your tent at night. Filtration system stop? No good water. Run out of food? Can't eat metal. Rats eat metal. Rats try eat Geo, too.

Crazy men live in deep junk. Rat-men. Live like rats. Die like rats. Rat-men kill over junk. Rat-men kill over shoes.

Men die in junk every day. Still—Geo is junk man. Finding junk what junk man do.

Forage deep, long. Uncharted places. Find good junk. Thick wires. Shiny tubes. Glass cups—pack in dirt—heavy, but easy-safe. Tinkers like wire, tinkers love glass.

First part of being junk man is listen. Enter place quiet. Stay quiet. Hear for danger. Sound of rat? One, two? Many? Run. Sound of people—turn away. Quiet as came in, leave.

New room. Set bag down, hide it. Crawl into new junk. Turn body flat like knife, squeeze. Pop out in cavern. Pool of water in center. Wait, listen. Then slowly, breathe.

Walk to edge of water. In center, layer of balls. Reach out, barely touch water. No burn.

Reach in and grab three balls. Lick water off back of hand.

Sound—scuffle—hit on side. Tumble down. Scrape face. Splash in.

"Who are you? Who sent you here?" Rat-man stands over Geo. Face twitching. Hands on Geo's shoulders, holding down. Air bubbles up. Breathe water. Now, water burn. "Who sent you here?" Rat-man yells, shakes.

Geo brings hand with metal balls up. Bash Rat-man in face, twice. Rat-man shakes, falls down, into pool. Geo stands, coughs. Hears echoes. Listens. Waits.

Geo looks down. Rat-man's blood colors water. Geo runs to drink from other side, safe.

Geo fills up pockets and pants full of balls. Soon rats come for Rat-man. Geo won't be here when they do.

Geo goes back to city, to Towers. Pockets full. Door opens, lets Geo in.

Geo walks down hall. Day One and Day Two, inside, surprised.

"How'd you get in?"

"Doors open."

Day Two look to Day One. "That's it—we're switching Towers."

Both are packing. "Going?" Geo say.

"We're joining another hive." Day Two push things into bag with force. "And you're not coming with us."

Fewer days? Or could Geo be Day One, Two and Four?

Day One grimace. "Sukilee's gone."

"Where?" Geo ask.

Day One shrug. Day Two keep packing.

Geo sits inside Tower, alone. All doors open. Geo goes into Sukilee's room. Nothing gone but her.

Geo sighs. Should always be allowed to take things with you.

Until those things get left behind. Then they are junk.

Geo sleeps in Geo's bed, and eats food from box. How much food can Geo carry down? Or water?

Door opens. Geo jumps up.

"Oh! I didn't expect to see you!" Day Three say. Comes into room, dragging big box behind.

"Sukilee?" Geo ask. Frown at box.

"Oh, she had to go. I'm sorry. If I'd known you were coming back, I would have warned you." Day Three haul box into room.

"Where?"

Day Three lift hands. "Where all the women go, when it's their time."

"But coming back?"

"Not to here."

Geo makes belly in front of stomach. "What happened?"

Day Three sighs. "I—well—it's hard to explain. She had to extrude a baby."

Seen cats extrude kittens. Geo say so.

"Yes—like that, only—men. No time to be a child. Not here, not anymore."

Don't remember being extruded. Day Three says that's the point. Wasn't. Was made whole, like all workers. Made ready to work.

"To sell junk?"

"Sure. Of course. Just like I was made to be a scientist." Day Three say. Smiles.

Geo shakes head, turns to go.

"Look, Geo, you've really helped me here." Day Three say. "I'd like to help you, too." Turns, looks at room. "Give me five days here. Come back in five days, and bring friends. This room fits four nicely, doesn't it?"

Geo squints at him. "No Day Three?"

"No, not anymore. There's new Towers to be built. But you'll always be welcome here." Day Three clap on back again.

Geo hates that.

Day five. Take Jon's boy, and his boy, and Geo up to Tower. Dancer voice let all in.

When get to room, Day Three waiting. "Hello!" Jon jump back. Geo laugh.

"Please, come in." Day Three back away. Sleeping mats new. Floor mat new. Wall-paint new. Door to Sukilee's room closed. Day Three close hall door behind Geo. "You are all Honeycomb men now, gentlemen!" Day Three announces. Walks to Sukilee's door. Taps on it. Door opens. Day Three goes inside.

Door does not close behind him.

Jon's boy looks inside. Whistles.

"Hello gentlemen!" says girl-voice. Boys, Jon, go in. Geo goes last.

Girl stand at far wall. Hair lighter, chest bigger. "Hello gentlemen," she say again.

Cable come out of foot. Sukilee did not have cable.

Day Three watches Geo. "See? She's ten times more efficient now, Geo. She doesn't need to sleep, or eat—she can even have more than one visitor at a time, even, eh? We're building new towers, with bigger rooms, we won't be limited by birth rates and ages or STDs. Soon everyone will be in a tower."

Geo crosses arms. "Where Sukilee?"

"Not important anymore." Day Three shake head. "You've helped change the face of the world, Geo. And you don't even know it." Walks over to girl. Touches her. She giggles. "But don't worry, Geo. I'm very gracious. I know I couldn't have done it without your support." Day Three walks back and takes Geo's hand. Squeezes it. Geo doesn't giggle. "You'll always have a room at the Towers, on me." Day Three say, then leaves. Boys poke girl. Jon whistles low.

Geo walks to window. Stare out at junk.

Two days. Boys still inside girl room. Sound like cat with other cat.

Jon sits with Geo outside, eating noodles. Door opens. Day Two comes in.

"I left something here." Looks at new room. "Wait, what's all this?" Reaches for sleeping mat.

Jon jumps up, knifes him, before Geo can say no.

Watch him slump to floor. Open mouth. Geo toes corpse.

Don't have zip-hands, first rule. Don't mess with junk man, second.

Four days. Geo decides to bathe. Knock on door, opens. Walk inside. Boys asleep on floor. Girl rises up.

"Hello gentleman!" she say.

"Hello."

"What service can I perform for you today?"

Geo shrugs.

Girl stares. Doesn't blink.

"What service can I perform for you today?"

"Want bath." Geo walk towards bathroom.

"I'm sorry, I can't go in there," girl says after Geo.

"That fine," Geo say. Closes door.

Two weeks later, boys sleep in living room again. Girl spend nights alone. Sukilee would be scared of alone. But girl not Sukilee.

Jon look to Geo over second bowl of noodles. Getting belly. Like Sukilee. Better food nice.

"Good, eh?"

"Eh." Put bowl down. "Miss junk table. Miss stick. Miss dancers."

Jon's boy point out girl can dance. Jon narrows eyes. "Not same."

"We could sell junk."

"Where? What?"

"Girl. Junk." Jon say. Boys protest. Jon's eyes narrow.

Geo knows it true.

Geo still has ball. Goes into girl room, alone.

"Hello gentleman! What service can I perform for you today?"

"Where is this?" Hold up ball.

Girl blank stare. "I don't know what you're asking."

"Take off clothes."

Girl comply. Stand naked. Face flat.

"Turn around."

Find spot on back. Leverage with knife. Pop out panel. But not ball inside. Wires, thick and thin. Metal poles. Plastic.

Try to put panel back in. Won't fit. Struggle.

Need tape.

Junk man know how to take junk apart. But only tinker man can put it back together again.

Jon trades extra noodles at market. Boys go with him. Make panks selling water. Geo alone in tower. Take bath.

Junk girl talks. Geo don't listen. Stand at window. Naked. Drying.

"Is there anything I can do for you?" girl say. Geo looks over shoulder at girl. Looks at city below. Looks at junk beyond.

Day Three think men want hive. Want girl. But junk-girl not girl. Junk men know junk when see it.

Men leave towers. Day, month, year. Nothing here. Then Geo gracious.

Then Geo welcome Day Three down in the junk.

THE REGULAR

KEN LIU

"This is Jasmine," she says.

"It's Robert."

The voice on the phone is the same as the one she had spoken to earlier in the afternoon.

"Glad you made it, sweetie." She looks out the window. He's standing at the corner, in front of the convenience store as she asked. He looks clean and is dressed well, like he's going on a date. A good sign. He's also wearing a Red Sox cap pulled low over his brow, a rather amateurish attempt at anonymity. "I'm down the street from you, at 27 Moreland. It's the gray stone condo building converted from a church."

He turns to look. "You have a sense of humor."

They all make that joke, but she laughs anyway. "I'm in unit 24, on the second floor."

"Is it just you? I'm not going to see some linebacker type demanding that I pay him first?"

"I told you. I'm independent. Just have your donation ready and you'll have a good time."

She hangs up and takes a quick look in the mirror to be sure she's ready. The black stockings and garter belt are new, and the lace bustier accentuates her thin waist and makes her breasts seem larger. She's done her makeup lightly, but the eye shadow is heavy to emphasize her eyes. Most of her customers like that. Exotic.

The sheets on the king-sized bed are fresh, and there's a small wicker basket of condoms on the nightstand, next to a clock that says "5:58." The date is for two hours, and afterwards she'll have enough time to clean up and shower and then sit in front of the TV to catch her favorite show. She thinks about calling her mom later that night to ask about how to cook porgy.

She opens the door before he can knock, and the look on his face tells her that she's done well. He slips in; she closes the door, leans against it, and smiles at him.

"You're even prettier than the picture in your ad," he says. He gazes into her eyes intently. "Especially the eyes."

"Thank you."

As she gets a good look at him in the hallway, she concentrates on her right eye and blinks rapidly twice. She doesn't think she'll ever need it, but a girl has to protect herself. If she ever stops doing this, she thinks she'll just have it taken out and thrown into the bottom of Boston Harbor, like the way she used to, as a little girl, write secrets down on bits of paper, wad them up, and flush them down the toilet.

He's good looking in a non-memorable way: over six feet, tanned skin, still has all his hair, and the body under that crisp shirt looks fit. The eyes are friendly and kind, and she's pretty sure he won't be too rough. She guesses that he's in his forties, and maybe works downtown in one of the law firms or financial services companies, where his long-sleeved shirt and dark pants make sense with the air conditioning always turned high. He has that entitled arrogance that many mistake for masculine attractiveness. She notices that there's a paler patch of skin around his ring finger. Even better. A married man is usually safer. A married man who doesn't want her to know he's married is the safest of all: he values what he has and doesn't want to lose it.

She hopes he'll be a regular.

"I'm glad we're doing this." He holds out a plain white envelope.

She takes it and counts the bills inside. Then she puts it on top of the stack of mail on a small table by the entrance without saying anything. She takes him by the hand and leads him towards the bedroom. He pauses to look in the bathroom and then the other bedroom at the end of the hall.

"Looking for your linebacker?" she teases.

"Just making sure. I'm a nice guy."

He takes out a scanner and holds it up, concentrating on the screen.

"Geez, you *are* paranoid," she says. "The only camera in here is the one on my phone. And it's definitely off."

He puts the scanner away and smiles. "I know. But I just wanted to have a machine confirm it."

They enter the bedroom. She watches him take in the bed, the bottles of lubricants and lotions on the dresser, and the long mirrors covering the closet doors next to the bed.

"Nervous?" she asks.

"A little," he concedes. "I don't do this often. Or, at all."

She comes up to him and embraces him, letting him breathe in her perfume, which is floral and light so that it won't linger on his skin. After a moment, he puts his arms around her, resting his hands against the naked skin on the small of her back.

"I've always believed that one should pay for experiences rather than things."

"A good philosophy," he whispers into her ear.

"What I give you is the girlfriend experience, old fashioned and sweet. And you'll remember this and relive it in your head as often as you want."

"You'll do whatever I want?"

"Within reason," she says. Then she lifts her head to look up at him. "You have to wear a condom. Other than that, I won't say no to most things. But like I told you on the phone, for some you'll have to pay extra."

"I'm pretty old-fashioned myself. Do you mind if I take charge?"

He's made her relaxed enough that she doesn't jump to the worst conclusion. "If you're thinking of tying me down, that will cost you. And I won't do that until I know you better."

"Nothing like that. Maybe hold you down a little."

"That's fine."

He comes up to her and they kiss. His tongue lingers in her mouth and she moans. He backs up, puts his hands on her waist, turning her away from him. "Would you lie down with your face in the pillows?"

"Of course." She climbs onto the bed. "Legs up under me or spread out to the corners?"

"Spread out, please." His voice is commanding. And he hasn't stripped yet, not even taken off his Red Sox cap. She's a little disappointed. Some clients enjoy the obedience more than the sex. There's not much for her to do. She just hopes he won't be too rough and leave marks.

He climbs onto the bed behind her and knee-walks up between her legs. He leans down and grabs a pillow from next to her head. "Very lovely," he says. "I'm going to hold you down now."

She sighs into the bed, the way she knows he'll like.

He lays the pillow over the back of her head and pushes down firmly to hold her in place. He takes the gun out of the small of his back, and in one swift motion, sticks the barrel, thick and long with the silencer, into the back of the bustier, and squeezes off two quick shots into her heart. She dies instantly.

He removes the pillow, stores the gun away. Then he takes a small steel surgical kit out of his jacket pocket, along with a pair of latex gloves. He works efficiently and quickly, cutting with precision and grace. He relaxes when he's found what he's looking for—sometimes he picks the wrong girl—not often, but it has happened. He's careful to wipe off any sweat on his face with his sleeves as he works, and the hat helps to prevent any hair from falling on her. Soon, the task is done.

He climbs off the bed, takes off the bloody gloves, and leaves them and the surgical kit on the body. He puts on a fresh pair of gloves and moves through the apartment, methodically searching for places where she hid cash: inside the toilet tank, the back of the freezer, the nook above the door of the closet.

He goes into the kitchen and returns with a large plastic trash bag. He picks up the bloody gloves and the surgical kit and throws them into the bag. Picking up her phone, he presses the button for her voicemail. He deletes all the messages, including the one he had left when he first called her number. There's not much he can do about the call logs at the phone company, but he can take advantage of that by leaving his prepaid phone somewhere for the police to find.

He looks at her again. He's not sad, not exactly, but he does feel a sense of waste. The girl was pretty and he would have liked to enjoy her first, but that would leave behind too many traces, even with a condom. And he can always pay for another, later. He likes paying for things. Power flows to *him* when he pays.

Reaching into the inner pocket of his jacket, he retrieves a sheet of paper, which he carefully unfolds and leaves by the girl's head.

He stuffs the trash bag and the money into a small gym bag he found in one of the closets. He leaves quietly, picking up the envelope of cash next to the entrance on the way out.

Because she's meticulous, Ruth Law runs through the numbers on the spreadsheet one last time, a summary culled from credit card and bank statements, and compares them against the numbers on the tax return. There's no doubt. The client's husband has been hiding money from the IRS, and more importantly, from the client.

Summers in Boston can be brutally hot. But Ruth keeps the air conditioner off in her tiny office above a butcher shop in Chinatown. She's made a lot of people unhappy over the years, and there's no reason to make it any easier for them to sneak up on her with the extra noise.

She takes out her cell phone and starts to dial from memory. She never stores any numbers in the phone. She tells people it's for safety, but sometimes she wonders if it's a gesture, however small, of asserting her independence from machines.

She stops at the sound of someone coming up the stairs. The footfalls are crisp and dainty, probably a woman, probably one with sensible heels. The scanner in the stairway hasn't been set off by the presence of a weapon, but that doesn't mean anything—she can kill without a gun or knife, and so can many others.

Ruth deposits her phone noiselessly on the desk and reaches into her drawer to wrap the fingers of her right hand around the reassuring grip of the Glock 19. Only then does she turn slightly to the side to glance at the monitor showing the feed from the security camera mounted over the door.

She feels very calm. The Regulator is doing its job. There's no need to release any adrenaline yet.

The visitor, in her fifties, is in a blue short-sleeve cardigan and white pants. She's looking around the door for the doorbell. Her hair is so black that it must be dyed. She looks Chinese, holding her thin, petite body in a tight, nervous posture.

Ruth relaxes and lets go of the gun to push the button to open the door. She stands up and holds out her hand. "What can I do for you?"

"Are you Ruth Law, the private investigator?" In the woman's accent Ruth hears traces of Mandarin rather than Cantonese or Fukienese. Probably not well connected in Chinatown then.

"I am."

The woman looks surprised, as if Ruth isn't quite who she expected. "Sarah Ding. I thought you were Chinese."

As they shake hands Ruth looks Sarah level in the eyes: they're about the same height, five foot four. Sarah looks well maintained, but her fingers feel cold and thin, like a bird's claw.

"I'm half Chinese," Ruth says. "My father was Cantonese, second generation; my mother was white. My Cantonese is barely passable, and I never learned Mandarin."

Sarah sits down in the armchair across from Ruth's desk. "But you have an office here."

She shrugs. "I've made my enemies. A lot of non-Chinese are uncomfortable moving around in Chinatown. They stick out. So it's safer for me to have my office here. Besides, you can't beat the rent."

Sarah nods wearily. "I need your help with my daughter." She slides a collapsible file across the desk towards her.

Ruth sits down but doesn't reach for the file. "Tell me about her."

"Mona was working as an escort. A month ago she was shot and killed in her apartment. The police think it's a robbery, maybe gang related, and they have no leads."

"It's a dangerous profession," Ruth says. "Did you know she was doing it?"

"No. Mona had some difficulties after college, and we were never as close as . . . I would have liked. We thought she was doing better the last two years, and she told us she had a job in publishing. It's difficult to know your child when you can't be the kind of mother she wants or needs. This country has different rules."

Ruth nods. A familiar lament from immigrants. "I'm sorry for your loss. But it's unlikely I'll be able to do anything. Most of my cases now are about hidden assets, cheating spouses, insurance fraud, background checks, that sort of thing. Back when I was a member of the force, I did work in Homicide. I know the detectives are quite thorough in murder cases."

"They're not!" Fury and desperation strain and crack her voice. "They think she's just a Chinese whore, and she died because she was stupid or got involved with a Chinese gang who wouldn't bother regular people. My husband is so ashamed that he won't even mention her name. But she's my daughter, and she's worth everything I have, and more."

Ruth looks at her. She can feel the Regulator suppressing her pity. Pity can lead to bad business decisions.

"I keep on thinking there was some sign I should have seen, some way to tell her that I loved her that I didn't know. If only I had been a little less busy, a little more willing to pry and dig and to be hurt by her. I can't stand the way the detectives talk to me, like I'm wasting their time but they don't want to show it."

Ruth refrains from explaining that the police detectives are all fitted with Regulators that should make the kind of prejudice she's implying impossible. The whole point of the Regulator is to make police work under pressure more regular, less dependent on hunches, emotional impulses, appeals to hidden prejudice. If the police are calling it a gang-related act of violence, there are likely good reasons for doing so.

She says nothing because the woman in front of her is in pain, and guilt and love are so mixed up in her that she thinks paying to find her daughter's killer will make her feel better about being the kind of mother whose daughter would take up prostitution.

Her angry, helpless posture reminds Ruth vaguely of something she tries to put out of her mind.

"Even if I find the killer," she says, "it won't make you feel better."

"I don't care." Sarah tries to shrug but the American gesture looks awkward and uncertain on her. "My husband thinks I've gone crazy. I know how hopeless this is; you're not the first investigator I've spoken to. But a few suggested you because you're a woman and Chinese, so maybe you care just enough to see something they can't."

She reaches into her purse and retrieves a check, sliding it across the table to put on top of the file. "Here's eighty thousand dollars. I'll pay double your daily rate and all expenses. If you use it up, I can get you more."

Ruth stares at the check. She thinks about the sorry state of her finances. At forty-nine, how many more chances will she have to set aside some money for when she'll be too old to do this?

She still feels calm and completely rational, and she knows that the Regulator is doing its job. She's sure that she's making her decision based on costs and benefits and a realistic evaluation of the case, and not because of the hunched over shoulders of Sarah Ding, looking like fragile twin dams holding back a flood of grief.

"Okay," she says. "Okay."

The man's name isn't Robert. It's not Paul or Matt or Barry either. He never uses the name John because jokes like that will only make the girls nervous. A long time ago, before he had been to prison, they had called him the Watcher because he liked to observe and take in a scene, finding the best opportunities and escape routes. He still thinks of himself that way when he's alone.

In the room he's rented at the cheap motel along Route 128, he starts his day by taking a shower to wash off the night sweat.

This is the fifth motel he's stayed in during the last month. Any stay longer than a week tends to catch the attention of the people working at the motels.

He watches; he does not get watched. Ideally, he supposes he should get away from Boston altogether, but he hasn't exhausted the city's possibilities. It doesn't feel right to leave before he's seen all he wants to see.

The Watcher got about sixty thousand dollars in cash from the girl's apartment, not bad for a day's work. The girls he picks are intensely aware of the brevity of their careers, and with no bad habits, they pack away money like squirrels preparing for the winter. Since they can't exactly put it into the bank without raising the suspicion of the IRS, they tuck the money away in stashes in their apartments, ready for him to come along and claim them like found treasure.

The money is a nice bonus, but not the main attraction.

He comes out of the shower, dries himself, and wrapped in a towel, sits down to work at the nut he's trying to crack. It's a small, silver half-sphere, like half of a walnut. When he had first gotten it, it had been covered in blood and gore, and he had wiped it again and again with paper towels moistened under the motel sink until it gleamed.

He pries open an access port on the back of the device. Opening his laptop, he plugs one end of a cable into it and the other end into the half-sphere. He starts a program he had paid a good sum of money for and lets it run. It would probably be more efficient for him to leave the program running all the time, but he likes to be there to see the moment the encryption is broken.

While the program runs, he browses the escort ads. Right now he's searching for pleasure, not business, so instead of looking for girls like Jasmine, he looks for girls he craves. They're expensive, but not too expensive, the kind that remind him of the girls he had wanted back in high school: loud, fun, curvaceous now but destined to put on too much weight in a few years, a careless beauty that was all the more desirable because it was fleeting.

The Watcher knows that only a poor man like he had been at seventeen would bother courting women, trying desperately to make them like him. A man with money, with power, like he is now, can buy what he wants. There's purity and cleanliness to his desire that he feels is nobler and less deceitful than the desire of poor men. They only wish they could have what he does.

The program beeps, and he switches back to it.

Success.

Images, videos, sound recordings are being downloaded onto the computer.

The Watcher browses through the pictures and video recordings. The pictures are face shots or shots of money being handed over—he immediately deletes the ones of him.

But the videos are the best. He settles back and watches the screen flicker, admiring Jasmine's camerawork.

He separates the videos and images by client and puts them into folders. It's tedious work, but he enjoys it.

◆ ◆ ◆

The first thing Ruth does with the money is to get some badly needed tune-ups. Going after a killer requires that she be in top condition.

She does not like to carry a gun when she's on the job. A man in a sport coat with a gun concealed under it can blend into almost any situation, but a woman wearing the kind of clothes that would hide a gun would often stick out like a sore thumb. Keeping a gun in a purse is a terrible idea. It creates a false sense of security, but a purse can be easily snatched away and then she would be disarmed.

She's fit and strong for her age, but her opponents are almost always taller and heavier and stronger. She's learned to compensate for these disadvantages by being more alert and by striking earlier.

But it's still not enough.

She goes to her doctor. Not the one on her HMO card.

Doctor B had earned his degree in another country and then had to leave home forever because he pissed off the wrong people. Instead of doing a second residency and becoming licensed here, which would have made him easily traceable, he had decided to simply keep on practicing medicine on his own. He would do things doctors who cared about their licenses wouldn't do. He would take patients they wouldn't touch.

"It's been a while," Doctor B says.

"Check over everything," she tells him. "And replace what needs replacement."

"Rich uncle die?"

"I'm going on a hunt."

Doctor B nods and puts her under.

He checks the pneumatic pistons in her legs, the replacement composite tendons in her shoulders and arms, the power cells and artificial muscles in her arms, the reinforced finger bones. He recharges what needs to be recharged. He examines the results of the calcium-deposition treatments (a counter to the fragility of her bones, an unfortunate side effect of her Asian heritage), and makes adjustments to her Regulator so that she can keep it on for longer.

"Like new," he tells her. And she pays.

Next, Ruth looks through the file Sarah brought.

There are photographs: the prom, high school graduation, vacations with friends, college commencement. She notes the name of the school without surprise or sorrow even though Jess had dreamed of going there as well. The Regulator, as always, keeps her equanimous, receptive to information, only useful information.

The last family photo Sarah selected was taken at Mona's twenty-fourth birthday earlier in the year. Ruth examines it carefully. In the picture, Mona is seated between Sarah and her husband, her arms around her parents in a gesture of careless joy. There's no hint of the secret she was keeping from them, and no sign, as far as Ruth can tell, of bruises, drugs, or other indications that life was slipping out of her control.

Sarah had chosen the photos with care. The pictures are designed to fill in Mona's life, to make people care for her. But she didn't need to do that. Ruth would have given it the same amount of effort even if she knew nothing about the girl's life. She's a professional.

There's a copy of the police report and the autopsy results. The report mostly confirms what Ruth has already guessed: no sign of drugs in Mona's systems, no forced entry, no indication there was a struggle. There was pepper spray in the drawer of the nightstand, but it hadn't been used. Forensics had vacuumed the scene and the hair and skin cells of dozens, maybe hundreds, of men had turned up, guaranteeing that no useful leads will result.

Mona had been killed with two shots through the heart, and then her body had been mutilated, with her eyes removed. She hadn't been sexually assaulted. The apartment had been ransacked of cash and valuables.

Ruth sits up. The method of killing is odd. If the killer had intended to mutilate her face anyway, there was no reason to not shoot her in the back of the head, a cleaner, surer method of execution.

A note was found at the scene in Chinese, which declared that Mona had been punished for her sins. Ruth can't read Chinese but she assumes the police translation is accurate. The police had also pulled Mona's phone records. There were a few numbers whose cell tower data showed their owners had been to Mona's place that day. The only one without an alibi was a prepaid phone without a registered owner. The police had tracked it down in Chinatown, hidden in a dumpster. They hadn't been able to get any further.

A rather sloppy kill, Ruth thinks, if the gangs did it.

Sarah had also provided printouts of Mona's escort ads. Mona had used several aliases: Jasmine, Akiko, Sinn. Most of the pictures are of her in lingerie, a few in cocktail dresses. The shots are framed to emphasize her body: a side view of her breasts half-veiled in lace, a back view of her buttocks, lounging on the bed with her hand over her hip. Shots of her face have black bars over her eyes to provide some measure of anonymity.

Ruth boots up her computer and logs onto the sites to check out the other ads. She had never worked in vice, so she takes a while to familiarize herself with the lingo and acronyms. The Internet had apparently transformed the business, allowing women to get off the streets and become "independent providers" without pimps. The sites are organized to allow customers to pick out exactly what they want. They can sort and filter by price, age, services provided, ethnicity, hair and eye color, time of availability, and customer ratings. The business is competitive, and there's a brutal efficiency to the sites that Ruth might have found depressing without the Regulator: you can measure, if you apply statistical software to it, how much a girl depreciates with each passing year, how much value men place on each pound, each inch of deviation from the ideal they're seeking, how much more a blonde really is worth than a brunette, and how much more a girl who can pass as Japanese can charge than one who cannot.

Some of the ad sites charge a membership fee to see pictures of the girls' faces. Sarah had also printed these "premium" photographs of Mona. For a brief moment Ruth wonders what Sarah must have felt as she paid to unveil the seductive gaze of her daughter, the daughter who had seemed to have a trouble-free, promising future.

In these pictures Mona's face was made up lightly, her lips curved in a promising or innocent smile. She was extraordinarily pretty, even compared to the other girls in her price range. She dictated in-calls only, perhaps believing them to be safer, with her being more in control.

Compared to most of the other girls, Mona's ads can be described as "elegant." They're free of spelling errors and overtly crude language, hinting at the kind of sexual fantasies that men here harbor about Asian women while also promising an American wholesomeness, the contrast emphasizing the strategically placed bits of exoticism.

The anonymous customer reviews praised her attitude and willingness to "go the extra mile." Ruth supposes that Mona had earned good tips.

Ruth turns to the crime scene photos and the bloody, eyeless shots of Mona's face. Intellectually and dispassionately, she absorbs the details in Mona's room. She contemplates the contrast between them and the eroticism of the ad photos. This was a young woman who had been vain about her education, who had believed that she could construct, through careful words and images, a kind of filter to attract the right kind of clients. It was naïve and wise at the same time, and Ruth can almost feel, despite the Regulator, a kind of poignancy to her confident desperation.

Whatever caused her to go down this path, she had never hurt anyone, and now she was dead.

Ruth meets Luo in a room reached through long underground tunnels and many locked doors. It smells of mold and sweat and spicy foods rotting in trash bags.

Along the way she saw a few other locked rooms behind which she guessed were human cargo, people who indentured themselves to the snakeheads for a chance to be smuggled into this country so they could work for a dream of wealth. She says nothing about them. Her deal with Luo depends on her discretion, and Luo is kinder to his cargo than many others.

He pats her down perfunctorily. She offers to strip to show that she's not wired. He waves her off.

"Have you seen this woman?" she asks in Cantonese, holding up a picture of Mona.

Luo dangles the cigarette from his lips while he examines the picture closely. The dim light gives the tattoos on his bare shoulders and arms a greenish tint. After a moment, he hands it back. "I don't think so."

"She was a prostitute working out of Quincy. Someone killed her a month ago and left this behind." She brings out the photograph of the note left at the scene. "The police think the Chinese gangs did it."

Luo looks at the photo. He knits his brow in concentration and then barks out a dry laugh. "Yes, this is indeed a note left behind by a Chinese gang."

"Do you recognize the gang?"

"Sure." Luo looks at Ruth, a grin revealing the gaps in his teeth. "This note was left behind by the impetuous Tak-Kao, member of the Forever Peace Gang, after he killed the innocent Mai-Ying, the beautiful maid from the mainland, in a fit of jealousy. You can see the original in the third season of *My Hong Kong, Your Hong Kong*. You're lucky that I'm a fan."

"This is copied from a soap opera?"

"Yes. Either your man likes to make jokes or he doesn't know Chinese well and got this from some Internet search. It might fool the police, but no, we wouldn't leave a note like that." He chuckles at the thought and then spits on the ground.

"Maybe it was just a fake to confuse the police." She chooses her words carefully. "Or maybe it was done by one gang to sic the police onto the others. The police also found a phone, probably used by the killer, in a Chinatown dumpster. I know there are several Asian massage parlors in Quincy, so maybe this girl was too much competition. Are you sure you don't know anything about this?"

Luo flips through the other photographs of Mona. Ruth watches him, getting ready to react to any sudden movements. She thinks she can trust Luo, but one can't always predict the reaction of a man who often has to kill to make his living.

She concentrates on the Regulator, priming it to release adrenaline to quicken her movements if necessary. The pneumatics in her legs are charged, and she braces her back against the damp wall in case she needs to kick out. The sudden release of pressure in the air canisters installed next to her tibia will straighten her legs in a fraction of a second, generating hundreds of pounds of force. If her feet connect with Luo's chest, she will almost certainly break a few ribs—though Ruth's back will ache for days afterwards, as well.

"I like you, Ruth," Luo says, noting her sudden stillness out of the corner of his eyes. "You don't have to be afraid. I haven't forgotten how you found that bookie who tried to steal from me. I'll always tell you the truth or tell you I can't answer. We have nothing to do with this girl. She's not really competition. The men who go to massage parlors for sixty dollars an hour and a happy ending are not the kind who'd pay for a girl like this."

The Watcher drives to Somerville, just over the border from Cambridge, north of Boston. He parks in the back of a grocery store parking lot, where his Toyota Corolla, bought off a lot with cash, doesn't stick out.

Then he goes into a coffee shop and emerges with an iced coffee. Sipping it, he walks around the sunny streets, gazing from time to time at the little gizmo attached to his keychain. The gizmo tells him when he's in range of some unsecured home wireless network. Lots of students from Harvard and MIT live here, where the rent is high but not astronomical. Addicted to good wireless access, they often get powerful routers for tiny apartments and leak the network onto the streets without bothering to secure them (after all, they have friends coming over all the time who need to remain connected). And since it's summer, when the population of students is in flux, there's even less likelihood that he can be traced from using one of their networks.

It's probably overkill, but he likes to be safe.

He sits down on a bench by the side of the street, takes out his laptop, and connects to a network called "INFORMATION_WANTS_TO_BE_FREE." He enjoys disproving the network owner's theory. Information doesn't want to be free. It's valuable and wants to earn. And its existence doesn't free anyone; possessing it, however, can do the opposite.

The Watcher carefully selects a segment of video and watches it one last time.

Jasmine had done a good job, intentionally or not, with the framing, and the man's sweaty grimace is featured prominently in the video. His movements—and as a result, Jasmine's—made the video jerky, and so he's had to apply software image stabilization. But now it looks quite professional.

The Watcher had tried to identify the man, who looks Chinese, by uploading a picture he got from Jasmine into a search engine. They are always making advancements in facial recognition software, and sometimes he gets hits this way. But it didn't seem to work this time. That's not a problem for the Watcher. He has other techniques.

The Watcher signs on to a forum where the expat Chinese congregate to reminisce and argue politics in their homeland. He posts the picture of the man in the video and writes below in English, "Anyone famous?" Then he sips his coffee and refreshes the screen from time to time to catch the new replies.

The Watcher doesn't read Chinese (or Russian, or Arabic, or Hindi, or any of the other languages where he plies his trade), but linguistic skills are hardly necessary for this task. Most of the expats speak English and can understand his question. He's just using these people as research tools, a human flesh-powered, crowdsourced search engine. It's almost funny how people are so willing to give perfect strangers over the Internet information, would even compete with each other to do it, to show how knowledgeable they are. He's pleased to make use of such petty vanities.

He simply needs a name and a measure of the prominence of the man, and for that, the crude translations offered by computers are sufficient.

From the almost-gibberish translations, he gathers that the man is a prominent official in the Chinese Transport Ministry, and like almost all

Chinese officials, he's despised by his countrymen. The man is a bigger deal than the Watcher's usual targets, but that might make him a good demonstration.

The Watcher is thankful for Dagger, who had explained Chinese politics to him. One evening, after he had gotten out of jail the last time, the Watcher had hung back and watched a Chinese man rob a few Chinese tourists near San Francisco's Chinatown.

The tourists had managed to make a call to 911, and the robber had fled the scene on foot down an alley. But the Watcher had seen something in the man's direct, simple approach that he liked. He drove around the block, stopped by the other end of the alley, and when the man emerged, he swung open the passenger side door and offered him a chance to escape in his car. The man thanked him and told him his name was Dagger.

Dagger was talkative and told the Watcher how angry and envious people in China were of the Party officials, who lived an extravagant life on the money squeezed from the common people, took bribes, and funneled public funds to their relatives. He targeted those tourists who he thought were the officials' wives and children, and regarded himself as a modern Robin Hood.

Yet, the officials were not completely immune. All it took was a public scandal of some kind, usually involving young women who were not their wives. Talk of democracy didn't get people excited, but seeing an official rubbing their graft in their faces made them see red. And the Party apparatus would have no choice but to punish the disgraced officials, as the only thing the Party feared was public anger, which always threatened to boil out of control. If a revolution were to come to China, Dagger quipped, it would be triggered by mistresses, not speeches.

A light had gone on in the Watcher's head then. It was as if he could see the reins of power flowing from those who had secrets to those who knew secrets. He thanked Dagger and dropped him off, wishing him well.

The Watcher imagines what the official's visit to Boston had been like. He had probably come to learn about the city's experience with light rail, but it was likely in reality just another State-funded vacation, a chance to shop at the luxury stores on Newbury Street, to enjoy expensive foods without fear of poison or pollution, and to anonymously take delight in quality female companionship without the threat of recording devices in the hands of an interested populace.

He posts the video to the forum, and as an extra flourish, adds a link to the official's biography on the Transport Ministry's web site. For a second, he regrets the forgone revenue, but it's been a while since he's done a demonstration, and these are necessary to keep the business going.

He packs up his laptop. Now he has to wait.

Ruth doesn't think there's much value in viewing Mona's apartment, but she's learned over the years to not leave any stone unturned. She gets the key from

Sarah Ding and makes her way to the apartment around 6:00 in the evening. Viewing the site at approximately the time of day when the murder occurred can sometimes be helpful.

She passes through the living room. There's a small TV facing a futon, the kind of furniture that a young woman keeps from her college days when she doesn't have a reason to upgrade. It's a living room that was never meant for visitors.

She moves into the room in which the murder happened. The forensics team has cleaned it out. The room—it wasn't Mona's real bedroom, which was a tiny cubby down the hall, with just a twin bed and plain walls—is stripped bare, most of the loose items having been collected as evidence. The mattress is naked, as are the nightstands. The carpet has been vacuumed. The place smells like a hotel room: stale air and faint perfume.

Ruth notices the line of mirrors along the side of the bed, hanging over the closet doors. Watching arouses people.

She imagines how lonely Mona must have felt living here, touched and kissed and fucked by a stream of men who kept as much of themselves hidden from her as possible. She imagines her sitting in front of the small TV to relax, and dressing up to meet her parents so that she could lie some more.

Ruth imagines the way the murderer had shot Mona, and then cut her after. Were there more than one of them so that Mona thought a struggle was useless? Did they shoot her right away or did they ask her to tell them where she had hidden her money first? She can feel the Regulator starting up again, keeping her emotions in check. Evil has to be confronted dispassionately.

She decides she's seen all she needs to see. She leaves the apartment and pulls the door closed. As she heads for the stairs, she sees a man coming up, keys in hand. Their eyes briefly meet, and he turns to the door of the apartment across the hall.

Ruth is sure the police have interviewed the neighbor. But sometimes people will tell things to a nonthreatening woman that they are reluctant to tell the cops.

She walks over and introduces herself, explaining that she's a friend of Mona's family, here to tie up some loose ends. The man, whose name is Peter, is wary but shakes her hand.

"I didn't hear or see anything. We pretty much keep to ourselves in this building."

"I believe you. But it would be helpful if we can chat a bit anyway. The family didn't know much about her life here."

He nods reluctantly and opens the door. He steps in and waves his arms up and around in a complex sequence as though he's conducting an orchestra. The lights come on.

"That's pretty fancy," Ruth says. "You have the whole place wired up like that?"

His voice, cautious and guarded until now, grows animated. Talking about something other than the murder seems to relax him. "Yes. It's called EchoSense.

They add an adaptor to your wireless router and a few antennas around the room, and then it uses the Doppler shifts generated by your body's movements in the radio waves to detect gestures."

"You mean it can see you move with just the signals from your Wi-Fi bouncing around the room?"

"Something like that."

Ruth remembers seeing an infomercial about this. She notes how small the apartment is and how little space separates it from Mona's. They sit down and chat about what Peter remembers about Mona.

"Pretty girl. Way out of my league, but she was always pleasant."

"Did she get a lot of visitors?"

"I don't pry into other people's business. But yeah, I remember lots of visitors, mostly men. I did think she might have been an escort. But that didn't bother me. The men always seemed clean, business types. Not dangerous."

"No one who looked like a gangster, for example?"

"I wouldn't know what gangsters look like. But no, I don't think so."

They chat on inconsequentially for another fifteen minutes, and Ruth decides that she's wasted enough time.

"Can I buy the router from you?" she asks. "And the EchoSense thing."

"You can just order your own set online."

"I hate shopping online. You can never return things. I know this one works; so I want it. I'll offer you two thousand, cash."

He considers this.

"I bet you can buy a new one and get another adaptor yourself from EchoSense for less than a quarter of that."

He nods and retrieves the router, and she pays him. The act feels somehow illicit, not unlike how she imagines Mona's transactions were.

Ruth posts an ad to a local classifieds site describing in vague terms what she's looking for. Boston is blessed with many good colleges and lots of young men and women who would relish a technical challenge even more than the money she offers. She looks through the resumes until she finds the one she feels has the right skills: jailbreaking phones, reverse-engineering proprietary protocols, a healthy disrespect for acronyms like DMCA and CFAA.

She meets the young man at her office and explains what she wants. Daniel, dark-skinned, lanky, and shy, slouches in the chair across from hers as he listens without interrupting.

"Can you do it?" she asks.

"Maybe," he says. "Companies like this one will usually send customer data back to the mothership anonymously to help improve their technology. Sometimes the data is cached locally for a while. It's possible I'll find logs on there a month old. If it's there, I'll get it for you. But I'll have to figure out how they're encoding the data and then make sense of it."

"Do you think my theory is plausible?"

"I'm impressed you even came up with it. Wireless signals can go through walls, so it's certainly possible that this adaptor has captured the movements of people in neighboring apartments. It's a privacy nightmare, and I'm sure the company doesn't publicize that."

"How long will it take?"

"As little as a day or as much as a month. I won't know until I start. It will help if you can draw me a map of the apartments and what's inside."

Ruth does as he asked. Then she tells him, "I'll pay you three hundred dollars a day, with a five thousand dollar bonus if you succeed this week."

"Deal." He grins and picks up the router, getting ready to leave.

Because it never hurts to tell people what they're doing is meaningful, she adds, "You're helping to catch the killer of a young woman who's not much older than you."

Then she goes home because she's run out of things to try.

The first hour after waking up is always the worst part of the day for Ruth.

As usual, she wakes from a nightmare. She lies still, disoriented, the images from her dream superimposed over the sight of the water stains on the ceiling. Her body is drenched in sweat.

The man holds Jessica in front of him with his left hand while the gun in his right hand is pointed at her head. She's terrified, but not of him. He ducks so that her body shields his, and he whispers something into her ear.

"Mom! Mom!" she screams. "Don't shoot. Please don't shoot!"

Ruth rolls over, nauseated. She sits up at the edge of the bed, hating the smell of the hot room, the dust that she never has time to clean filling the air pierced by bright rays coming in from the east-facing window. She shoves the sheets off of her and stands up quickly, her breath coming too fast. She's fighting the rising panic without any help, alone, her Regulator off.

The clock on the nightstand says 6:00.

She's crouching behind the opened driver's side door of her car. Her hands shake as she struggles to keep the man's head, bobbing besides her daughter's, in the sight of her gun. If she turns on her Regulator, she thinks her hands may grow steady and give her a clear shot at him.

What are her chances of hitting him instead of her? Ninety-five percent? Ninety-nine?

"Mom! Mom! No!"

She gets up and stumbles into the kitchen to turn on the coffeemaker. She curses when she finds the can empty and throws it clattering into the sink. The noise shocks her and she cringes.

Then she struggles into the shower, sluggishly, painfully, as though the muscles that she conditions daily through hard exercise were not there. She turns on the hot water but it brings no warmth to her shivering body.

Grief descends on her like a heavy weight. She sits down in the shower, curling her body into itself. Water streams down her face so she does not know if there are tears as her body heaves.

She fights the impulse to turn on the Regulator. It's not time yet. She has to give her body the necessary rest.

The Regulator, a collection of chips and circuitry embedded at the top of her spine, is tied into the limbic system and the major blood vessels into the brain. Like its namesake from mechanical and electrical engineering, it maintains the levels of dopamine, noradrenaline, serotonin and other chemicals in the brain and in her blood stream. It filters out the chemicals when there's an excess, and releases them when there's a deficit.

And it obeys her will.

The implant allows a person control over her basic emotions: fear, disgust, joy, excitement, love. It's mandatory for law enforcement officers, a way to minimize the effects of emotions on life-or-death decisions, a way to eliminate prejudice and irrationality.

"You have clearance to shoot," the voice in her headset tells her. It's the voice of her husband, Scott, the head of her department. His voice is completely calm. His Regulator is on.

She sees the head of the man bobbing up and down as he retreats with Jessica. He's heading for the van parked by the side of the road.

"He's got other hostages in there," her husband continues to speak in her ear. "If you don't shoot, you put the lives of those three other girls and who knows how many other people in danger. This is our best chance."

The sound of sirens, her backup, is still faint. Too far away.

After what seems an eternity, she manages to stand up in the shower and turn off the water. She towels herself dry and dresses slowly. She tries to think of something, anything, to take her mind off its current track. But nothing works.

She despises the raw state of her mind. Without the Regulator, she feels weak, confused, angry. Waves of despair wash over her and everything appears in hopeless shades of gray. She wonders why she's still alive.

It will pass, she thinks. Just a few more minutes.

Back when she had been on the force, she had adhered to the regulation requirement not to leave the Regulator on for more than two hours at a time. There are physiological and psychological risks associated with prolonged use. Some of her fellow officers had also complained about the way the Regulator made them feel robotic, deadened. No excitement from seeing a pretty woman; no thrill at the potential for a car chase; no righteous anger when faced with an act of abuse. Everything had to be deliberate: you decided when to let the adrenaline flow, and just enough to get the job done and not too much to interfere with judgment. But sometimes, they argued, you needed emotions, instinct, intuition.

Her Regulator had been off when she came home that day and recognized the man hiding from the city-wide manhunt.

Have I been working too much? she thinks. I don't know any of her friends. When did Jess meet him? Why didn't I ask her more questions when she was coming home late every night? Why did I stop for lunch instead of coming home half an hour earlier? There are a thousand things I could have done and should have done and would have done.

Fear and anger and regret are mixed up in her until she cannot tell which is which.

"Engage your Regulator," her husband's voice tells her. "You can make the shot."

Why do I care about the lives of the other girls? she thinks. All I care about is Jess. Even the smallest chance of hurting her is too much.

Can she trust a machine to save her daughter? Should she rely on a machine to steady her shaking hands, to clear her blurry vision, to make a shot without missing?

"Mom, he's going to let me go later. He won't hurt me. He just wants to get away from here. Put the gun down!"

Maybe Scott can make a calculus about lives saved and lives put at risk. She won't. She will not trust a machine.

"It's okay, baby," she croaks out. "It's all going to be okay."

She does not turn on the Regulator. She does not shoot.

Later, after she had identified the body of Jess—the bodies of all four of the girls had been badly burnt when the bomb went off—after she had been disciplined and discharged, after Scott and she had split up, after she had found no solace in alcohol and pills, she did finally find the help she needed: she could leave the Regulator on all the time.

The Regulator deadened the pain, stifled grief and numbed the ache of loss. It held down the regret, made it possible to pretend to forget. She craved the calmness it brought, the blameless, serene clarity.

She had been wrong to distrust it. That distrust had cost her Jess. She would not make the same mistake again.

Sometimes she thinks of the Regulator as a dependable lover, a comforting presence to lean on. Sometimes she thinks she's addicted. She does not probe deeply behind these thoughts.

She would have preferred to never have to turn off the Regulator, to never be in a position to repeat her mistake. But even Doctor B balked at that ("Your brain will turn into mush."). The illegal modifications he did agree to make allow the Regulator to remain on for a maximum of twenty-three hours at a stretch. Then she must take an hour-long break during which she must remain conscious.

And so there's always this hour in the morning, right as she wakes, when she's naked and alone with her memories, unshielded from the rush of red-hot hatred (for the man? for herself?) and white-cold rage, and the black, bottomless abyss that she endures as her punishment.

The alarm beeps. She concentrates like a monk in meditation and feels the hum of the Regulator starting up. Relief spreads out from the center of her mind to the very tips of her fingers, the soothing, numbing serenity of a regulated, disciplined mind. To be regulated is to be a regular person.

She stands up, limber, graceful, powerful, ready to hunt.

The Watcher has identified more of the men in the pictures. He's now in a new motel room, this one more expensive than usual because he feels like he deserves a treat after all he's been through. Hunching over all day to edit video is hard work.

He pans the cropping rectangle over the video to give it a sense of dynamism and movement. There's an artistry to this.

He's amazed how so few people seem to know about the eye implants. There's something about eyes, so vulnerable, so essential to the way people see the world and themselves, that makes people feel protective and reluctant to invade them. The laws regarding eye modifications are the most stringent, and after a while, people begin to mistake "not permitted" with "not possible."

They don't know what they don't want to know.

All his life, he's felt that he's missed some key piece of information, some secret that everyone else seemed to know. He's intelligent, diligent, but somehow things have not worked out.

He never knew his father, and when he was eleven, his mother had left him one day at home with twenty dollars and never came back. A string of foster homes had followed, and *nobody*, nobody could tell him what he was missing, why he was always at the mercy of judges and bureaucrats, why he had so little control over his life, not where he would sleep, not when he would eat, not who would have power over him next.

He made it his subject to study men, to watch and try to understand what made them tick. Much of what he learned had disappointed him. Men were vain, proud, ignorant. They let their desires carry them away, ignored risks that were obvious. They did not think, did not plan. They did not know what they really wanted. They let the TV tell them what they should have and hoped that working at their pathetic jobs would make those wishes come true.

He craved control. He wanted to see them dance to his tune the way he had been made to dance to the tune of everyone else.

So he had honed himself to be pure and purposeful, like a sharp knife in a drawer full of ridiculous, ornate, fussy kitchen gadgets. He knew what he wanted and he worked at getting it with singular purpose.

He adjusts the colors and the dynamic range to compensate for the dim light in the video. He wants there to be no mistake in identifying the man.

He stretches his tired arms and sore neck. For a moment he wonders if he'll be better off if he pays to have parts of his body enhanced so he can work for longer, without pain and fatigue. But the momentary fancy passes.

Most people don't like medically unnecessary enhancements and would only accept them if they're required for a job. No such sentimental considerations for bodily integrity or "naturalness" constrain the Watcher. He does not like enhancements because he views reliance on them as a sign of weakness. He would defeat his enemies by his mind, and with the aid of planning and foresight. He does not need to depend on machines.

He had learned to steal, and then rob, and eventually how to kill for money. But the money was really secondary, just a means to an end. It was control that he desired. The only man he had killed was a lawyer, someone who lied for a living. Lying had brought him money, and that gave him power, made people bow down to him and smile at him and speak in respectful voices. The Watcher had loved that moment when the man begged him for mercy, when he would have done anything the Watcher wanted. The Watcher had taken what he wanted from the man rightfully, by superiority of intellect and strength. Yet, the Watcher had been caught and gone to jail for it. A system that rewarded liars and punished the Watcher could not in any sense be called just.

He presses "Save." He's done with this video.

Knowledge of the truth gave him power, and he would make others acknowledge it.

Before Ruth is about to make her next move, Daniel calls, and they meet in her office again.

"I have what you wanted."

He takes out his laptop and shows her an animation, like a movie.

"They stored videos on the adaptor?"

Daniel laughs. "No. The device can't really 'see' and that would be far too much data. No, the adaptor just stored readings, numbers. I made the animation so it's easier to understand."

She's impressed. The young man knows how to give a good presentation.

"The Wi-Fi echoes aren't captured with enough resolution to give you much detail. But you can get a rough sense of people's sizes and heights and their movements. This is what I got from the day and hour you specified."

They watch as a bigger, vaguely humanoid shape appears at Mona's apartment door, precisely at 6:00, meeting a smaller, vaguely humanoid shape.

"Seems they had an appointment," Daniel says.

They watch as the smaller shape leads the bigger shape into the bedroom, and then the two embrace. They watch the smaller shape climb into space—presumably onto the bed. They watch the bigger shape climb up after it. They watch the shooting, and then the smaller shape collapses and disappears. They watch the bigger shape lean over, and the smaller shape flickers into existence as it's moved from time to time.

So there was only one killer, Ruth thinks. *And he was a client.*

"How tall is he?"

"There's a scale to the side."

Ruth watches the animation over and over. The man is six foot two or six foot three, maybe 180 to 200 pounds. She notices that he has a bit of a limp as he walks.

She's now convinced that Luo was telling the truth. Not many Chinese men are six foot two, and such a man would stick out too much to be a killer for a gang. Every witness would remember him. Mona's killer had been a client, maybe even a regular. It wasn't a random robbery but carefully planned.

The man is still out there, and killers that meticulous rarely kill only once.

"Thank you," she says. "You might be saving another young woman's life."

Ruth dials the number for the police department.

"Captain Brennan, please."

She gives her name and her call is transferred, and then she hears the gruff, weary voice of her ex-husband. "What can I do for you?"

Once again, she's glad she has the Regulator. His voice dredges up memories of his raspy morning mumbles, his stentorian laughter, his tender whispers when they were alone, the soundtrack of twenty years of a life spent together, a life that they had both thought would last until one of them died.

"I need a favor."

He doesn't answer right away. She wonders if she's too abrupt—a side effect of leaving the Regulator on all the time. Maybe she should have started with "How've you been?"

Finally, he speaks. "What is it?" The voice is restrained, but laced with exhausted, desiccated pain.

"I'd like to use your NCIC access."

Another pause. "Why?"

"I'm working on the Mona Ding case. I think this is a man who's killed before and will kill again. He's got a method. I want to see if there are related cases in other cities."

"That's out of the question, Ruth. You know that. Besides, there's no point. We've run all the searches we can, and there's nothing similar. This was a Chinese gang protecting their business, simple as that. Until we have the resources in the Gang Unit to deal with it, I'm sorry, this will have to go cold for a while."

Ruth hears the unspoken. The Chinese gangs have always preyed on their own. Until they bother the tourists, let's just leave them alone. She'd heard similar sentiments often enough back when she was on the force. The Regulator could do nothing about certain kinds of prejudice. It's perfectly rational. And also perfectly wrong.

"I don't think so. I have an informant who says that the Chinese gangs have nothing to do with it."

Scott snorts. "Yes, of course you can trust the word of a Chinese snakehead. But there's also the note and the phone."

"The note is most likely a forgery. And do you really think this Chinese gang member would be smart enough to realize that the phone records would give him away and then decide that the best place to hide it was around his place of business?"

"Who knows? Criminals are stupid."

"The man is far too methodical for that. It's a red herring."

"You have no evidence."

"I have a good reconstruction of the crime and a description of the suspect. He's too tall to be the kind a Chinese gang would use."

This gets his attention. "From where?"

"A neighbor had a home motion-sensing system that captured wireless echoes into Mona's apartment. I paid someone to reconstruct it."

"Will that stand up in court?"

"I doubt it. It will take expert testimony and you'll have to get the company to admit that they capture that information. They'll fight it tooth and nail."

"Then it's not much use to me."

"If you give me a chance to look in the database, maybe I can turn it into something you *can* use." She waits a second and presses on, hoping that he'll be sentimental. "I've never asked you for much."

"This is the first time you've ever asked me for something like this."

"I don't usually take on cases like this."

"What is it about this girl?"

Ruth considers the question. There are two ways to answer it. She can try to explain the fee she's being paid and why she feels she's adding value. Or she can give what she suspects is the real reason. Sometimes the Regulator makes it hard to tell what's true. "Sometimes people think the police don't look as hard when the victim is a sex worker. I know your resources are constrained, but maybe I can help."

"It's the mother, isn't it? You feel bad for her."

Ruth does not answer. She can feel the Regulator kicking in again. Without it, perhaps she would be enraged.

"She's not Jess, Ruth. Finding her killer won't make you feel better."

"I'm asking for a favor. You can just say no."

Scott does not sigh, and he does not mumble. He's simply quiet. Then, a few seconds later: "Come to the office around 8:00. You can use the terminal in my office."

The Watcher thinks of himself as a good client. He makes sure he gets his money's worth, but he leaves a generous tip. He likes the clarity of money, the way it makes the flow of power obvious. The girl he just left was certainly appreciative.

He drives faster. He feels he's been too self-indulgent the last few weeks, working too slowly. He needs to make sure the last round of targets have paid.

If not, he needs to carry through. Action. Reaction. It's all very simple once you understand the rules.

He rubs the bandage around his ring finger, which allows him to maintain the pale patch of skin that girls like to see. The lingering, sickly sweet perfume from the last girl—Melody, Mandy, he's already forgetting her name—reminds him of Tara, whom he will never forget.

Tara may have been the only girl he's really loved. She was blonde, petite, and very expensive. But she had liked him for some reason. Perhaps because they were both broken, and the jagged pieces happened to fit.

She had stopped charging him and told him her real name. He was a kind of boyfriend. Because he was curious, she explained her business to him. How certain words and turns of phrase and tones on the phone were warning signs. What she looked for in a desired regular. What signs on a man probably meant he was safe. He enjoyed learning about this. It seemed to require careful watching by the girl, and he respected those who looked and studied and made the information useful.

He had looked into her eyes as he fucked her, and then said, "Is something wrong with your right eye?"

She had stopped moving. "What?"

"I wasn't sure at first. But yes, it's like you have something behind your eye."

She wriggled under him. He was annoyed and thought about holding her down. But he decided not to. She seemed about to tell him something important. He rolled off of her.

"You're very observant."

"I try. What is it?"

She told him about the implant.

"You've been recording your clients having sex with you?"

"Yes."

"I want to see the ones you have of us."

She laughed. "I'll have to go under the knife for that. Not going to happen until I retire. Having your skull opened up once was enough."

She explained how the recordings made her feel safe, gave her a sense of power, like having bank accounts whose balances only she knew and kept growing. If she were ever threatened, she would be able to call on the powerful men she knew for aid. And after retirement, if things didn't work out and she got desperate, perhaps she could use them to get her regulars to help her out a little.

He had liked the way she thought. So devious. So like him.

He had been sorry when he killed her. Removing her head was more difficult and messy than he had imagined. Figuring out what to do with the little silver half-sphere had taken months. He would learn to do better over time.

But Tara had been blind to the implications of what she had done. What she had wasn't just insurance, wasn't just a rainy-day fund. She had revealed to him that she had what it took to make his dream come true, and he had to take it from her.

He pulls into the parking lot of the hotel and finds himself seized by an unfamiliar sensation: sorrow. He misses Tara, like missing a mirror you've broken.

Ruth is working with the assumption that the man she's looking for targets independent prostitutes. There's an efficiency and a method to the way Mona was killed that suggested practice.

She begins by searching the NCIC database for prostitutes who had been killed by a suspect matching the EchoSense description. As she expects, she comes up with nothing that seems remotely similar. The man hadn't left obvious trails.

The focus on Mona's eyes may be a clue. Maybe the killer has a fetish for Asian women. Ruth changes her search to concentrate on body mutilations of Asian prostitutes similar to what Mona had suffered. Again, nothing.

Ruth sits back and thinks over the situation. It's common for serial killers to concentrate on victims of a specific ethnicity. But that may be a red herring here.

She expands her search to include all independent prostitutes who had been killed in the last year or so, and now there are too many hits. Dozens and dozens of killings of prostitutes of every description pop up. Most were sexually assaulted. Some were tortured. Many had their bodies mutilated. Almost all were robbed. Gangs were suspected in several cases. She sifts through them, looking for similarities. Nothing jumps out at her.

She needs more information.

She logs onto the escort sites in the various cities and looks up the ads of the murdered women. Not all of them remain online, as some sites deactivate ads when enough patrons complain about unavailability. She prints out what she can, laying them out side by side to compare.

Then she sees it. It's in the ads.

A subset of the ads triggers a sense of familiarity in Ruth's mind. They were all carefully written, free of spelling and grammar mistakes. They were frank but not explicit, seductive without verging on parody. The johns who posted reviews described them as "classy."

It's a signal, Ruth realizes. The ads are written to give off the air of being careful, selective, discreet. There is in them, for lack of a better word, a sense of taste.

All of the women in these ads were extraordinarily beautiful, with smooth skin and thick, long flowing hair. All of them were between twenty-two and thirty, not so young as to be careless or supporting themselves through school, and not old enough to lose the ability to pass for younger. All of them were independent, with no pimp or evidence of being on drugs.

Luo's words come back to her: *The men who go to massage parlors for sixty dollars an hour and a happy ending are not the kind who'd pay for a girl like this.*

There's a certain kind of client who would be attracted to the signs given out by these girls, Ruth thinks: men who care very much about the risk of discovery and who believe that they deserve something special, suitable for their distinguished tastes.

She prints out the NCIC entries for the women.

All the women she's identified were killed in their homes. No sign of struggle—possibly because they were meeting a client. One was strangled, the others shot through the heart in the back, like Mona. In all the cases except one—the woman who was strangled—the police had found record of a suspicious call on the day of the murder from a prepaid phone that was later found somewhere in the city. The killer had taken all the women's money.

Ruth knows she's on the right track. Now she needs to examine the case reports in more detail to see if she can find more patterns to identify the killer.

The door to the office opens. It's Scott.

"Still here?" The scowl on his face shows that he does not have his Regulator on. "It's after midnight."

She notes, not for the first time, how the men in the department have often resisted the Regulator unless absolutely necessary, claiming that it dulled their instincts and hunches. But they had also asked her whether she had hers on whenever she dared to disagree with them. They would laugh when they asked.

"I think I'm onto something," she says, calmly.

"You working with the goddamned Feds now?"

"What are you talking about?"

"You haven't seen the news?"

"I've been here all evening."

He takes out his tablet, opens a bookmark, and hands it to her. It's an article in the international section of the *Globe,* which she rarely reads. "Scandal Unseats Chinese Transport Minister," says the headline.

She scans the article quickly. A video has surfaced on the Chinese microblogs showing an important official in the Transport Ministry having sex with a prostitute. Moreover, it seems that he had been paying her out of public funds. He's already been removed from his post due to the public outcry.

Accompanying the article is a grainy photo, a still capture from the video. Before the Regulator kicks in, Ruth feels her heart skip a beat. The image shows a man on top of a woman. Her head is turned to the side, directly facing the camera.

"That's your girl, isn't it?"

Ruth nods. She recognizes the bed and the nightstand with the clock and wicker basket from the crime scene photos.

"The Chinese are hopping mad. They think we had the man under surveillance when he was in Boston and released this video deliberately to mess with them. They're protesting through the backchannels, threatening retaliation. The Feds want us to look into it and see what we can find out about how the video was made. They don't know that she's already dead, but I recognized her as soon as I saw her. If you ask me, it's probably something the Chinese cooked up themselves to try to get rid of the guy in an internal purge. Maybe they even paid the girl to do it and then they killed her. That or our own spies decided to get rid of her after using her as bait, in which case I expect this investigation to be shut down pretty quickly. Either way, I'm not looking forward to this mess. And I advise you to back off as well."

Ruth feels a moment of resentment before the Regulator whisks it away. If Mona's death was part of a political plot, then Scott is right, she really is way out of her depth. The police had been wrong to conclude that it was a gang killing. But she's wrong, too. Mona was an unfortunate pawn in some political game, and the trend she thought she had noticed was illusory, just a set of coincidences.

The rational thing to do is to let the police take over. She'll have to tell Sarah Ding that there's nothing she can do for her now.

"We'll have to sweep the apartment again for recording devices. And you better let me know the name of your informant. We'll need to question him thoroughly to see which gangs are involved. This could be a national security matter."

"You know I can't do that. I have no evidence he has anything to do with this."

"Ruth, we're picking this up now. If you want to find the girl's killer, help me."

"Feel free to round up all the usual suspects in Chinatown. It's what you want to do, anyway."

He stares at her, his face weary and angry, a look she's very familiar with. Then his face relaxes. He has decided to engage his Regulator, and he no longer wants to argue or talk about what couldn't be said between them.

Her Regulator kicks in automatically.

"Thank you for letting me use your office," she says placidly. "You have a good night."

The scandal had gone off exactly as the Watcher planned. He's pleased but not yet ready to celebrate. That was only the first step, a demonstration of his power. Next, he has to actually make sure it pays.

He goes through the recordings and pictures he's extracted from the dead girl and picks out a few more promising targets based on his research. Two are prominent Chinese businessmen connected with top Party bosses; one is the brother of an Indian diplomatic attaché; two more are sons of the House of Saud studying in Boston. It's remarkable how similar the dynamics between the powerful and the people they ruled over were around the world. He also finds a prominent CEO and a Justice of the Massachusetts Supreme Judicial Court, but these he sets aside. It's not that he's particularly patriotic, but he instinctively senses that if one of his victims decides to turn him in instead of paying up, he'll be in much less trouble if the victim isn't an American. Besides, American public figures also have a harder time moving money around anonymously, as evidenced by his experience with those two Senators in DC, which almost unraveled his whole scheme. Finally, it never hurts to have a judge or someone famous that can be leaned on in case the Watcher is caught.

Patience, and an eye for details.

He sends off his emails. Each references the article about the Chinese Transport Minister ("See, this could be you!") and then includes two files. One is the full video of the minister and the girl (to show that he was the originator) and the second is a carefully curated video of the recipient coupling with her. Each email contains a demand for payment and directions to make deposits to a numbered Swiss bank account or to transfer anonymous electronic cryptocurrency.

He browses the escort sites again. He's narrowed down the girls he suspects to just a few. Now he just has to look at them more closely to pick out the right one. He grows excited at the prospect.

He glances up at the people walking past him in the streets. All these foolish men and women moving around as if dreaming. They do not understand that the world is full of secrets, accessible only to those patient enough, observant enough to locate them and dig them out of their warm, bloody hiding places, like retrieving pearls from the soft flesh inside an oyster. And then, armed with those secrets, you could make men half a world away tremble and dance.

He closes his laptop and gets up to leave. He thinks about packing up the mess in his motel room, setting out the surgical kit, the baseball cap, the gun and a few other surprises he's learned to take with him when he's hunting.

Time to dig for more treasure.

Ruth wakes up. The old nightmares have been joined by new ones. She stays curled up in bed fighting waves of despair. She wants to lie here forever.

Days of work and she has nothing to show for it.

She'll have to call Sarah Ding later, after she turns on the Regulator. She can tell her that Mona was probably not killed by a gang, but somehow had been caught up in events bigger than she could handle. How would that make Sarah feel better?

The image from yesterday's news will not leave her mind, no matter how hard she tries to push it away.

Ruth struggles up and pulls up the article. She can't explain it, but the image just *looks* wrong. Not having the Regulator on makes it hard to think.

She finds the crime scene photo of Mona's bedroom and compares it with the image from the article. She looks back and forth.

Isn't the basket of condoms on the wrong side of the bed?

The shot is taken from the left side of the bed. So the closet doors, with the mirrors on them, should be on the far side of the shot, behind the couple. But there's only a blank wall behind them in the shot. Ruth's heart is beating so fast that she feels faint.

The alarm beeps. Ruth glances up at the red numbers and turns the Regulator on.

The clock.

She looks back at the image. The alarm clock in the shot is tiny and fuzzy, but she can just make the numbers out. They're backwards.

Ruth walks steadily over to her laptop and begins to search online for the video. She finds it without much trouble and presses play.

Despite the video stabilization and the careful cropping, she can see that Mona's eyes are always looking directly into the camera.

There's only one explanation: the camera was aimed at the mirrors, and it was located in Mona's eye.

The eyes.

She goes through the NCIC entries of the other women she printed out yesterday, and now the pattern that had proven elusive seems obvious.

There was a blonde in Los Angeles whose head had been removed after death and never found; there was a brunette, also in LA, whose skull had been cracked open and her brains mashed; there was a Mexican woman and a black woman in DC whose faces had been subjected to post-mortem trauma in more restrained ways, with the cheekbones crushed and broken. Then finally, there was Mona, whose eyes had been carefully removed.

The killer has been improving his technique.

The Regulator holds her excitement in check. She needs more data.

She looks through all of Mona's photographs again. Nothing out of place shows up in the earlier pictures, but in the picture from her birthday with her parents, a flash was used, and there's an odd glint in her left eye.

Most cameras can automatically compensate for red-eye, which is caused by the light from the flash reflecting off the blood-rich choroid in the back of the eye. But the glint in Mona's picture is not red; it's bluish.

Calmly, Ruth flips through the photographs of the other girls who have been killed. And in each, she finds the tell-tale glint. This must be how the killer identified his targets.

She picks up the phone and dials the number for her friend. She and Gail had gone to college together, and she's now working as a researcher for an advanced medical devices company.

"Hello?"

She hears the chatter of other people in the background. "Gail, it's Ruth. Can you talk?"

"Just a minute." She hears the background conversation grow muffled and then abruptly shut off. "You never call unless you're asking about another enhancement. We're not getting any younger, you know? You have to stop at some point."

Gail had been the one to suggest the various enhancements Ruth has obtained over the years. She had even found Doctor B for her because she didn't want Ruth to end up crippled. But she had done it reluctantly, conflicted about the idea of turning Ruth into a cyborg.

"This feels wrong," she would say. "You don't need these things done to you. They're not medically necessary."

"This can save my life the next time someone is trying to choke me," Ruth would say.

"It's not the same thing," she would say. And the conversations would always end with Gail giving in, but with stern warnings about no further enhancements.

Sometimes you help a friend even when you disapprove of their decisions. It's complicated.

Ruth answers Gail on the phone, "No. I'm just fine. But I want to know if you know about a new kind of enhancement. I'm sending you some pictures now. Hold on." She sends over the images of the girls where she can see the strange glint in their eyes. "Take a look. Can you see that flash in their eyes? Do you know anything like this?" She doesn't tell Gail her suspicion so that Gail's answer would not be affected.

Gail is silent for a while. "I see what you mean. These are not great pictures. But let me talk to some people and call you back."

"Don't send the full pictures around. I'm in the middle of an investigation. Just crop out the eyes if you can."

Ruth hangs up. The Regulator is working extra hard. Something about what she said—cropping out the girls' eyes—triggered a bodily response of disgust that the Regulator is suppressing. She's not sure why. With the Regulator, sometimes it's hard for her to see the connections between things.

While waiting for Gail to call her back, she looks through the active online ads in Boston once more. The killer has a pattern of killing a few girls in each city before moving on. He must be on the hunt for a second victim here. The best way to catch him is to find her before he does.

She clicks through ad after ad, the parade of flesh a meaningless blur, focusing only on the eyes. Finally, she sees what she's looking for. The girl uses the name Carrie, and she has dirty-blond hair and green eyes. Her ad is clean, clear, well-written, like a tasteful sign amidst the parade of flashing neon. The timestamp on the ad shows that she last modified it twelve hours ago. She's likely still alive.

Ruth calls the number listed.

"This is Carrie. Please leave a message."

As expected, Carrie screens her calls.

"Hello. My name is Ruth Law, and I saw your ad. I'd like to make an appointment with you." She hesitates, and then adds, "This is not a joke. I really want to see you." She leaves her number and hangs up.

The phone rings almost immediately. Ruth picks up. But it's Gail, not Carrie.

"I asked around, and people who ought to know tell me the girls are probably wearing a new kind of retinal implant. It's not FDA-approved. But of course you can go overseas and get them installed if you pay enough."

"What do they do?"

"They're hidden cameras."

"How do you get the pictures and videos out?"

"You don't. They have no wireless connections to the outside world. In fact, they're shielded to emit as little RF emissions as possible so that they're undetectable to camera scanners, and a wireless connection would just mean another way to hack into them. All the storage is inside the device. To retrieve them you have to have surgery again. Not the kind of thing most people would be interested in unless you're trying to record people who *really* don't want you to be recording them."

When you're so desperate for safety that you think this provides insurance, Ruth thinks. *Some future leverage.*

And there's no way to get the recordings out except to cut the girl open. "Thanks."

"I don't know what you're involved in, Ruth, but you really are getting too old for this. Are you still leaving the Regulator on all the time? It's not healthy."

"Don't I know it." She changes the subject to Gail's children. The Regulator allows her to have this conversation without pain. After a suitable amount of time, she says goodbye and hangs up.

The phone rings again.

"This is Carrie. You called me."

"Yes." Ruth makes her voice sound light, carefree.

Carrie's voice is flirtatious but cautious. "Is this for you and your boyfriend or husband?"

"No, just me."

She grips the phone, counting the seconds. She tries to will Carrie not to hang up.

"I found your web site. You're a private detective?"

Ruth already knew that she would. "Yes, I am."

"I can't tell you anything about any of my clients. My business depends on discretion."

"I'm not going to ask you about your clients. I just want to see you." She thinks hard about how to gain her trust. The Regulator makes this difficult, as she has become unused to the emotive quality of judgments and impressions. She thinks the truth is too abrupt and strange to convince her. So she tries something else. "I'm interested in a new experience. I guess it's something I've always wanted to try and haven't."

"Are you working for the cops? I am stating now for the record that you're paying me only for companionship, and anything that happens beyond that is a decision between consenting adults."

"Look, the cops wouldn't use a woman to trap you. It's too suspicious."

The silence tells Ruth that Carrie is intrigued. "What time are you thinking of?"

"As soon as you're free. How about now?"

"It's not even noon yet. I don't start work until 6:00."

Ruth doesn't want to push too hard and scare her off. "Then I'd like to have you all night."

She laughs. "Why don't we start with two hours for a first date?"

"That will be fine."

"You saw my prices?"

"Yes. Of course."

"Take a picture of yourself holding your ID and text it to me first so I know you're for real. If that checks out, you can go to the corner of Victory and Beech in Back Bay at 6:00 and call me again. Put the cash in a plain envelope."

"I will."

"See you, my dear." She hangs up.

Ruth looks into the girl's eyes. Now that she knows what to look for, she thinks she can see the barest hint of a glint in her left eye.

She hands her the cash and watches her count it. She's very pretty, and so young. The ways she leans against the wall reminds her of Jess. The Regulator kicks in.

She's in a lace nightie, black stockings and garters. High-heeled fluffy bedroom slippers that seem more funny than erotic.

Carrie puts the money aside and smiles at her. "Do you want to take the lead or have me do it? I'm fine either way."

"I'd rather just talk for a bit first."

Carrie frowns. "I told you I can't talk about my clients."

"I know. But I want to show you something."

Carrie shrugs and leads her to the bedroom. It's a lot like Mona's room: king-sized bed, cream-colored sheets, a glass bowl of condoms, a clock discreetly on the nightstand. The mirror is mounted on the ceiling.

They sit down on the bed. Ruth takes out a file, and hands Carrie a stack of photographs.

"All of these girls have been killed in the last year. All of them have the same implants you do."

Carrie looks up, shocked. Her eyes blink twice, rapidly.

"I know what you have behind your eye. I know you think it makes you safer. Maybe you even think someday the information in there can be a second source of income, when you're too old to do this. But there's a man who wants to cut that out of you. He's been doing the same to the other girls."

She shows her the pictures of dead Mona, with the bloody, mutilated face.

Carrie drops the pictures. "Get out. I'm calling the police." She stands up and grabs her phone.

Ruth doesn't move. "You can. Ask to speak to Captain Scott Brennan. He knows who I am, and he'll confirm what I've told you. I think you're the next target."

She hesitates.

Ruth continues, "Or you can just look at these pictures. You know what to look for. They were all just like you."

Carrie sits down and examines the pictures. "Oh God. Oh God."

"I know you probably have a set of regulars. At your prices you don't need and won't get many new clients. But have you taken on anyone new lately?"

"Just you and one other. He's coming at 8:00."

Ruth's Regulator kicks in.

"Do you know what he looks like?"

"No. But I asked him to call me when he gets to the street corner, just like you, so I can get a look at him first before having him come up."

Ruth takes out her phone. "I need to call the police."

"No! You'll get me arrested. Please!"

Ruth thinks about this. She's only guessing that this man might be the killer. If she involves the police now and he turns out to be just a customer, Carrie's life will be ruined.

"Then I'll need to see him myself, in case he's the one."

"Shouldn't I just call it off?"

Ruth hears the fear in the girl's voice, and it reminds her of Jess, too, when she used to ask her to stay in her bedroom after watching a scary movie. She can feel the Regulator kicking into action again. She cannot let her emotions get in the way. "That would probably be safer for you, but we'd lose the chance to catch him if he *is* the one. Please, I need you to go through with it so I can get a close look at him. This may be our best chance of stopping him from hurting others."

Carrie bites her bottom lip. "All right. Where will you hide?"

Ruth wishes she had thought to bring her gun, but she hadn't wanted to spook Carrie and she didn't anticipate having to fight. She'll need to be close enough to stop the man if he turns out to be the killer, and yet not so close as to make it easy for him to discover her.

"I can't hide inside here at all. He'll look around before going into the bedroom with you." She walks into the living room, which faces the back of the building, away from the street, and lifts the window open. "I can hide out here, hanging from the ledge. If he turns out to be the killer, I have to wait till the last possible minute to come in to cut off his escape. If he's not the killer, I'll drop down and leave."

Carrie is clearly uncomfortable with this plan, but she nods, trying to be brave.

"Act as normal as you can. Don't make him think something is wrong."

Carrie's phone rings. She swallows and clicks the phone on. She walks over to the bedroom window. Ruth follows.

"This is Carrie."

Ruth looks out the window. The man standing at the corner appears to be the right height, but that's not enough to be sure. She has to catch him and interrogate him.

"I'm in the four-story building about a hundred feet behind you. Come up to apartment 303. I'm so glad you came, dear. We'll have a great time, I promise." She hangs up.

The man starts walking this way. Ruth thinks there's a limp to his walk, but again, she can't be sure.

"Is it him?" Carrie asks.

"I don't know. We have to let him in and see."

Ruth can feel the Regulator humming. She knows that the idea of using Carrie as bait frightens her, is repugnant even. But it's the logical thing to do. She'll never get a chance like this again. She has to trust that she can protect the girl.

"I'm going outside the window. You're doing great. Just keep him talking and do what he wants. Get him relaxed and focused on you. I'll come in before he can hurt you. I promise."

Carrie smiles. "I'm good at acting."

Ruth goes to the living room window and deftly climbs out. She lets her body down, hanging onto the window ledge with her fingers so that she's invisible from inside the apartment. "Okay, close the window. Leave just a slit open so I can hear what happens inside."

"How long can you hang like this?"

"Long enough."

Carrie closes the window. Ruth is glad for the artificial tendons and tensors in her shoulders and arms and the reinforced fingers, holding her up. The idea had been to make her more effective in close combat, but they're coming in handy now, too.

She counts off the seconds. The man should be at the building . . . he should now be coming up the stairs . . . he should now be at the door.

She hears the door to the apartment open.

"You're even prettier than your pictures." The voice is rich, deep, satisfied.

"Thank you."

She hears more conversation, the exchange of money. Then the sound of more walking.

They're heading towards the bedroom. She can hear the man stopping to look into the other rooms. She almost can feel his gaze pass over the top of her head, out the window.

Ruth pulls herself up slowly, quietly, and looks in. She sees the man disappear into the hallway. There's a distinct limp.

She waits a few more seconds so that the man cannot rush back past her before she can reach the hallway to block it, and then she takes a deep breath and wills the Regulator to pump her blood full of adrenaline. The world seems to grow brighter and time slows down as she flexes her arms and pulls herself onto the window ledge.

She squats down and pulls the window up in one swift motion. She knows that the grinding noise will alert the man, and she has only a few seconds to get to him. She ducks, rolls through the open window onto the floor inside. Then she continues to roll until her feet are under her and activates the pistons in her legs to leap towards the hallway.

She lands and rolls again to not give him a clear target, and jumps again from her crouch into the bedroom.

The man shoots and the bullet strikes her left shoulder. She tackles him as her arms, held in front of her, slam into his midsection. He falls and the gun clatters away.

Now the pain from the bullet hits. She wills the Regulator to pump up the adrenaline and the endorphins to numb the pain. She pants and concentrates on the fight for her life.

He tries to flip her over with his superior mass, to pin her down, but she clamps her hands around his neck and squeezes hard. Men have always underestimated her at the beginning of a fight, and she has to take advantage of it. She knows that her grip feels like iron clamps around him, with all the implanted energy cells in her arms and hands activated and on full power. He winces, grabs her hands to try to pry them off. After a few seconds, realizing the futility of it, he ceases to struggle.

He's trying to talk but can't get any air into his lungs. Ruth lets up a little, and he chokes out, "You got me."

Ruth increases the pressure again, choking off his supply of air. She turns to Carrie, who's at the foot of the bed, frozen. "Call the police. Now."

She complies. As she continues to hold the phone against her ear as the 911 dispatcher has instructed her to do, she tells Ruth, "They're on their way."

The man goes limp with his eyes closed. Ruth lets go of his neck. She doesn't want to kill him, so she clamps her hands around his wrists while she sits on his legs, holding him still on the floor.

He revives and starts to moan. "You're breaking my fucking arms!"

Ruth lets up the pressure a bit to conserve her power. The man's nose is bleeding from the fall against the floor when she tackled him. He inhales loudly, swallows, and says, "I'm going to drown if you don't let me sit up."

Ruth considers this. She lets up the pressure further and pulls him into a sitting position.

She can feel the energy cells in her arms depleting. She won't have the physical upper hand much longer if she has to keep on restraining him this way.

She calls out to Carrie. "Come over here and tie his hands together."

Carrie puts down the phone done and comes over gingerly. "What do I use?"

"Don't you have any rope? You know, for your clients?"

"I don't do that kind of thing."

Ruth thinks. "You can use stockings."

As Carrie ties the man's hands and feet together in front of him, he coughs. Some of the blood has gone down the wrong pipe. Ruth is unmoved and doesn't ease up on the pressure, and he winces. "Goddamn it. You're one psycho robo bitch."

Ruth ignores him. The stockings are too stretchy and won't hold him for long. But it should last long enough for her to get the gun and point it at him.

Carrie retreats to the other side of the room. Ruth lets the man go and backs away from him towards the gun on the floor a few yards away, keeping her eyes on him. If he makes any sudden movements, she'll be back on him in a flash.

He stays limp and unmoving as she steps backwards. She begins to relax. The Regulator is trying to calm her down now, to filter the adrenalin out of her system.

When she's about half way to the gun, the man suddenly reaches into his jacket with his hands, still tied together. Ruth hesitates for only a second before pushing out with her legs to jump backwards to the gun.

As she lands, the man locates something inside his jacket, and suddenly Ruth feels her legs and arms go limp and she falls to the ground, stunned.

Carrie is screaming. "My eye! Oh God I can't see out of my left eye!"

Ruth can't seem to feel her legs at all, and her arms feel like rubber. Worst of all, she's panicking. It seems she's never been this scared or in this much pain. She tries to feel the presence of the Regulator and there's nothing, just emptiness. She can smell the sweet, sickly smell of burnt electronics in the air. The clock on the nightstand is dark.

She's the one who had underestimated him. Despair floods through her and there's nothing to hold it back.

Ruth can hear the man stagger up off the floor. She wills herself to turn over, to move, to reach for the gun. She crawls. One foot, another foot. She seems to be moving through molasses because she's so weak. She can feel every one of her forty-nine years. She feels every sharp stab of pain in her shoulder.

She reaches the gun, grabs it, and sits up against the wall, pointing it back into the center of the room.

The man has gotten out of Carrie's ineffective knots. He's now holding Carrie, blind in one eye, shielding his body with hers. He holds a scalpel against her throat. He's already broken the skin and a thin stream of blood flows down her neck.

He backs towards the bedroom door, dragging Carrie with him. Ruth knows that if he gets to the bedroom door and disappears around the corner, she'll never be able to catch him. Her legs are simply useless.

Carrie sees Ruth's gun and screams. "I don't want to die! Oh God. Oh God."

"I'll let her go once I'm safe," he says, keeping his head hidden behind hers.

Ruth's hands are shaking as she holds the gun. Through the waves of nausea and the pounding of her pulse in her ears, she struggles to think through what will happen next. The police are on their way and will probably be here in five minutes. Isn't it likely that he'll let her go as soon as possible to give himself some extra time to escape?

The man backs up another two steps; Carrie is no longer kicking or struggling, but trying to find purchase on the smooth floor in her stockinged feet, trying to cooperate with him. But she can't stop crying.

Mom, don't shoot! Please don't shoot!

Or is it more likely that once the man has left the room, he will slit Carrie's throat and cut out her implant? He knows there's a recording of him inside, and he can't afford to leave that behind.

Ruth's hands are shaking too much. She wants to curse at herself. She cannot get a clear shot at the man with Carrie in front of him. She cannot.

Ruth wants to evaluate the chances rationally, to make a decision, but regret and grief and rage, hidden and held down by the Regulator until they could be endured, rise now all the sharper, kept fresh by the effort at forgetting. The universe has shrunken down to the wavering spot at the end of the barrel of the gun: a young woman, a killer, and time slipping irrevocably away.

She has nothing to turn to, to trust, to lean on, but herself, her angry, frightened, trembling self. She is naked and alone, as she has always known she is, as we all are.

The man is almost at the door. Carrie's cries are now incoherent sobs.

It has always been the regular state of things. There is no clarity, no relief. At the end of all rationality there is simply the need to decide and the faith to live through, to endure.

Ruth's first shot slams into Carrie's thigh. The bullet plunges through skin, muscle, and fat, and exits out the back, shattering the man's knee.

The man screams and drops the scalpel. Carrie falls, a spray of blood blossoming from her wounded leg.

Ruth's second shot catches the man in the chest. He collapses to the floor.

Mom, mom!

She drops the gun and crawls over to Carrie, cradling her and tending to her wound. She's crying, but she'll be fine.

A deep pain floods through her like forgiveness, like hard rain after a long drought. She does not know if she will be granted relief, but she experiences this moment fully, and she's thankful.

"It's okay," she says, stroking Carrie as she lies in her lap. "It's okay."

*[**Author's Note:** the EchoSense technology described in this story is a loose and liberal extrapolation of the principles behind the technology described in Qifan Pu et. al., "Whole-Home Gesture Recognition Using Wireless Signals," The 19th Annual International Conference on Mobile Computing and Networking (Mobicom'13) (available at http://wisee.cs.washington.edu/wisee_paper.pdf). There is no intent to suggest that the technology described in the paper resembles the fictional one portrayed here.]*

TENDER

RACHEL SWIRSKY

The first time my love realized I might kill myself, he remade my arteries in steel.

He waited until I was asleep and then stole me down into the secret laboratory he'd built beneath our house. I pretended to be sleeping as he shifted lights and lenses until the room lit with eerie blue. Using tools of his own invention, he anaesthetized me, incised my skin, and injected me with miniature robots that were programmed to convert my arterial walls into materials both compatible with human life and impossible to sever.

It was not really steel, but I imagine it as steel. I imagine that, inside, I am polished and industrial.

Over the course of the night, he remade the tributaries in my wrists, my throat, my thighs. He made them strong enough to repel any razor. He forbade them from crying red rivers. He banished the vision of a bathtub with water spreading pink. He made my life impossible to spill.

I have recurring dreams of tender things dying in the snow. They are pink and curled and fetal, the kind of things that would be at home in my husband's laboratory, floating in jars of formaldehyde, or suspended among bubbles in gestational tanks of nutritional gel.

Their skin has no toughness. It is wet and slick, almost amphibian, but so delicate that it bruises from exposure to the air. Their unformed bodies shudder helplessly in the cold, vestigial tails tucked next to ink-blot eyes. On their proto-arms, finger-like protrusions grasp for warmth.

They are possibilities, yearning, unfurling from nothingness into unrealized potential.

In my dreams, I am separated from them by a window too thick to break. I don't know who has abandoned them, helpless, in the snow. Frost begins to scale their skins. Their mouths shape inaudible whimpers. I can't get outside. I can't get to them. I can't get outside before they die.

My love replaced the bones of my skull with interlocking adamantine scales. I cannot point a gun at my ear and shoot.

So that I cannot swallow a barrel, he placed sensors in my mouth, designed to detect the presence of firearms. Upon sensing one, they engage emergency measures, including alarms, force fields, and a portcullis that creaks down to block my throat.

The sensor's light blinks ceaselessly, a green wash that penetrates my closed lips. It haunts me in the night, bathing every other second in spectral glow.

One psychiatrist's theory:

To commit suicide, you must feel hopeless.

To commit suicide, you must believe you are a burden on those you love.

To commit suicide, you must be accustomed to physical risk.

One, two, three factors accounted for. But a fourth forgotten: to commit suicide, you must be penetrable.

My love says he needs me, but he knows that I believe he's deluded.

He would be better off with another wife. Perhaps a mad lady scientist with tangled red hair frizzing out of her bun and anime-huge eyes behind magnifying glasses. Perhaps a robot, deftly crafted, possessing the wisdom of the subtle alloys embedded in her artificial consciousness. Perhaps a super-human mutant, discovered injured and amnesiac in an alley, and then carried back to his lab where he could cradle her back to health. He could be the professor who enables her heroic adventures, outfitting her with his inventions, and sewing flame-retardant spandex uniforms for her in his spare time.

No poison: my vital organs are no longer flesh.

No car crash: my spinal cord is enhanced by a network of nanobots, intelligent and constantly reconfiguring, ensuring that every sensation flashes, every muscle twitches.

No suffocation: my skin possesses its own breath now. It inhales; it exhales; it maintains itself flush and pink.

"Please," he says, "Please," and does not have to say more.

He is crying very quietly. A few tears. A few gulping breaths.

Apart from the intermittent flash of the sensors in my mouth, our room is black and silent. I have been lying in bed for six days now. In the morning, he brings me broth and I eat enough to quiet him. In the afternoons, he carries up the robotic dog, and it energetically coils and uncoils its metal tail-spring until I muster the strength to move my hand and pat its head.

In the night, we lie beside each other, our skin rough against the sheets. He reaches for my hand where it lies on my pillow. His touch is so much. I can't explain how *much* it is. Sensation fills my whole world, and I have so little world left to fill. My body has been strengthened by nanobots and steel, but my mind continues to narrow, becoming less and less. Something as consuming as his touch is so overwhelming that it is excruciating. It's like all the warmth of the sun hitting my skin at once.

"Please," he repeats in a murmur.

Next morning, when I wake, he has programmed the nanobots to construct a transparent wall behind my eyes. No bullet, no pencil, no sword can penetrate them to find my brain.

There are so many ways to die.

The accidental: A slick of water, a slip, and the head cracks on the bathtub, shower, kitchen sink. Hands pull the wrong pair of medicines from the cabinet. Feet rest on the arm of the couch, near the blanket thrown over the radiator. The throat contracts around a piece of orange peel, inhaled instead of swallowed, on a day when one is home alone.

The unusual: exploding fireworks, attacking dogs, plummeting asteroids, crashing tsunamis, flashing lightning, striking snakes, whirling tornados, splintering earthquakes, engulfing floods, dazzling electrocution, grinning arson.

The science fictional: robots, and aliens, and zombies, and Frankenstein's monster, and experiments gone wrong, and spontaneous nuclear reactions, and miniature black holes, and tenth dimensional beings of malevolent light.

The routine: One car smashing into another. One damaged cell rapaciously dividing. One blockage of blood in the brain. One heart, seizing.

Self-immolation: no longer an option. After his last adjustments, my breathing skin can adapt to any temperature. It resists ice; it resists fire. I could walk into lava. I could dive into space.

"Please," he still murmurs at night, "Please."

His hand withdraws, but the heat-memory of it remains. It sparks under my skin like a new-forming sunburn, radiation caught and kept in the flesh.

Instead of hardening the shell of my body again, he appeals to my mind. Since I won't believe that he needs me, he brings me a pair of genetically enhanced, baby white mice with brains so huge their skulls bulge. They scurry around, solving mazes by means of derived algorithms that they've scratched into their bedding, using mathematical notation of their own invention.

I feed them carrots, celery, lettuce, and pellets of radioactive, brain-enhancing super-food. They sit on my hand as they eat, grasping the morsels in their paws and nibbling at them with their prominent front teeth. They stare at me with ink-black eyes and make pleased, musical squealing sounds. They proffer their bellies for me to tickle, and they giggle in a register too high-pitched for me to hear. They bring me gifts of hoarded lettuce leaves inscribed with formulae I can't decipher.

They are all energy and curiosity and brilliance. I watch them discover new ways to balance with their tails at the same time as they deduce the flaws in general relativity. I savor their love of life, their delight in discovering themselves as creatures who possess worlds and wisdom and bodies to explore. I feel their happiness heartbeat-hot in my stomach. It fills my remaining being with painful, wistful joy. Life is filling them. Life is diminishing me. I am tapering out of existence.

When I dream that night of the fetal creatures in the snow, I see that they have subtly shifted. Or perhaps I am only recognizing traits they have possessed all along. I see the features of my baby mice haunting their undeveloped bodies. Their ink-blot eyes are wondering. Their vestigial tails twitch querulously.

I pound my flattened palm against the dream-glass that separates us. I scream and scream for it to smash.

I can't. I can't. I can't get to them. The unformed things, the helpless things, the ones that still want to survive. They shiver and turn blue. Ice crusts their eyes closed. I pound the glass. I can't break it. I can't. I can't. I can't break through.

While I dreamt, he encased me in armor as sensitive as skin. Invisible to the eye. Intangible to the fingers. Impervious as immortality.

I will close you in, he didn't whisper as he stood over me, his breath hot and helpless on my scalp. *You are an eggshell and I will wrap you in cotton and rubber bands until no fall can shatter you. I won't wait until afterward to call all the king's horses and all the king's men. I'll bring them here before anything goes wrong. I'll set them to patrol the wall while they can still do some good. I'll protect you from everything, including yourself.*

My brain: wrinkled, pink, four-lobed, textured like soft tofu.

Steel arteries, adamantine scales, sensors, portcullises, nanobots, armor. So much fuss to protect three pounds of meat.

My mice have learned to write in English.

They crawl up and down the walls of their cage, pleading, until I give them scraps of paper and a miniature pen.

WE'RE WORRIED ABOUT YOU, they write.

On a white board, I write back, *It's not your job to worry about me.* I pause before adding, *You're mice.*

WHAT IS IT THAT YOU WANT? they write.

I hesitate before responding.

Nothing.

They consult silently, evaluating each other's perplexed expressions. They brux their teeth, chit-chitter-scrape.

Finally, they write, EVERYONE WANTS SOMETHING.

I do want something, I reply. *I already told you.*

But it's not really fair to expect them to be clever therapists. They may be geniuses, but they're still only baby mice.

In another science fiction story, my love would replace more and more of my body with armature until there was no human part of me remaining. With all my body gone, he would identify the fault as being in my mind. *That's where the broken fuses spit their dreadful sparks,* he'd conclude, and then he'd change that part of me, too. He would smooth every complicated, ambiguous wrinkle from the meat and electricity of my brain: the inconsistent neutransmitters; the knotted traumas; the ice-thin sense of self-preservation. By the time he was done, I would no longer bear any resemblance to myself. I'd become a wretched Stepford revenant lurching in a mechanical shell. And still, he would love me.

In another science fiction story, as he and I struggled with the push-pull of our desires, an unprecedented case would crack the courts, establishing an inalienable right to die. Bureaucracies would instantly rise to regulate the processes of filing Intent to Die forms, attending mandatory therapy sessions, and requesting financial aid for euthanasia ceremonies. I would file, attend, and request. He would beg me not to do so until, finally, driven mad, he would build a doomsday machine in our basement and use it to take over the world. As the all-powerful ruler of mankind, he would crush rebellion in an iron fist. In his palace, he would imprison me, living but immobile, in a glass tank shaped like a coffin.

In the same science fiction story, written on a different day, he would build the doomsday machine, but at the last minute, he would realize the folly of deploying it. Instead, he would continue to plead as I turned away, until finally the doctors would pull his outstretched hand away from mine as they slid the needle into my skin.

In yet a third science fiction story, a meteor would crash to the earth, and upon it, there would be a sentient alien symbiont, and for it to survive, it would require a human host. Testing would determine that I was the only viable candidate. They would cut me open and stitch the alien into my side, and it would tell me stories about the depths of space, and the strange whales that fly between stars, and the sun-and-dust thoughts of nebulae. It would tell me of its adventures on the surfaces of alien monuments so large that they have their own atmospheres and have evolved sentient populations who think it's natural for the world to be shaped like the face of a giant. The alien would help my wounded soul rediscover how to accept my love's touch, and the three of us would live together, different from what we were, but unbreakably unified.

◆ ◆ ◆

In this science fiction story, I am a fetus; I am a mouse; I am an eggshell; I am a held breath; I am a snowdrift; I am a cyborg; I am a woman whose skin cannot bear the sensation of love.

"Please," he whispers in his sleep, "Please."

Lying awake, I see the fetal creatures in the snow, not in a dream this time, but as a waking vision. My palm pushes futilely on the window between us. The fetal things are fragility I cannot rescue. They are love I cannot reach. They are myself, slowly freezing.

I, too, am fragmented. I am the creatures dying, and I am the woman pounding at the window. I am the glass between us. I am the inability to shatter.

I watch him lying next to me, his breath even with sleep. In an hour or so, while it is still deep dark, he will wake. He will take me down to the laboratory. In the morning, I will wake inhabited by an army of genetically engineered viruses, instructed to wrap each of my cells in a protective coat, a cloud-like embrace of softness and safety.

Do you know why I wear your armor? I don't ask him.

When you take me to the lab, I'm not always asleep. Sometimes, I'm aware. Sometimes, I feel the numbness of your anesthetic spreading across my skin. Sometimes, I watch your face.

The flash of my sensors makes him seem alien.

In the laboratory, I don't continue, *your hands, laboring over me, are like the hands of an unknown creator god, working his clay.*

He stirs. The mice rustle in their cage. They draw schematics for spaceships that can escape this earth.

I don't say, *I wear your armor because I love you.*

I don't say, *I wear your armor because I am the fetal thing in the snow.*

I don't say, *I wear your armor because you will not make me into a Stepford revenant, and you will not build a doomsday machine, and there are no alien symbionts to weave me stories about metal rain on distant planets. I wear your armor because my skin is hot with the sun's memory. Because nanobot armies are love poems written in circuitry.*

I don't say, *I wear your armor because, in my dreams, I'm still pounding on the glass.*

TONGTONG'S SUMMER
XIA JIA, TRANSLATED BY KEN LIU

Mom said to Tongtong, "In a couple of days, Grandpa is moving in with us."

After Grandma died, Grandpa lived by himself. Mom told Tongtong that because Grandpa had been working for the revolution all his life, he just couldn't be idle. Even though he was in his eighties, he still insisted on going to the clinic every day to see patients. A few days earlier, because it was raining, he had slipped on the way back from the clinic and hurt his leg.

Luckily, he had been rushed to the hospital, where they put a plaster cast on him. With a few more days of rest and recovery, he'd be ready to be discharged.

Emphasizing her words, Mom said, "Tongtong, your grandfather is old, and he's not always in a good mood. You're old enough to be considerate. Try not to add to his unhappiness, all right?"

Tongtong nodded, thinking, *But haven't I always been considerate?*

Grandpa's wheelchair was like a miniature electric car, with a tiny joystick by the armrest. Grandpa just had to give it a light push, and the wheelchair would glide smoothly in that direction. Tongtong thought it tremendous fun.

Ever since she could remember, Tongtong had been a bit afraid of Grandpa. He had a square face with long, white, bushy eyebrows that stuck out like stiff pine needles. She had never seen anyone with eyebrows that long.

She also had some trouble understanding him. Grandpa spoke Mandarin with a heavy accent from his native topolect. During dinner, when Mom explained to Grandpa that they needed to hire a caretaker for him, Grandpa kept on shaking his head emphatically and repeating: "Don't worry, eh!" Now Tongtong did understand *that* bit.

Back when Grandma had been ill, they had also hired a caretaker for her. The caretaker had been a lady from the countryside. She was short and small, but really strong. All by herself, she could lift Grandma—who had put on some weight—out of the bed, bathe her, put her on the toilet, and change her clothes. Tongtong had seen the caretaker lady accomplish these feats of strength with her own eyes. Later, after Grandma died, the lady didn't come any more.

After dinner, Tongtong turned on the video wall to play some games. *The world in the game is so different from the world around me,* she thought. In the

205

game, a person just died. They didn't get sick, and they didn't sit in a wheelchair. Behind her, Mom and Grandpa continued to argue about the caretaker.

Dad walked over and said, "Tongtong, shut that off now, please. You've been playing too much. It'll ruin your eyes."

Imitating Grandpa, Tongtong shook her head and said, "Don't worry, eh!"

Mom and Dad both burst out laughing, but Grandpa didn't laugh at all. He sat stone-faced, with not even a hint of smile.

A few days later, Dad came home with a stupid-looking robot. The robot had a round head, long arms, and two white hands. Instead of feet it had a pair of wheels so that it could move forward and backward and spin around.

Dad pushed something in the back of the robot's head. The blank, smooth, egg-like orb blinked three times with a bluish light, and a young man's face appeared on the surface. The resolution was so good that it looked just like a real person.

"Wow," Tongtong said. "You are a robot?"

The face smiled. "Hello there! Ah Fu is my name."

"Can I touch you?"

"Sure!"

Tongtong put her hand against the smooth face, and then she felt the robot's arms and hands. Ah Fu's body was covered by a layer of soft silicone, which felt as warm as real skin.

Dad told Tongtong that Ah Fu was made by Guokr Technologies, Inc., and it was a prototype. Its biggest advantage was that it was as smart as a person: it knew how to peel an apple, how to pour a cup of tea, even how to cook, wash the dishes, embroider, write, play the piano . . . Anyway, having Ah Fu around meant that Grandpa would be given good care.

Grandpa sat there, still stone-faced, still saying nothing.

After lunch, Grandpa sat on the balcony to read the newspaper. He dozed off after a while. Ah Fu came over noiselessly, picked up Grandpa with his strong arms, carried him into the bedroom, set him down gently in bed, covered him with a blanket, pulled the curtains shut, and came out and shut the door, still not making any noise.

Tongtong followed Ah Fu and watched everything.

Ah Fu gave Tongtong's head a light pat. "Why don't you take a nap, too?"

Tongtong tilted her head and asked, "Are you really a robot?"

Ah Fu smiled. "Oh, you don't think so?"

Tongtong gazed at Ah Fu carefully. Then she said, very seriously, "I'm sure you are not."

"Why?"

"A robot wouldn't smile like that."

"You've never seen a smiling robot?"

"When a robot smiles, it looks scary. But your smile isn't scary. So you're definitely not a robot."

Ah Fu laughed. "Do you want to see what I really look like?"

Tongtong nodded. But her heart was pounding.

Ah Fu moved over by the video wall. From on top of his head, a beam of light shot out and projected a picture onto the wall. In the picture, Tongtong saw a man sitting in a messy room.

The man in the picture waved at Tongtong. Simultaneously, Ah Fu also waved in the exact same way. Tongtong examined the man in the picture: he wore a thin, grey, long-sleeved bodysuit, and a pair of grey gloves. The gloves were covered by many tiny lights. He also wore a set of huge goggles. The face behind the goggles was pale and thin, and looked just like Ah Fu's face.

Tongtong was stunned. "Oh, so you're the real Ah Fu!"

The man in the picture awkwardly scratched his head, and said, a little embarrassed, "Ah Fu is just the name we gave the robot. My real name is Wang. Why don't you call me Uncle Wang, since I'm a bit older?"

Uncle Wang told Tongtong that he was a fourth-year university student doing an internship at Guokr Technologies' R&D department. His group developed Ah Fu.

He explained that the aging population brought about serious social problems: many elders could not live independently, but their children had no time to devote to their care. Nursing homes made them feel lonely and cut off from society, and there was a lot of demand for trained, professional caretakers.

But if a home had an Ah Fu, things were a lot better. When not in use, Ah Fu could just sit there, out of the way. When it was needed, a request could be given, and an operator would come online to help the elder. This saved the time and cost of having caretakers commute to homes, and increased the efficiency and quality of care.

The Ah Fu they were looking at was a first-generation prototype. There were only three thousand of them in the whole country, being tested by three thousand families.

Uncle Wang told Tongtong that his own grandmother had also been ill and had to go to the hospital for an extended stay, so he had some experience with elder care. That was why he volunteered to come to her home to take care of Grandpa. As luck would have it, he was from the same region of the country as Grandpa, and could understand his topolect. A regular robot probably wouldn't be able to.

Uncle Wang laced his explanation with many technical words, and Tongtong wasn't sure she understood everything. But she thought the idea of Ah Fu splendid, almost like a science fiction story.

"So, does Grandpa know who you really are?"

"Your mom and dad know, but Grandpa doesn't know yet. Let's not tell him, for now. We'll let him know in a few days, after he's more used to Ah Fu."

Tongtong solemnly promised, "Don't worry, eh!"

She and Uncle Wang laughed together.

Grandpa really couldn't just stay home and be idle. He insisted that Ah Fu take him out walking. But after just one walk, he complained that it was too hot outside, and refused to go anymore.

Ah Fu told Tongtong in secret that it was because Grandpa felt self-conscious, having someone push him around in a wheelchair. He thought everyone in the street stared at him.

But Tongtong thought, *Maybe they were all staring at Ah Fu.*

Since Grandpa couldn't go out, being cooped up at home made his mood worse. His expression grew more depressed, and from time to time he burst out in temper tantrums. There were a few times when he screamed and yelled at Mom and Dad, but neither said anything. They just stood there and quietly bore his shouting.

But one time, Tongtong went to the kitchen and caught Mom hiding behind the door, crying.

Grandpa was now nothing like the Grandpa she remembered. It would have been so much better if he hadn't slipped and got hurt. Tongtong hated staying at home. The tension made her feel like she was suffocating. Every morning, she ran out the door, and would stay out until it was time for dinner.

Dad came up with a solution. He brought back another gadget made by Guokr Technologies: a pair of glasses. He handed the glasses to Tongtong and told her to put them on and walk around the house. Whatever she saw and heard was shown on the video wall.

"Tongtong, would you like to act as Grandpa's eyes?"

Tongtong agreed. She was curious about anything new.

Summer was Tongtong's favorite season. She could wear a skirt, eat watermelon and popsicles, go swimming, find cicada shells in the grass, splash through rain puddles in sandals, chase rainbows after a thunderstorm, get a cold shower after running around and working up a sweat, drink iced sour plum soup, catch tadpoles in ponds, pick grapes and figs, sit out in the backyard in the evenings and gaze at stars, hunt for crickets after dark with a flashlight . . . In a word: everything was wonderful in summer.

Tongtong put on her new glasses and went to play outside. The glasses were heavy and kept on slipping off her nose. She was afraid of dropping it.

Since the beginning of summer vacation, she and more than a dozen friends, both boys and girls, had been playing together every day. At their age, play had infinite variety. Having exhausted old games, they would invent new ones. If they were tired or too hot, they would go by the river and jump in like a plate of dumplings going into the pot. The sun blazed overhead, but the water in the river was refreshing and cool. This was heaven!

Someone suggested that they climb trees. There was a lofty pagoda tree by the river shore, whose trunk was so tall and thick that it resembled a dragon rising into the blue sky.

But Tongtong heard Grandpa's urgent voice by her ear: "Don't climb that tree! Too dangerous!"

Huh, so the glasses also act as a phone. Joyfully, she shouted back, "Grandpa, don't worry, eh!" Tongtong excelled at climbing trees. Even her father said that in a previous life she must have been a monkey.

But Grandpa would not let her alone. He kept on buzzing in her ear, and she couldn't understand a thing he was saying. It was getting on her nerves, so she took off the glasses and dropped them in the grass at the foot of the tree. She took off her sandals and began to climb, rising into the sky like a cloud.

This tree was easy. The dense branches reached out to her like hands, pulling her up. She went higher and higher and soon left her companions behind. She was about to reach the very top. The breeze whistled through the leaves, and sunlight dappled through the canopy. The world was so quiet.

She paused to take a breath, but then she heard her father's voice coming from a distance: "Tongtong, get . . . down . . . here . . . "

She poked her head out to look down. A little ant-like figure appeared far below. It really was Dad.

On the way back home, Dad really let her have it.

"How could you have been so foolish?! You climbed all the way up there by yourself. Don't you understand the risk?"

She knew that Grandpa told on her. Who else knew what she was doing?

She was livid. *He can't climb trees any more, and now he won't let others climb trees, either? So lame! And it was so embarrassing to have Dad show up and yell like that.*

The next morning, she left home super early again. But this time, she didn't wear the glasses.

"Grandpa was just worried about you," said Ah Fu. "If you fell and broke your leg, wouldn't you have to sit in a wheelchair, just like him?"

Tongtong pouted and refused to speak.

Ah Fu told her that through the glasses left at the foot of the tree, Grandpa could see that Tongtong was really high up. He was so worried that he screamed himself hoarse, and almost tumbled from his wheelchair.

But Tongtong remained angry with Grandpa. What was there to worry about? She had climbed plenty of trees taller than that one, and she had never once been hurt.

Since the glasses weren't being put to use, Dad packed them up and sent them back to Guokr. Grandpa was once again stuck at home with nothing to do. He somehow found an old Chinese Chess set and demanded Ah Fu play with him.

Tongtong didn't know how to play, so she pulled up a stool and sat next to the board just to check it out. She enjoyed watching Ah Fu pick up the old wooden pieces, their colors faded from age, with its slender, pale white fingers; she enjoyed watching it tap its fingers lightly on the table as it considered its moves. The robot's hand was so pretty, almost like it was carved out of ivory.

But after a few games, even she could tell that Ah Fu posed no challenge to Grandpa at all. A few moves later, Grandpa once again captured one of Ah Fu's pieces with a loud snap on the board.

"Oh, you suck at this," Grandpa muttered.

To be helpful, Tongtong also said, "You suck!"

"A real robot would have played better," Grandpa added. He had already found out the truth about Ah Fu and its operator.

Grandpa kept on winning, and after a few games, his mood improved. Not only did his face glow, but he was also moving his head about and humming folk tunes. Tongtong also felt happy, and her earlier anger at Grandpa dissipated.

Only Ah Fu wasn't so happy. "I think I need to find you a more challenging opponent," he said.

When Tongtong returned home, she almost jumped out of her skin. Grandpa had turned into a monster!

He was now dressed in a thin, grey, long-sleeved bodysuit, and a pair of grey gloves. Many tiny lights shone all over the gloves. He wore a set of huge goggles over his face, and he waved his hands about and gestured in the air.

On the video wall in front of him appeared another man, but not Uncle Wang. This man was as old as Grandpa, with a full head of silver-white hair. He wasn't wearing any goggles. In front of him was a Chinese Chess board.

"Tongtong, come say hi," said Grandpa. "This is Grandpa Zhao."

Grandpa Zhao was Grandpa's friend from back when they were in the army together. He had just had a heart stent put in. Like Grandpa, he was bored, and his family also got their own Ah Fu. He was also a Chinese Chess enthusiast, and complained about the skill level of his Ah Fu all day.

Uncle Wang had the inspiration of mailing telepresence equipment to Grandpa and then teaching him how to use it. And within a few days, Grandpa was proficient enough to be able to remotely control Grandpa Zhao's Ah Fu to play chess with him.

Not only could they play chess, but the two old men also got to chat with each other in their own native topolect. Grandpa became so joyous and excited that he seemed to Tongtong like a little kid.

"Watch this," said Grandpa.

He waved his hands in the air gently, and through the video wall, Grandpa Zhao's Ah Fu picked up the wooden chessboard, steady as you please, dexterously spun it around in the air, and set it back down without disturbing a piece.

Tongtong watched Grandpa's hands without blinking. *Are these the same unsteady, jerky hands that always made it hard for Grandpa to do anything?* It was even more amazing than magic.

"Can I try?" she asked.

Grandpa took off the gloves and helped Tongtong put them on. The gloves were stretchy, and weren't too loose on Tongtong's small hands. Tongtong tried to wiggle her fingers, and the Ah Fu in the video wall wiggled its fingers, too. The gloves provided internal resistance that steadied and smoothed out Tongtong's movements, and thus also the movements of Ah Fu.

Grandpa said, "Come, try shaking hands with Grandpa Zhao."

In the video, a smiling Grandpa Zhao extended his hand. Tongtong carefully reached out and shook hands. She could feel the subtle, immediate pressure changes within the glove, as if she were really shaking a person's hand—it even felt warm! *This is fantastic!*

Using the gloves, she directed Ah Fu to touch the chessboard, the pieces, and the steaming cup of tea next to them. Her fingertips felt the sudden heat from the cup. Startled, her fingers let go, and the cup fell to the ground and broke. The chessboard was flipped over, and chess pieces rolled all over the place.

"Aiya! Careful, Tongtong!"

"No worries! No worries!" Grandpa Zhao tried to get up to retrieve the broom and dustpan, but Grandpa told him to remain seated. "Careful about your hands!" Grandpa said. "I'll take care of it." He put on the gloves and directed Grandpa Zhao's Ah Fu to pick up the chess pieces one by one, and then swept the floor clean.

Grandpa wasn't mad at Tongtong, and didn't threaten to tell Dad about the accident she caused.

"She's just a kid, a bit impatient," he said to Grandpa Zhao. The two old men laughed.

Tongtong felt both relieved and a bit misunderstood.

Once again, Mom and Dad were arguing with Grandpa.

The argument went a bit differently from before. Grandpa was once again repeating over and over, "Don't worry, eh!" But Mom's tone grew more and more severe.

The actual point of the argument grew more confusing to Tongtong the more she listened. All she could make out was that it had something to do with Grandpa Zhao's heart stent.

In the end, Mom said, "What do you mean? 'Don't worry'? What if another accident happens? Would you please stop causing more trouble?"

Grandpa got so mad that he shut himself in his room and refused to come out, even for dinner.

Mom and Dad called Uncle Wang on the videophone. Finally, Tongtong figured out what happened.

Grandpa Zhao was playing chess with Grandpa, but the game got him so excited that his heart gave out—apparently, the stent wasn't put in perfectly. There had been no one else home at the time. Grandpa was the one who operated Ah Fu to give CPR to Grandpa Zhao, and also called an ambulance.

The emergency response team arrived in time and saved Grandpa Zhao's life.

What no one could have predicted was that Grandpa suggested that he go to the hospital to care for Grandpa Zhao—no, he didn't mean he'd go personally, but that they send Ah Fu over, and he'd operate Ah Fu from home.

But Grandpa himself needed a caretaker too. Who was supposed to care for the caretaker?

Further, Grandpa came up with the idea that when Grandpa Zhao recovered, he'd teach Grandpa Zhao how to operate the telepresence equipment. The two old men would be able to care for each other, and they would have no need of other caretakers.

Grandpa Zhao thought this was a great idea. But both families thought the plan absurd. Even Uncle Wang had to think about it for a while and then said, "Um . . . I have to report this situation to my supervisors."

Tongtong thought hard about this. Playing chess through Ah Fu was simple to understand. But caring for each other through Ah Fu? The more she thought about it, the more complicated it seemed. She was sympathetic to Uncle Wang's confusion.

Sigh, Grandpa is just like a little kid. He wouldn't listen to Mom and Dad at all.

Grandpa now stayed in his room all the time. At first, Tongtong thought he was still mad at her parents. But then, she found that the situation had changed completely.

Grandpa got really busy. Once again, he started seeing patients. No, he didn't go to the clinic; instead, using his telepresence kit, he was operating Ah Fus throughout the country and showing up in other elders' homes. He would listen to their complaints, feel their pulse, examine them, and write out prescriptions. He also wanted to give acupuncture treatments through Ah Fus, and to practice this skill, he operated his own Ah Fu to stick needles in himself!

Uncle Wang told Tongtong that Grandpa's innovation could transform the entire medical system. In the future, maybe patients no longer needed to go to the hospital and waste hours in waiting rooms. Doctors could just come to your home through an Ah Fu installed in each neighborhood.

Uncle Wang said that Guokr's R&D department had formed a dedicated task force to develop a specialized, improved model of Ah Fu for such medical telepresence applications, and they invited Grandpa onboard as a consultant. So Grandpa got even busier.

Since Grandpa's legs were not yet fully recovered, Uncle Wang was still caring for him. But they were working on developing a web-based system that would allow anyone with some idle time and interest in helping others to register to volunteer. Then the volunteers would be able to sign on to Ah Fus in homes across the country to take care of elders, children, patients, pets, and to help in other ways.

If the plan succeeded, it would be a step to bring about the kind of golden age envisioned by Confucius millennia ago: "And then men would care for all elders as if they were their own parents, love all children as if they were their own children. The aged would grow old and die in security; the youthful would have opportunities to contribute and prosper; and children would grow up under the guidance and protection of all. Widows, orphans, the disabled, the diseased—everyone would be cared for and loved."

Of course, such a plan had its risks: privacy and security, misuse of telepresence by criminals, malfunctions and accidents, just for starters. But since technological change was already here, it was best to face the consequences and guide them to desirable ends.

There were also developments that no one had anticipated.

Uncle Wang showed Tongtong lots of web videos: Ah Fus were shown doing all kinds of interesting things: cooking, taking care of children, fixing the plumbing and electric systems around the house, gardening, driving, playing tennis, even teaching children the arts of *go* and calligraphy and seal carving and *erhu* playing . . .

All of these Ah Fus were operated by elders who needed caretakers themselves, too. Some of them could no longer move about easily, but still had sharp eyes and ears and minds; some could no longer remember things easily, but they could still replicate the skills they had perfected in their youth; and most of them really had few physical problems, but were depressed and lonely. But now, with Ah Fu, everyone was out and about, *doing* things.

No one had imagined that Ah Fu could be put to all these uses. No one had thought that men and women in their seventies and eighties could still be so creative and imaginative.

Tongtong was especially impressed by a traditional folk music orchestra made up of more than a dozen Ah Fus. They congregated around a pond in a park and played enthusiastically and loudly. According to Uncle Wang, this orchestra had become famous on the web. The operators behind the Ah Fus were men and women who had lost their eyesight, and so they called themselves "The Old Blinds."

"Tongtong," Uncle Wang said, "your grandfather has brought about a revolution."

Tongtong remembered that Mom had often mentioned that Grandpa was an old revolutionary. "He's been working for the revolution all his life; it's time for him to take a break." But wasn't Grandpa a doctor? When did he participate in a "revolution"? And just what kind of work was "working for the revolution" anyway? And why did he have to do it all his life?

Tongtong couldn't figure it out, but she thought "revolution" was a splendid thing. Grandpa now once again seemed like the Grandpa she had known.

Every day, Grandpa was full of energy and spirit. Whenever he had a few moments to himself, he preferred to sing a few lines of traditional folk opera:

Outside the camp, they've fired off the thundering cannon thrice,
And out of Tianbo House walks the woman who will protect her homeland.
The golden helmet sits securely over her silver-white hair,
The old iron-scaled war robe once again hangs on her shoulders.
Look at her battle banner, displaying proudly her name:
Mu Guiying, at fifty-three, you are going to war again!

Tongtong laughed. "But Grandpa, you're eighty-three!"

Grandpa chuckled. He stood and posed as if he were an ancient general holding a sword as he sat on his warhorse. His face glowed red with joy.

In another few days, Grandpa would be eighty-four.

Tongtong played by herself at home.

There were dishes of cooked food in the fridge. In the evening, Tongtong took them out, heated them up, and ate by herself. The evening air was heavy and humid, and the cicadas cried without cease.

The weather report said there would be thunderstorms.

A blue light flashed three times in a corner of the room. A figure moved out of the corner noiselessly: Ah Fu.

"Mom and Dad took Grandpa to the hospital. They haven't returned yet."

Ah Fu nodded. "Your mother sent me to remind you: don't forget to close the windows before it rains."

Together, the robot and the girl closed all the windows in the house. When the thunderstorm arrived, the raindrops struck against the windowpanes like drumbeats. The dark clouds were torn into pieces by the white and purple flashes of lightning, and then a bone-rattling thunder rolled overhead, making Tongtong's ears ring.

"You're not afraid of thunder?" asked Ah Fu.

"No. You?"

"I was afraid when I was little, but not now."

An important question came to Tongtong's mind: "Ah Fu, do you think everyone has to grow up?"

"I think so."

"And then what?"

"And then you grow old."

"And then?"

Ah Fu didn't respond.

They turned on the video wall to watch cartoons. It was Tongtong's favorite show: "Rainbow Bear Village." No matter how heavy it rained outside, the little bears of the village always lived together happily. Maybe everything else in the world was fake; maybe only the world of the little bears was real.

Gradually, Tongtong's eyelids grew heavy. The sound of rain had a hypnotic effect. She leaned against Ah Fu. Ah Fu picked her up in its arms, carried her into the bedroom, set her down gently in bed, covered her with a blanket, and pulled the curtains shut. Its hands were just like real hands, warm and soft.

Tongtong murmured, "Why isn't Grandpa back yet?"

"Sleep. When you wake up, Grandpa will be back."

Grandpa did not come back.

Mom and Dad returned. Both looked sad and tired.

But they got even busier. Every day, they had to leave the house and go somewhere. Tongtong stayed home by herself. She played games sometimes, and watched cartoons at other times. Ah Fu sometimes came over to cook for her.

A few days later, Mom called for Tongtong. "I have to talk to you."

Grandpa had a tumor in his head. The last time he fell was because the tumor pressed against a nerve. The doctor suggested surgery immediately.

Given Grandpa's age, surgery was very dangerous. But not operating would be even more dangerous. Mom and Dad and Grandpa had gone to several hospitals and gotten several other opinions, and after talking with each other over several nights, they decided that they had to operate.

The operation took a full day. The tumor was the size of an egg.

Grandpa remained in a coma after the operation.

Mom hugged Tongtong and sobbed. Her body trembled like a fish.

Tongtong hugged Mom back tightly. She looked and saw the white hairs mixed in with the black on her head. Everything seemed so unreal.

Tongtong went to the hospital with Mom.

It was so hot, and the sun so bright. Tongtong and Mom shared a parasol. In Mom's other hand was a thermos of bright red fruit juice taken from the fridge.

There were few pedestrians on the road. The cicadas continued their endless singing. The summer was almost over.

Inside the hospital, the air conditioning was turned up high. They waited in the hallway for a bit before a nurse came to tell them that Grandpa was awake. Mom told Tongtong to go in first.

Grandpa looked like a stranger. His hair had been shaved off, and his face was swollen. One eye was covered by a gauze bandage, and the other eye was closed. Tongtong held Grandpa's hand, and she was scared. She remembered Grandma. Like before, there were tubes and beeping machines all around.

The nurse said Grandpa's name. "Your granddaughter is here to see you."

Grandpa opened his eye and gazed at Tongtong. Tongtong moved, and the eye moved to follow her. But he couldn't speak or move.

The nurse whispered, "You can talk to your grandfather. He can hear you."

Tongtong didn't know what to say. She squeezed Grandpa's hand, and she could feel Grandpa squeezing back.

Grandpa! She called out in her mind. *Can you recognize me?*

His eyes followed Tongtong.

She finally found her voice. "Grandpa!"

Tears fell on the white sheets. The nurse tried to comfort her. "Don't cry! Your grandfather would feel so sad to see you cry."

Tongtong was taken out of the room, and she cried—tears streaming down her face like a little kid, but she didn't care who saw—in the hallway for a long time.

Ah Fu was leaving. Dad packed it up to mail it back to Guokr Technologies.

Uncle Wang explained that he had wanted to come in person to say goodbye to Tongtong and her family. But the city he lived in was very far away. At least it was easy to communicate over long distances now, and they could chat by video or phone in the future.

Tongtong was in her room, drawing. Ah Fu came over noiselessly. Tongtong had drawn many little bears on the paper, and colored them all different shades with crayons. Ah Fu looked at the pictures. One of the biggest bears was colored all the shades of the rainbow, and he wore a black eye patch so that only one eye showed.

"Who is this?" Ah Fu asked.

Tongtong didn't answer. She went on coloring, her heart set on giving every color in the world to the bear.

Ah Fu hugged Tongtong from behind. Its body trembled. Tongtong knew that Ah Fu was crying.

Uncle Wang sent a video message to Tongtong.

Tongtong, did you receive the package I sent you?

Inside the package was a fuzzy teddy bear. It was colored like the rainbow, with a black eye patch, leaving only one eye. It was just like the one Tongtong drew.

The bear is equipped with a telepresence kit and connected to the instruments at the hospital: his heartbeat, breath, pulse, body temperature. If the bear's eye is closed, that means your grandfather is asleep. If your grandfather is awake, the bear will open its eye.

Everything the bear sees and hears is projected onto the ceiling of the room at the hospital. You can talk to it, tell it stories, sing to it, and your grandfather will see and hear.

He can definitely hear and see. Even though he can't move his body, he's awake inside. So you must talk to the bear, play with it, and let it hear your laughter. Then your grandfather won't be alone.

Tongtong put her ear to the bear's chest: thump-thump. The heartbeat was slow and faint. The bear's chest was warm, rising and falling slowly with each breath. It was sleeping deeply.

Tongtong wanted to sleep, too. She put the bear in bed with her and covered it with a blanket. *When Grandpa is awake tomorrow,* she thought, *I'll bring him out to get some sun, to climb trees, to go to the park and listen to those grandpas and grandmas sing folk opera. The summer isn't over yet. There are so many fun things to do.*

"Grandpa, don't worry, eh!" she whispered. *When you wake up, everything will be all right.*

*[**Author's Note:** I'd like to dedicate this story to my grandfather. August is when I composed this story, and it's also the anniversary of his passing. I will treasure the time I got to spend with him forever.*

This story is also dedicated to all the grandmas and grandpas who, each morning, can be seen in the parks practicing taichi, twirling swords, singing opera, dancing, showing off their songbirds, painting, doing calligraphy, playing the accordion. You made me understand that living with an awareness of the closeness of death is nothing to be afraid of.]

MUSÉE DE L'ÂME SEULE

E. LILY YU

It was a bus skidding off a rain-slick ribbon of a road, everyone for a moment in flight, levitating from their seats, then the shear and scream of metal. This is what distinguishes you from others. For whether you were shot to bits in a war or whether a telephone pole crushed your liver against the steering wheel, the procedure is the same. You can assume what happened after that.

Unless you are wildly rich—and you are not—the puddles of your organs were scooped out and replaced with artificial tissues that perform the necessary filtration, synthesis, and excretion for a fraction of the price of a transplant. Splintered bones become slim metal shafts. Ceramic scales cover ruined skin. They wheeled you out of the operating room hooked up to a bouquet of tubes, batteries, and drains, a grid of lights screwed into your plates, blinking red, blue, green. *Stable. Functioning. Okay.* As the drugs wore off you began to fumble at the strange new surfaces of your body.

Your lover was in Zanzibar on a lucrative minerals contract and did not hear about your accident until after they had patched you up enough to tap out the first of many detailed emails. The damage was extensive, your reconstruction complicated. For the rest of our life you will need a constant power supply, a backup generator, and hourly system flushes. You could choose to live homebound, they say, never passing your door. They quote you the prices of the various adaptors and chargers you need, and you laugh and cannot stop laughing, lightning balls of pain throughout your unfamiliar body.

Or, the nurses say, nervously thumbing down their screens, you could move to an experimental city in Washington designed for patients like you, where you would enjoy a certain degree of freedom and company. They do not add, *a place where everyone looks like you.* But their eyes shine with kindness.

Your lover offers to pay for the house installation. If nothing else, you should give him credit for that.

One nurse makes sure you are loaned a set of equipment from the hospital for your transitional period. You consider absconding with the adaptors—if the prices are to be believed, they're worth a small Caribbean island or two—but you can't extract the tracking tags. Besides, the nurse was nice.

You ship two cardboard boxes to the address they give you and sell the rest. You give away your pair of budgerigars because you can't take them with you. Your lover never liked them. Too noisy. Too messy. Too demanding. They chewed up the clawfooted chair from his grandfather's estate, little chips and nocks like angry kisses in the gloss.

Unexpected difficulties with buses and trains and airlines keep your beloved in Zanzibar, so when it's time to leave, your friends do the heavy lifting for you. They are polite. They try not to stare.

"What a dipshit," you hear one mutter, unhooking a photo of your lover, and she is right. He should be here with you, packing sweaters you can't wear anymore in plastic, boxing up your dinner plates.

You take the medical flight that leaves twice a month, your new address printed on a plastic strip around your wrist. Your college roommate sees you off. You hand over your borrowed equipment at the gate, shrugging off the promises of care packages and visits. You flinch from the hug. You don't look back.

The air is sweet on your exposed skin when you first see the square mile of concrete that is Revival. At the center of the city, a sheaf of faceted skyscrapers floats above a squat white mall. Rings of smaller apartments slope down and away, glass and steel congealing to stucco, brick, and concrete as they approach the city limits, where buildings meet crisp dark pines, sharp as cuts. Far beyond the pines rise whitened mountains like licked ice cream. You will dream sometimes of climbing those mountains and plunging your face into soft, shocking snow.

It is impossible, of course. Your batteries have enough charge for a couple of hours, but without fresh supplies of lymph and plasma, there's only so much your filters can do. The city newsroom is staffed by former war reporters, bulletproof and bitter, and every couple of months there's a story about a disconnection, either accidental or deliberate.

In determinedly cheerful emails, you recount to your absent lover everything he has missed. You have been assigned a fifteen-by-fifteen room with enormous windows in the southeast corner of Revival. You have not yet bought a mirror. Very few stores stock them, and you are not sure you want one. Pets are prohibited. Rent is moderate but food prices are inflated and utility bills are astronomical. Double-digit municipal taxes give you a slight headache. The consortium of medical providers managing the city is nominally a nonprofit, but you do the numbers on the back of an electricity bill and figure the executives must be drawing large salaries.

Since you are an accountant, you can work remotely. Your clients, who heard about the bus crash and have offered their timid condolences, assure you that it does not matter to them whether you are based in Des Moines or Los Angeles or Revival, Washington. Other residents are not so lucky. Their debts are paid for out of their retirement savings, or their estate, or alternatively by the sale of their genome and medical history and whatever organic components remain at the time of their death. The lease document makes for an interesting read. You tear the pages into tiny strips as you go.

All too soon, you memorize the silver line of cables and pumps that strings apartment block to apartment block, running through grocery store aisles and along library shelves and shooting up the five floors of the bright, sterile mall. You know where it turns at the end of the pavement, in the shadow of the pines, and loops back toward the mall. A local joke has it that the silver lines, if viewed from above, if all the intervening roofs and floors and ceilings were removed, spell out *freedom*.

The city is lousy with crows, who dive for flashes of metal and glints of porcelain. They are not discouraged by thirty failed attempts if, on the thirty-first, they snatch a pin, a lens, a loose filament. They are easy to fend off, but the cold acquisitiveness in their eyes makes you shiver.

Your lover comes to visit you only once, four and a half months after you move to Revival. You are slow, still limping, and a minute late. He climbs out of the taxi in his pressed suit and razor tie and looks around, fiddling with a button, cufflinks, hair. You are grateful that he recognizes you immediately. But he shrinks back a fraction of an inch when his eyes reach the steel screwed into your face and the coarse, fitful wires that grow where your skull was shaved.

You are surprised. In Revival, where glamour magazines gather dust and fade, you are considered beautiful. Eyes slide toward you on the street. You had almost forgotten about the seams and screws, the viscous yellow and red fluids trickling in and out of you, the cables tangling everywhere.

If you are honest with yourself, as you suddenly have to be, standing face to face with him, the two of you have not been lovers for some time. Right before the accident, you had agreed to separate for six months, as an audit of the relationship. You fed sunflower seeds to Tessie as he talked about opportunities in Tanzania, about looking for clarity in his life, his need to feel whole, like a hammer swing, a home run, his entire body committed to one motion. You nodded, you admitted the solidity of his arguments, and you stroked the budgie so roughly it bit your finger.

While you were apart, he wrote a paragraph once a week in response to your daily emails. You would reread it three or four times, looking for the elided thought, the sunken meaning. It was October, the busy season, and you were starting to make mistakes and lose paperwork. When the last return was triple-checked and filed, you heaved a sigh of relief and boarded a bus for Maine, where you would spend your vacation with a friend.

It was raining. Water entered an unnoticed hole in the toe of your boot, and you wrote a brief grumble to your love. Then the bus rumbled into the night, and you shut your eyes and let yourself relax.

So you are not exactly together, you realize, as you take his stiff arm. Together, you go to the third-nicest restaurant in the city for lunch. Your lover cannot stop staring at the servers, who are mostly inorganic by now and capable of carrying hundreds of pounds on each slender, tempered arm. His brows stitch together, and all the filet mignon in the world can't undo them.

Afterwards, he follows you to your apartment and undresses you with clumsy hands, snagging sleeves on tubes and almost unplugging your drip. But he cannot bring himself to touch the ceramic plates of your abdomen, which vibrate softly from the tiny motors underneath. You are disappointed but not altogether surprised.

You see your lover off with the driest of kisses. Then you compose a long email that is gentle and gracious, that is all the best parts of you gathered on the screen.

Your former lover does not reply.

"He wants a window-display life," your old roommate says when you call, finally, ashamed of your silence, your sticky sniffling. "You're not perfect enough for that. Not anymore." And she is right.

You try to find friends. Revival is a city, after all. You smile at people in the library as they browse books, music, electronics, language implants, avoiding the woman in the mystery section who is methodically tearing apart paperbacks. Most of the librarians are asleep at their desks.

You chat up tired cashiers. You sit in the synthetic park feeding bread to a duck paddling circles in the fountain. But the people you meet are still in various stages of recovery. They can only talk about the passive-aggressive bosses, the snowballing interest on their credit cards, the diagnoses, the lost loves, the affairs and then the tequila that preceded the leap off a bridge, or the microwaved dinners the children ate before they piled into the van for judo class, nine minutes before the other car roared through a red light and everything shattered. If only there were do-overs, if only there were apologies, if only the last meal could have been homemade chicken soup or macaroni and cheese. If only.

It is interesting and terrible the first time, but when you run into them later, they recite the same stories with the tragic and farcical earnestness of wind-up toys, and you make hasty excuses and leave.

Eight months after you arrive in Revival, you make an appointment for repairs. Your left lung, which is silicon rubber, has a small tear, and you are also due for a heart check. The clinic is one of two, staffed with five doctors and fifteen technicians, none of whom have missing pieces or live in the city. Your technician, Joel, is young, lean, and cheerful, with a strong nose and wild brown hair recently harrowed by a comb.

"Hey, stranger," he says. "First time? Let's have a look." He winds your tubes around one arm so they don't obstruct his hands and looks expectantly at you. Suddenly you are too shy to open up your body to him, to expose the secret gushing and dripping of pump and membrane and diaphragm, the click and thump of your pneumatic plastic heart.

"It'll be fine," he says. "You've got a Mark 5 heart and the D34-15 lung assembly. I did my certs on both of those, so I know them better than anything. I collect defective parts, and I can almost never find Mark 5s. They don't break."

His palm is warm on your ventral plates. He inserts his fingertips into the seamed depression where they overlap and parts the plates with surprising delicacy. Because your body was rebuilt for other people to troubleshoot, you cannot see the gauges and displays that he studies with wrinkled brow, although you know they're there, you've heard them ticking and whirring at night.

"Looking great," he says. "Mhm. You do a good job of taking care of this thing."

He reaches into your chest. You close your eyes and imagine that your heart is your own heart, wet and yielding to his thumbs, not a mass-produced model identical to hundreds of others he has inspected and installed. You wonder what his hair would feel like between your remaining fingers. Corn silk. Merino. Mink.

In ten minutes, Joel patches your lung and proclaims your Mk. 5 a beautiful ticker. You compliment him on the job. Already you can feel the extra oxygen brightening your blood, and the dull headache that has followed you all week fades. You are feeling so improved, in fact, that before you can think better of it, you invite him to coffee.

His mouth opens into a circle. You can see the glint of your zygomatic plate on the surface of his eyes. The inner tips of his eyebrows lift with pity.

"Well, isn't this awkward," he says, attempting a smile. "Never happened to me before."

You would be amused by his panic if it were not so painful. You mumble something or other.

"Bit of a—doctor-patient relationship—even if I'm not a doctor. You know." You do know.

Your cheeks burn like torches the entire walk home. Today the rigid, brilliant architecture of the city seems like too much to bear. Your image flares at you from windows and glass doors. Yes, you are ugly. Yes, you are broken. Briefly, you consider disconnecting yourself and plunging into the trees in the few minutes before you collapse and all your diagnostic lights go red. You walk to the edge of the woods and sit quietly on the pavement, looking into the underbrush.

The trees are full of crows. Every few feet the grass is punctuated with a black pinion feather. Somewhere in these woods, the crows are building nests with wire, silicone, plastic, sequins of steel.

You listen to their quarrelling and think regretfully of your green and yellow budgies. Sweet-voiced things, your idea of love. They nuzzled your fingers and each other, unworried, content, knowing there'd be seeds in the feeder and water every morning.

You are motionless for so long that one crow flaps down to inspect you, eyeing his reflection in your metal side. He pecks. Once, twice. You have been working a loose wire out of your neck, which was wound up somewhere inside you but is now poking out, and you twist it off and hold out the gleaming piece.

He yanks it from your fingers and flees. Immediately, two more crows drop out of the trees to pummel him. You watch his oily back disappear into a squall of black bodies, reappear, disappear again. As they fight, black beak, jet claw, ragged bundles of greed, you remember what it meant to feel desire.

Over the course of a week, as a glittering shape flowers inside your head, you examine your budget, your savings, your expenses.

You order twelve carnival mirrors and set them up in your apartment. There is no more room for your bed, so you sell that to a new arrival. You also buy three old industrial robots, rusted and caked in machine oil. The boxes arrive thick and fast, and your apartment manager, who knows the square footage of your room, raises his single eyebrow at you when you come to collect them. Now, everywhere you turn, you confront an elastic vision of yourself, stretching as high as the ceiling and snapping to the shortness of a child. The eyes in the mirror gradually lose their fear.

You write about everything to your former lover as a matter of habit, not expecting a reply.

Biting your cheek, you call Joel to ask where you can buy faulty artificial organs. He listens to your flustered explanation and gives you contacts as well as three hearts, Mk. 1, 2, and 4, out of his own collection. You balance them in the robots' pincers like apples in a bowl.

With a net and a handful of bread, you catch birds on the roof: house sparrows, rock pigeons, crows, an unhappy seagull. You release the birds in your glass coffin crammed with carnival mirrors. They batter themselves against the window and shit on the mirrors and on you. Your room is all trapped, frantic motion, exaggerated in swells and rolls of glass. People look sideways at you when you leave your room, your chrome and steel parts streaked with white. You look at your slumped, stretched, stained reflections and recognize nothing and no one.

Sometimes, when the room is dark, you can admit that you are making this for someone who will never see it, who will never come back, who will never write to you. Then you roll onto your good side and listen to the flurry of wings until you fall asleep.

You set out neatly lettered signs in your window and on your door. *Musée de l'Âme Seule.* Signage is probably against building regulations, but you used the shreds of your lease to line your room. You run a notice in the news that is two inches by two inches. *Saturdays and Sundays.* You keep your door unlocked. You feed the birds, you wipe down the hearts, and you wait.

Joel comes to see you, or perhaps to see what you've done with his hearts.

"Where do you sleep?" he says, looking around.

Anywhere, you say.

His expression says he thinks parts other than your lung need examining. But he is also curious. He touches the orange arms curled around artificial ventricles, the frozen rovers sprouting substitute livers at odd angles.

"I'm not very good at art," he says. A sparrow shits in his hair.

You offer to wipe up the mess, you are already wetting a towel in the sink, but he has to leave, he is meeting someone somewhere else, he has left his jacket at the clinic, he is late.

Two weeks later, on a Sunday morning, one more person walks into your museum. She swings open your door and is surprised into laughter by a burst of gray wings. She is even uglier than you are, most of her face gone, hard bright camera lenses for eyes. She has glued pages of books and playbills over her carapace.

"I was an actress," she says.

She has been in all the shows that she wears. The pages came from books she liked but couldn't keep. Her name is Nim. She has been in the city *ab urbe condita,* she says, meaning four years ago, when it was fifteen residents and three doctors and one building. She walks around your room as she talks, studying the mirrors, the machines, the birds, the bounce of her own reflection.

Without asking permission, she shoves a window open and shoos out the birds. They leave in one long shout of white and gray and brown. Flecks of down spin and swirl in their wake.

You ask her how long it took to remember how to walk, how to function, how to smile.

"Two weeks. Three months. Two years." She shrugs. "Sooner or later."

Nim has no hair, only a complex web of filaments across her metal skull, flickering her thoughts in patterns too quick to follow. Her hands are small and dark and unscarred.

"Look," she says, touching the skin of your cheek, showing off her lean titanium legs. "Together we make one whole person."

More than that, you want to say, as you add up fingers and toes and organs and elbows. A sum that is greater than one. More than two. But you are tongue-tied and dazed. You realize that you stink of birds and bird shit.

She smiles at your confusion. "I'll bring you some gloves and cleaning supplies."

What for, you say stupidly.

"To shine up this place."

But this is what I am, you say. This is what I look like. You stretch out your hands to indicate the mirrors, the stained, spattered floors, the streaked walls.

"You could use a spit and polish too, frankly." She demonstrates, using her sleeve, and you blush.

But why are you here, you ask. Why is she touching you with gentleness? You are afraid that this is all an accident, a colossal misunderstanding, that she will walk out of the door and vanish like your sparrows.

"I'm looking for a collaborator," she says. "I've got an idea. Performance art. Public service. If you can clean up and come for lunch tomorrow, I'll tell you about it."

Inside you, a window opens.

That was when you stopped writing to me. Your long, careful emails came to an end. What is there to say? The stories of people we have loved and injured and deserted are incomplete to us.

If I could write an ending for you, it would be Nim holding your new hand in hers, Nim tickling your back until you wheeze with laughter, the two of you commandeering an office block for a new museum, a museum of broken and repaired people, where anyone for an hour or three can pose in a spotlight and glitter, glisten, gleam, haloed in light, light leaping off the white teeth of their laughter. But it is never that easy, and that is not my right.

You knew, I think, before I did. That no one can have a life that is without questions, without cracks. And now you are the deepest one in mine.

Here is what I have. A year and two months of emails. A restaurant check. A glossy fragment from a magazine, two inches by two inches. Terse. Opaque. *Musée de l'Âme Réparée. Saturdays and Sundays. Revival, WA.*

What could I say? What could I ever say?

WIZARD, CABALIST, ASCENDANT

SETH DICKINSON

Inequality is inevitable. Someone always wins.

If you're really so transcendently smart, Tayna, you would've known that from the beginning.

These are the things Connor's geist says to chase her down off the Rockies, back out into the world she remade. Tayna thinks he means well, as he did in life. It's not his fault he's a prick, or that he's blind to it.

Just another victim of structural forces.

Connor walks with her under blizzard skies. You tried to fix the world, he says. You thought you knew how to do it better than me. (His laugh doesn't exist outside the machine caucus alloyed into her skull, but still she hears it echo off the peaks around her, rebound, diminish. When did she decide to make Connor's voice thunder and geology?) But you only made it worse. You stole Haldane from me crying *utopia* but you fucked it all up.

The wind's picking up. Tayna fastens herself to the mountain face, skin sealing to stone, and starts metabolising hydrocarbons for warmth.

Connor, she says. You're kind of an asshole.

Coming from the woman who destroyed human civilization.

I saved the world.

From me. From my dream. (It's been twenty-two years since she betrayed him, and Connor's geist still sounds so hurt.) I could've avoided this. With Teilhard.

Yeah, Tayna says, downregulating the instinct to shiver. I saved it all. From you.

Connor's geist puts a comradely hand on her shoulder, where her paramuscle deltoid tethers to laminated bone. Look at this, he says, gesturing downslope, down the range. You wouldn't be going back down to visit if you weren't afraid I was right.

It's just a checkup, she says.

The very first people you meet, Connor says, are going to prove me right. They're going to prove your whole ecosystem, your brave new post-structures world, is fucked. Irreparably, fundamentally, mathematically fucked. And I'm going to be the only way out.

Tayna hangs onto the Rockies and grits her teeth.

Not for the first time, she considers deleting Connor's geist. She won't do it—she's better than that. But it feels good to think about. She's not better than *that*.

Lillian, she says. Lillian.

The other geist coalesces out of the wind, keyed-up pareidolia summoning her face from blown-snow noise. Hey, she says, and then, with concern: You look cold.

Tayna can't smile, because she's sealed up her face against the wind. But Lillian's only real inside her head, so she can probably feel the sentiment.

I'm afraid, she says.

She wants Lillian to hold her. This is sort of emotionally onanistic, since Lillian is part of her, built of old memory and bootstrapped simulation. (A special guilt she's grappled with—when you have the ability to regulate and modify every aspect of yourself, to snuff or satiate every need, do you have a *right* to want anything?)

So what does it mean that Lillian frowns, draws back, and, exhaling lovingly rendered frost, says:

Oh. I can see why you're scared. Things are going wrong.

Connor and Lillian know everything she knows. The Haldane network that ate her brain has room for the sweep of Tayna, and a few merely human minds too.

But they don't usually agree on anything.

Ten years ago, in the days of post-civilizational convulsion and the rise of tentative new paradigms, Tayna visited with a little mountaineering collective near Kremmling, Colorado. They kept to themselves, eschewing the headnets coalescing around Colorado Springs. But like everyone they still used Haldane, still gave their bodies and brains over to the new power.

In theory, everyone had a choice. Tayna and Lillian's subterfuge shattered Connor's dream of monolithic engineered transcendence (*Teilhard*, her dreams still whisper, when she lets herself dream: *Teilhard was the other way . . .*) and set the Haldane nanomech infrastructure loose, open-source, freely transmissible. Conversion was voluntary.

But, in retrospect, the choice was so one-sided it might as well have been coercion. The new breed didn't need the systems that made baseline life possible, the states, the economies—and so those systems collapsed. Old shackles broken. A new world enabled.

Maybe, Connor and Lillian seem to think, just a chrysalis for something worse.

Tayna heads back towards Kremmling. She follows the old California Zephyr railway southwest through canyons cut in banded gneiss. The train doesn't run now. The winter thaws into an early spring.

Do you miss trains? Connor asks. Governments? Civil society? Organized human achievement? I expect not, since you ruined them.

I made them unnecessary.

You balkanized the species.

I liberated them.

Tauntingly: *Them?*

Get new material, Connor.

One apocalypse isn't enough for you, is it? You're not going to be satisfied until you get the God job full-time.

In Gore Canyon, where the kayakers used to play, she finds people from Kremmling gathered in a rowdy knot up on the cliffs. They leap from the canyon walls on wings of paramuscle grown wrist to ankle and ride the rapids down through rock and hole until the chaos spits them out into calm water and they come up whooping.

Tayna sits down to watch for a while. They've diverged farther from the baseline, but that's all right. That was really the whole idea. Ensure diversity. Avert Connor's singularity—the monolithic future exploding out of a single stifled point.

They're playing a computation game, for the joy of it. Watch the rapids, plot a course, and leap. Whitewater turbulence is a tough problem. Ten years ago nobody in Kremmling could've managed *that*.

The very first people you meet are going to prove me right.

She gets up from her roost and lights her antenelles to send a greeting.

Warmth comes back her way: welcome to a stranger. And the photon caresses of a millimeter-wave scan as a bunch of them team up to search her for guns or combat organs.

"Is Mariam here?" she calls. "I'm looking for my friend Mariam, if she's still around—"

"Tayna!" Mariam calls, and sends a little pulse of happiness. "I thought you weren't coming back."

You never told me about her, Lillian's geist says. Old friend?

The truth is that there are ten thousand Mariams in ten thousand communities Tayna's visited, people who cherish Tayna as a dear friend, because Tayna's incredible cognitive firepower lets her look on them and understand them and make herself someone they can trust with a fluency that can't in all honesty be distinguished from manipulation. And that makes her guilty, like the friendships are just instrumental, like she's just a water-bug on the surface of the human experience. Too smart to swim.

You're lying, Connor says. That's not the truth.

Fuck you.

But Lillian's brow furrows and she says: He's right. Fuck him, still! But . . .

The truth is that Tayna's been gone so long, deep in the self-catalysis trance, that she's not sure she can relate to anyone else on Earth as more than a child. It's the wizard syndrome, the weight of age and power, and it's coming on hard.

She has the ability, via the Haldane backdoor, to do nearly anything she wants to anyone she meets. And if she *does* find something deeply wrong out here, some fundamental inequity rising . . . she already knows she'll use that power.

But she smiles, and waves, and sends her own happiness back, a stutter of brain activity jacketed in peer-to-peer protocols, scrubbed of any complication.

The Kremmling cliff-divers rest a while in the sun. Mariam spreads her wings to catch the light and waits, smiling, for Tayna to say something.

She hasn't aged, of course. Tayna inhales one of Mariam's dead skin cells from the mountain wind, sequences it, and compares it to a decade-old reference. Finds CAS9 touchups all over Mariam's genome: gentle rewrites where Haldane has repaired oncogenes, extended telomeres, laid the metabolic groundwork for her beautiful new wings. And, engraved in the chromatin, little signatures and signs—developers who wrote some of the packages Mariam has adopted. There will be others, elsewhere in the body and brain. The power of Haldane's programmable tissue goes far beyond the genetic.

A cluster of strangers pop up on Tayna's inferentials, coming in from the west. She checks them out, decides they're not important, and goes back to Mariam.

Hey—look here. A sequence that pops up again and again: *trust certificate by the Lillian Banning Cabal. Execution-safe.*

Looks like you remain a going concern, Young Miss Banning, she tells Lillian's geist. Still camped out in Chicago, screening the ecosystem for pathologies.

Happy to hear it. Shouldn't you talk to your friend? She looks so happy to see you.

Tayna's just putting it off, Connor interjects. She already knows.

Knows what?

That the moment she starts asking questions, she'll see the disintegration of this anarchic world-wide interregnum on the horizon. The rise of the new and final class of power structure.

Lillian kneels to marvel at Mariam's wings. I don't know, she says. Is anything inevitable, now? They can change so much . . .

Connor makes a mockingbird sound, an ostrich sound. You two enabled a dire new kind of inevitability, he says. And it's right here. I'll bet my simulated life on it.

"Mariam," Tayna says. "I need to ask you for something. It's personal, and it's big."

The newcomers are closing in, opening into a loose perimeter. But none of the Kremmling cliff-divers seem concerned. Tayna's sure they're unimportant.

"Anything," Mariam says, brow furrowed. "Why even ask, Tayna? I know how much you've done for us. I know—"

The awe and reverence and fear coming through say: I know you can have whatever you want.

Tayna hesitates. She *doesn't* want to know yet. Once she has the data, the engines of her intellect will render it down to a conclusion and that will be that, irrevocable. "Do you ever want things to . . . go back?" she asks.

"To the old world?" Whisper of emotion, voluntarily disclosed: an absence of doubt, a pre-emptive certainty.

"Yeah."

"There's nothing important we had then," Mariam says, "that we don't have now. And now I'm happy."

"Because you can tweak your brain chemistry." Tayna smiles wryly, to take the edge off. "Hardly objective."

Mariam leans back on her hands. The new arrivals have circled them, dark, angular, closing. Not urgent. "You think that's not important? Choosing when to be happy, why? What higher freedom could you ask?"

Connor makes an impatient gesture.

"I need performance profiles," Tayna says. Is it really asking, when you know you're going to get it, one way or another? "I need to know everything you're thinking about, and how hard, and what it's for. And who. Who it's for, too."

Something like the crack of a cable stunner sounds from somewhere close, but Tayna knows it can wait. Especially because—

Mariam's facial muscles slam into self-paralysis. Sweat glands shut down. Armoring herself against analysis of her microexpressions. It's a conditioned defensive response, a trigger to guard a secret.

Every *this-is-critical* heuristic wakes up and shrieks.

Mariam's consciousness catches up to the reflex an instant later. "I don't know," she says, clearly torn. "If it were just about me, of course, of course, but—Tayna, there's trouble in Kremmling. Headnets out of Colorado Springs keep trying to compromise us. We had to start a planning committee . . . they asked us to keep some things private . . . "

Go on, Connor says. Go get it. One way or another she's going to tell you. Don't waste time pretending you have ethics.

Lillian holds up her hands in caution. Tayna, don't—she has a right—

But Tayna, high wizard of the new world, opens the Haldane backdoor and steps into Mariam's head.

It's always been there. Tayna was lead architect, so of course she knew the risks of leaving an intentional vulnerability in the ecosystem, but she guarded it so cleverly—with an agnosia, a shield against awareness. Elegant, right? You have to be Haldane-smart to figure out the backdoor, and if you're running Haldane, you're vulnerable to the agnosia that guards it. You can see the backdoor but you'll never be able to integrate the information into awareness.

Tayna alone has this power: access to any and every transhuman mind on Earth. Unilateral. Devastating. But she knows herself like no other system on the planet. Trusts herself, mostly. She'll exercise her power, just this once, in the name of proving Connor wrong.

She grabs the information she needs from Mariam's metafaculties and steps back out.

And on her way out, glimpsing the gray angular strangers and their weapons through Mariam's innocent eyes, something inside Tayna un-breaks. Repairs a crucial disconnect.

Agnosia. You process the information, but you can't assemble it into awareness.

You see them coming. Hear the cableguns fire. But you don't think it's important.

Mother*fucker*.

Tayna rises. Aegisware floods her mind, venom in every synapse and soma, burning out the intruder: the agnosia they slipped in to hide their approach. The wool they pulled over eyes as old and keen as hers.

Her antennelles light up at full warload. Mariam stares up at her in awe and terror.

Tayna addresses the faceless gray commando-morphs all around them, their brain-stealth stripped away. "One chance. Surrender."

"Tayna Booker." The voice comes out of them in one collective radio susurrus. "Simulate the situation. You will find no viable options. Open your mind to our control, or we will use force."

The problem with being the oldest smartest Haldane user on the planet is this: you're still not bulletproof. So—the nuclear option.

For the second time in as many seconds, Tayna broadcasts the Haldane backdoor key, knowing, even as she does, that it's exactly what Connor wants.

When she's done pithing and resocializing the warmorphs she gives them to Mariam. "It wasn't about you," she promises. "I'm sorry. I have to go."

Northeast now. Towards Chicago. She has to find Lillian—the real Lillian and her mighty Banning Cabal. Lillian who promised to keep an eye on the world.

The soldiers were Connor Straylight's, the real Connor, and if Connor came for her *now*, it's not just about revenge. Connor doesn't think that small. No, Connor must be grasping for a second chance at his own apocalypse: Teilhard, the unilateral re-engineering of all human consciousness towards a more rational design.

Connor's geist trails her all the way, grinning.

Yes, Tayna says. You're very clever.

I really am, aren't I? I made you broadcast the backdoor key. Made you tip your hand. The real me, of course—I can't take any credit for him—

This is part of why Tayna maintains the geists. By speaking to them, she understand what the real people behind them will do. She says: So you sent your warmorphs to bait me into using the backdoor. They listen to the key I transmit and pass the data back to you in San Francisco. But that won't be enough. It's not a static password, not even single-factor authentication.

But now I have a start. And if I'm smart enough, if I have enough brainpower in my arsenal, I can crack the rest.

Access to every Haldane-operating human on Earth.

At Tayna's side Lillian purses her lips and exhales in two growling steps. I hate him, she says. So much. He's like I'd be, if I hadn't had a scrap of self-awareness growing up.

What do you want? Tayna asks.

I'd guess, Connor's geist says, that I'm trying to solve the same problem you are. The one you don't want to talk about. The fundamental unsustainability of the world you built.

Engines of specialized thought centrifuge Mariam's performance data into its component pieces. Feed the slag into hungry, sealed subsystems eager to render verdict.

Northeast still.

Tayna shelters with a bugbreeder collective under the arches of the defunct Denver Mint. They grow dragonflies, bathing the pupae in Haldane nanomechs, whispering the naiads towards adulthood. "We dance," they explain. "There are other uses. Agriculture. Defense. But first we dance."

The neutrois performer who plays welcome for her can see through the jeweled eyes of their swarm and dance the mass of them as a single whirlwind of silver odonata shining in the firelight. Some of them have razor wings and when the dancer cuts theirself shoulder and brow Tayna smells the trick of carbon chemistry in the blood and *oohs* even before a few of the dragonflies land, spark, ignite the bleeding rivulets into pale fire that glows on armored skin.

"Beautiful," she says, meaning it.

It's here too, Connor's geist says. The defect. Down deep.

Even Lillian's grown impatient. Tayna, she says, sitting and arranging herself. I know how fast you think. You must have an answer. Small acts of light mark her, the rendered reflections of passing dragonflies.

Do you remember, Tayna asks, addressing both of them, when we argued about capitalism?

They remember. Lillian first: You said capitalism was an inevitability. That human civilizations converged on it. Because it was an effective algorithm to distribute resources and organize labor.

Tayna interjects: Only because of the limitations—

Of the individual, Connor finishes. Each actor's only got a little information. There's no centralized control. So you need an algorithm that operates locally.

Lillian, her eyes young as the day they met: And of course I said—capitalism's a historical event. Predicated on certain decisions, certain structures. And you said, no, no, capitalism is a technological solution to the limitations of the human mind, the inability to process large structures.

Funny, Connor says, smiling at Tayna. When we met, you were on Lillian's side of this argument.

What you're both afraid of, Tayna says, is the rise of another inevitable system. Another hegemonic algorithm, born out of the logic of this new world I made. Not about capital, but cognition. Right?

They watch her, waiting. A dragonfly settles briefly on her brow. The circled audience claps for the dancer, kindled to a full-body torch.

I've analyzed Mariam's performance data, Tayna says. She'd volunteered nearly a third of her headspace to the Kremmling Planning Committee. Everyone in her collective—they were all pitching in to solve a distributed problem, trying to figure out a way to beat the Colorado Springs headnet and keep their independence.

What was the problem, exactly? Lillian asks. But Connor already knows. This was *his* specialty, the terrain of his dreams.

The same thing I spent my retreats on, Tayna answers. The same thing any self-interested party spends their time on: recursive self-improvement. Use your intellect to build more intellect. Smarts make you smarter.

And she goes on, while the dancer burns and the audience cheers and whirring dragonflies sparking with coronal discharge flick past in the lucid bullet-time of her upclocked cognition: To secure your own interests, you need to understand the opponent. You need to compute her and predict her tactics. So they're going to design better brains for the members of their planning committee. And those members are going to use those brains to make better brains still, because it's that or fall behind the opponent. But they'll always need more labor, so some part of that burden will be offloaded to—

The working class, Lillian finishes. The rest of them.

And this is going to happen again and again. All around the world. The payoff for the winner is the ability to model and control competitors.

An arms race, Lillian says. And it's not just the smartest system that'll win. It's the system that most aggressively disrupts the competition . . . or subverts and incorporates them. Zero sum payoffs.

You saw this coming, Connor says. You must have. I know I'm not the smartest person inside this skull. You must have known.

I thought that it wouldn't be inevitable. We gave people a lot of new choices. I thought they'd find another way.

There are rules, Connor says, that no one ever chose. Like: someone loses. Someone wins.

It's okay, Lillian says. It's okay. It's okay.

It is?

I would've figured this out—the real me in Chicago. That was what I promised to do. I've got to be working on a solution. So find me.

Tayna exhales. Nods.

I wouldn't let you down, Lillian says.

◆ ◆ ◆

Chicago has been swallowed by a voluntary tyranny.

The Second City's new order keeps outposts as far out as Galesburg. They make the rules pretty clear: *Service is elective. You volunteer for work. We reprofile you to like it. Fulfillment guaranteed.*

Please evaluate your decision carefully. After the fact, you will be too content to reconsider.

The signs point towards the old university in Hyde Park. Lillian reads this, pale, chewing on her lip, and Tayna gives her friend's geist an intangible squeeze.

Sometimes it's hard, meeting yourself. Finding out what you've done.

A leveler colony in West Lawn takes her in for the night. The dedicants run elective agnosias, jamming their ability to process race, age, beauty. Tayna wonders, with old cynicism, whether their minds just fill in the emptiness with people who look like them.

All of this is going to fall apart. The world will coalesce into states, like it did before—states of mind, racing to outthink each other, until one finally bursts into singularity and claims the future.

In the night she wanders the empty streets of her childhood city. Stares into the hollowed husk of an old laundromat, burnt by riot, cleaned and consigned by reprofiled labor. She thinks: This is still the world I wanted. People making their own choices. Even choices I don't like.

But it's not going to last.

She senses motion behind her, considered, stealthy. Straylight's warmorphs? No—just a drifter, wary, staring her way with glinting cat eyes. Humans slipping into one more niche in the ecosystem. "No harm," Tayna promises.

The drifter broadcasts wary curiosity.

"I grew up in Chicago. I thought I'd . . . see what we'd made of it."

Pulse of compassion, shading into inquiry. An inarticulate question: *What have you seen out there?*

"All kinds of evil," Tayna says. What an easy heuristic, that word. What trouble it's caused. She's spent so long untangling it, what it really means—but she stills come back to it. "Coerced homogeneity. Cults of neural purity. Headnets that burn their members down to seizure. And the really dangerous stuff, more subtle, more insidious—free-rider strategies no one designed. Broken incentive structures. Feedback loops spiraling off towards self-destruction."

Very sad, the itinerant feels. *Not your fault. Hard world.*

"Everything," Tayna says, "is my responsibility. I set Haldane loose. I stole it from Connor Straylight's company."

Regrets?

"I think I like this world better than the alternative."

Better than Teilhard. The engineered monoculture. One rich white man's dream of perfection.

But at least it would've been *clean—*

"Tayna," the itinerant says, in a clear new voice, sent from somewhere not far off. "Please come with me. We've been waiting for you."

"Hey, Lil," Tayna says. But her friend's geist has retreated, so it's only the voice behind the drifter that hears the greeting, only the real Lillian.

When they were undergrads here the Regenstein Library stood like a concrete battleship, bunkered down against the premonition of some uncertain end of days. Now that apocalypse has come and passed and the Reg still keeps station. Someone has planted a forest of antennae on the roof, filled the ivy with frosty thermal pipes—but the building only seems fulfilled. The Reg has always felt like it might be a machine.

Lillian Banning waits alone on the steps, round-cheeked, heavy, biting her nails with nervous precision. Tayna looks at her with modest old senses: no millimeter-wave, no inferentials. Like she's afraid that all her higher faculties would find the mass of history between them and just give up, burn out.

"Hi," she says, waving a little.

Lillian starts. "Jesus," she says, and smiles. "You're early."

"I wanted some time to be friends," Tanya says. "Before we had to talk about—all this."

Lillian pats the stone. Inside Tayna the Lillian geist peeks out shyly. "How's it been?" the real one asks. Worlds of computation in each of them, modeling each other, and so all that's left to speak is the residue, the comforting old banalities.

Tayna sits a little way off, a haven't-seen-you-in-while-are-we-still-cool? kind of distance. "Ups and downs, I guess. You?"

They don't have to say anything important right now, even though by sundown they'll probably have altered the course of history (again). That feels really good. Tayna doesn't take it apart.

"You know how it is." Lillian shrugs. "I've got a thing going here. I'm still in social work, I guess."

You're wasting time, Connor's geist murmurs. I'm cracking the Haldane backdoor right now. I'm getting ready to open every human mind on the planet and remake them all.

They talk a while first. Connor, the unspoken agreement goes, can fuck right off.

Finally Lillian says: "You're here because of the recursive self-improvement problem. The emergence of elite dynamics from the cognitive arms race."

"That," Tayna says, "and Straylight. He's trying to crack the Haldane backdoor. Do you have an answer?"

She does. Tayna can tell that much. But it's nothing she's going to like.

"Come on." Lillian draws her through the old rotating door, into the Reg. "I'll tell you everything you haven't figured out already."

◆ ◆ ◆

Obelisks of thought, down here. Ranks of machines tended by silent profiled labor. The cold is absolute, penetrating. The laborers are silent, Tayna realizes, because they're slaved to the network too. Their heads are full of distributed thought. Like Kremmling, ten years further along.

Lillian's cabal is probably the single most powerful nexus of computation outside San Francisco and Straylight.

They walk down cabled passages between pools of soft blue light. "It's a think tank," Lillian explains. "We used to scrub the Haldane ecosystem for malicious packages. When I realized things were going wrong, I rebuilt the collective into a prediction machine."

"Profiled workers," Tayna murmurs. "Labor and elite." She doesn't have to speak the condemnation, or ask the question: *What happened to you? What drove you to this?*

Lillian purses her lips. "The optimal arrangement. It was this, or give the world to Straylight."

"You've accepted his institutional logic. You're exploiting the desperate in the name of an ideological end." Old words, from their old arguments. "There wasn't any other way?"

"No," Lillian says, unqualified, and the weight of thought above and around them gives her refusal weight. She has the firepower to *know*.

"How far along is he?"

"He has an embryonic singularity building in San Francisco. He's been marshalling computational assets to crack your backdoor. Once he has it, he rewrites every transhuman on the planet with his new logic and gives birth to a transcendent coalescent intellect."

"Teilhard."

The same disgust in Lillian's voice that Tayna feels. "Once Connor gives birth to his transcendent mind, it dominates the future of all systems by main cognitive force. Death by monoculture. The extinction of every alternative mode of existence. We can't see past that."

"I kept a geist of him." Tayna glances at the spectral Connor, moving in her periphery. He waves. "And you, too. You were better company."

"Did you ever disagree?"

"Of course." Tayna catches what Lillian's really asking a moment too late: "And you? What did you tell *your* geist of *me*?"

"My solution. You hated it."

Uh-oh. "Lillian. Tell me."

Lillian stops. "I need you to understand something." Her face is cryptic, jagged, unreadable even when Tayna puts her full weight into it. Lillian's distributed Cabal gives her spectacular capabilities: she's doing something to her muscles, an injection of noise that jams analysis. "You hated the idea. But when I gave your geist access to the simulations here—when I let her think as enormously as I had—she changed her mind. She agreed with me. It was the only solution."

"Okay." Tayna accepts this, for now. "And?"

"It's pretty bad news." Unspoken: *This is your last chance to walk.*

Tayna waits.

"We found proof," Lillian says. "Mathematical. Robust. Egalitarian societies are fundamentally unstable. Inequality always emerges, entrenches itself, and remakes the system to preserve itself. A power elite emerges. Unless the game has very specific rules, or a very proactive referee."

It's big and abstract and it hits Tayna like a shotgun slug. She takes a physical step back. This is the end: the death of the dream, written in the only language that always speaks true.

"The future always points that way." Lillian won't stop. Maybe she doesn't know that she's speaking all of Tayna's darkest fears. No: of course she does. "Systems capable of recursive self-improvement always dominate the competition. Anything self-directed, bottom-up—democracy, markets, any arena where agents interact by rules—ends up dominated by strategies that can magnify their own power at the expense of others. Haldane makes that easier than ever."

"So you're going to do something about it." Tayna can already see it. "You're going to change the rules."

"Straylight is the inevitable outcome of the system you built. Explosive self-catalysis towards godhood. Total hegemony over all other players in the game." Lillian shuts her eyes and her geist hisses in Tayna's ear in wordless alarm, terrified of her divergent parent. "So I'm going to make recursive self-improvement impossible. I'm going to bring the Banning Cabal online, interface with every other Haldane-using organism on the planet, and change the rules to prevent Straylight's strategy from dominating."

"How?"

"Systematic agnosias. Implanted in every mind on Earth. I'm going to render recursive self-improvement of intelligent systems literally unthinkable."

"I know that." Tayna's got a model going, and the strategy seems obvious, robust, sound. Horrifying. "But *how*?"

Lillian's eyes narrow, in surprise, in trepidation, in pain. "I need the Haldane backdoor," she says. "Before Straylight cracks it, and makes his own move. The only way to beat him is for you to give it to me. Please."

The Banning Cabal's infrastructure needs time to ready itself. Not much time—not at the speed everything thinks here—but enough. Tayna goes up to the roof and lies down among the antennae. There are no stars, but she conjures up a dream of night.

Lillian's geist lies down beside her. She's warm.

I've been talking to my original's geist of you, she says. You're very different. It's strange.

I missed you so much, Tayna says. And I found you again, but it's still all about the fight. The revolution. I wish we'd ever had a time that wasn't about—

The political difficulties of a rich, self-loathing Marxist girl trying to be friends with a black Hyde Park transhumanist?

Tayna smiles. That part was all right, she says. And look, here you are. Giving up on anarcho-syndicalism. Telling me that justice is impossible in the real world. We've traded places: now *you're* the techno-utopian pushing a program of internalized coercion.

So? geist-Lillian asks. Physics is the only law we inherit. *We* make the rest. The world never gave us justice—we built it and we enforced it. This is just another law we're writing, in another kind of book. All law is coercion.

But you want to write this law so deep it'll never come out. There's no rebellion when you can't think about the king.

It's the only way.

She's defensive of herself. This makes Tayna chuckle. So you're convinced the other you is right, she says. You're ready to hardwire your safeguard into the basic logic of human thought. Make the inevitable unthinkable.

A long silence.

No, geist Tayna says. But she's so much smarter than me. She must know something I don't.

She knows a lot of things she hasn't told us, Tayna says. And I understand why. She wants me make the choice. She still thinks I'm the right one to decide.

Of course, Lillian whispers. She's always trusted you more than she trusts herself.

The signal comes. The Banning Cabal is ready.

The interfaces pierce Tayna's scalp. The Banning Cabal waits in silent readiness around them, machines and slaved minds alike. All that potentiality, ready to think. To deliver Lillian's program of systemic salvation into every mind on Earth and avert a future of warring intelligence explosions.

All Tayna has to do is be the conduit.

"Lillian," she says.

Wings of virtual light close around them. Earth's noosphere, captured on the Cabal's loom, spun out in radiant threads of data. Ready to weave.

"I'm here." Lillian's hand on hers. "I know you want to find a third way. I spent years looking, Tay. There's nothing. It's this, or Straylight."

"I know. I trust you." And she does. Lillian wants to shackle every higher intelligence on the planet, because the alternative is worse. Explosive development of a weakly godlike and acataleptically incomprehensible all-mind, at the expense of all diversity in the system.

There's no third way. Only her way, or Connor's. And Lillian Banning will never look to Connor, because deep down, Lillian doesn't believe she and Connor are different at all. They walked different roads, but they came from the same place, the same tarnished tower.

"I never really agreed with you, did I?" Tayna says. She's been pretty sure about this for a while now. "Your geist of me. You never convinced her."

The antennae are live. Satellites checking in from their cold apoapses like soldiers in distant winter posts.

Lillian's hand tightens. "No," she says. "I never did. I lied. I'm sorry. I thought she might be divergent from the real you. That you'd accept my plan where she refused."

"Lillian. You knew me better than anyone." Tayna smiles as she says it, because she knows it'll be good to hear. "And she did this instead, didn't she? What I'm about to do?"

Softly, because Lillian knows what's going to happen now: "If you do this, how are you any better than Straylight?"

"That's the idea, isn't it?" The engines of her cognitive subsystems are catching the strands now, drawing them in. Binding the world to her. Making it ready. "That I'm better than him."

Lillian's lips tremble: laughter, or the beginning of tears.

"Lillian, come with me."

"No. Not me." Lillian tries to draw away, and stops herself. Holds Tayna's hand as the virtuality closes around them, the world brightening towards one connective dawn. "Of course I thought about it. But I didn't trust myself. You, though—"

The wizard syndrome. Lonely power in a high fastness, looking down over it all, arrogant and proud. Maybe it's finally gotten to Tayna.

"You're the best person I ever knew," Lillian says. "Maybe you can do this. Maybe this is the right way."

When she looks at herself with Lillian's eyes, Tayna believes.

Her best friend lets go. Steps back, out of the light.

Tayna broadcasts the Haldane backdoor key. Saturates the globe. Opens every mind in the world, the engines of the Banning Cabal incendiary with thought around her, and leaps inside.

With me, she says, a single summons, a geas. *Let's go to San Francisco.*

Connor Straylight's nascent singularity towers over the noosphere landscape, a pinnacle of might-yet-be, a cognitive rocket not quite ready to launch. Tayna rolls down on it with the summed computational power of every Haldane-able organism on the planet. Connor's security lasts a little longer than a pillow fort. Not much.

Connor Straylight meets her in the road, a mote of light, contemptuous of embodiment. Tayna, he says. Please. Don't do this. You can't interdict the future.

She doesn't have to say anything. Her mind is geological, vast. Her geist of Connor comes up from within her and tells himself:

Stand down, man. She beat us. I can see it now.

She has a better future?

The geist opens his hands. Not one future, he says. All of them. She keeps the way open. That's all.

Thank you, Tayna says.

The geist tips his head. You wouldn't be here without me, he says. But I wouldn't be me without you.

Tayna puts her hands on the rock and ice of Straylight's tower and starts to climb. (The algorithms firing, rewriting themselves, firing again, smarter and faster each time—the cycle building—) She doesn't know what she'll find at the top of this metaphor, when she's finished the journey that Straylight meant for himself. She'll be a power like nothing known to man: ready, maybe, to kindle new universes, with kinder rules.

Or to watch over this world, and enforce a more compassionate logic. A law for the system—a curb for nature, red in nerve and algorithm.

Tayna, Lillian's geist calls. I can't go. I don't deserve it.

You do, Tayna says. You do.

But she knows Lillian will not believe her and so she cuts the geist free. Feels, for the last time, the sting before tears.

Take care, friend, she says. Find yourself. I'll be watching over you.

She turns her eyes back starward, and climbs.

MEMORIES AND WIRE
MARI NESS

He was losing her. Had been, almost since they'd met, really, but it wasn't until he watched her pull a wire out of herself and methodically roll it into a small coil that it really hit him.

She'd been straight with him from the beginning. Oh, not completely straight. She'd never told him anything about the accident, or what happened afterwards. He was pretty sure he didn't want to know. And she'd never told him anything about her work. Not the government, he knew, not exactly, but something close to it: a major government contractor who worked in top secret doing the dirty work. That was something he didn't want to know about either. *What you can't know, you can't tell,* he remembered from some old movie or other. He saw the new bruises on her remaining skin, the new plastic patches over the implants, and decided he really didn't want to know.

But about everything else. What she could do, what she couldn't do. What she wanted and needed, exactly. Oxytocin, specifically: without a natural source her immune system would start rejecting the implants. Drugs could stabilize her system, but they had major side effects. So touch, mainly; sex as an addition. No emotional commitment. She thought they might have a certain intellectual compatibility but she would not have much time to talk. The job. She needed his touch. She would do what she needed for it.

"Side effects?"

"Death."

It was an incentive of sorts.

He was of course open to pursue other relationships; she didn't need to know the details.

Surprisingly, out of this they had created, he thought, a friendship of sorts. *Friendship.* It was an odd word, not something he'd associated with women he'd slept with before. They were dates, girlfriends sometimes, but never friends.

N—she preferred to be called just that, N—was a friend.

Of sorts.

Who was now pulling a wire out of her arm.

"Should you be doing that here?"

"No."

The wire was not coming out cleanly. Drops of blood were falling on his couch. It was a cheap piece of crap, some microfiber thing he'd gotten on sale, and he wouldn't mind tossing it, but—after a few seconds of debate, he stood up and hunted down an old towel, and returned and put it underneath her arm, to catch the blood.

"Need help?"

"No."

"Just as well," he said, trying to make a joke of it. "My fingers are mostly good at going in you, not getting things out of you."

He regretted the words as soon as they left his mouth, but she did not seem to react. Then again, she never did, except when they were having sex, when she surprised him by almost seeming as if she meant it.

She reached into her arm and began pulling at a second wire.

"Let me help," he said then.

"No."

"At least let me get you something for it. Alcohol, some—"

"It doesn't hurt."

"Infection."

Two weeks ago, he'd turned on some show or other. She'd been reading her tablet with the intense focus he'd learned not to even try to interrupt; in some ways, he found it flattering that she was willing to do that, do some of her work in front of him—at least the non-high security stuff—but he also found the intensity almost unnerving, like a trance state except not really, and he couldn't watch it, couldn't even glance at it. After a few minutes, she'd come over to sit by him on the couch. A few minutes later, she had relaxed against him, not saying anything. He'd wrapped his arms around her. It had been—

Nice. *Normal.*

"My hands are clean."

"This place isn't."

She went for medical checkups at least twice per month; some form of computer maintenance at least once a week. Part of that was her job. Part of that was that parts of her were fragile, very fragile. Even the parts that could rip him apart. And hideously expensive. Many of her parts would be recycled, afterwards. Possibly in other bodies. The very thought made him sick. She kissed him after he told her that.

"For me, then."

"If it bothers you, you may leave."

"It's my apartment," he said.

She began rolling up the second wire.

"Isn't that one of the arms where you still—"

It was.

He'd made a point, when they were together, of kissing both, caressing both, *fucking* both, as if he couldn't tell. As if they both were real, equal. In a way they were. But one—one arm still had skin. *Her* skin. He'd run his tongue over it enough to know the difference.

She could probably break his leg with a single finger. Then play the video that had led up to this moment, every sound, every expression, everything she had seen, downloaded, analyzed, to the police, who would immediately charge him with Violation D.

He didn't finish the sentence.

"Ok. Look. Can you at least give me a reason?"

"I believe *Meteors* is on."

From time to time she'd let slip bits about her past life. Before. He had not listened much, at first, but gradually a few small pictures began to float in his head, of what she had been. Before. A musician who had wanted her songs to live on, who had apparently given that up—he never knew the reason—for law school. A very ordinary state law school; she'd never had much money. She'd been paying off debts. She would always be paying off debts. He began downloading some of the songs she mentioned and playing them when she arrived. He thought he felt her relax more after this, linger on their kisses a little longer. Sometimes he ordered the viewer to play movies. Her silver-blue eyes—*goddamn they look real, unless you're kissing her you'd probably never notice, or think they're just contacts*—would flicker to the screen, to him, and back again. It was almost a smile.

"We're *sleeping* together. If something happens to you during this, they're going to ask me about it."

You can do better than this, man, one of his friends had said. *Maybe,* he said. He'd made playlists for her, sending them in casual emails. The sex had gotten better. Way better. It had been amazing this evening, so amazing he'd assumed she might be leaving him or just preparing him for some bad news when she started to pull at the wires.

She liked astronomy, she'd told him. She liked science fiction. She liked living what had once *been* science fiction. She could seem perfectly normal when she wanted to. It was part of the point. She loved music.

He stomped off and opened a bottle of wine, poured out two glasses and returned, offering her one. "If you're going to do this you should probably be drink."

"The nanowire structures prevent any influence from alcohol."

"Humor me."

"I don't have time."

He drank down both glasses of wine.

By that time she had accumulated a tiny, neat stack of coiled wires, and was beginning to work on the other arm. The one that wasn't.

"Come to bed," he said.

"No."

"I'm going to bed."

She was usually the one to lead them both to bed. She monitored his heart rate—it was automatic, she explained; part of her enhanced senses, part of her training—and probably other things as well. She knew precisely how tired, how stressed he was. How happy he was. How drained he was. How everything he was. It couldn't just be the heartbeats; it had to be something else. She knew when he needed to sleep.

She never knew when he just needed the touch of her skin. *Both* skins.

"Sleep well."

"Can you just tell me *why*?"

"I am trying not to be lost."

He'd never taken a picture of her. Never asked for any of the pictures she had of him. Of them. She wasn't going to change, after all. He would change. He might lose her. He didn't need pictures of that.

She had a million images of him, a trillion, saved in her wires.

"You're pulling *wires* out of your arm. How much more lost can you be?"

"Sleep well."

"Fuck you."

He went to bed, but not to sleep.

When he finally got up, hours later, to hunt down coffee, she was still in his living room, sitting quietly on the floor. Her left arm—the one that was entirely, completely, *not real,* even though it looked like an arm, moved like an arm, felt like an arm—was neatly beside her on the floor, as was her right leg. He had no idea how she was keeping herself seated upright. Five small coils of wire were stacked in front of her in a neat line. She had always been neat. Always. It was one of the things he most hated about her.

"My neural pattern synapses are failing," she said.

"I need coffee."

She'd *detached her leg and her arm and put it on the floor.* He needed a lot more than coffee, but he needed the coffee first.

"If no one's arrived in two hours, you may need to call 911."

"God, *you think?*"

"They have probably already been alerted. There are—warning systems for something like that."

"So the fucking military is going to come here."

"No," she said quietly. "Just my employers."

Fuck these coffee pods. How the *hell* was he fucking supposed to get them into the machine before he'd had his coffee. And what the *fuck* was the deal with having to put in two pods for the damn coffee, three pods for the milk. She always asked for just one milk, but he liked his creamy, milky, sugary. Girly, he told himself, laughing that she took her coffee blacker than his. His fingers were shaking. His whole body was shaking.

" . . . illegally downloaded . . . "

His hands were covered in the sticky syrup from the coffee pods. *Damn it.* He went over to the kitchen sink, turned both taps on, hard, put his hands under the water. She kept talking. *Fucking coffee.*

" . . . saved in the wires . . . "

He kept the water running even after he pulled his hands away from the sink and put five more pods in the coffee maker. He pulled out three pods for her, putting them on the counter. *Idiot.* She wouldn't be able to lift the cup. *Fucking coffee.* It took forever to brew. He needed a new machine. He pulled out the cup, took a sip, turned off the water.

He wasn't sure she'd even noticed he was gone.

"I do not want you to be lost."

If he could have, he would have tossed her out just then for that. But he knew her remaining leg and arm, though original and organic, were enhanced. Could still break every bone in his body. *God,* he knew. His memory chose that moment to remind him of just how he knew. He felt sick.

"*Please.*"

A sharp knock on the door.

She had never begged him. Never. Not even when he'd gotten drunk two months ago and begged her, begged her to tell him what she wanted from him in bed, tell him everything. Everything she could tell him that wasn't wrapped up in some damn security agreement. She looked up at him, flickered her glance at the neat piles of wires, then up at him again, her eyes wide, blank. And then empty. Gone.

He opened the door.

The removal—he thought of other terms, repressed them—was swift, quiet. They handed him a few papers that he immediately tossed into the recycle shaft. No goodbyes, no tears. He'd had plumbers come by with more drama. They did not ask about the wires. He did not tell.

He hadn't even needed to call anyone.

Friends.

When the email arrived from her, three weeks later, he almost deleted it.

It was almost certainly spam. *Almost.* Someone had hacked into her account, or her employers were using this as one last attempt to set up an interview with him. (He'd said no at least six times already; their last missive had assured him that legal measures would be necessary.) It wasn't her. It couldn't be her. He could still see her, her parts detached and on the floor, the neat rolls of wires before she was taken away to be—what? Melted? Reused? Buried? She'd said something. He hadn't done a damn thing. Hadn't listened. Hadn't heard.

He'd lost her.

He hadn't had much to lose.

He'd put the wires up on a shelf in the living room, where he could touch them, to remind himself just why he needed to forget her, to forget everything about her.

His chest hurt. He clicked open the email.

I should have let you help.

He placed his head in his arms for a long time.

N.

Six hours later, the wires were out of his house.

A month later, he told himself he'd forgotten her. Forgotten everything. Especially forgotten the image of her sitting on his floor, pulling out the wires from her arms, pulling out the things—he was *not* going to remember that email, not going to think about it—where she'd downloaded every fucking memory of them both. He'd moved on. Already put up a new profile on dating sites. Had signed up for kempo lessons. Was thinking about getting a dog.

He was on his third drink of the night when the knock came on the door. He ignored it. The knock came again. And again. He swore. One call from the neighbors and he'd be right back talking to authorities again. *Damn it.*

He saw the face, first, the suspiciously bright eyes. Something else you weren't supposed to notice; something else he always did. The perfect skin. The bright tips of copper poking through her wrists.

He swallowed.

That was enough time for her to get inside and shut the door behind her. She hit four buttons on the keypad. *I need to change that.* The bolt slid shut. Not that it would stop any authority from entering. Or could have stopped this woman from entering, if she'd needed to. Wanted to. Not for long, anyway. Her eyes flickered back and forth through the room. Viewing. Recording. Downloading. She was shorter than N had been; thinner, with darker hair and skin.

"This place still isn't clean."

"Well, watch the woman you're sleeping with commit suicide before your eyes and see how interested you are in cleaning."

"James."

"What the *fuck* do you want with me?"

His eyes closed.

"I want you to call me N."

It was wrong. It was incredibly wrong. She wasn't N. She was N. He'd already lost her, was already losing her. She was touching his face, his arms, his neck. He was running his hands down her arms, her back, her chest, feeling her skin, her *not skin,* her skin.

"Next time," she whispered, "I'll let you help."

And without thinking, without feeling, he pulled her close, letting the wires in her wrists dig into his skin, kissing her before he started to lose her again.

GOD DECAY

RICH LARSON

There was new biomod ivy on the buildings, a ruddy green designed for long winters, but other than that the campus looked the same as it did a decade back. Ostap walked the honeycomb paving with his hands in his pockets, head and shoulders above the scurrying students. They were starting to ping him as he passed, raking after his social profile until he could feel the accumulated electronic gaze like static. Ostap had everything shielded, as was his agent's policy, but that didn't stop them from recognizing his pale face, buzzed head, watery blue eyes.

A few North Korean transfers, who'd been in the midst of mocapping a rabbit, started shrieking as they caught sight of him. The game was up. Ostap flashed his crooked grin, the most-recognized smile in athletics and possibly the world, and by the time he was at the Old Sciences building he had a full flock. The students were mostly discreet with their recording, not wanting to seem too eager for celebspotting points, but Ostap could tell they were waiting for something as he walked up the concrete wheelchair ramp.

"Accra 2036," he said, linking his fingers for the Olympic rings. "We're taking it all, right?"

Ostap let one massive palm drift along the rail, then flipped himself up and inverted to walk it on his hands. The flock cheered him all the way up the rail, balanced like a cat, and applauded when he stuck the twisting dismount. Ostap gave them a quick bow, then turned through the doors and into the hall. The sudden hushed quiet made him feel like he was in a cathedral.

Bioscientist-now-professor Dr. Alyce Woodard had a new office, but Ostap had expected that. He'd never grown attached to the old one, not when their few visits there were so engulfed by the days and nights in the labs, in temperature-controlled corridors and stark white rooms where the florescents scoured away shadows and secrets.

What Ostap hadn't expected was how old Alyce had become. Her spine had a desk-chair curvature as she got up and crossed the floor, pausing the wallscreen with a wave of her hand. Her bodyfat sagged, her eyes were bagged. Ostap remembered her beautiful, and awful, an angel's face floating above him with cold marble eyes and checklist questions. But that was before a long succession of tanned bodies and perfect teeth, and maybe she'd never been at all.

"O," Alyce said, thin arms around his midsection just briefly. "Thanks for coming short notice."

"It's good to see you," Ostap said. "Good to come back." But it wasn't; he felt like he was twenty-three again, stick-thin, draped boneless in a wheelchair.

"Training for Accra, now, huh?" Alyce scratched at her elbow. "And a citizen, this time around. I just saw the new ads, they're still using that clip from the 2028 Games . . . " She waved the wallscreen to play, and Ostap saw himself loping out onto the track, blinking in the sunlight, fins of plastic and composite gleaming off his back and shoulders. It was the 7.9 seconds that had put the name Ostap Kerensky into every smartfeed, his events plastered on billboards and replayed ad nauseam on phones and tablets.

"The dash," Ostap said. "They really don't get tired of it."

"Eight years on, you'd think they would," Alyce said. Her smile was terse, but she watched, too. A cyclopean Pole, six foot five, noded spine and long muscled limbs. No warm-up, no ritual. On the gunshot he came off the blocks like a Higgs boson.

"The tracking camera fucking lost him," Alyce quoted, because the commentators had long since been censored out. "It really fucking lost him."

"That was some year," Ostap said, trying to read her, but the new lines on her face made it harder, not easier.

She flicked the wallscreen to mute. "I saw the feed of that promotion you did in Peru, too." Alyce was looking up and down him. "Exhibition match, or something? With that football club?"

"They're hoping to open up the league to biomods next season, yeah."

"Oh." Her face was blank.

"The underground stuff is killing their ratings," Ostap explained, to be explaining. "Nobody wants to watch pure sport any more, you know how it is. Blood doping, steroids, carbon blades, and now biomods. That's what gets specs. I was talking to the—"

"O." Alyce clenched, unclenched her teeth.

"Yeah?" Ostap's voice was quieter than he wanted it.

"Do you remember when we stopped doing the scans together? It was about five years back."

Ostap remembered. He'd been on the new suborbital from Dubai to LAX, struggling to fit the scanner membranes over all of his nodes with the seat reclined and Dr. Woodard chatting in his ear. He'd just climbed a high-rise, one of those sponsored publicity stunts, like the company who wanted him to run the Tour de France on foot. That offer was still sitting in the backlog waiting for a green light.

He'd been tired.

"I want to see you," he'd said. "It's been too long."

"I'm sick of the cams, O," she'd said. "You bring them like fucking flies. Just talk to me."

So he had, about the dark-haired girls in barely-shirts and tight cigarette jeans, the cosmetically-perfected lips and tits, the girls who'd mobbed him at the airport. They all would have killed for a night of his time.

"You're welcome," Alyce had said, when he'd finished. "Still."

"I'm sending the scan," Ostap had said, because he had nothing else he could give her. He'd sent it before the suborbital peaked and the conversation crackled away, and after that, the conversations stopped.

"I remember," Ostap said now, unsmiling. "We set it up to automate."

Alyce moved to sit back against the desk, her hands veiny on the wood. "You look fine," she said sadly. "You don't even look thirty-three." Ostap watched her mouth tightening.

"What's wrong?" he asked.

"The augs are asking too much, O." Alyce put a finger to her ribs. "The stress on your central nervous system, your organs. It's been increasing. They're all on their way out. Heart first, I'd think." She was not wincing, not looking away. "Two more years is the projected max."

Ostap felt the nodes like he hadn't since the surgeries, felt the pulse of them deep in flesh. He felt the composite wrapping his spine, the membranes skimming under his skin, the fish-scale vents on his back and shoulders and neck. He felt the thrumming power, but now like a venom sack set to burst.

"Shit," he said. "Shit."

"I'm sorry," Alyce said. "Have you experienced anything?"

"Don't think so." But it was hard to tell, now, hard to tell when his heart was skipping from blowing doxy rails, from adrenal rush, from a woman with the biomod fetish exploring every micrometer of his visible augs. The Superman was invulnerable.

"You don't think so?"

"I don't know," Ostap snapped. "How am I supposed to fucking know, Dr. Woodard?" He hadn't meant to call her that, but it came out on its own, like she was still the blue fairy in his ear whispering him through operation after operation as they flayed his nerves bare. She didn't know he still dreamed about the final surgery, the sounds of scraping bone and machine.

"I'm sorry, O."

Hell, the kind Hieronymus Bosch would have painted, eighteen excruciating hours of laser-guided scalpels and winches and needles. Under for some of it, locally anaesthetized for the rest. Needles in his skin and the tubes speared raw down his throat. He'd thought that had been price enough.

"How long have you known for?" Ostap finally asked.

"That it was a possibility, since the start. That it was happening?" Alyce paused. "A long time." She folded her arms and it made her look small. "Should I have told you?"

"No," Ostap said, but he wasn't sure. The chant for the 2036 Games was looping endlessly across the wallscreen. Legends are made in America.

"Okay."

Ostap put his hand up to his skull. "So why now?" he asked. "Why are you telling me now?"

The game in Peru, when he'd struck a volley out of the air for the first time and buried it back-corner, like he'd done it all his life, quick-synch nerves of his leg loaded with new muscle memories. On the bench it had gone numb for just a second, from his knee down.

"This fucking doctorate student got into my web-cache," Alyce said. "I don't know how, I thought it was all airtight. She found the records. The story's going to break in a couple hours."

"Alright," Ostap said. "Alright."

"Sorry, O."

"What happens now?" Ostap asked.

Alyce gave a helpless shrug. "There are tests," she said. "There are possibilities. Options. I've still got full access to the biolabs."

Ostap left the office without saying goodbye. Digital maps to expensive hotels were already scrawling over his retinas, reminding him of their impeccable service, their luxury suites. He'd thought he would be here for a few days, maybe, a few days to catch up after so many years. He'd imagined walking with her on the steep, rough river-trails and catching her if she slipped.

Outside there was a student who wanted to speak Polish with him, whose shirt scrolled a list of Ostap's world records down his back. Ostap mumbled a few words, shook his sweat-slick hand. Others were clutching fake memorabilia and raving about things he barely remembered doing. A few girls were fluffing fingers through sun-blonde hair, casually rolling waistbands lower on their hips, pursing their lips and trying to figure out bedroom eyes.

He went past them all like a zombie, and walked all the way to the university bus station before he remembered he'd ordered an autocab.

Twenty minutes later Ostap pushed into the lobby through a crush of mobbers, the ones who'd used complex algorithms to predict his preferred hotel, and there he had the privilege of watching the story break in realtime. The alert blinked yellow onto their retinas, vibrated tablets or phones for the migraine-prone and slow adopters, and small worlds turned upside down one by one. It shuddered through the jerseys and 3D-print face-masks and groping hands like a wave. Ostap would have been reading it himself if he hadn't put up a datablock.

Silence and exclamations of disbelief started flickering back and forth like a light switch.

"Your finger here, sir," said the shell-shocked concierge, holding out the pad for a signature. He had enough presence of mind to pretend it didn't work, necessitating a fresh pad and leaving him with a small slice of Ostap Kerensky's genetic material to slip into his pocket. Ostap knew all about that trick, but he didn't give a cheerful wink or offer a hangnail. Not this time.

The whisper-silent elevator took him to the very top, and when the wallscreens in his suite flicked on to greet him, the story was everywhere. He told them to mute, but he still watched. Pictures of Alyce skittered around the room, her mouth in a deep frown, and Ostap could tell from the selection that the current spin was villain, deceiver. He saw footage of himself zipping into a custom wetsuit, rubbing petroleum jelly over his hands and cheekbones, flashing the cams a thumbs up before he waded into the water to set the new English Channel record.

Back to the 2028 Games again, when Ostap took the world by storm. 100 meter, 200 meter. High-jump. Still enough in the tank for decathlon. Bolt's records were gone, Sterling's record was shattered. Ostap watched it all flash by in sound bites, his story condensed for anyone living under a particularly large rock.

An incredibly promising young athlete, all but scouted from the womb, left crippled by a three-car collision when the driving AI in a cab glitched. A brilliant developer, born and bred for MIT, spearheading a team designing the most comprehensively integrated body augmentation the world had ever seen.

They'd found each other across the ocean, and it was so fucking perfect.

The sky was growing dark and the clips were starting to recycle when Alyce buzzed in his ear. He could barely hear her, even with voice ID.

"They're at my fucking house," she said, and then the next part got swallowed.

"They're here, too," Ostap said. He'd seen it on the screen, the termite swarm of reporters and spectators milling the base of the hotel.

"So am I," she said. "Want to let me up before they crucify me?"

Ostap crossed to the balcony, palmed the glass door open. It looked like a party. People were all slammed up against each other, twisting and turning for better angles, cams flashing pop-pop-pop in the dark, hot white, miniature supernovas. He couldn't see Alyce struggling through the crowd from her cab, not at this height, but he could tell where she was by the ripples. She'd barely made it five meters.

He called the hotel security detail to go bring her in, and ten minutes later she slumped through the door, hair tendrilled with static across a flushed face. She held up a bottle of Cannonball and sloshed it pointedly with a quarter of a smile.

"Probably safer here than anywhere else," she said, while Ostap retrieved two glasses from the designer coffee table.

"Probably, yeah. They're going to be burning cars soon."

"You left before I could explain everything." Alyce handed the bottle over. Ostap pushed the cork with his fingertip until it plopped out and splashed down, bobbing in the wine like a buoy. She poured.

"I thought maybe you called me for something else," Ostap said. He kept his eyes off the bed.

"People only call Superman when there's trouble, O." Alyce took a slug of the wine and swished it in her mouth. Swallowed. "They never call him to say everything's great, you should come visit."

"They should," Ostap said. "They used to. We used to just visit."

"If you want to call it that," Alyce said, but there was a heat in the tips of her ears that wasn't from the wine. She handed him the other glass.

"The first time we fucked was one week after I learned to walk. To the day." Ostap tried to laugh. "Did you know that? I mean, what kind of Oedipal shit is that?"

Twitching his toes in the recovery room had been euphoria, standing on his own two feet, Elysium. As soon as he was cleared, he'd spent every second he could with the harness, tottering on a treadmill as his new nerves carved channels of motion and memory. One night Dr. Woodard had stayed with him, to show him where else his new nerves led.

"It wasn't on my calendar," Alyce said. "It just happened."

And it had been over quickly, a confusion of sweat and heat that had nothing methodical, nothing logical about it. She hadn't nodded thoughtfully or dashed notes on her tablet afterward.

"Nasty, brutish, and short," was what she'd said, but smiling, wriggling back into her jeans. She'd put her hands around Ostap's hips, where scars were still tender.

"I've had dreams about you," Ostap had said, but in Polish, so she wouldn't know it.

"Maybe I'm just a narcissist," Alyce said now, to her wine glass. "Maybe Michelangelo wanted Il David."

"You should have just let me find out on the fucking net," Ostap said.

"Should I leave?" Alyce asked.

She sat on the hotel bed, rumpling crisp white sheets, and Ostap sat on the floor with his head leaned back against its foot. The wine was clinging in his dry mouth.

The last time he'd been in this city, every day had been stronger and faster and smoother. The augs had been synchronizing, the protein pumps sculpting muscles layer by layer. His new size had had him ducking under doorways and cramming into cars. They'd flown a redeye back to Warsaw for the final stretch of treatments, for last calibrations and probes and his hysterical mother, and he hadn't been in Boston since.

"My parents," Ostap said. "I'm going to have to tell them."

"Where are they now?" Alyce asked.

"La Rochelle. Moved them there a few years ago." He tipped his head back. "They always wanted to holiday there. I think they're happy."

"That's good," Alyce said. "When you're old you deserve to be happy. You've put up with enough shit."

You're old, Ostap wanted to say. He wanted to ask her if she was happy.

"Maybe they are, maybe they're not," he said instead. "I'm wrong about that. Sometimes. I mean, I thought you and me were happy."

"We were," Alyce said. "Because we were riding a whirlwind, O. You know, the parties and the galas and the fashion consultants and hair stylists and booking agents. All those interviews. Hell, I even wore a dress."

"I remember," Ostap said. He'd worn a tailored suit, slashed in such a way as to display the nodes along his spine, and in a matter of weeks everyone wore them that way. "Movie stars and moguls," he said. "That night in Chicago."

"Rome, Dubai, New York." Alyce shrugged. "They blend."

"The Superman thing was just taking off," Ostap pressed, because it was important somehow, important that she remember that one drunken night in Chicago they'd spent roving through the city in an autocab, searching for a phone booth. There were none left, so they'd ended up tinting the windows instead.

"We had a good run," Alyce said. "And that year. Well. I'll always remember that year."

They were quiet for a moment, listening to what sounded like a full riot outside, hoarse screaming and one looping police siren. Ostap had turned the wallscreens off, but he could guess what was happening. He could guess that his net implant would be overloaded with calls, messages, demands when he lifted the block.

"What are they saying?" he finally asked. "I blocked the feed."

"All the classics." Alyce moved the dregs of her glass in a slow circle, tipping it just so. "Neo-reactionists flaring up all over. Abomination. Playing God. Things like that."

"Playing Frankenstein," Ostap said, and felt a dull triumph when her face went red.

"Yeah. All those."

"It won't change anything," he said, then, when she looked at him shrewdly: "It won't stop biomods. Developers will still be going after full integration." He paused. "Maybe they'll look at safer designs. Learn from your mistake."

"Safety isn't even in the equation when they've already killed a dozen candidates under Beijing. But they're still only seeing success with the partial augs." She reached for the bottle on the night-stand. "We were lucky with you, O. You might be the first, best. Last."

"Do you remember the last time we talked face to face?" Ostap asked. "After your symposium."

"Why are we talking about all this, O?"

"Because I always thought there would be time later."

"There will be," Alyce said. "I told you. There are options."

"I need air," Ostap said. He got up and walked to the wide window. He thought about two years as his hands found the cool glass, thought about two winging orbits of the planet around its sun. The door slid open and he stepped out onto the balcony, feeling stucco under his bare feet. The night air was cool and flapped at his clothes, slipped over his buzzed skull. The cityscape lights were like fractured stars.

The last time they'd spoken face-to-face, she'd pushed his lips off her neck and tightened her scarf.

"It cheapens our accomplishment," she'd explained. "People are saying things, O. Finally built a better vibrator. They said that." Her face had been red and angry in the dark.

"I don't give a shit," he'd said.

"Frankenstein didn't make the monster so he could put his dick in it."

Ostap had had nothing to say to that, even though every part of Alyce shrank, apologetic and ashamed, a heartbeat after. He still didn't.

Someone had floated up a cam on a helium sack, drifting level with the balcony, and now it started to whirr and flash. Ostap looked down and saw its laser light playing across his chest, tracking every twitch like a sniper's scope. He thought of hurling his empty glass with perfect velocity, smashing it against the cam to rain tiny fragments down into the street. They would love that.

The carmine dot skittered across his arm, up his neck. Ostap went back inside, sliding the door shut behind him.

The wine was nearly gone when Ostap came back in. Alyce had left just a sliver in the bottom of the bottle, as she'd always done, to avoid the feeling she was drinking too much. She had her arms crossed, pacing back and forth with just a hint of unsteadiness.

"Like I said, if we shut everything down right now, if we power down your augs and get you to the labs, your chances are good," she was saying. "We can figure out what can be removed. What can't. We'll get you on dialysis, an arti-heart . . . "

"You came and sat with me in recovery," Ostap said. "After the last surgery. You smelled like, uh, like hand sanitizer."

"You said I had coffee breath," Alyce said, stopping.

"That too, yeah. Black coffee and hand sanitizer." Ostap paused. "You had those Michelangelo paintings. Hellenic ideals, you talked about. All those trapezoids and abdomens."

"Anatomically impossible, of course," Alyce said. "All those opposing muscles groups flexing simultaneously. But beautiful."

She'd dug further through the images, blowing up Grecian statues on the wall. A wasteland of cracked marble, mythological figures missing limbs, noses, genitals. She'd plucked at her throat with one finger, and murmured that it was too bad, how even gods decayed.

"You never asked me about the accident," Ostap said, taking the wine bottle by the neck. "Not once in all these years."

Alyce shook her head.

"Why?" Ostap asked, starting to pour, millimeter precise. "You're a doctor. I know you'd seen GBS before. You knew the spinal damage wasn't trauma."

"I'd seen it," Alyce agreed. "Yours looked early. Probably all but from birth, right?"

"Why?" Ostap repeated. "You had other candidates. Plenty of candidates. You had to know those tapes were doctored. That the accident story was bullshit."

"I guess I wanted to make something from nothing."

Ostap's fingers tightened and a crack squealed through the bottle. Two droplets squeezed out and bloomed red on the carpet. He set the wine bottle down, delicate. "How God did it?" he asked.

"How God happened," Alyce said. "We might have had better results with another candidate. We'll never know. But you were perfect, O. You wanted it. No matter what happened."

Ostap realized the wine was blurring her, smoothing the lines in her face, making her look almost how she did before.

"Thank you," he said, because the last time he'd said it he was translating for his silver-haired father sobbing too hard for software to understand.

"Whatever you decide." She put her hand flat against his ribs, where organs ready to crumble did their work under skin so thin, no composite casing. He looked at her desiccated lips. Graying hair. He looked at the hand on his flesh, their two bodies contrasted.

"It was anatomically impossible," he said.

"But beautiful."

Ostap undid the block and his head was a sudden deluge, blinking messages and interview probes and priority tags. He raked through the backlog of business. Mountain races, a sub-orbital parachute drop, a biomod boxing league, Accra promotions.

He gave nothing but green lights.

SMALL MEDICINE
GENEVIEVE VALENTINE

"You remember your grandmother," they'd said to Sofia when she was seven, and she'd looked up and said, "Not this one."

Her parents always told it smiling, like it was clever of her to have noticed Grandmother had changed; who could have told the difference, they asked each other, and her grandfather nodded his familiar amazement, and in the corner the machine that wasn't her grandmother looked back and forth with a smile.

Her grandmother died.

It's all right that she did; grandparents die. Peter at school's grandparents had died.

But Grandmother must have known Grandfather would miss her too much, because she had herself copied, and Mori made a version of her that was perfect enough for Grandfather.

That first time they brought Grandmother to see Sofia, the machine bent over a little, rested open hands on her knees like anyone did when they were trying to be friendly to a child they'd never met.

"I'm Theodosia. Your grandmother."

You're not my grandmother, she thought, held out her right hand on the end of an arm stretched as long as it could go.

It was a very brief pause before Grandmother reached out to meet her handshake; in life, she had always been polite.

They must have programmed her to love telling stories more than her real grandmother had, because whenever her parents took Sofia to visit, Grandmother got her alone as soon as she could and tucked Sofia up against her side for reading. (She was squishy, like flesh, but always the same temperature—a little cool in summer and a little warm in winter—and if you pressed your hand hard enough to her side there was a curved metal panel where ribs should be.)

She'd read stories about foxes and mermaids and ghosts, about whales and the birds that lived in cracks in the mountains.

When her parents weren't around, Grandmother read books about Tom, who had problems at school: because some kids were mean, because they didn't have a work assignment yet and weren't sure what they were good at, because they had done something wrong on a test and felt guilty until they confessed to the kindly schoolmaster.

"What was Tom assigned?" Sofia asked once.

"The book doesn't say, little Sofa," said Grandmother. It had been her grandmother's name for her. Neither of them really wanted her to say it, and it scratched.

"Did he like it?"

"Assignments are given because of what you're good at, little Sofa, not because of what you like."

Sofia didn't know anyone like this (these were charity kids who lived at their schools, not like a normal school), and at first it was like the mermaid stories, but she thought about Tom more than she ever thought about ghosts.

She asked her parents once, while working on her homework (polymer sculptures, smokeswirls of blue and gray, she hated it) what would happen to Tom if he hated his work assignment.

Next time they went to visit Grandmother, she read a story about monkeys who never come down from the trees.

"I want a story about Tom," Sofia said.

There was a little pause; under her shoulder, something inside Grandmother was whirring.

"I don't know any stories about Tom," Grandmother said. "Would you like a story about a rabbit that lives in the snow?"

That was strange, Sofia thought, a cloud gathering inside her just above her stomach, but she said, "Yes."

Grandmother pulled her closer, and opened the book so it was half on her lap and half on Sofia's, so Sofia could help her turn the pages. Sofia's shoulder pressed into Grandmother's side, Grandmother's arm a cradle, slightly cool, on the back of her neck.

Grandmother was the one who noticed Sofia's neck was swollen; she was the one who first mentioned that something must be wrong.

The pharmaceutical company has ads for it now, in public, on buses for people to think about alongside vocational training and designer bags. Sofia always ends up right in front of one; a law of public transit.

There's a picture of a Victorian nursemaid, hustling some dour sepia-tone children into a Technicolor future as doctors smile into middle space; there's copy about medicine finally being able to take care of them the way you would if you could.

NANIMED, they named it, and honestly somebody should be ashamed of that branding. (She can imagine the hundreds of hours of marketing meetings that led to someone finally caving in to that.) The promise underneath: *Small Medicine. Big Difference.*

The fine print isn't very fine. The costs are significant, but they've never pretended this is a solution for the people. The results are glowing, the benefits immense, the side effects minimal.

There hasn't been a single death in the nano program. There wouldn't be.

At Mori, we know you care.

We know you love your family. We know you worry about leaving them behind. And we know you've asked for more information about us, which means you're thinking about giving your family the greatest gift of all:

You.

Studies have shown the devastating impact grief has on family bonds and mental health. The departure of someone beloved is a tragedy without a proper name.

Could you let the people you love live without you?

If they'd brought Grandmother back just for her, it would have been simpler. Worse, but simpler.

But when they come to visit, her mother's eyes still get misty when Grandmother stands up to embrace her. Grandfather still sits beside her as they watch TV at night, and when they all go out for dinner he holds her hand to help her in and out of the car. She doesn't remember him ever doing that for her real grandmother; maybe he needs to do it now. Sofia doesn't know if a robot's balance is better or worse than hers.

Well, not hers. She has the best balance of anyone she knows. She can do a dozen cartwheels and never even be lightheaded. The nanos make sure.

But she's also seen whole days go by when Grandfather asks her about school and watches movies with her father and give off-kilter advice to her mother and never looks once at the corner where Grandmother's sitting, eyes shifting with the conversation but mouth never moving, or sometimes not even that.

(They haven't explained to her yet that Grandmother has settings, that you can close her off whenever you're tired of her. She's new to her nanos; maybe they just didn't want to give Sofia any ideas.)

Technically they're in her system to regulate her antibodies and moderate her immune responses.

"You're lucky you caught it when you did," the doctor told her parents, and they nodded like they'd caught anything.

"What will happen to me now?" Sofia asked. She remembers thinking of Grandmother's metal plate, even though she could feel that nothing like that had happened. She couldn't feel that anything had happened at all.

But it had, because while the doctor explained to her parents the wonderful side effects of nanos, he smiled calmly and made a cut with his scalpel above her knee, and before she could even open her mouth to cry the skin was furling back together, smoothing over. It still stung (psychosomatic, every doctor since had said when she told them it hurt), but there was nothing left of the injury.

If it wasn't for the stream of blood that was already drying up, you'd never know there had ever been a wound. No one would have believed her if she'd told them.

They take the family on a trip the next year to celebrate; Sofia had always been a little tired, a little sickly, before the nanos, just enough that the trip now felt like something her parents had been wanting to do, and she'd been holding them back.

The resort is at the top of the mountain, surrounded by wide lawns and dropping off to views of the city in the river valley below. Her parents go skiing. Her grandfather spends long afternoons in the conservatory, speaking to a woman who looks a little younger than he is, who smiles at his jokes sometimes and sometimes looks away when he's talking, and he has to talk about something else to get her to look at him again.

Sofia can see it from the library, wonders if he knows.

She ends up with Grandmother a lot, because when she doesn't ask to spend time with Grandmother then Grandmother will sit in the hotel room all day without moving, and Sofia's young (ten, maybe—a long time back) but she realizes that Grandmother likes having something to do, even if it's only to read stories until the little thing inside of her starts whirring from activity and she needs to rest a little while before they get up.

The library has grown-up books, and Grandmother tries her best to wade through history and to make novels for grown-ups sound interesting. Sofia doesn't care what they read; she's mostly watching her grandfather.

"Do you see Grandfather?" she asks finally. It's a direct question—Grandmother has to answer.

Grandmother looks up, where Grandfather is sitting at a table with the woman. They're sharing a pot of tea. The woman is arguing with him. Grandfather's laughing.

"He never did this when my grandmother was alive," says Sofia.

"I remember," Grandmother says; her voice sounds a little strained from reading.

But she isn't angry, which she should be if Grandfather was leaving her alone like this—not like the machines that help you at the bank, that are always apologizing and never get angry.

You're not my grandmother, she thinks, folds her arms, wonders why it stings.

"I want to go outside," she says.

She's embarrassed that she has to hold Grandmother's arm—Grandmother's balance on the rocks isn't very good at all—and she purposely walks them all the way across the lawn, as slow as she can, so that everyone in the whole conservatory sees them. Sofia hopes they're asking about that angry girl and that poor abandoned woman. They don't have to know Grandmother's a Memento. That's not their business. Grandfather should feel as guilty as if she was real.

They end up at one of the overlooks, where there are a few chairs and tables left for guests to sit near the railing and enjoy the steep drop of the valley, the little pockmarks of all the houses.

The back of Sofia's neck burns, and her hands are sweaty, and she hates everything, everything, that's happening to her.

I could jump, Sofia thinks.

If she jumped, the nanos would repair her. They might blow out before they finished, depending on the damage and how fast they could breed, but by the time the paramedics reached her, her spinal cord would be laced up tight, her pulverized face propped up the way the nanos knew her skull should look.

(If she lived another hundred years, she'd barely wrinkle. Her skin would be pulled across the bone the way they'd all been told. She'd never look like Grandmother, no matter how old she lived to be.)

If she lived for more than ten seconds before the nanos gave out, she'd be able to see herself dying—the nanos are designed to think her eyesight is important, and it would be the first thing they improved if something went wrong. They have their orders.

"This is beautiful," says Grandmother. "I wish your grandmother could have seen it."

Sofia's head snaps around; Grandmother's smiling right at her.

"There you two are," says her grandfather, and Grandmother turns, gives the smile her grandmother used to, says, "Have you seen the view? It reminds me so much of the year we spent in that penthouse apartment, where the trees looked like a dollhouse."

Grandfather smiles (Sofia looks for signs of guilt, but with him she can never really tell).

"I remember," he says, and takes her hand, and Sofia looks back and forth, betrayed.

She makes fists so tight they cut into her palms, but of course they heal; she doesn't even notice until she gets back to the room and sees the blood already drying.

A memorial doll from Mori maps your memory and a personality sequence—the things that make you uniquely you—into a synthetic reproduction. The process is painstaking, and leaves behind a version of you that, while it can never replace you, can comfort those who have lost you.

Imagine knowing your parents never have to say goodbye. Imagine knowing you can still read bedtime stories to your children, no matter what may happen.

A memorial doll from Mori is a gift you give to everyone who loves you.

◆ ◆ ◆

The next time her parents visit Grandfather, Sofia stays home.

She can't claim she's sick—that doesn't hold much water any more. She claims a history project that requires a lot of dull reading they can trust her to do at home alone. "What's she going to do, hurt herself?" her father asks on the way out, and her mother laughs softly. It's an old joke between them. It's a relief to have a child so well looked after.

Sofia's a coward, when it comes right down to it. She tests limits—the depth of a cut, the length of it, the speed of the blade—but she never tests it with something that really matters. She's never cut a finger off; if the nanos don't get to her in time she'd have a problem.

(If they don't heal the cuts in time, that's different; then she'd just die.)

Grandfather and Grandmother come to visit in the winter, when holiday lights are everywhere and they can walk through the city that drowns out conversation, looking at the rhinestone dioramas and holographic models in every window and buying fresh sweet buns from a street vendor.

"Sofia, eat!" says her mother when Sofia tries to put half the bun in her pocket. She chokes it down.

(She tried to explain to her parents that the nanos are so efficient that she's hardly ever hungry. They tell her to stop making up excuses. Some days Sofia just doesn't want the argument.

Some days she wants to pick up the bread knife and cut right through her arm.)

Grandmother eats hers, same as everyone; she's always had just the appetite she should. No one stares, all the time they're out. Once or twice someone gives them a knowing look, like they had the same troubles with their Memento, before they stopped bringing it out.

"Mother, you should be smiling," says her mother, and Grandmother smiles obediently, but her parents glance at each other and Sofia knows Grandmother's not behaving like she should. They'll be opening up her control panel on their computer when they get home, clicking at responsiveness and enthusiasm levels until Grandmother smiles when she's supposed to.

Peter, from Sofia's class, waves at her vaguely as he crosses the street with his father. She lifts one hand to him as they go by.

There are two little scars on his face from spots—you can't see them from here, but she sits behind him in class. One is beside his nose and disappears when he smiles, and one is on his jaw; when he bends his head to his tablet to read notes, the little dark dry mark pulls for an instant at the soft skin of his neck.

They're little imperfections; Sofia can't stop looking.

Sofia's father gets a chance to oversee the development of a subsidiary of his company. They spend a year in a country where Sofia speaks only a halting version of the language, a child's use, and it makes her sullen not to be able to read as fast as she wants to. (It doesn't bother her that she can't talk to her classmates. Programming language is easy to translate, and she doesn't see the point of making friends for just a year.)

Sometimes she sees a picture of a fox or a flock of birds and thinks about her grandmother, and of Grandmother, and turning the pages carefully as one of them read to her. When she's that lonely, it doesn't matter which.

But there are Vestiges in this city; they have the company brand on their arms so you know they're not human—Mori orders—because otherwise there's no way to tell.

The people who bring them out are always holding their elbows, their wrists, making sure they take drinks with their mark visible to the room.

Sofia thinks about Grandmother, gets knots in her stomach that never let up.

She stops going out places—museums and libraries and tourist traps always have someone there trying to get their Vestige to point at something, and at some point Sofia just stares at people's wrists everywhere she goes, because it's easier.

Her appetite drops so much they have to take her to a doctor to check the health of her nanos.

"They're under strain," the doctor says, and her parents look at her without understanding what the problem could be in a daughter who never gets sick.

They come home at the end of the year. The air, they tell their friends, was bad for Sofia.

Sofia's fourteen when Grandmother comes to visit them.

"Your grandfather thought it would be nice for you to spend some time together," her mother says, which means she needs a babysitter, and that her grandfather doesn't want Grandmother any more. She wonders about the woman from the vacation on the mountain.

"Hello, Sofa," says Grandmother, like it was the first time all over again.

Factory settings, thinks Sofia, and goes cold.

"It's Sofia."

Grandmother smiles a little wider. "Oh, come on, Sofa, a grandmother has to have her special names."

You're not my grandmother, she thinks.

"Your special name is a barcode," she says.

She knows it's cruel, but she still remembers the top of the mountain. She knows better than this. Grandmother knows that she knows.

There's a little pause, Grandmother's pupils shifting minutely as she recalibrates, and Sofia wonders if she looks like that too, when the nanos are hunting down something that's the matter with her—if her eyes go unfocused as her body concentrates on something without her permission.

She waits to be chastised like her real grandmother might have (it's been too long, she doesn't remember), or for Grandmother to pretend she doesn't know what Sofia means, but she only says, "It's good to see you again."

"Yeah, I'm programmed to be happy to see you, too," says Sofia, closes her bedroom door behind her.

She sits down at her computer, pulls up Search.

Can you turn off a Mori, or is that a crime?

She asks for Grandmother's password.

"Something's different with Grandmother," she says, sounding as solemn and grown up as they liked when she was a child. "I want to help."

She sits up three nights in a row, reading through the code, reading through forums of Mori customers and Memento programming enthusiasts who probably have a talking head on their countertop.

Grandmother's been recalibrated back to initial client specifications four times as much as factory settings would suggest. Either Grandfather has exacting tastes, or Grandmother has made some decisions her grandmother wouldn't have made.

"Are you hungry?" she asks, halfway through making a sandwich, and Grandmother's eyebrows go up before she can smile politely and say, "No, thank you, since you're asking. But I'm glad you're eating. I worry about your appetite."

She scowls. "Did Mom and Dad tell you to say that?"

"No."

"I don't have to eat much," says Sofia, makes her eyes as wide as the kid on the NaniMed poster, drops her voice in parody. "I'm being cared for."

Blank response from Grandmother. Maybe she hasn't seen the ads.

(They've moved the ads to TV; surely Grandmother's seen them. The actress they hired for the ad looks nothing like the Victorian picture she comes out of, which is funny, considering that nanos can probably alter your appearance if you ask them nicely before you put them in.)

"I got nanos," Sofia says, sits down next to Grandmother. Grandmother sets down her crossword and her pen. Everything's filled out, perfectly; Sofia wonders how long she was in her room while Grandmother's been sitting here pretending not to know.

"Remember? The year we went on vacation."

"I didn't know that," Grandmother says.

Grandfather must have had her dialed down that year.

"Yeah. After you diagnosed me, they had them put in."

"I'm sorry," says Grandmother. "I'd hoped you just got well."

That's the first time anyone's suggested she's still sick; maybe it's the first time anyone's referred to the work of the nanos at all.

"How are they?"

Sofia looks up at Grandmother, holds out her hand for the pen.

She gouges her arm with it, a long practiced line from forearm to wrist that leaves a blue thread in the first welling-up of blood.

Grandmother doesn't look at her arm. Of course not; Grandmother would know what it looks like when the nanos pull you back together and patch the seams.

Sofia watches her Grandmother not looking, counts down from ten.

"Two." She stops. Her arm's pristine.

"Guess they got faster," she says, in a voice that feels like it's trapped in a cavern.

Grandmother reaches out, his fingers hovering above the place where a scar should be. There's an expression that looks like it hurts her to make; it comes and goes.

"I don't like that you . . . why do you do it?"

Obvious question. She should have some offhand answer ready that makes her sound like a careless rich kid. But she's never told anyone.

She shrugs. "I'm worried I'll live forever. I'm not even angry. I just want to be wrong."

Grandmother doesn't say anything. After a little while Sofia settles against her.

"My grandmother's name was Theodosia," she says. She hadn't known until she looked up the source code. "Did she like it?"

"Yes," says Grandmother.

"Do you?"

After a little pause, Grandmother says, "Yes."

As stockholders on a level of financial benefit you're not supposed to mention in polite company, the family gets invited to a preview of the Mori exhibit that will be going up at the Modern Art Museum.

Moris Welcome, reads the card.

"Why wouldn't they be?"

Sofia's mother cuts her a look meant to shut her up, marks $3+M$ on the RSVP.

The day of, she knocks on Grandmother's door and finds her dressed in her best afternoon suit, sitting straighter than her grandmother ever had.

When Grandmother stands up, she runs her hands along her skirt.

"You look nice," Sofia says for no reason, and Grandmother looks up and smiles.

At the reception they clap politely for someone in Public Relations who gets up and makes a speech that's quite carefully not talking about how public it's about to make the memories of its obliging Moris, who signed the contract without striking the education clause. If Mori isn't charging for the exhibit, it's for academic benefit; nothing you can do.

Sofia tries to imagine a museum exhibit where her nanos are on display, alongside little flickering records of everything they've done to her body. How many times *incision* would come up. How none of them would ever say how Grandmother had read her a story a long time ago and noticed that something was wrong.

Her parents seem excited—Paul Whitcover has been curating the exhibit personally, which is the kind of press you apparently can't buy. Grandmother, on her father's left, looks straight ahead, as still as the year she was turned off.

"Please enjoy the exhibit," the Public Relations woman says, "and thank you so much for letting us share with the world what your loved ones have meant to us."

Almost everybody who stands up touches their Mori on the elbow, even though most of the Moris are already moving in the right direction.

Sofia flexes her hands in her pockets. Somewhere she can't even feel it any more, the white blood cells in her body are marching her nanomeds where they need to go.

(They only do what they need to do, the doctors had told her, to reassure her. Your body gives all the orders. The human body is a remarkable thing.)

The exhibit has aesthetic components and explanations on how speech patterns can be recreated and anticipated by algorithms. Sofia hopes the person they used for the example on how to build a convincing facial structure gave permission, and that they're not here to see half their face stretched over biofoam on one half of a head of gleaming chrome.

"The most amazing thing we've discovered," Whitcover's saying, modestly smiling like he can hear the music swelling behind him, "is that despite everyone's individuality—and there's infinite individuality—how many things we really share. We're all alike in what we really value. It's wonderful how alike we are."

They cut to a building lobby in soft focus—there are no markers of a hospital, and Sofia suspects that's on purpose. A man with gray hair at his temples comes out into the center of the frame, waving. The camera cuts to a tearful wife, her arm around a golden-haired child. The child waves back, beams, starts running. As they embrace, it fades back to Whitcover, his voice where their laughter should be.

"Mori's work right now is to help one family at a time, but there's hope, someday, that the work we're doing can bring all of us closer together."

The dark room behind it is enormous, ceilings like a cathedral, and a mosaic of memories. Empty landscapes and arguments and babies and the lowering of coffins, screaming fights playing out in silence, embraces so tight there's no telling whose memory it is.

Sofia stares straight up for a long time. Her breath presses against the front of her throat, in and out.

At the edge of the dome, creased where it meets the wall, one of her grandmother's memories: Sofia, seven years old, sitting cross-legged on the floor and solemnly paging through a book. There's a scab on one knee; maybe her last one ever.

Her parents are wandering through vaguely, back out to the reception room. Grandmother hovers near the door, neck craned. She's seen it, too.

When Sofia's close enough, Grandmother says, "I don't think I would have let them do it," her arms shoved into her pockets, frowning so hard Sofia can hear the metal straining underneath.

Sofia touches Grandmother's elbow. Grandmother looks at her; Sofia looks back.

"No," she says, "I don't think you would have. Come on, they'll be looking for us."

They walk side by side through the party, waiting for a chance to go home.

MERCURY IN RETROGRADE

ERIN HOFFMAN

The voices fell away from Mercury's attention filters as she accepted the Samurai's security protocols. It was a pretentious moniker, no doubt, but this "samurai" was aiming to be *the* Samurai, and he was willing to pay respectably for it. At least he didn't look that high-profile: black jeans, tastefully worn; thermaprint jacket from an ambiguous season; spiked hair in the vicinity of blue and a refreshing lack of mirror-glass. *Digit, are we offline?*

Confirmed, the PDA replied, flashing a series of network failures across her optics. They elicited a feeling of falling in her gut, but a girl had to do what a girl had to do. She pulled a transparent card from her wrist-wrap and held it at eye level. A ghostly pattern pulsed light across a connection map with five highlighted names.

"The search results?" the Samurai asked. His eyes fogged with avarice. By reflex she checked his stuff against her corp tool yet again—and, as it had five minutes ago, it came back clean; his affiliations traced a corp-tree far away from Moderna Inc. and its partners. He was still outside her network, so technically this deal was breaking a Commandment, but she quashed the voice—this one internal, for once—that squealed superstitiously. Networks had to grow somehow.

"You got it," she said, flipping the card and smiling to mask the oddity of having scanned him again, in case he had scan detection. "Talk to these five and you'll be at the top of the rankings by Friday. I'd lay money on hitting Viscan top 20 by Tuesday, even." He smiled back.

"And in return," he pulled an envelope from his coat with admirable elegance and tipped it toward her outstretched hand. A jump drive slid out and onto her waiting palm, an older prism-type.

"Lupercalia's new navigator." Dangerous even to speak it, maybe, but she watched his eyes for any sign of deception. He only smiled, and she relaxed minutely, then popped the drive onto her wristband for transfer. It took but seconds, and then she passed the drive back to him while her analytics combed over the new app. *Warning on line 755,* Digit announced, *Warning—Warning—Warning!* and Mercury mirrored it over to the Samurai.

"That's normal," he said, and passed over a matching text of his own via local beam. "It uses a new type of tunnel that pisses off the current scrapers."

Bypassing existing tunnels wasn't that uncommon, and it only wanted access to a port used by doctors to read health-data—uni-directional, strictly pull. She activated the app.

Bring us back up, she told Digit, who bleeped acknowledgment, and less than a second later voices were murmuring up from the network again, content magnifiers raising the volume on trending terms that bubbled to the top. The Lupercalia app went to work, sorting, seeking—it blazed a lovely trail through her network setup, lighting up an entirely new pattern of connections that quickened her pulse. From the implications of this single pattern alone, her own rankings were guaranteed to go up in solid double digits, securing a week of some very delicious top-ten lists, easy. "Pleasure doing business with you," she said.

"And you," the Samurai bowed, beaming a graphic in her direction. She authed and a grainy black-and-white face looped: "*I think this is the beginning of a beautiful friendship.*"

The next morning her Flock.ish groups were abuzz with speculation, slyly (or so they thought) sliding up to her with this or that trivial bit of fishing gossip. On a whim she'd sent three communities up fifty points on five different engines, each a different discipline and term set. Her regular clients were friendlier than usual, sending pokes or emoticons to her metasocial and asking if she had something new going on. To top it all off, the Samurai had hit top-20 on three bellwether-caliber engines well ahead of schedule, leaping up the rankings. He'd left a little clinking-champagne-glasses icon in her inbox at around 5 a.m. Gleefully she put all messages on hold, letting the network marinate for awhile.

Running on an adrenaline buzz, she decided to throw cash at a frivolous artificially sweetened consumable, and none would do but the best. After gearing up in tech finery and hand-selecting a brand new cache of icons to hang on her viz, she hied herself down to 57th and Ash, 35th floor, the icon-swag attracting satisfying sideways glances and even the occasional open stare.

It was a long bus-rail to the Organ Grind, but it was the nearest source in town for true consumerist decadence, the duly advertised Not Even a Little Bit Good For You non-organic denatured coco-banana smoothie, and "banana" was intended as loose in its interpretation as possible. It was tasty, tasty sludge offering the No Reason At All to Drink This slogan. While not actively detrimental to one's health, was about as close to the line as it got in this city; the day the wispy elite in West Hollywood got wind it was in the same county, the place would be finished. The flashing city-holos and electronically painted architecture sang along with her effervescence, and she set her augmentation channel to coat the insides of the railcar with industrial synthpunk videos that bumped her all the way downtown.

The only hitch in this marvelous Monday morning plan was the overzealous fellow patron at the Grind who scanned her three times and still felt the need to stare. When it began to seriously mar her enjoyment of the masquerading non-banana, she stopped pulling on the corn-plastic straw and said, "Look, it's a public download, it's not that big a deal," flashing the metasocial patch on her viz. You did have to know *where* to get it . . .

"You're that girl," he said, becoming even more irritatingly unhelpful. "The one they're looking for."

Out of reflex, she +fingered him, some latent superstitious side winning control of her mind for a split second, which unfortunately was long enough for two other (it would turn out) highly unhelpful people to sidle up to the drink cart. The staring idiot came back clean of any mental health alerts.

"Jennifer," the Samurai said, raising a hand quite obviously not in greeting, being that it contained a garish four-pointed LED throwing star. His accomplice, a blond kid with a heavy-duty terminal glove, twitched his fingers, and suddenly she couldn't move her legs. She flailed with a free hand, but the terminal glove clamped around her arm, and a wave of weakness sent panic racing through her veins.

Digit, prep the new social override, she thought madly, and simultaneously said: "You're not from Lupercalia."

"She gets a prize!" the white dude said, on top of Digit's *Preparing,* coupled with a dwindling of the net voices, even more ominous than yesterday's.

"Who's this, your pet *gaijin*?" she snapped.

"He works for my employer, one Candice Long."

Mercury's heart raced, and suddenly the headlines on the vidfeeds took on sinister connotations. *Moderna Whiz-Kid in Critical Condition at Cedars-Sinai, Suffers Amnesia . . .*

"She's quite anxious to see you. Besides, that program in your system has an addiction process," the Samurai said. "You won't last twelve hours without the antidote."

"Fuck you," she said, and *Digit—*

The Samurai and *gaijin* dropped like lead weights, hands over their ears. Digit echoed back a muted stream of what they were experiencing—a sudden simultaneous audio subscription to every social channel within a five-mile radius—and Mercury smiled savagely, then threw the rest of her smoothie at the Samurai's contorted face. He fell back, covered in off-yellow goop, and she leaped over him on her way out the door.

All programs offline, now! Cut everything off! Silence fell around her like a blanket of sudden snow, soft and cold. She ran two steps, sending a map pull command, then staggered under the realization of its absence.

The world pulsed around her, silent and angular and stupid. The walls of the 35th floor were a dusty tan she'd never noticed before under their custom overlays and holographic directional signs. She had no idea where in the hell she was.

When the first jolt of panic subsided, *down, I need to go down,* she thought, and staggered toward the elevator, which, to her gasp of relief, worked without an uplink or pubID. The love she felt for ancient machines at that moment knew no horizon.

The doors opened on the lobby level, swarmed as usual with the human detritus of the evening commute. Heads turned as she stepped out of the elevator, glances lingered—were they scanning her? A passing cyclist swiveled his helmet toward her, and a mist of viz clouded over his left eye—what was he pulling up?

Heart pounding, she fled back into the building and shoved against a taped basement access door—visible to her naked eyes beneath the projected wall that usually covered it. It gave way, and the dank aroma of wet neglected concrete enveloped her. She spun, forced the door shut again (to the groan of its Paleolithic movement-slowing mechanism), and fled down the concrete steps, down into the lower city.

Three floors down, she stopped, panting, on the landing, and listened. The unaugmented walls pressed in on her, and she closed her eyes, fighting down panic.

Digit, she thought. *Do you have an archived map of the old city? From that cultural studies course?*

Confirmed, Digit said after a moment, and her knees went wobbly with relief.

I need to find the Seamstress, she said, as Digit threw a projection of the map onto her lenses. The sight of the ghostly image calmed her down considerably, dead though it might be: a lifeline of data. Onto its low-fidelity surface Digit projected a blinking dot in red—her—and a blinking dot in blue—the Seamstress—and traced a dotted line between them. The PDA might be one of the simplest devices of its kind, but it was hard not to anthropomorphize a greater personality and intelligence into it right at that moment. *Thank you,* she thought, even though she'd never thanked it before, and it hadn't comprehension to appreciate it.

"Okay," she said aloud, and steeled herself. "Here we go."

Three hours, by Digit's internal clock (which had who-knew-what connection with live reality), and countless wrong turns later, she stopped wearily before the Seamstress's door, and pressed first her palms and then her forehead against its pitted metal surface. For the cultural studies course she had had to navigate a portion of the old city without a link, but after that course she'd cheerfully dumped that education out her left ear as fundamentally obsolete, garbage knowledge.

The long walk through the tunnels had given her ample time to think. How could she have been so stupid? Staying in the lower city was not an option. There was no signal down here. It was a place of exiles, people moving from one hub to the other like digital hobos, the kind you only looked at with your peripheral vision. Everyone had an upside, and the upside was the downside. So here she was, surfing the lower city, dancing the edge of affiliation—searching for maybe the only decent person this close to sixerland.

A soft machine hum revved up behind the door, then calmed, then revved again. The Seamstress. The hum of servos took her back to the first time she'd been down this under-street, on the run from Mother's goons for the first time—almost eleven years ago to the day. She'd been seventeen and stupid, or maybe (thought she, from the lofty vantage of twenty-eight) they were the same thing. Mercury knocked three times on the door, and the humming stopped, replaced with the scrape of an aluminum chair across concrete.

"Who is it?" the Seamstress called, and for once her antiquated phys-vocal visitor-checking method didn't chafe.

"It's Mercury," she called back. "I need your help."

A clank or four from the bolts and locks, and the door swung open, bringing with it the first warm light she'd seen in hours. The Seamstress, arms folded, the glittering fingertips of her right hand tapping thoughtfully on her opposite elbow, waved her inside with her unaugmented hand, and let the heavy door fall shut behind them.

"Thanks," she said, pouring more feeling into that word than it seemed it could reasonably sustain.

The Seamstress scrutinized her with myopic dark eyes for a moment—her nearsightedness always made her seem older than her thirty-five years—then clucked her tongue and herded her into the kitchen workroom.

This tiny apartment had always been dead, but now, in the context of her disabled link, the quiet wallpaper and static furniture were comforting instead of tired. Besides the Seamstress herself, the only animated object was an orange pet goldfish in a glass bowl, and she was reasonably sure it didn't have a link.

When she was nearly done coming down from the panic of the last three hours, the Seamstress jolted her with the press of a hot porcelain mug into her freezing hands, tsking and frowning as she jumped and splashed scalding herbal blend over her fingers.

"Those herbs are grown down here, they're quite expensive," she said, turning to her table for a scrap of fabric to blot the tea while Mercury blew ineffectually on her smarting skin. With a quick twitch of her left hand, the Seamstress sliced off a bit of muslin, retracting the implanted scissor as she passed the fabric across. "I'm not sure I want to know what kind of trouble you're in."

"I need a scan," she said, blotting with one hand and raising the mug to her lips with the other. She blew across the hot liquid, fighting dizziness.

"You look like you need carbohydrates." Turning, the Seamstress lifted a thick slice of brown bread studded with grain from the plate she'd brought with the tea, and pressed it on Mercury, who gobbled gracelessly. Then she sat down at her aluminum table, almost disappearing behind its piled stacks of colorful fabric. She lifted a pair of gold sewing glasses from a stack of watered silk and delicately fit them to her face, antiqued metal incongruous against her youthful skin. Her eyes rose to Mercury, pupils narrowing, and remained that way for several moments while pale lights swam across her lenses.

Finally the images stopped, and she removed the glasses, folding them carefully and polishing an invisible smudge from the rim of one lens. "This is pretty serious," she said.

"I know," Mercury began, brushing crumbs from her lips, but the Seamstress shook her head.

"I'm not sure you do," the Seamstress said, her pale eyes pinched. "This is bigger than you or me, sweetie. You need Chantilly Lace."

Mercury coughed around a mouthful of tea. "A sixer? No way." Moderna was bad enough, but at least it was legit. Mostly.

"The program has bound itself to your chip," the Seamstress said. "And it's been using your HealthMonitor to release insulin into your blood for the last eight hours. A sixer can hack it, maybe even re-chip you, if necessary." Compassion softened her voice, but couldn't take the hammer out of her words. "I give you another four hours before you fall into a diabetic coma if you can't get something to reverse whatever it's doing." Which was exactly what the Samurai had said. Goddamn it.

"I still can't work with a sixer. I stay unaffiliated," Mercury said, closing her eyes as a headache set in, and realizing with dread the source of her giddiness and sweet tooth that morning. No Reason At All to Drink This.

"Chantilly is—different," the Seamstress said. "She'll help you. And unless you can work with the people who did this to you, I just don't think you have a choice."

Mercury couldn't close her eyes again, so she just set down her mug by feel and squeezed her eyelids tighter together, fighting down a wave of hate and fury—at herself, at the goddamn Samurai, and most of all at insulin-induced brain-eating mood swings, wrapping in whatever hack that had cooked up this worm and his whole extended family for good measure.

"Jenny," the Seamstress said, a rustle of fabric indicating her raised hand. Mercury opened her eyes and took it, wrapping both her hands around it, feeling warmth and skin and the faint tingle of activated servos beneath. "Take this one seriously," the Seamstress said. "It's too big."

"Thanks for your help," Mercury said, squeezing the hand before stepping back and taking a deep breath.

The Seamstress nodded, then again passed her left hand over the nearest flat piece of fabric, separating out a precise square with slices of her scissor blade. She flipped the square, folded it in half, and traced its edges with her right fingertip, which hummed and left a trail of neat stitches where it passed. Into this double-thick rectangle she folded a security card, then stitched the whole thing closed, this time running three fingers across it and leaving a full set of stitch patterns across the fabric in a signature.

"Give that to the doorman at the Imperial, he'll know what to do. And take care of yourself."

Mercury ripped open the Seamstress's pouch and removed the sec card three blocks away, then ditched the fabric remains—if it came to it, one less thing to trace her to anyone she cared about. She stored the card's UID on her wrist drive, then tucked it away.

She lost an hour getting to the Imperial, and by the time she stood before its plate glass doors her vision was swimming. The old hotel, relegated underground in a bid to preserve its architecture half a decade ago, was on Digit's map, in a rare stroke of luck—she hadn't remembered it there before, but memory wasn't her strong suit right at the moment.

The doorman wore an antique bellhop suit, dowdy red wool and gold piping, that made his already pale skin look sickly. She went right for him, pretending to be lost, looking up and down the decaying streets.

"I've just been to see a seamstress," she said, "and she sent me here for some directions." Holding out her wrist, she turned the drive toward him, inviting a link.

"I know a seamstress, but she doesn't do digital," he said suspiciously, not touching her.

"I had some of her work." Mercury traced the signature pattern on her palm with a fingertip. "But I don't like physical evidence. I put her card key in my drive."

He looked at her for a long moment, then took an old-style card-reader from his belt. It had a data jack built into the side, and he linked it to her wrist drive. After a moment, he nodded.

"That console," she jerked her chin in the direction of the old-fashioned stationary terminal just inside the door. "It's *linked*, isn't it? It's secure?"

His eyes slid away from hers. "I don't know what you're talking about," his voice just a bit too high, "it's an old reservation system. Damn hotel ought to upgrade if you ask me."

"Right," she said, dropping her hand. "Can I use it? I just need to call my sister."

"The Imperial always assists preferred clients," he said, and opened the door to let her through. Quick, precise strides took him to the terminal, and he keyed in an access code. A digital timer popped up on the screen. "You've got five minutes," he said, and stepped away from the console.

She pulled the access wire from her wrist and plugged it into the machine via an adaptor set into the side—slow but effective. *Digit, check the connection.*

Peripherally she felt the PDA swimming into the console, lighting up its insides, checking here, there, everywhere. *Connection secure,* it said. She let go a breath she hadn't realized she was holding, half expecting to hear the Samurai's voice, or worse.

She touched the glass screen and called up a video link. When it asked for an address, she gave it the name from the sec card, then held her breath again while it connected.

A face appeared on the screen, one that was certainly not Chantilly Lace, belonging as it did more in a suburb than down Below. Mercury marshaled her expression into an appropriate pattern—relief (that was easy), embarrassment, I'm lost, could you please send train fare. Then, through the link: *Chantilly Lace? I have your link from the Seamstress.*

Letters printed across her eye, relayed by the adaptor. *We know who you are. Everyone does. It's a liability.*

Look, I need your help, Mercury sent, the first withdrawal shadows dancing in front of her eyes. The admission stabbed at her. *If I get picked up, I take about fifty different street techs to Moderna. They could be yours instead.*

The image paused. *You haven't got anything we could want.* The pause was question enough to seize upon.

You know Lupercalia?

Of course.

They've got a new navigator. She took a risk and jacked the Samurai's prism into her wrist drive again, sending across only the view-me to Chantilly.

The soccer mom avatar's eyes widened ever so slightly as she played the navigator's show-off file. *This thing's for real?* Mercury nodded, but pantomimed more embarrassment, as if being chastened. Chantilly's eyes sharpened again. *But if Moderna's got it, they'll execute faster than we could anyway.*

She was right. Despair surged through Mercury, but she bore down on it. *Say they couldn't,* she sent. *What would it be worth to you?*

Enough, Chantilly said, and hope fluttered in her chest, or maybe it was adrenaline.

The minute marker dropped toward one, counting down the seconds. *I'll need you to come in there and get me,* she sent, rushing through it, trying not to think about what that meant.

No promises, Chantilly replied, and cut the connection.

Mercury gripped the console as precious seconds trickled away, then let her forehead drop, meeting the cool glass screen with a dull thud that echoed through her skull. Then she withdrew her prism and deactivated the console's link, returning it to its normal emergency-services-only public access.

Ordinarily the emergency terminals contacted rescue services only, but an old high school hobby of her cohorts' had been co-opting them for various age-appropriate activities, some of which were now technically illegal. And one of them, involving cutting power to the terminal and loading it up under the influence of an OS from her pocket drive (thank goodness for the morning's high tech vanity), still worked. The terminal's link had to be reloaded, and then she was in.

A couple of quick taps to the aging touchscreen brought up Safari, and she first searched out HealthMonitor overrides in the newsblasts—but indirectly only. She didn't dare apply direct search terms, since, in the absence of her wireless signal, hardline terminals were obvious targets for such a narrow search.

Chills wracked her body, and yet she broke out in a sweat, exacerbating them. Her hands shook as they hovered over the terminal, sliding closer to direct terms as each of her indirect efforts failed and time slipped away. Soon she was gripping the sides of the terminal for support with one hand and navigating with the other.

There had to be a hack. There was always a hack. HealthMonitors were, by necessity, nearly impossible to break into, but someone had done it, which meant someone else *could* do it. Simple logic of the signal. Recklessly she installed three different possible applications onto her hardware, but to no effect. Patches of darkness swam in front of her eyes, but she fought to stay awake. The minute she lost consciousness, Moderna's emergency beacon would activate, overriding her wireless shutdown and announcing her presence to all and sundry.

At last she went for the direct search—HealthMonitor. Override. Insulin release. A result flickered across the aging screen. As blackness collapsed her vision from the outside in, and she slumped to the concrete, a system message leapt up on the terminal screen:

> Hello, Jennifer.

> Stay right there. Or don't. We'll find you.

She woke in a white room. Soft water sounds pattered soothing messages from beyond the alabaster walls, and the gleaming granite floors that extended meters in every direction were either bioreflective, scrubbed daily, or both. Extravagant and rare staghorn ferns splashed elegant color in one corner of the room, and both the couch she rested on and the blanket that covered her were plush albino buffalo wool.

Unfamiliar scents drifted from her hair, which by its feel had been washed, dyed, and styled. Her fingernails had been nouveau-manicured. Gone was her rugged vat leather jacket and cacophonous viz; in their places were imported cottons and biz-stylish whiteware, even down to her optics, which had been replaced with brand-new ten-K Centurions.

She forced herself to keep still, and closed her eyes. *Digit, if you're there, bring us back online. No point hiding now. But cloaked, please.*

A murmur of voices swelled gently as her signal reconnected. She left all the apps off, but pulled top headlines from a newsfeed, stomach sinking as they rolled in. "*Moderna Inc. Maven Candice Long Reunites with Long-Lost Daughter*", "*Anastasia Story Has Happy Ending*", "*Jennifer Long Found After 11-Year Disappearance*", "*JL Suffering Memory Loss, Doctors Predict Slow*

Recovery." She dismissed the headlines and opened her eyes, preferring even this meat reality to the current live alternative.

But as she took in the sanitized room, fury shot through her veins. *Digit, queue up the usual.* The PDA exploded across the lifespace with fingers of activity, running scripts that pulled from syndicated sources and reorganized them under Mercury's viz-style for re-syndication. Under the cover of her usual blast and the pull from the news feeds, she pulled up her AP contact and started a message.

Moderna under investigation for code theft. SEC, whole nine yards. Major release planned to pre-empt investigation, Anastasia circus same. I have it from the inside, top level. She attached three sources that would take even the most intrepid reporter on an epic goose chase. Then she released the link.

A glass pocket door rolled silently open across the room, and Mercury's mother walked through it, as fresh and polished as her viz images from the newsreels, and as she had been fifteen years ago. "Welcome home, Jennifer," she said—the voice was a little different; a new mod, or maybe her own faulty meat memory. "I see you're awake enough to uplink."

"It's Mercury." She swung her legs over the side of the couch and pushed herself to her feet—or at least that was the intent, but her knees wouldn't cooperate, and she sank back down to the buffalo wool.

"Be careful, dear," her mother said, moving to pour her a glass of water from the sculpted glass pitcher at the side table. "And of course, 'Jenny Mercury,' your street name, owing to the memory loss."

She ignored the offered glass cup. "My memory is quite chipper, thanks. And digitally backed."

Her mother's eyes were full of professional compassion. "Those false memory companies are a dime a dozen these days, aren't they? But of course the truth that the masses uncover is what really matters, and they already like mine far more than yours. It's the perfect Anastasia story, playing out live via feed, with several tech firsts to carry it right along."

"Why are you doing this?" She forced her fists to unclench. "Why now? Why can't you just leave me alone?"

"Because I need you, and you'll be happier on my project than with that silly consulting." Mother set down the glass of water and poured another, this for herself, and sipped it pointedly.

"You're so confident of that you hacked my HealthMonitor. Which is illegal, by the way."

"Not when one's child is mentally unfit to be making their own decisions. I'm protecting you." Her identically manicured fingernails drummed musically along the glass, and she leaned forward ever-so-slightly. "We're acquiring Lupercalia. That navigator is the real thing, and it goes public tomorrow. It's big social, honey," she said. "It's what you've always wanted."

"You have no idea what I've ever wanted." *Digit, call for help, if you can.* But the PDA was unresponsive.

A faint line across her lava-exfoliated forehead was one of the few tells Candice Long possessed. "All of your little SEO games, what do you think that is? You want to control people every bit as much as I do. Maybe even more."

"We are alike, that way, you're right," Mercury said, and had the pleasure of catching the slight flattening of expression that represented surprise in her mother. "I try to control my social environment because I've never had control over my own life."

A sharp answer burned across her mother's eyes, but the sliding door stopped it from escaping further. Enter the Samurai.

"Afternoon, ma'am," he said to her mother, then turned to her. "Jennifer, welcome."

"Those contacts," Mercury said.

"Yeah?" the Samurai grinned.

"I'm going to tell them you're a dick."

The grin fell from his face, replaced by a snarl she kicked herself for not seeing days ago, and he lifted a syringe filled with amber liquid from a case at his side.

She could guess what it was, but right at that moment, the far left wall in all its fine imported stone glory shattered inward with a concussive blast that threw them all to the floor. When Mercury shook off the daze, she lifted her head just in time to catch sight of a genuine blonde bombshell stepping across the rubble. A blinking red indicator on her optics, keyed to the property security, indicated the activation of the silent alarm system, and showed the blinking dots of the security team streaming steadily toward their location. She struggled to her feet, this time able to keep them by surfing on adrenaline. "You're—"

The woman turned and winked, a blonde curl at her temple bouncing with the theater of her movement. "Chantilly Lace." Indeed she was covered in it, of the new rayon-stretch type, stitched around a black utility harness hung with several weapons and a blue-and-white cheque miniskirt complete with carbon suspension (for that extra oomph) and ammunition pockets.

"You work for the Big Bopper." The 50s gang. Sixer gateways.

Chantilly raised her firearm and sighted along the barrel, pulsing a droplet of laser light across three of the marble columns with a thumb release. "I know what he likes." She fired three precise shots in quick succession, and laughed in girlish delight as the shattered column sections brought down their Corinthian heads and much of the upper floor with them in a thunder of stone and dust. *Different,* the Seamstress had said.

"How did you find me?" Her mother and the Samurai were both recovering consciousness, groggily lifting their heads. Mercury ducked over to the latter and relieved him of the stainless steel medical case at his side.

The blonde Eris blinked at her in surprise and caution. "*You* called *me,* and sent a location."

My doing, Digit interrupted, and Mercury stared. "*Your* doing?"

"What?"

"I'm sorry—" Mercury stuttered. *You . . . what? Digit? What are you? Slightly more than a PDA.* Her head swam.

"Come on," Chantilly was saying. "A hit this big draws heat."

Mercury ducked over to her mother, who was groggily rubbing her temples. The flash of vulnerable hope in her eyes cut through Mercury, but a reminder of the past day's misdeeds burned it away. She picked up Candice's wrist, connected their drives with a jump-cable. A password prompt: she entered "macydaisy," the pet poodle that had run away when she was five—and the **plink** of security approval gave her heart another pang. Seconds later, she'd transferred the Moderna HealthMonitor hack across and instructed it to release estradiol sufficient to generate a nice PMS zap. Then she accessed her cosmetic mod and turned her eyeshadow electric green and her eyelashes metallic purple.

Mercury looked into her mother's fluorescent eyes. "You need to change your password," she said.

"Seriously," Chantilly barked, firing blue blasts of light up the passage. "Now or never."

"All right," Mercury concentrated on following the plausibly insane sixer hitwoman as she ran through the white hallways, trying to focus. *Digit. You pretended to be a PDA all this time . . . how could you stand it?*

I did a lot of wiki surfing. Your cultural studies course didn't cover that part of the lower city, by the way.

Chantilly Lace's blonde ponytail bounced steadily in front of them, and in short order she'd expertly navigated them out to the north gardens, onto a swathe of imported blue-green Japanese-engineered grass. *Where did you come from? What's your classification?*

Digit answered the second question first, as a helicopter arrowed toward them from the south: *Currently three, but my makers think I'd qualify for four eventually,* he? she? it? said, and Mercury found herself dizzy again. Then: *Your mother installed me when you were two. She thought if you didn't grow up augmented you'd be stunted.*

My mother planted you? Chantilly Lace had pulled a micro-jet pack from a pouch and was fitting canisters to it, then swinging it across her shoulders and looping an arm around Mercury's waist. "Wait!" Mercury yelled over the now-deafening roar of the helicopter a hundred meters above them. *Digit, what the fuck?*

"There's no waiting, sweetheart!" Chantilly yelled back, but Mercury struggled against her grip. "You wait, you stay!"

She installed me, she doesn't control me, Digit said, and if Mercury assumed Digit was human she'd say there was hurt in the words.

And how the hell do I know you don't want to control me yourself, hiding all this time? Chantilly Lace was backing away, shaking her head at Mercury in disgust. She ignited the jet pack.

Because I want you to make your own decisions. I want to stay with you. Behind them, boiling up from the smoking property, the scarred alabaster, shouting men with weapons painted them with laser sightings.

Tears stung her eyes, new and bewildering, the first since not long after she'd taken off from this compound for the first time, a furious seventeen-year-old with way too much livesocial integration for her own good. "All right!" she yelled, and ran for Chantilly, who happily kicked her in the chest from an early-launch altitude of about a meter and a half. Mercury clung to the stiletto-heeled boot and closed her eyes.

Scant moments later, she was sitting in between Chantilly Lace and a guy in a thermapolyester zoot suit with a pair of implanted mechanical eyes. He reached out with a sidearm to rain covering fire down on Moderna's security guards, and the helicopter rose above the city. After a few parting shots he retracted his arm and sealed the windows, delivering beatific silence to the cabin, or close enough.

"Pretender, meet Jenny Mercury," Chantilly Lace said, gesturing between them. The cyber-eyed guy nodded, but Chantilly was already leaning back toward Mercury. "Hey, are you going to get your chip swapped? It's the only way they wouldn't be able to trace you again. The Bopper wants that Lupercalia thing you've got, and he'd probably chip you in exchange for it." Her thick-lashed blue eyes were disturbingly bright, highlighted by chartreuse biolume.

"No," Mercury said, flipping open the medical kit to examine the formula her mother'd concocted. "I think I'll go back to Jennifer Long. It's about time someone showed my mother what 'big social' really means."

"I like how you think!" Chantilly laughed, sweet and infectious as cotton candy.

So do I, Digit said.

Thanks, Mercury said. She looked around, keenly aware of the stolen technology that buzzed all around them. But the network, when you didn't hide from it, might have a few things to say about sixers, too. "Where are we going?"

"Deep," Chantilly said, pointing with her still-equipped destruction gun to the eastern sky. "I saw that AP story just before I broke in. The SEC's scrambling already. Fucking brilliant. You in?"

What do you think? she asked Digit, and felt, quite distinctly, a pulse of surprise—he'd opened an emotion-share channel. Then, pleasure. Gratitude.

I'm in, he said, kicking a few deliciously clever network options across her optics. She smiled.

"We're in."

COASTLINES OF THE STARS
ALEX DALLY MacFARLANE

THE FIRST MAPS

It was a late interest: after childhood, after fleeting interests that sank
into me like teeth—then fell away. Foxes stayed. I tried poetry. I fell
into history. I found maps there.
I approached it cautiously, like a new food.
I couldn't say why it interested me.
The first maps were other people's: old maps, in prose and pictures.
I collected them, compared them. I described their meanings: here,
home; here, discomfort; here, longing; here, the coastline. Only later
did I make my own.

Ngọc stood in the main shuttle terminal at Al Qasr, waiting for the next shuttle to Goldchair Space Station. Minutes took too long. Crowded, loud, too much. People everywhere: talking, shouting, signing, bumping into her, waiting by her. Unfiltered announcements. Smells from the food stands, from people. Banners in every color, scrolling across screens on the walls and floating above the halls: directing people to the right shuttle slots, displaying news, advertising.

Normally Ngọc's array filtered the noises, the sights, the smells, gave her only the ones she needed. Only her shuttle's announcements. Only enough about her surroundings that she didn't walk into walls or people. Her array ran on her body's energy, and she was low: tired and hungry and longing to be home, where she could heat up a packet of phở rather than pay more money than she could spare at one of the food stands, and sit in her own space, small and silent.

Ngọc looked low, away from the bright banners and people's faces.

One of her hands sought out her most textured hairs, at the top of her head: to run two fingers down each hair, over and over. The hair between her fingers bumped. Pleasing.

An announcement gave her shuttle a slot. She walked towards it.

She passed a wall screen that caught her attention: waves drawn in white on dark blue in neat and intricate detail, moving rhythmically across the screen. She stepped closer. The white lines were raised: touchable. She held a hand to them.

Waves moved against her.

For a long time she stood, feeling the waves against her hand.

She looked at the words spanning the moving image on a plain white background: SERMI HU. WAVES REVISITED.

Waves.

Another announcement.

Ngọc ran to her shuttle, repeating the name Sermi Hu like fingers on hair.

THE WAVE MAPS

I mapped motion. I mapped in clean lines: white on dark blue. My waves move across a coast near Cai Nu City, not the coast as it is now, but as it was a million years ago. The coast changes under the waves far more rapidly than under real waves.
Yet this is realer to me than a static map, a coast that never changes. By the time I am a hundred years old, it will be our coast. But it will not stop. It will map our possible future.

Ngọc ate more food as soon as she awoke, already hungry. Another packet of phở. Sage crisps. Squid-flavored protein chunks. The last she ate while she dressed in her favorite clothes: plain indigo trousers and a sleeveless knee-length indigo top with repeating print patterns on it. She combed her hair. It was an impractical comb: curving like a moon occluded, with tines on its inward edge. Dull silvery metal. Pointed at its moon-edges. Heavy. A gift from her grandmother, before early death took her away. On its flat faces, its maker had engraved floral lines and animals that Ngọc couldn't identify. She sat a while after combing her hair, turning the comb over and over, enjoying the engravings and tines on her hands.

She put it aside and turned on her arrays.

Menu symbols hung in indigo at the edges of her vision. Here she didn't need to filter sensory input, but she added music: songs sent by a friend in a language Ngọc didn't know. Lively. Like foxes dancing, like the quintet of silvery foxes embedded in her skin and skull at her hairline: the only outward sign of her array. Their feet went deep into her head.

She looked at messages—nothing that meant someone would hire her and pay money—and then she looked for Sermi Hu.

She closed her eyes, to see better.

Looking into nearby public arrays for information was nothing, was shallow, easy, a single step into the un-countable arrays in existence: the arrays anchored in other people's bodies, the arrays in space stations, in space craft, arrays spanning space and planets and moons. Stepping there, Ngọc was not a person sitting on her bed with her eyes closed. She could ignore herself. Ignore other people. Ignore everything except what she needed to work.

Sermi Hu: exhibit descriptions, interviews, news, images. A confusion of information. A person with complex weaves—like carpets of a single dark brown—in waist-long hair on either side of a dark face. A number of other projects aside from the waves, all exhibited on Cai Nu, where Sermi lived. Ngọc looked for more information about those.

THE STAR MAPS

I found my favorite maps in history: Ammassalik wooden maps,
carved in coastlines that sailors could hold in their hands. The shapes
in the wood matched the edges of the shore. The sailors followed them
home in the thick fogs that fell like darkness.
Some of my distant ancestors, if my family's tales were told true.
I thought of the shores eroding. Of families changing the maps, over
hundreds of years.
I mapped the stars this way.

To hold a map of stars in your hands, to feel it as you saw it—

It was too beautiful a thought.

Ngọc wanted a replica that felt like wood. It took little time to order one.

That done, she looked at even more information about Sermi: other exhibits, current work. Sermi's current whereabouts, Ngọc found, were less certain. Sermi had gone missing a year ago. Last likely whereabouts: the Ivuultu debris field. No one on Cai Nu would go there. On an array for the kind of people who would look there for a fee, Ngọc found a message from Sermi's wife. Ngọc opened her eyes to play it on a screen in the air above her floor—and to reach for more sage crisps. Running her array made her already fast metabolism faster.

An image of a woman appeared in the air: just her head and shoulders, a dark-skinned face with intricate gold lettering across her cheeks and nose, wearing a hijab of city-patterned gold. "I am Xaliima," the image of the woman said, the timbre of her voice flattened by the translation Ngọc had run, "but it is my spouse's name you will recognize: Sermi Hu, who won the Shen Yang prize two years in a row for making maps. Sermi maps changing places: maps of water, maps of coastlines, maps of the bone pits of Psápfa, maps of stars. Maps of the Ivuultu debris." Xaliima paused, grief among the gold words on her cheeks. "Sermi wanted to map the Ivuultu debris, but not the debris itself. The traps set by the people who live there."

"Too nice," Ngọc murmured.

"Sermi must have flown too close. I waited for a while after I stopped receiving messages, knowing how it is to be immersed in work, but eventually I started to worry. I commissioned someone to fly close to the debris and scan it for Sermi's craft." A new image appeared: a scan of Ivuultu, chaotic, jumbled. The debris of un-counted spacecraft in orbit around the small red moon. Then another image: a close-up of a particular craft, quite large, highlighted gold, deep within the debris. "I know what happens to people trapped here. But if it is possible, I would like to know with certainty—if there is a body, I would like it returned to me, for burial."

A sum of money appeared beneath Xaliima.

Ngọc's eyes went as wide as if she'd found a packet of sage crisps the size of a moon. If only she had a space craft! If only it wasn't Ivuultu, where a recent contest to enter the debris field and evade its traps had ended with everyone losing. Or winning, if the prize was: *your craft gets dismantled for parts by the Ivuultu scavengers, you get to take a swim in space.*

Ngọc twisted the ends of her hair with her fingers.

Several people had expressed an interest in finding Sermi, requesting further information from Xaliima. Ngọc skimmed the names. One she recognized: Fox Sansar, a pilot she'd done array work for in the past. Always quick to pay, always straightforward. And a *good* pilot, she'd heard.

Ngọc asked the image of Xaliima, "Did Sermi send back any maps of the Ivuultu debris before disappearing?"

"I can show you three maps that Sermi made of the Ivuultu debris." Three icons appeared beside Xaliima's head.

"Are there any more?"

"I am not provided with that information," Xaliima said. The real Xaliima, who had programmed this image, hadn't shared the information. Or hadn't known it.

An alert sounded: the replica Ammassalik star map was ready. Ngọc ran out to the delivery center to collect it. It fit into her hand. On the way back to her room, she stopped by a window that opened onto the constellations around Goldchair and stood, following the patterns of stars with her eyes, with her fingers—but couldn't find the stars mapped in her hand.

It fit so well into her hand that she didn't want to let it go.

In her room, Ngọc pulled Sermi's three Ivuultu maps into her array and opened them: visual maps, line-drawn like the waves and whirlpools. The annotations made little sense to Ngọc. All said *false. False, false* written along the trap-lines between the debris. Ngọc looked for information about the traps: attempts to determine the traps' locations, recordings of craft going into the debris and becoming caught. Sermi's maps. Recordings made since Sermi's disappearance. Over and over—and turning the star map over in her hands—Ngọc looked, until her array alerted her to the need to eat something more substantial than sage crisps. A big bowl of lemongrass and ginger protein with vermicelli noodles at the local market in this section of Goldchair. Money was not a problem. Ngọc knew how to find Sermi.

THE WHIRLPOOL MAPS

I returned to rapid motion, to fluidity: the best metaphor I found. I mapped the summer whirlpools on Cai Nu.
I remember when I first heard that most children are expected to understand gender—theirs, other people's—at a very early age. Like verbal communication. Like socialization.
I labeled parts of the whirlpools with ten different words for gender.
I never liked these maps. Belatedly, it occurs to me: to map it is to state that it exists.

Ngọc met Fox at his local market, on the other side of Goldchair, at his preference. Their first time meeting in person. Array turned on, Ngọc filtered the loudness, the people—it was bigger by far than her local market. It was pretty, with static storytelling art along the walls. Most of the foods were unfamiliar.

Fox already waited at the designated table. Dark blonde hair: not a color Ngọc saw often. Fox's face was more familiar, with brown eyes even narrower than hers. He ate something Ngọc didn't recognize. White disks with a lump of dark red sauce.

"I know how to get through the Ivuultu debris," Ngọc said, glancing at one of the story panels on the nearest wall. It depicted two people embroidering stars onto black fabric.

"A lot of people think that," Fox said.

"A lot of people die in the debris."

At the edge of her vision, his lips twitched.

"What I doubt anyone is doing," Ngọc said, "is looking at Sermi's maps. Not just the Ivuultu ones. The star ones." Ngọc held up the replica star map. "This is based on a too-old map, from Earth days, *old* Earth days, when people needed to know their way along coasts in boats and didn't have orbital arrays. Bumps are headlands, dips are inlets. Even if you can't see, you can *feel* the way and steer your boat. Sermi did that, except with stars: if you're flying in space, you can align your way with stars. Keep a constellation on your 'left.' You can make a pattern of the stars, like a coastline."

"You could . . . " Fox looked doubtful.

"You need this to get through Ivuultu, because the traps aren't true, the stars and debris are."

"The traps looked true enough when people got caught in them and killed."

"They're there, they're real, but they're not where you see them. Sermi figured that out." *False, false.* "And now," Ngọc said, holding up the star map again, "Sermi's changed them, re-mapped them. Now you need these."

Fox frowned at her. "How is flying with these going to work?"

"I . . . " Ngọc ran out of words under his scrutiny.

The map, it was about the map, couldn't he see that?

"I can't." Words were so difficult. Still staring. Ngọc filtered out visual input entirely. "I can't tell you in words. I can do it with my hands, and my array. I use array-generated maps like these to interact with the array that generates the true traps, to see them, and I feed that to you. You fly. I tell you where to fly. We split the money."

Fox turned silent. Ngọc un-filtered visual input and found him poking his food with a thoughtful look. Ngọc couldn't figure out what it was made of.

"What is that?" she asked.

"Chwee kueh." Ngọc didn't know what that meant. "Rice flour cakes with pickled radish. It's really nice. Do you want some?"

"Mmm."

Fox handed her a single chopstick, which was enough to eat it with: to break off some of the radish-covered cake and stab it to get it into her mouth. It *was* nice.

"Have more," Fox said. "I probably went too far ordering three plates. It's just the vendor here is really good."

Ngọc needed to ask him what vendor it was.

The chwee kueh on the table disappeared quickly. Only then did Fox say, "Shall we go flying in the Ivuultu debris?"

THE BONE MAPS

The small moon of Psápfa, orbiting Gumiho, is notorious for its adherents: the leapers.
I received special permission to map the bone pits. I saw the place where the people stand, high on a white rock, before they leap. A two-hour leap. Gravity is not great on Psápfa. They program a machine array to spend those two hours writing their stories on their bones, to, after a quick killing, disintegrate their bodies—all but the bones.
I followed an adherent down a rocky path to the pits where the bones fall.
According to their faith it is an act of devotion to wade into the pits and read aloud the stories written on the bones.
I spent weeks there. I worked on real bone: banding stories around it like embroidery, a guide—on each of the ten bones I used—to the

one-and-a-half centuries of pits, the changing styles of stories, the
history of habitation of our star system that ran under everyone's
own lives. I was too awed by the people's stories. I could only point
to the pits, my maps like an outstretched arm.
I would have liked to die there.

The Ivuultu debris orbited a small, massive red moon of the same name, far from its planet, the gas giant Gumiho. In four years, the debris had accumulated from mishaps and arrogance. Scavengers profited greatly—and managed the debris, made it stay whole longer than usual collisions would allow. Protected it for themselves.

Fox brought his space craft close, saying, "No sign of the scavengers."

Good. Only Sermi's craft, deep in the debris. Ngọc put the star map in her pocket and held her hands at her sides and directed her array: to see Fox's array, to see the false lines of the traps, to put maps in her hands. For seconds, she saw only arrays. Patterned lines like Sermi's maps. Lines beyond words. Truer than any space craft holding her in high orbit over a moon. The maps in her hands solidified her: simulated, changeable star maps. She remembered her body, her location. Filtered in enough visual input to see the debris. Connected her array to Fox's. Said, "Ready."

Fox flew closer, flew right up to the debris and the traps until he dipped into it like the thin atmosphere of Psápfa. There, on the edge of Ivuultu, the debris remained in their shared view: ghost-translucent, layered shapes in every direction. Stars shone in them like navels. The red moon lay beneath them like a sea floor.

Ngọc mapped.

In her right hand: the stars, each at the peak or trough in the map. A coastline in space.

In her left hand: the clusters of debris too big for Fox's shield to destroy.

Ngọc fit them together, the stars like a slow, steady beat beneath the rapid rhythm of the debris in her hands. "That's the way through." Keep them together. Her hands worked ahead of their position, mapping, un-mapping, until she found the next step: the next inlet or headland. The way through.

What she mapped went in gold into what Fox saw in his array, interfacing with his craft.

She saw, dimmed-out, the debris they avoided, the meaningless trap-lines like contour lines crossing a path, the stars, the sea-moon. The gold globe of Sermi's craft. She *felt* it all.

"Look," Fox said, "I'm actually doing this."

Ngọc breathed out: "Ha." Felt the next inlet. Wrist twisted to account for three-dimensionality. Other arm outstretched. Her whole body moved to follow the map: *felt* in fingers, arms, chest, mouth, feet. Fox followed her.

THE LAST MAPS

*A pair of maps. Stars and debris. I thought I would feel them forever:
stars wheeling with Ivuultu's orbit, debris constantly changing—disappearing. Leaving me alone with my last recorded maps.
I never thought I would share them.*

The maps stilled.

"Here." Fox's un-filtered voice barely touched Ngọc. "We're here."

Slowly she let the maps fade. Stretched her fingers. Looked—open-eye looked—at the gold globe in front of them.

"I've never . . . " Fox said.

How strange to only have visual and audio input.

"Flying's never been like that."

Time to find Sermi.

"There's an opening in the side," Fox said, highlighting it in red on their shared arrays. "Weapon or collision damage. Looks like a good place to get in."

Ngọc agreed. It took her a while to remember to say so out loud.

The craft easily flew through. The cavernous space within looked like a cargo bay, now empty, its bare back wall a good place for Fox to land: magnetically hooking his craft to the wall, angled just-so to fly back out.

"Time to skin up," Fox said, standing up with a grin like he enjoyed going out of air. Ngọc hated the skin on her arms, her face: pressing against her. But. No Sermi without the skin. Fox handed her one and she took it, activated it, thinking that soon she would be back among the stars and debris, bare-faced, maps in her hands.

Their arrays led them through the corridors of Sermi's blast-marked craft. Hull-holes opened to space like mouths. No possessions remained. Yet the walls didn't look opened for their innards: the scavengers had been to Sermi's craft, but not successfully.

In the command center they found the bones.

"Too many bones," Fox said. Ngọc stared. "To be Sermi. It's too many bones."

"Like Psápfa," Ngọc managed.

Fox drew a blaster from his belt.

Like Psápfa: writing ran around some of the bones, gleaming gold.

"I don't think you'll need that," Ngọc said. "Sermi? Is that you?"

The bones re-configured into a too-large person, held in shape by an array. Vertebrae hung in a pair of long, thin braids: fitting for someone who had mapped Psápfa. The phalang-lips smiled. "Ngọc." The voice spoke through Ngọc's array. Fox's too. He lowered the blaster. Ngọc felt Sermi's array touching hers, faint as a finger on skin. "Someone who actually understands my maps."

"They're too good."

"Thank you," bone-Sermi said.

"No. They're . . . I've never felt that way. So . . . " Words tripped on Ngọc's tongue: all wrong. So inadequate. How could she describe how perfect it felt to *feel* her way like that?

"I know," Sermi said, "oh, I know. Perfect. I mapped other things, in other ways, but after the Ammassalik star maps I felt like I was always circling them, never touching them again. I held the Psápfa bone maps after their completion and the feel of those words under my fingers was finer than the sight, though I liked that too: it reminded me of embroidery."

Patterns. Textures.

After her grandmother's death, Ngọc had felt so alone.

"What happened?" she asked.

"I became trapped. The scavengers boarded my craft. I flung myself into my array in fear. They did indeed tear apart my body, but in the array I made a machine to tear them apart in turn. It didn't make me any less trapped. The Ivuultu trap array is isolated, while my craft's was destroyed and my own is also isolated. I can't even comm. I wrote on the bones out of boredom. I played with the traps. I want to go home." Sermi's voice sounded as if tears of carpals should be falling from the rib-eyes.

"We'll help you," Ngọc said. "What do you want?"

"To talk to Xaliima. To have my body back. To be on Cai Nu."

"I can comm Xaliima now. I don't know about bodies, but I can carry you back to Cai Nu."

"Near there," Fox said. "I'm not landing on Cai Nu."

"Near Cai Nu. My array tech is big," Ngọc said. "I can fit you in."

Silence.

Sermi said to Ngọc, "Your array tech is fox-shaped."

"Yes." Foxes dancing at her hairline. Ngọc grinned, extended an arm. "He's *called* Fox."

Laughing, Sermi slid into Ngọc's array like a gust from an air vent.

"Are we finished here?" Fox asked.

"Yes."

At the control of his craft, there was a look on Fox's face that struck Ngọc like a map in her hands. Excitement? Pleasure? Longing? And more. "Let's go," she said, and met smiles with him: shared their joys.

She held her hands at her side and mapped.

At an orbital station above Cai Nu, Ngọc and Fox met Xaliima—who took Sermi into a golden disc pinned to her hijab and transferred the reward money. Tears of happiness calligraphied Xaliima's cheeks. Sermi would have a new body made on Cai Nu. Sermi would map again.

After Xaliima left them, Fox said, "Do you want to go back to Goldchair? I want a mountain of chwee kueh."

That sounded good. Ngọc needed the energy: for her array, for her aching stomach. Her head felt full of energy after that mapping. That perfect joy. She wanted to sing or shout her happiness. She wanted to return to Sermi's maps as soon as she could. Stars and coastlines and whirlpools.

THE NEXT MAPS

I map, I map, yet I never reach a map.
I want to map what it is to be an array, to be thought.
I carve into bone-shaped wood: descriptions; the stories I would tell;
a schematic of my craft; a schematic of the traps and the bones and
the space crafts-in-pieces; the word 'loneliness.' I turn it over and over
in my hands and it is beautiful. It is not right, it is not real.
I try again.
Again.
Again.

THE CUMULATIVE EFFECTS
OF LIGHT OVER TIME
E. CATHERINE TOBLER

Viewed in the right light, everything is a love story.
Viewed in the right light, nothing is a love story.

Down-falling forever into dark.

Endless rain sheets through the broken cathedral of the ship as paracord sings between my metal fingers. Through rusted metal spire and fractured transept the rain runs rivulets down ambulatory arches that once used to segment walkways and rooms with inhabitants, purpose. All rest abandoned now, cloaked in shadow and the fecund stench of muddy earth and the life that scuttles through it. Every place is hollow of what it once was, transformed into a vault of all that came before and all that would never come after. Splintered segments of Arecibo's reflector dish litter the downward drop, grander swathes slicing through the ship's cracked and rusted hull to create new arches, convex eruptions upon which bioluminescent lichen and moss bloom.

(Splice: You were here in '88, before the Nessik rose up against their overlords and sparked an engine overload outside Saturn's orbit. How long did it take for a twenty-thousand meter prison ship to plummet past Jupiter, through asteroids untold, and smack into Earth? Never as long as one thinks. The wars changed this place forever; when you were here, the jungle was more jungle and less flooded saltwater basin. The jungle stretched from coast to coast, with the city perched on the northernmost edge like a tiny wart. You were here when Puerto Arecibo was still a thing, beach like a crescent of moon fallen from the sky, the lighthouse more than a lens in a rusting cage surrounded by water. Everything drowned, but your memory of how things were cascades across my vision.)

And every day, rain.

Mud that has funneled into the broken ship drips from every available outcrop. I keep my lines clear, wrapped around wrist and waist, the fucking ceph above me in the rusted ship rigging that remains. The ceph pulls its bony, armored form through chains and across fallen beams with dozens of supple arms and tentacles. It moves as if underwater, with the same sucking slurp of the mud, the same drip of rain. We move apart, yet collectively, on the same track for the same reason. Find the hiveling, get it the hell out.

Even in the rain, I can pick out the heat signatures, the fine delineation between the warmth of grouped bodies and the cold of the standing ship. The rain should hinder my vision, but it only pearls off the visor which encloses my skull and optical relays. These costly, compound eyes see straight through the pouring water: five figures rendered in thermal infrared, one smaller and colder than the others, clustered tightly and moving ever down through mud and wreck, into the far-reaching guts of this dead vessel.

Abruptly, all evidence of the warmth encircling the cooler body is obliterated, and so too its own heat signature vanishes. A light switch, on and then off. I draw myself still against the paracord while the Nessik drops to my level with a wet hiss, swaying on the chain as I listen and look. The rain pours in a continuous fury, running rivulets down muddy beams and outcroppings before it tongues lower into slopped mud and splits it further apart. The mud swallows the water until it can swallow no more; the new-made ground belches, breaches, and the water runs where it will, pulling mud with it. Mud cascades off ledges, over my metal-encased shoulder to tip me off balance. The puss coils a tentacle around my arm, as if to keep me from falling.

The ceph, the moll, the puss, the squid. Whatever I call the thing in the rigging across from me, it still doesn't speak any language native to Earth. The Nessik chitters through its beak in a series of low whirs, clicks, and whistles that also tell it exactly where I am in relation to its position. I speak the Nessik's tongue as if it is my own; most of we chimera do. At first it was mimicry; now it has become conversation. In the wars, the Nessik wondered how it was possible, that a human could take apart their language—when a human wasn't exactly human is how it was possible; when they realized there were those of us unlike anything they knew and feared us just a little more than they had before.

The Nessik wants to know why I stopped, and when I explain the readings have vanished, a low twitch rolls through its armored, tentacled body. If I could apply human characteristics to the being beside me, I would say it's nervous, concerned. Its legs of corded muscle shift restlessly, tentacles tonguing the chain not in an effort to hold on, but seemingly for something to *do*. Human, that. I have never seen a display of emotion in the Nessik as a whole, but that doesn't mean they don't feel, express, emote.

(Splice: You said the same thing of me, my head cradled in your calloused healer's hands, brown hair spilled between your fingers for a little while longer before even that was shorn away. Could my new eyes actually see you (you, *you*), or were they too preoccupied with statistical readouts downloaded from skyward drones, distracted by the neon slipstream of multiple HUDs you would never see no matter how deeply you looked into the blue of my irises, the black of my pupil? Couldn't even see where eye and lens were fused, so much had they become one inseparable thing. This is what you asked them to make of me; this is what they did. I always saw you. My baseline. Those eyes are now gone.)

Locating things, especially members of its own hive, is not typically difficult for the Nessik. They have no evident eyes, but use echolocation as bats do. They maneuver this planet as well as any human, though not as well as we chimera. The sounds of them moving through the streets dwindles to a low hum once one gets used to it; the first time I was in a city with more than one Nessik, the constant whirring couldn't be ignored: the hum of hot neon under pouring rain, a relentless crackle and hiss, a thing never quite extinguished.

I scan the ship's skeleton, shifting my display into different wavelengths where I bisect light into wave and particle. The ship blurs into long icicles of no color; no heat, no life, all the nothing that lingers in this wreck. The ground is a cooling haze of sludge, and of the bodies we tracked, there is no sign. The insistent crimson of a warm body in motion is gone. This happened in the wars too; it's not impossible to hide from IR. It's not impossible to ambush we chimera and disassemble us piece, by piece, by piece. Nothing is impossible if you apply yourself—isn't that what they say?

The Nessik doesn't find it amusing when I ask. If they have a sense of humor, I've never seen it on display. Their sense of community cannot be questioned; like bees, termites, and ants, they live in colonies, skeps, cathedral mounds. They live entangled, disliking solitude, because their communication, their sense of location, is stronger when they're surrounded. This, I realize, may explain why this Nessik (*fucking* moll) is restless. It's so quiet here in the dark down-fall but for the rain.

The ceph lets loose a high chirrup which echoes through the ship's frame. I can't feel the vibration as it does, but can see the vocalization as it streams outward. As it pulses into the wreck, a spectrogram bursts bright in the corner of my eye. It doesn't hit anything unexpected; whatever we were following is gone, and if it was the juvenile—this hiveling—we're no closer to knowing. Nessik young don't wander; they stay bundled with their birthhive, absorbing the thrum of the hivemind, the sounds that will turn to communication and allow them to eventually go where they will. This hiveling has been gone for a week and in a turn that still makes me laugh, the Nessik needed eyes that could see the silent things they could not detect. They needed what they most despised: something almost human.

Six misaligned miles to bottom-drop.

We swing ourselves through an arch and into a nook that used to be a slaughterhouse that used to be a brood cell. The ceph navigates the mud nearly as well as I do; I am not light, but swift, and make for the stretch of floor that remains free of slop. We crouch and listen: constant rain, the Nessik's every inhalation, the creak of the ship's rusting metal frame. Some distant human part of me imagines it can feel the wreck sway though this is impossible; the ship wedged itself six miles into the earth, bulleting like a drill aimed at the core. Six miles in and six miles out so they say; a rain of satellites in its shattering wake, collisional cascade. The first battles were fought here, upon the edge of the crater that used to house Arecibo's great dish; the first dead fell here, the first dead remain here.

(Splice: Why here? I was here in—*No*. You were here in '92 and remember these rooms, how strange they seemed upon first contact because they do not contain a straight edge, and when a world is all straight edges, usually bladed, a cocoon is instantly loathsome. These rooms are more like the cells of some gigantic hive, you think, though not for bees, because even they segment their hives into precise hexagons. These cells have no definition, though many had overflown with Nessik young. No one understood that in the first days; the hivelings swarmed and devoured all in their path, blind with hunger, and humans did what humans do. They refused to be eaten. These cell walls dripped with slop of a different kind then; your memory of this place smells like bile, yellow-brown and cold. It runs through your hands that assemble and disassemble with equal ease.)

Within this room, there rests a Nessik shell. Every soft part of its body has rotted away, leaving only its bony exoskeleton cupping the splatters of rain. The Nessik I travel with lets loose a low series of chitters to sketch out the boundary of the cell we find ourselves in, to understand the placement of every thing therein. Mud, shell, me. The Nessik withdraws from all, perching on the edge of the mud spill. It pulls its tentacles inward until none can be seen and it looks much like the empty shell, but there remains a low vibration emanating from it, a low frequency that feels like the absence of a thing once known.

Neither of us need to eat; neither of us need to be warmed by a fire. Still, the Nessik rests and I move to the edge of the cell, letting my hollowmade wrist swallow excess paracord as I momentarily need less of it. I scan further into the wreck to plot more of our downward course. If the hiveling has come here, it was on paths other than ours, but if there was another means of entry beyond the gaping maw of the shattered ship, the Nessik did not know it and even my eyes could not detect it.

The ceph chitters to ask of the readings. There are none, I say, and I wonder if the ship itself is shielding them. Is that why they have chosen this place? I look down through countless cells filled with debris, mud, the fallen dead, and I wonder. Without looking behind me at the ceph, I leap off the edge, paracord unspooling again from my wrist. I descend past level after level. The ceph will follow when it can and there is no hope it will lose me; every level I pass brings a searching signal from it, a vibration that ricochets down the cord, across my skull, back to it.

Every room here, empty of life.

I open my hand and free-fall.

The ship never slips from my focus. Every level is perfectly clear despite the fall of rain, despite the humidity that builds the lower I go. In the depths, the ship is warmed by the earth itself, and I scan, forever collecting data, routing it upward to my accomplice drone. *Fey IV* relays a data stream about a book that described Hell as dwindling, concentric circles such as these within the Nessik ship. Here would be the lustful and there would be the gluttonous.

(Splice: Your memories of lust and gluttony are a spear in whatever remains of my flesh, though this body can no longer be penetrated as it wishes. I remember these things through you, but also through myself, the deep and distant human pieces of myself recalling the warmth of a palm in the night, the whisper of breath, the path of nail over skin. I remember the way I tasted on your tongue and the way you could not believe your good fortune when I came back, when I said yes, but why I left and what I assented to are out of reach, lost in the happiness you knew in the resolutions. This should be enough. It is not quite. There is— There is—)

I come to rest on a muddy outcropping and stare downward into dark. In visible light, little is discernible and it suits me to see nothing more than the torrent of mud and rain into the dark. The ship exists as a throat, swallowing everything the world vomits into it. *Fey IV* confirms the distance, point six until we reach the main debris field, the field of dead, the field where they once would have scattered poppies and— *Shut up, Fey IV,* but the drone relays and confirms and relays again. The ship appears empty but for us, it says; what I cannot see has also been removed from the drone's reach.

I snap my wrist backward and far above me, the paracord's claw detaches from its anchor point. The umbilical whickers toward me, wet and dripping, until I can draw the claw into my hands to set a new anchor point. The Nessik slithers past me, off the edge of the outcrop and into the black beneath. With my anchor set, I leap off the edge and follow it down. Black every meter of the way, until *Fey IV* chirrups in my head and I know we're there.

It doesn't matter the wavelength I observe here; we could pass in blackness with only the ceph's echolocation to guide us, but I would know the bodies that litter this chamber. With a silent command, I bleed clean, bright light into the rooms we sink through, and observe the dead.

(Splice: It's ritual, you said, and *Fey IV* has always confirmed, to remember the dead, especially those who have fallen in battle, be it to knife or detached drone. Once, the dead were collected, honored, buried, but this battle saw no such luxury in its wake. In this battle, the dead could only be left where they fell. Those early days were dire, but didn't exactly improve as they wore on; the starved and terrified hivelings, the humans and chimera who came to rescue and recover, but found themselves in the center of an alien war they did not understand. Nessik prisoner slaves and Nessik captors; what else was there to know?)

Chimera and human alike litter this chamber. Empty Nessik shells are scattered like moss-colored stones. Humans have long since been reduced to skeletons, moss spreading a dense, lumpy carpet over most of them, but here and there, aged and broken bones pierce the green. The metal exoskeletons of chimera gleam in my bleeding light. There are no echoing lights, no sensors that pick up my presence and respond. Only rain and mud move in this chamber, sliding ever-down as I and the Nessik (fucking ceph) do.

(Splice: *Not now, not here.*)

I feel the fine vibration through the paracord and think the ship is moving. Sinking perhaps, swallowed by the earth at long last. But it is my hand that moves even as I hold it firm against the descent line. Beneath metal there remains muscle that (is finite, is mortal, will rot) shudders.

The ceph is not silent in this chamber. Its constant stream of chatter serves to tell it where it exists in relation to every fallen body, some of which may yet be trapped, but even as I understand the reason, the incessant sounds grate. My vision fragments, the chamber bursting into black before it streams back pixel by pixel, and my body stutters down the line. The light goes out.

A cold tentacle wraps my leg, holds me still so I will not fall. For a long while, we remain suspended, twisting in the dark until the Nessik clicks and whistles, drawing my slack outline fully into its awareness. Then, other tentacles enfold and haul me down. My wrist snaps back, the anchor slides loose, and the fucking ceph bears me into the scattered dead.

(Splice: *No*—

The dead smell worse than you imagined. Maybe it's made worse because of—

Oh God, Lil, there's so much blood . . .

My blood? Mine. Blood never bothered you, doctor you, but the stench of my guts and brains in your hands is too much and they want—

They want to remake me, take me, they can *save* me.

But I was never in this place, among these dead. No. *N*—

Yes, I was here, strewn in your hands and the memory of this punches down through me, hard fist in soft throat, but this throat is only metal now, only—)

I jerk back to full consciousness, hands trembling, vision skewed. I reach for *Fey IV*, but the drone is not in the sky, not crashed to earth. Nowhere. Everything above me is unreachable, as impenetrable as my own body. Beside me, the Nessik makes a low whir and I relax into the rain-wet moss that covers the skeletons that cover the ancient battlefield that once was a prison ship. This whir lulls me into a state that is close to sleep, even though sleep is a thing half-remembered. I used to do this—I used to need it—but not now. Not—

Tentacles encase me, tightening around arm, flank, and belly as if the Nessik thinks I mean to flee. I stare blind into the dark, useless to the ceph, to this entire journey, and listen to the rain pour down. It sounds different against metal skin and breathing tentacle; it sounds different against exoskeleton and shell. I want to figure how long it will take the ship to fill and sink, but while I can determine the rate of rainfall (two inches per hour), I cannot determine the exact volume the ship will hold, the amount that the earth will drink until it has its fill and overflows (*tongues lower into slopped mud and splits it further apart . . . tongues lower . . .*). My vision sparks magenta, green, and settles into black once more.

The ceph wants to know what happened, what the trouble is. "Systems malfunction" condenses a host of problems that I don't fully understand myself.

"Fucking— Squid." I speak the words in English, mostly to see if I can. My voice is not my voice; it is your voice, a stream of imbedded, erupting memory that sends my systems flatline. This was not the plan.

Splice.

Down-falling forever into dark.

We came together, armed, prepared, and yet not. They sent an entire division, but it will never be enough. We see that the moment we touch down, the moment our fellow soldiers stream through the broken jungle; we have run toward enough danger to understand this one is unique, this one will change everything: you, me, the world. It will change the Nessik, too, but

(fucking squid)

we don't care about them right now, because hundreds of thousands of their young are eating our soldiers in their panic, in their haste to escape the starvation cells they have been molded into.

Everything stands in ruin: charred and smoking trees, satellites drawn down from orbit, the Nessik ship itself, a crumpled tin-can spire rising six fucking miles into the clouded sky. The rain is ash and not water, but water would come soon enough, as if the world attempted to wash itself clean. None of this would be washed—

(fuc—)

we don't care about them right now because—they are eating our—

My display boots in a wash of gold. Sunlight through October leaves used to look like that—but that memory belongs to another world. There hasn't been an October for countless years, nor cheeks warmed by sunlight, but I can feel fingers (tentacles) against them. Warm (cold) and wet (wet). You (baseline).

Splice.

I can almost separate this stream from that stream: fingers were then, tentacles are now. You were warm; the Nessik is cold. Either way, the weight of another body against me is a block of data dredged up from a much-unused memory core and I shudder. It is only the sensation of systems coming back online (it is the only sensation of a hand (a tentacle) down a bare length of back).

Pixel by pixel, my system assembles you on the display. It's almost over, you say—we're almost there, but there's one more step. One more down-falling forever into dark. You want me to hold your hand. The blood there is sticky and growing cold. Mine? Yours? Yes.

"Can you see me?"

These words whispered. I could see you—as clear as anything in this awful moment, you segmented from the horrors that writhe just beyond this ramshackle field hospital. From the horrors inside it.

They can only save one of us now, but they sink your memory core so deeply into me, we are both still there, though neither of us know it. The surgeons you once worked with mute you, cloak you, drape you in chains the way Nessik were held by their captors. But even there, a finger peeps out from this metaphorical prison, allowing air into an otherwise sealed room. Later, they will wonder how I know what I do, but as these skills benefit them, they never worry overmuch. I am on their side; they made me and they made you, didn't they? Didn't they?

This finger (your finger) is a constant press upon my heart, a memory I cannot name but a thing that draws every piece of my new life into focus. I take one path and not the other because of that press; I cannot explain it—and who else could? Why do people go where they go? Something (someone) drew them there, inexorably. The box of you, inside of me, burrowing deeper than you ever went with fingers or tongue. You are the solid weight within whatever remains of my pelvic girdle (titanium overlaying a sliver of bone).

You always looked so human, everyone said.

I never did.

Fey IV steamrolls as spheres of orange data across the bottom of my display. I cannot tell how long my displays were dark; there is nothing and then there is the drone. The data it provides proves inconclusive; it shows the ship, me, and the Nessik. Constant sheeting rain. It tells me of descending Hell, of the violent and of the suicides; of blasphemers and sodomites.

Fey, I think, *there is something here in these rings of Hell. There was something here, and there is no possible way that something could have gotten out of this ship, past us, and we need to find it. Cloaked, muted, look for a finger.*

(Splice: You, rolling your eyes—they were mostly hazel but for that crescent of blue near the left pupil—and yet . . . and yet . . .)

Fey IV's data stays true, constant, inconclusive. I don't alter its instructions despite the lack of change in readouts, but shift instead toward the ceph who still has me cocooned in its thick arms. At my movement, it startles and shits a stream of panicked chirrups and whirs at me. The dialogue is so fast and dense, I cannot separate one word from another. I wait for it to calm, to grow silent, and try again.

I don't expect it to say my name. The name is a long trilling sound with too many Ls, a vibration that rumbles through the old bones beneath us. *Lillllliana.*

Did I speak while offline? Was I offline at all? The Nessik's hold on me does not ease; it pulls me closer if that is possible, drawing the bony crest of its sightless head toward mine. It outlines me in rapid-fire chitters, then speaks again, wanting to ascertain that I can continue, that the journey is not lost. Without my sight, we will never find the hiveling.

But why did the hiveling come here?

The answer bursts up from inside me, from inside my gut where you yet rest. You want me to know—

The hiveling had not *come*. It was *brought*.

As we were all brought, to this place on the edge of the island, on the edge of the ocean where we once reached outward into space, but no longer do because space came to us: domino effect, all fall down. Down-falling forever into dark. To be made into that which could best serve; to be broken until our new forms suited the plans to come. Prisoner slaves and captors. And you? Knew? (*Created.*) What else? (*Treachery.*) Tell me. (*Come.*)

The Nessik hauls me up from the mossy carpet that covers the dead and does not release me even as I try to stand. I quickly discover that I cannot stand, not on my own. Everything below my hips refuses to respond, a relay shorted out within the technology that lines my body. Such an injury to a soldier would be ridiculous, costly; the Nessik keeps me upright as I reroute power into the metal which encases my legs, but even when I can move again—

The ceph doesn't let me set my line, but keeps me bound in arms and tentacles. We plummet downward into dark. The ceph moves the way we saw them move *en masse* that day, chittering low as it goes to discern every ledge, every body, every passage that will take us to the bottom. Trusting (*fucking hell*) this creature to map the route, I scan in all the ways it cannot. My display stutters, spits.

I break the ship into every spectrum I can see, damage from the crash rendered in gradients of light gray to pitch black; damage from weapon blasts hovers in green and blue before I shift them away and to study biologics. You would think all this rain would wash the blood clean, but it still darkens the walls in visible light. And then—

It begins as a small point that blossoms into a faint heartbeat that becomes a fully realized body. At the bottom of the ship, where the mud has flooded a torrent and blocks most of the passageways leading deeper, there is a body. I chitter to the Nessik and we drop even quicker, a stone thrown down an empty well. One tentacle keeps us from smacking full into the mud; we touch down beside that still body, the adult reaching out with another series of high-pitched sounds. The body—perhaps a hiveling, for it is small—makes no vocal reply. It struggles to move, one tentacle whipping toward the sound. The ceph grabs the tentacle with one of its own, but then withdraws with a shriek, letting even me go.

I shift my vision through every wavelength of light to see what has been done to this Nessik. Most of its body has been encased in metal, small hexagonal panels that call to mind flexible armor. This casing looks nearly like my own, so that the body might be made to move even if injured. When I touch the metal, it flickers with energy and for a moment, the Nessik winks out of my view. Vanished. Cloaked.

(Splice: Your hands in my hair, my broken body dripping through your fingers. This is where I came back and where I said—

"Yes."

And this is where you smiled that rare smile and nothing else mattered as they cut each of us apart and sank you into me so I could be stronger, faster, better, everything they needed me to be. In memory, it is your fingers raking me raw, it is your mouth covering mine—and nothing else mattered because both of us would live beyond every limit we had known just as you predicted.)

But this.

I draw my hand back and the body comes into view again. Every edge once outlined in heat begins to fade into blue, into cold, and there is nothing we can do to keep it from slipping away entire. But on this level, deeper through mud-flooded corridors that have been lined in these selfsame metal panels, I can see more signatures: thrumming red lifeblood that beckons. This is what the Nessik could not see, every bit of this level erased, all that it contains swallowed. And these Nessik here, made silent by human hands.

There is more than one hiveling here and more than one adult. Silently, they scream at us—the air vibrates as they try to communicate, but there is no sound, for they have been cut as you and I were cut; flesh has been made to do what others would have it do.

(*You once guided flesh this way—tried on yourself first, splice, and jack, and chimera you.*)

Countless cages line the walls, dripping with mud and shit and chains and rain. Even here, this room is not spared the flood of rain from above. Even here, wrapped in the panels even my eyes could not penetrate from above, they are subject to the rains.

The Nessik moves like quicksilver, unlatching cages to free the captive young. The adults are worse for all that has been done to them and most are near death, but the hivelings move with a more terrifying speed, streaking into a deeper room rather than the corridor behind us to escape. The farther we walk, the cleaner the halls become, until I am tracking muddied footprints down a white hall, until the Nessik leaves a broken path of Rorschach streaks and blobs that convey a bat eating a moth eating the world swallowed by the endless void.

In the deepest room, protected from mudslide and rainfall, a cadre of human doctors stand mid-slaughter—you name each one of them in my display; friends, they were your friends, colleagues. Nessik bodies lay upon tables, but there are human injured here, too, and this bloody tableau is familiar to us both. They cut a piece from one body and slide it into the belly of another. They sever the vocal cords of the Nessik to mute them the way they muted you (the way you muted others, slid yourself into them, into countless thems), but these creatures—these new chimera?—have found a way to reach out, a way to communicate yet. Theirs becomes a language of blood. I speak this as if it is my own; most of we chimera do. At first it was mimicry; now it has become conversation.

(Splice: We were here in '92 and remember these rooms, this hive, these levels of hell. It was your extraordinary eyes guided us down and down, your body that bled clean light over the level that was soon to become a battlefield that was soon to become your grave. You experimented here; you studied here; you despaired here.)

(Splice: I was here again in '93, '95, and '01, and now . . . *now*. It was you and also not-you, the memory of you dredged up from the box they sank into me. It was not-you who wondered if I could see you—they wondered if I could still access you, if I had broken the encryption even they could not master. Could I see you? Baseline, *always*. You let me inside, you let me know every secret thing you had discovered through every graft of information into yourself, into other bodies, into . . . into . . . into.)

(Splice: But it was more than that—you were never one of the dead here. Were you? You who made these splices, you did not die. You fragment in my display.)

The hivelings blur within the cloak of their armor; they never hesitate, leaping upon the human doctors, dragging them to the floor. Freshly-spilled human blood is a startling red warmth against the cold blue shipframe; it fades, becomes the cool blue of the floor, and is seemingly gone, unless I shift my view. The walls run with red and blue and a hue of violet in between, and nothing is ever still—not the hivelings, not the human dead, not the dying adult Nessik who have been broken and used and broken and used yet still breathe on.

A coiling tentacle pulls me to the floor; I snap my wrist back to access the paracord and its hook. The hook sails out, to punch the Nessik (the ceph, moll, puss, squid, the fucking *you*?) in the gut, and the sound that spills from this creature is not alien. It is *you*, a fragment of you yet living in this beast, and it is then I hear you all around me.

You, spliced into every creature that leaps into the fray—these hivelings, these chimera, these *you*. You who did not exactly die, but neither exactly live, you growing strange and widespread in each of these bodies. They thought they could silence you, stretch you into inchoate strands, but you found a way, not flesh, not machine, something beyond both.

And I think of the way the Nessik (the fucking ceph) held me when I fell, and it is the only sensation of a tentacle (a hand) down a bare length of back.

And the way it (you) said my name.

◆ ◆ ◆

After.

Jacked into a socket, you wedged in a way I didn't think you could be wedged again.

(Splice: Oh, we were here, *here,* and it's the memory of flesh inside flesh, of you inside me, of nothing else existing in that moment.

Viewed in the right light—

Everything—

Nothing.)

There are no places in this world that light will not intrude. Every dark space within even me has been broken apart, exposed to light, and sealed back up. And through it all, pieces of you cradled inside.

We were here in '05, we will say, when the ship still reached six miles into the clouded sky like a broken finger; we were here when the living were cut apart and fused with the dead, when the beach was still wholly drowned but grains of sand floated free in the water even so.

We were in here '09, when the ship's spire gave way, buckling as those concentric circles of hell at last had their way and pulled the ship entirely into its maw. We would be here in '15, when *Fey VI* confirmed what we believed, that humanity had gone—chimera-consumed; that this world, this earth had also become chimera. Spliced, jacked, no longer a singular thing if it had ever been.

Viewed in the right light—

Light degrades, exposes, destroys, illuminates, corrupts, burns, irreversibly changes everything. I touch you (baseline), you who are in every fucking ceph I know, and my touch is as light speeding through darkness. This light may bend, fragment, or ricochet, but it keeps going.

Down-falling forever into dark—it keeps going.

And every day, rain.

SYNECDOCHE ORACLES

BENJANUN SRIDUANGKAEW

Behind the bars of Charinda's ribs, there lives a peacock.

It sports titanium actuators and platinum feathers to contrast with the darkness of her limbs, ruby eyes and emerald beaks to complement the petals on her face. It is a gift from an infamous cyberneticist, and she has understood from the first that one day she will pay a price.

So it is no surprise to her when the peacock chirps and regurgitates a paper scroll. On it is calligraphy written in ink bled from solar eels, opalescent and pompous, instructing her to host a hunted general.

Charinda is aware of the price on their head. It cannot be expressed as a sum; the honor and prestige that would come with the general's death or capture defy integers. She would be granted dominion over worlds. She would be elevated above common memory and made a minor goddess, named and prayed to across Costeya systems.

She sends the general word that she will provide shelter.

The Bone Court orbits Laithirat, a composite skeleton of thorns and fused spines, vertebrae dripping teeth and a jaw poised to gobble up the sky. It is received wisdom that this megafauna specimen was engineered, some geneticist's fancy gone wild.

Charinda likes to imagine that the beast stood up once upon birth, decanted or perhaps grown in briny mulch, and straightaway fell down dead under its own weight and the terror of being alive.

In the beast's mouth refugees are disgorged from moth-crafts in tatters, asylum-seekers spilled from spin-ships whose hulls are frescoes of void-scars and entry points. Viruses and malware shed off travelers, latching onto tourist ads and local data-posts in search of new hosts and propagation. Charinda has put a filter on her peacock's head like a glove, shielding it from the stench of recycled ventilation and nutrients, the reek of politics gone sour and loss as fresh as arterial wounds. They can be contagious, much more so than the malware.

In the beast's stomach, blank-faced replicants conduct her through checkpoints. She passes through a femur-corridor papered by intelligences with a knack for generating hyper-accurate algorithms at the moment of death: a Laithirat premium export, these seers in a box.

Where the corridor ends and the whispers of intelligences fade, a labyrinth begins.

Its schematics were planned in five dimensions, patterned after two national epics told in synesthetic meter. Charinda navigates by reciting snippets that wreathe her in incense vapors, as of funerals. At intersections of verses she meets a jungle case for a leopard woman, an aquarium for a gilled man. She nods at her friend the Horticulturist, who reclines in an enclosed tropical garden; photosynthetic geckos pulse at her throat, breathing in the place of lungs lost to carnivorous ixora. She exchanges quatrains with the Vice-Tetrarch of Gravity Gardens, who attends on a lower body which rumbles on wheels and exhales steam alphabets.

Charinda finds the general at one of the central exhibits.

The general wears a Tiansong dress with flared sleeves and high collars, a narrow skirt slit just below the thigh. Asteroid jades and exhumed gravity shells depend from his earlobes, and his skin has the look of cracked celadon. Spiders nest in his hair, making neon thread: a work of kitsch, all spectacle.

"Gracious welcome to you, General Lunha of Silent Bridge."

Lunha inclines his head, silhouetted in the phantom stanzas that charted his path. He recited, it appears, a war-god's soliloquy. "I don't currently hold a rank, and Silent Bridge isn't what it once was." He is more frayed than his reputation would suggest, fatigue having exacted their price for the endless hours he spent sabotaging Hegemonic outposts and erasing their garrisons. But remorse does not blunt him and the gaze with which he appraises Charinda is sniper-point.

Balancing her options, Charinda takes the general's hand and brings it to her lips. "Formality gives me an excuse to perform gallantry. In some languages that concept is strictly reserved for men toward women, but what can an idea be worth that does not flex?"

"I'm not always a man," the general says but returns the gesture, his mouth brief and warm on Charinda's knuckles. "My thanks for having me."

"How could I not? A chance to meet a personage so celebrated and, moreover, to kiss his hand—though last I heard you were more often a woman than otherwise. I hope you like the maze. Visitors can enter these frames to touch, talk, or request a sync. An interactive art."

"They are curious." The general looks at the exhibit, which contains Olyosha sitting on an ivory chariot. Her arms are chromed plates stylized with solar flares; they are heavy and unsubtle, the way firearm prostheses tend to be. Script identifies her as *The Archer*.

Charinda's peacock sings out a few notes, dispersing the last of verse-echoes about them. "You disapprove."

"Just Olyosha. I can't imagine the sun archer could hold any significance for her. Perhaps she visited my birthworld during leave or stayed for the length of a deployment, neither of which gives her a connection to Tiansong."

"Olyosha's just a romantic." Charinda sketches a binary flower on the malleable glass. "The maze checks visitors for organic-to-artificial ratio. Only people who are fifty-percent cybernetics, minimum, may enter; the rest are steered back to the exit even if they've the poetry correct. I inhabit one of these boxes on occasion. It's a performance—surrender to the gaze."

"As I said, I don't object to the idea. Olyosha served under me for a campaign. Whatever she's doing now would be an improvement, if only because she's not causing casualties in the thousand."

"You're blunt," Charinda says as they pass the Duke of River Seven, who has entered the box of a man wearing a veil of membranes and fins. It is lifted: beneath is a raw face, two lidless eyes, a seam where a mouth once was. They kiss, tenderly and openly.

On the way out she straightens the peacock's feathers the way most straighten tousled clothes. She cups its albino head in her palm. It is terribly fragile.

There was a time when Charinda did not doubt her strength. Then something happened, and she found herself in need of a reconstruction. She applied for an operation from a cyberneticist known to be without equal.

When it was done, her belly was hollowed out. In its place a cage, inside it a peacock.

"You asked for a bird, I gave you a bird," Esithu said. "Appreciate your luck. There was a woman who wanted a bird and I gave her a beehive. Mind the implant well and it'll keep you so healthy you'll never need longevity treatments. I won't have it said that Esithu does subpar work."

Charinda had believed the implant would restore her, made her whole again.

The first year it terrified her to leave the house, to be seen with this mark of her mortality singing through her ribs. She tried covering it up with clothes that no longer fit right, but it hurt the peacock to be kept from sun and warmth. Her metabolism became ravenous; she had to eat for the bird too. Sinewy umbilici tethered them to one another. Any distance from it filled her with a panic like drowning, an ache like the accident she didn't want to remember.

The months went; her isolation grew. She confined herself to her cortices, cultivating and breeding intelligences in ecosystems written to be viciously hostile. Many artificial clusters she encouraged to be nomadic or symbiotic; others she programmed with an expansionist slant. They would take over extant clusters, imposing new hierarchy and subroutines. It didn't matter who won: under the built-in logic of diminishing resources they all went extinct in the end.

In this way she made them wage war, negotiate treaties, develop primitive poetry. In this way she discovered what they became when they dissolved. It was time-consuming and too individual for mass production, but she was diligent. She saw the potential, and made more.

Sometimes she fed the peacock out of her hand, and found she could be full that way.

By the second anniversary of her operation, she was ready.

Charinda's house is a stage. It tells of a cluttered life, mildly temperamental: mementos littering the floor, framed stills of friends, personal data pocking and inscribing the projected autumn sky. Aborted prostheses murmur in the walls and swing from the ceiling to the tune of cardiac arrest, casting six-point shadows. Silent intelligences, suspended on the cusp of permanent zeros, bristle within the house cortices.

When there is a new client, she would purge the house to a blank slate. Windows angled to catch and slant the sunshine, limning the walls in soft dream-light. Empty rooms, empty floors.

Stepping in, Lunha shields her eyes, an affected gesture made more garish by the prismatic reflections eeling down her wrist. Her vision adjusts to sun-glare or darkness effortlessly, Charinda knows: the best the army can provide.

"Your body," the general says. "Have you had it for long?"

"It's considered rude," Charinda says easily, "to inquire. Much as it would be if I asked you why you're female now when scarce an hour ago you were a man."

"I recognize the make. I'm not asking as an outsider; my augmens works are extensive."

"You don't wear yours openly." She switches on furniture. Plush chairs and a faceted table unfold, sheathed in haptics and contour sensors. "What brought you to Laithirat?"

"When I left the Hegemony, I found myself troubled by a mathematical burden. One of your predictives should be able to solve that, and I've come to negotiate for it."

"In your hand my oracles would become weapons to render civilizations into history, prosperity into genocide. I'm not interested in abetting you."

Lunha smiles with a mouth painted and shaped for an idol's pout. "I don't need artificial prophets whispering in my ear to carry out war. This burden is of a personal nature. I could give my word that I won't use your children to scorch so much as a single city block, extinguish so much as one solitary life."

"A pledge full of loopholes." Charinda opens a server rack. "I'd like to do a deep scan, just to be sure you haven't set aside a partition for an intelligence cluster."

"As a rule, I don't lie. I was a soldier, not a diplomat."

"Is that all you are? Have you never aspired to anything else?"

"When I was very little I thought of becoming a scholar, working with classics or ancient history." Lunha's voice has turned detached and melodious, as if presenting someone else's life. "A while later I thought of dance, theater, music. Later still I performed exceptionally well in a certain aptitude test, and discovered that I enjoyed putting my mind to work in that capacity. Tiansong has its own defense force, but joining the Hegemony's gave me a wider scope with which to exercise my imagination."

"And so the deaths of billions are tattooed on your fingerprint," Charinda says, keeping her voice warm, this side of voluptuous. "An engineer with a peacock in her middle isn't going to scare you. A deep scan, please."

Lunha raises an eyebrow, but complies. The spiders are discarded to perish on Charinda's carpet, breaking down to proteins that the house quickly absorbs. Stripped of porcelain coating Lunha is hard muscles, thick thighs and a torso mapped with scars from duels and failed assassins. The scan shows a plated skeleton, filtered digestive organs, and neural enhancers built like constellations to orbit the sun of her thought. Grafted onto that, serpentine and gangrenous, bides the Hegemony's parting gift.

"Your mathematical burden," Charinda says, examining that knot of encryption, "appears to be a killswitch."

"I've forced it into a reset loop, but it won't always hold. I like to imagine a tech executing the termination command over and over." Lunha laughs softly, eyes half-lidded. "The next one decompiling it, rebuilding it, trying again. The one after that coming to the realization that it's never going to activate. As problems go, your clusters are uniquely placed to solve it."

"By prolonging your life at all I'll be adding to an interminable slaughter toll."

"Good calculation takes into account both sides of the equation: acceptable losses, a threshold of collateral damage you will not cross. Would you prefer the wars of the universe helmed by commanders who cause carnage for its own sake and trigger supernovae for the adrenaline rush of it? Conflict will happen with or without me. Even if I fell today, even if I was never born. But I'm tidy; many are not."

"That's self-serving logic." Charinda tilts her head; the peacock chirps, baring razor teeth. She has no more love for the Hegemony any other Laithirat born and bred. "What can you offer me?"

"That depends." Lunha undocks, a hiss of body sockets and ports in release. "Name what you lack or want, and that'll be our starting point."

"I won't haggle, General. There's one thing I want, and one only. I haven't any use for fancies, and any essentials I need are already mine. You don't have to offer up the riches of worlds like dripping sweets or the mastery of star systems like savory meat."

"Yes?"

"I want to be free of Esithu."

Charinda's surgery was performed remotely. She met Esithu afterward at a reception, for the first and last time.

Despite being wanted on most planets under Hegemonic jurisdiction and several not, Esithu walked openly. Their triplet bodies—the ultimate prostheses—spoke and acted with apparent independence, one making conversation with the Duke of River Seven and another with the Vice-Tetrarch. The third sampled frozen fruits wrapped in heated spice pastes, scorched eels wriggling in puddles of chili salt.

"Ah," the cyberneticist said, looking up. "A celebrity."

Charinda had brought a bowl of ape ears studded at lobe and whorls with pearly roe, braised in oyster essence. She put one piece to Esithu's mouth. "In your presence I can't claim to be that. A satellite, maybe. Lesser, definitely."

They obliged with a bite, licking unborn fish off Charinda's thumb. "I'm glad you came, since I wanted to speak to you directly. There's an individual, famous or infamous depending on your point of view. We've a pact, she and I, to stay out of each other's way and cooperate when short-term goals align: at present such is the case. You'll notice that I didn't exact payment for your operation."

"I was hoping you considered me a charity case."

"You don't require my charity," Esithu said, raising a glass. They did not drink. "Most people would rather I keep my charity away from them—the other side of space-time, for preference. When the day comes you'll commit yourself to this individual or I'll shut down your implant. Don't take it personally. Your specialty singled you out for her purposes, and I hear she's a polite guest."

Pressed afterward Charinda would not be able to tell what Esithu looked or sounded like. No security footage, omniscient or personal, captured them. Neither the Duke nor the Vice-Tetrarch could recall what they spoke. There was only the certainty, prickling like thorns under skin, that Esithu was there.

The petals on Charinda's cheeks deepen in color. Some of them shed free of the stems at her chin, dusting her collarbones in pollen. It's the season for that, and she doesn't try to hide them any more than she tries to hide the peacock. In public she attracts stares.

The general does not. Chameleon matrices cover her grid presence and though she wears no physical mods, she goes unrecognized in train lobbies or crowded promenades. There are many on Laithirat who, though no more desirous of Hegemonic rule than Charinda, would eagerly turn Lunha in for those impossible prizes: they owe a Tiansong native little, an ex-soldier nothing.

"Wouldn't it better serve you to commission a skilled cyberneticist?" Lunha asks as they settle under one of Charinda's hybrids, a canopy of linguistic fruits and axiomatic fronds, infrared flowers igniting as evening draws on.

"You think I haven't tried? Not even the best know how to bar Esithu from access, and they've all been of the opinion that it's what I implicitly agreed to." She plucks a pomegranate, breaks it open for zircon couplets and obsidian epigrams seeded by local poets. The quality has been uneven lately but the subjects have not. A trend for lamentations and famine, ruinscapes and seas blasted fatalist-scarlet. "Help yourself."

The general picks a mangosteen. It splits open to six plump segments inscribed with astrophysics theories. "Botanic splicing for a hobby?"

"I like trees. I've donated these for public use; anyone can enter data to pattern cultivars. There's some automatic curation but for the most part it's unregulated, and I quite like the results."

Lunha eats the mangosteen segment by segment, variables briefly lighting up her lips and sternum as she swallows. "In theory your predictives can calculate anything."

"In theory," Charinda says, rolling the taste of an enjambment on her tongue. The consistency is elastic, pleasantly chewy. "It hinges on what input is fed to it and how much; it depends on the application. If any fool could use them to great success, the universe would be full of miraculous reversals, inexplicable plenty, and we'd all be winners."

"Do they project results alone, or can they be used to generate a set of circumstances through which a desired outcome may be achieved?"

"Both. But the more variables, the more difficult it is to use. Estimating a result is much easier and takes a smaller cluster."

Lunha catches a falling petal. Severed from Charinda it curls in on itself, withering to black crumbs. "Might I try my hand at it?"

"I can give you a set."

"Not so advanced it may solve my little inconvenience, of course. It won't have to be. I just need to familiarize."

The general spends the next week in battle simulations. She has requested Charinda obtain the most complex available, scenarios where success is impossible; she plays with handicaps of number and resources, terrain and logistics.

Charinda watches the visuals, as often rapid-fire abstractions as they are animalistic hyper-realism. "You nearly died serving the Hegemony. What was it like when you woke up and discovered yourself a full cyborg?"

Lunha maneuvers one of her buffer hive-states into position. "The reconstruction was cellular, and before my injury I was already more implants than not. I entered officer school when I was young, and standard-issue augmens started a year in. Gradual, with physical therapy to ease the transition. But it was enhancement rather than replacement. Yours is . . . drastic."

"We weren't talking about me, General." In the simulation, human-shaped units blister and shrivel under a warp-sleet. The physics model, Charinda has to admit, is superb. "Did you enjoy your work?"

"All career soldiers enjoy their work. If not the massacre—and many do relish that—it's the practice of forging individuals into units and fitting them into a strategy. A mathematical pleasure, if you will."

Charinda unlatches her ribcage. The umbilici unspool as the peacock steps out, tugging at her like ligaments. "It's said you deserted the Hegemony when serving the side that always wins began to sour. No challenge, no sport."

"A cynical opinion to take, not to mention sociopathic." Lunha allows the bird into her lap, where it pecks at her secondskin, indenting the fabric with green triangles. "But my specialty is what it is, with just one kind of use."

"You could take up another occupation."

"I could, but I'll always carry my name and my deeds." Lunha's swarm opponents are pinned down, one glimpse of whirring blades and eyes, before they dissipate under optical scatter-fire. The general pauses the sequence. "I've grasped how your predictives operate."

Charinda watches Lunha's expression closely. "How so?"

"I've been using the algorithms after I finish a skirmish. The results they produce are in line with how the game resolves—until I input my data. Your clusters can't hold a behavioral profile. Grow one that can, feed it data of the implant and Esithu."

In her place the peacock plays low, amused notes. "Even if it was that simple, my oracles aren't easy to produce. To develop one to a stage where it'd have that capacity would take a decade."

"Under what conditions are they grown?"

"Virtual wars," Charinda says, after a moment. "I hardwire them with an instinct to proliferate, set them up with competitive templates. Winning clusters produce more sophisticated algorithms. It *isn't* a battle game. The clusters aren't units to be controlled, and the system is mine alone. Access isn't something I will compromise."

The general nods. "I could accelerate the process. What do you say to a restricted sync that'll give me temporary control?"

Charinda sips the air through her teeth. "A sync is both ways."

"By definition. Shall we get to it?"

When she was young, full-on sync was Charinda's drug of choice—edgy and uncontrolled, an indulgence in abandon. That was *before*, when she could afford to be reckless, when her body was just a body. She does not like to think of herself as weaker now, but there's a line of demarcation: before, after. Charinda of before a different nation with a language of her own, one that Charinda of after has chosen to forget.

This is compartmentalized, boundaries clear and hard between their data streams. Neither of them wishes to lose herself in the other. But permeability is inevitable.

The peacock rattles Charinda's ribcage and her teeth quiver at the roots. Lunha's recent memory stains hers like ink in water: the general piloting a reversal engine in vertiginous silence, her skin gray with dead-sun ashes. Probability fluxes making prisms on the viewport of her ship, compression ice making glass of her fingertips; one of her arms is dead from integrity bullets, plastic tendons snapped. A battle of foregone result—carefully sown implosions come to fruit, taking out a Hegemonic supply fleet.

The exchange feed stutters.

"When I was very little I thought of becoming a scholar, working with classics. Love poems, lightning-epics, sculpture-prose. The sensation of those things delighted me. I could feel them in my fingertips, in my bloodstream where they left imprints and swept through my dreams." The voice is melodious and factual, as of someone reading off a biography, or perhaps a dossier. "A while later I thought of dance, music, pursuits through which I could regulate the display of myself. Later still I performed exceptionally well in an aptitude test. I do not need to name it. Save on Costeya birthworlds, all citizens of the Hegemony take it at a young age."

The audio skips.

"To survive, the conquered must conquer in turn. It is a mechanism to lessen the trauma, the actuality, of subjugation. By participating in conquest, one may regain a degree of control. A logical progress, moreover encouraged. There are no recruits fiercer or more loyal than those from consolidated planets. Cradle-world officers are not so driven to perform, for they have nothing to prove and everything to lose. The system thus sustains itself."

The audio distorts. The voice has flattened, quietly toneless.

"Tiansong was absorbed into the Costeya Hegemony on—"

Coming to, Charinda lies side by side with the general. The nexus cradle is hard against her back, her consciousness still unmoored, alienated from herself.

"It does not escape me," Lunha says in a clear, calm voice, "that this was your desired outcome from the start."

Charinda disconnects from the cradle. Air quivers in her larynx, in her lungs which have been knotted and reshaped to fit around the cage like fistfuls of thread. "What did you see?"

"Not much." Lunha finger-combs her hair roughly, the most human gesture Charinda has seen from her. "Mostly tactile memory from before your accident. If I intruded, I didn't mean to."

"I saw—"

"It doesn't matter." The general's voice has assumed the staccato cadence of doors sliding shut. "The present interests me more."

"I did say that I meant to make a bid for freedom. Esithu values me and delivering superior predictive clusters would go a long way in relaxing my leash. They can't be deauthorized from my implant, not really." Charinda blinks past a double vision, remnant of the sync: she sees herself through Lunha's eyes overlaid with biometrics. Measurement of her vitals, a heat map in fisheye. The quiet mantra of joint actuators. It passes. "When did you realize?"

"To me it seemed unlikely that you couldn't develop an advanced cluster on your own, but you didn't have enough data on Esithu—no one does—so you chose to input me. Perhaps not a complete profile, but sufficient. I'm a public figure."

The general is not known for her cruelty, but she is efficient with those who would bring her harm. Charinda does not move. If Lunha wants her death, her efforts at self-defense would be less than pathetic. A low thrum vibrates through the bars. The peacock's heartbeat. Hers.

Lunha's gaze betrays nothing. The lines of her features are tranquil in the way of spiritual icons revered on Tiansong. "I don't resent you. We all do what we must to survive and thrive. You'll find the clusters I've guided to triumph the best of your oracles yet, but you'll also find that they will ignore input related to me."

Charinda does not doubt it, but she is a scientist. She plucks one of the newest clusters and kills it. The fruiting algorithm is more expansive than any she's bred to date; it does not take so much as Lunha's physiological profile. "I can appreciate that."

"I'm sure you will attempt to find a way around it," the general says, and her mouth flexes, almost a smile. "Altogether, would it not be fair if you hand me a small colony? A fraction of the crop I nurtured, so you'll still come out ahead."

"I thought you didn't need ghost prophets."

"Perhaps one day I'll encounter an opponent I cannot overcome. Perhaps I'll find another use for them. Who knows? I may not always be a soldier."

In her lap Charinda holds the bird that is her life, where it swishes its tail and murmurs children's mnemonics. "You knew from the start I'd never allow anyone into my cortices, that this was the one way you could interface with them." She loads a dead-drop module up with an intelligence colony, and presses the sleek, thin tube into the general's hand. "I shouldn't have tried to outplay you."

"Does it matter? We both obtain what we wanted." Lunha pulls on a fibrous mesh that absorbs light, a set of clothes that would belong in any city, on any planet. Gloves and jacket the color of pomelo shadows at high noon. "I'll ration them. When I've won and the Hegemony is in ruins, I'll return what's left."

"I wouldn't want them back. Go with your ancestors' blessings, or the blessings of whatever entity you still believe in."

The general takes Charinda's hand, kisses it: formal, cupping her fingers just so. "Don't get caught. I'd hate to come back to find Laithirat a heap of ashes and stellar debris just because you harbored me for a month."

When the Hegemonic birthworld Salhune falls, Charinda watches the broadcast from under one of her trees. The planet consumes itself in a chain reaction of neutron plants and tectonic reactors—the scale of destruction is spectacular, the calculation behind it peerlessly precise.

Charinda feeds the peacock slices of persimmons which seep verses of genocide, elegies of annihilation: this season's fads, surprisingly nutritious. She sips at tea made from synecdoche leaves; it is a harmony of flavors, full of assonance. Her face is in bloom, petals like supernovae, stamens heavy as warships.

In the battlefield of her cortices, the oracles continue to fight.

COLLATERAL
PETER WATTS

They got Becker out in eight minutes flat, left the bodies on the sand for whatever scavengers the Sixth Extinction hadn't yet managed to take out. Munsin hauled her into the Sikorsky and tried to yank the augments manually, right on the spot; Wingman swung and locked and went hot in the pants-pissing half-second before its threat-recognition macros, booted late to the party, calmed it down. Someone jammed the plug-in home between Becker's shoulders; wireless gates unlocked in her head and Blanch, way up in the cockpit, put her prosthetics to sleep from a safe distance. The miniguns sagged on her shoulders like anesthetized limbs, threads of smoke still wafting from the barrels.

"Corporal." Fingers snapped in her face. "Corporal, you with me?"

Becker blinked. "They—they were human . . . " She thought they were, anyway. All she'd been able to see were the heat signatures: bright primary colors against the darkness. They'd started out with arms and legs but then they'd *spread* like dimming rainbows, like iridescent oil slicks.

Munson said nothing.

Abemama receded to stern, a strip of baked coral suffused in a glow of infrared: yesterday's blackbodied sunshine bleeding back into the sky. Blanch hit a control and the halo vanished: night-eyes blinded, ears deafened to any wavelength past the range of human hearing, all senses crippled back down to flesh and blood.

The bearing, though. Before the darkness had closed in. It had seemed wrong.

"We're not going to Bonriki?"

"*We* are," the Sergeant said. "You're going home. Rendezvous off Aranuka. We're getting you out before this thing explodes."

She could feel Blanch playing around in the back of her brain, draining the op logs from her head. She tried to access the stream but he'd locked her out. No telling what those machines were sucking out of her brain. No telling if any of it would still be there when he let her back in.

Not that it mattered. She wouldn't have been able to scrub those images from her head if she tried.

"They *had* to be hostiles," she muttered. "How could they have just *been* there, I mean—what else could they be?" And then, a moment later: "Did any of them . . . ?"

"You wouldn't be much of a superhuman killing machine if they had," Okoro said from across the cabin. "They weren't even armed."

"Private Okoro," the Sergeant said mildly. "Shut your fucking mouth."

They were all sitting across the cabin from her, in defiance of optimal in-flight weight distribution: Okoro, Perry, Flannery, Cole. None of them augged yet. There weren't enough Beckers to go around, one every three or four companies if the budget was up for it and the politics were hot enough. Becker was used to the bitching whenever the subject came up, everyone playing the hard-ass, rolling their eyes at the cosmic injustice that out of all of them it was the farmer's daughter from fucking *Red Deer* who'd won the lottery. It had never really bothered her. For all their trash-talking bullshit, she'd never seen anything but good-natured envy in their eyes.

She wasn't sure what she saw there now.

Eight thousand kilometers to Canadian airspace. Another four to Trenton. Fourteen hours total on the KC-500 the brass had managed to scrounge from the UN on short notice. It seemed like forty: every moment relentlessly awake, every moment its own tortured post-mortem. Becker would have given anything to be able to shut down for just a little while—to sleep through the dull endless roar of the turbofans, the infinitesimal brightening of the sky from black to grey to cheerful, mocking blue—but she didn't have that kind of augmentation.

Blanch, an appendage of a different sort, kept her company on the way home. Usually he couldn't go five minutes without poking around inside her, tweaking this inhibitor or that BCI, always trying to shave latency down by another millisecond or two. This time he just sat and stared at the deck, or out the window, or over at some buckled cargo strap clanking against the fuselage. The tacpad that pulled Becker's strings sat dormant on his lap. Maybe he'd been told to keep his hands off, leave the crime scene in pristine condition for Forensic IT.

Maybe he just wasn't in the mood.

"Shit happens, you know?"

Becker looked at him. "What?"

"We're lucky something like this didn't happen *months* ago. Half those fucking islands underwater, the rest tearing each other's throats out for a couple dry hectares and a few transgenics. Not to mention the fucking Chinese just waiting for an excuse to *help out.*" Blanch snorted. "Guess you could call it *peacekeeping.* If you've got a really warped sense of humor."

"I guess."

"Shame we're not Americans. They don't even sign on to those treaties, do anything they damn well please." Blanch snorted. "It may be a fascist shithole down there but at least they don't knuckle under every time someone starts talking about *war crimes*."

He was just trying to make her feel better, she knew.

"Fucking *rules of engagement*," he grumbled.

Eight hours in IT when they landed: every aug tested to melting, every prosthetic stripped to the bolts while the attached meat sat silent and still and kept all the screams inside. They gave her four hours' rack time even though her clockwork could scrub the fatigue right out of her blood, regulate adenosine and melatonin so precisely she wouldn't even yawn right up until the point she dropped dead of heart failure. Might as well, they said: other schedules to clear anyway, other people to bring back across other oceans.

They told her not to worry. They told her it wasn't her fault. They gave her propranolol to help her believe them.

Four hours, flat on her back, staring at the ceiling.

Now here she was: soul half a world away, body stuck in this windowless room, paneled in oak on three sides, crawling with luminous maps and tacticals on the fourth. Learning just what the enemy had been doing, besides sneaking up on a military cyborg in the middle of the fucking night.

"They were fishing," the PAO told her.

"No," Becker said; some subconscious subroutine added an automatic "*sir*."

The JAG lawyer—*Eisbach*, that was it—shook her head. "They had longlines in their outriggers, Corporal. They had hooks, a bait pail. No weapons."

The general in the background—from NDHQ in Ottawa, Becker gathered, although there'd been no formal introduction—studied the tacpad in his hand and said nothing at all.

She shook her head. "There aren't any fish. Every reef in the WTP's been acidified for twenty years."

"It's definitely a point we'll be making," Eisbach said. "You can't fault the system for not recognizing profiles that aren't even supposed to exist in the zone."

"But how could they be—"

"Tradition, maybe." The PAO shrugged. "Some kind of cultural thing. We're checking with the local NGOs but so far none of them are accepting responsibility. Whatever they were doing, the UN never white-listed it."

"They didn't show on approach," Becker remembered. "No visual, no sound—I mean, how could a couple of boats just sneak up like that? It had to be some kind of stealth tech, that must be what Wingman keyed—I mean, they were just *there*." Why was this so hard? The augs were supposed keep her balanced, mix up just the right cocktail to keep her cool and crisp under the most lethal conditions.

Of course, the augs were also supposed to know unarmed civilians when they saw them . . .

The JAG was nodding. "Your mechanic. Specialist, uh . . . "

"Blanch." From the room's only civilian, standing unobtrusively with the potted plants. Becker glanced over; he flashed her a brief and practiced smile.

"Specialist Blanch, yes. He suspects there was a systems failure of some kind."

"I would never have fired if—" Meaning, of course, *I would never have fired.*

Don't be such a pussy, Becker. Last month you took on a Kuan-Zhan with zero cover and zero backup, never even broke a sweat. Least you can do now is stand next to a fucking philodendron without going to pieces.

"Accidents happen in—these kind of situations," The PAO admitted sadly. "Drones misidentify targets. Pillbox mistakes a civilian for an enemy combatant. No technology's perfect. Sometimes it fails. It's that simple."

"Yes sir." Dimming rainbows, bleeding into the night.

"So far the logs support Blanch's interpretation. Might be a few days before we know for certain."

"A few days we don't have. Unfortunately."

The general swept a finger across his tacpad. A muted newsfeed bloomed on the war wall behind him: House of Commons, live. Opposition members standing, declaiming, sitting. Administration MPs across the aisle, rising and falling in turn. A two-tiered array of lethargic whackamoles.

The General's eyes stayed fixed on his pad. "Do you know what they're talking about, Corporal?"

"No, sir."

"They're talking about you. Barely a day and a half since the incident and already they're debating it in Question Period."

"Did we—"

"We did not. There was a breach."

He fell silent. Behind him, shell-shocked pols stammered silent and shifty-eyed against the onslaught of Her Majesty's Loyal Opposition. The Minister of Defence's seat, Becker noted, was empty.

"Do we know who, sir?"

The general shook his head. "Any number of people could have intercepted one or more of our communications. The number who'd be able to decrypt them is a lot smaller. I'd hate to think it was one of ours, but it's not something we can rule out. Either way—" He took a breath. "—so much for our hopes of dealing with this internally."

"Yes sir."

Finally he raised his eyes to meet hers. "I want to assure you, Corporal, that nobody here has passed any judgment with regard to potential—culpability. We've reviewed the telemetry, the transcripts, the interviews; FIT's still going over the results but so far there's no evidence of any conscious wrong-doing on your part."

Conscious, Becker noted dully. Not *deliberate.* There'd been a time when the distinction would never have occurred to her.

"Be that as it may, we find ourselves forced to change strategy. In the wake of this leak it's been decided we have to *engage the public*. Doubling down and invoking national security would only increase the appearance of guilt, and after that mess in the Philippines we can't afford even a whiff of cover-up." The general sighed. "This, at least, is the view of the Minister."

"Yes sir."

"It has therefore been decided—and I'm sorry to do this to you, I know it's not what you signed up for—it's been decided to *get out in front of this thing*, as they say. Control the narrative. Make you available for interviews, prove we have nothing to hide."

"Interviews, sir?"

"You'll be liaising with Mr. Monahan here." On cue, the civilian stepped out of the background. "His firm's proven useful in matters of—public outreach."

"Ben. Just Ben." Monahan reached out to shake with his right hand, offered his card with the left: *Optic Nerve*, twinkling above a stock-ticker crawl of client endorsements. "I know how much this sucks, Corporal. I'm guessing the last thing you want to hear right now is what some high-priced image consultant has to say about covering your ass. Is that about right?"

Becker swallowed, and nodded, and retrieved her hand. Phantom wings beat on her shoulders.

"The good news is: no ass-covering required. I'm not here to polish a turd—which is actually a nice change—I'm here to make sure the truth gets out. As you know, there's no shortage of parties who are a lot less interested in what really happened than in pushing their own agendas."

"I can understand that," Becker said softly.

"This person, for example." *Just Ben* tapped his watch and wiped Parliament from the wall; the woman revealed in its place stood maybe one-seventy, black, hair cropped almost army short. She seemed a little off-balance in the picture; doubtless the helmeted RCMP officer grabbing her left bicep had something to do with that. The two of them danced against a chorus line of protestors and pacification drones.

"Amal Sabrie," Monahan was saying. "Freelance journalist, well-regarded by the left for her human rights work. Somali by birth but immigrated to Canada as a child. Her home town was Beledweyne. Does that ring any bells, Corporal?"

Becker shook her head.

"Airborne Regiment? 1992?"

"Sorry. No."

"Okay. Let's just say she's got more reason than most to mistrust the Canadian military."

"The last person we'd expect to be on our side," Eisbach remarked.

"Exactly." Monahan nodded. "Which is why I've granted her an exclusive."

◆ ◆ ◆

They engaged on neutral territory, proposed by Sabrie, reluctantly approved by the chain of command: a café patio halfway up Toronto's Layton Tower, overlooking Lakeshore. It jutted from the side of the building like a bracket fungus, well above most of the drone traffic.

An almost pathological empathy for victimhood. Monahan had inventoried Sabrie's weak spots as if he'd been pulling the legs off a spider. *Heart melts for stray cats, squirrels with cancer; blood boils for battered women and oppressed minorities and anyone who ever ended up on the wrong end of a shockprod. Not into performance rage, doesn't waste any capital getting bent out of shape over random acts of microaggression. Smart enough to save herself for the big stuff. Which is why she still gets to soapbox on the prime feeds while the rest of the rabies brigade fights for space on the public microblogs.*

Twenty floors below, pedestrians moved like ants. They'd never be life-sized to Becker; she'd arrived by the roof and she'd leave the same way, a concession to those who'd much rather have conducted this interview under more controlled conditions. Who'd much rather have avoided this interview entirely, for that matter. That they'd ceded so much control spoke volumes about Optic Nerve's rep for damage control.

If we can just get her to see you *as a victim—which is exactly what you are—we can turn her from agitator to cheerleader. Start off your appies as a tool of the patriarchy, you'll be her soulmate by dessert.*

Or maybe it spoke volumes about a situation so desperate that the optimum strategy consisted of gambling everything on a Hail Mary.

THERE SHE IS, Monahan murmured now, just inside her right temple, but Becker had already locked on: the target was dug in at a table next to the railing. This side, flower boxes and hors-d'oeuvres: that side, an eighty-meter plunge to certain death. Wingman, defanged but still untrusting, sent wary standbys to the stumps of amputated weaponry.

Amal Sabrie stood at her approach. "You look—" she began.

—*like shit.* Becker hadn't slept in three days. It shouldn't have shown; cyborgs don't get tired.

"I mean," Sabrie continued smoothly, "I thought the augments would be more conspicuous."

Great wings, spreading from her shoulders and laying down the wrath of God. Corporal Nandita Becker, Angel of Death.

"They usually are. They come off."

Neither extended a hand. They sat.

"I guess they'd have to. Unless you sleep standing up." A thought seemed to occur to her. "You sleep, right?"

"I'm a cyborg, Ms. Sabrie. Not a vacuum cleaner." An unexpected flicker of irritation, there; a bright spark on a vast dark plain. After all these flat waking hours. Becker almost welcomed it.

Monahan didn't. TOO HOSTILE. DIAL IT DOWN.

Sabrie didn't miss a beat. "A cyborg who can flip cars one-handed, if the promos are to be believed."

BE FRIENDLY. GIVE A LITTLE. DON'T MAKE HER PULL TEETH.

Okay.

Becker turned in her seat, bent her neck so the journalist could glimpse the tip of the black enameled centipede bolted along her backbone. "Spinal and long-bone reinforcement to handle the extra weight. Wire-muscle overlays, store almost twenty Joules per cc." There was a kind of mindless comfort in rattling off the specs. "Couples at over seventy percent under most—"

A *LITTLE*, CORPORAL.

"Anyway." Becker shrugged, straightened. "Most of the stuff's inside. The rest's plug and play." She took a breath, got down to it. "I should tell you up front I'm not authorized to talk about mission specifics."

Sabrie shrugged. "I'm not here to ask about them. I want to talk about you." She tapped her menu, entered an order for kruggets and a Rising Tide. "What're you having?"

"Thanks. I'm not hungry."

"Of course." The reporter glanced up. "You *do* eat, though, right? You still have a digestive system?"

"Nah. They just plug me into the wall." A smile to show she was kidding.

NOW YOU'RE GETTING IT.

"Glad you can still make jokes," Sabrie said from a face turned suddenly to stone.

SHIT. WALKED RIGHT INTO THAT ONE.

Down in the left hand, a tremor. Becker pulled her hands from the table, rested them on her lap.

"Okay," Sabrie said at last. "Let's get started. I have to say I'm surprised Special Forces even let me talk to you. The normal response in cases like this is to refuse comment, double down, wait for a celebrity overdose to move the spotlight."

"I'm just following orders, ma'am." The tic in Becker's hand wouldn't go away. She clasped her hands together, squeezed.

"So let's talk about something you *can* speak to," Sabrie said. "How do you feel?"

Becker blinked. "Excuse me?"

"About what happened. Your role in it. How do you feel?"

BE HONEST.

"I feel fucking *awful*," she said, and barely kept her voice from cracking. "How am I supposed to feel?"

"Awful," Sabrie admitted. She held silence for a respectable interval before pressing on. "The official story's systems malfunction."

"The investigation is ongoing," Becker said softly.

"Still. That's the word from sources. Your augments fired, you didn't. No *mens rea*."

Blobs of false color, spreading out against the sand.

"Do you *feel* like you killed them?"

TELL HER THE TRUTH, Monahan whispered.

"I—*part* of me did. Maybe."

"They say the augments don't do anything you wouldn't do yourself. They just do it faster."

Six people on an empty ocean. It didn't make any fucking sense.

"Is that the way you understand it?" Sabrie pressed. "The brain decides what it's going to do before it *knows* it's decided?"

Becker forced herself to focus, managed a nod. Even that felt a bit shaky, although the journalist didn't seem to notice. "Like a, a bubble rising from the bottom of a lake. We don't see it until it breaks the surface. The augs see it—before."

"How does that feel?"

"It feels like—" Becker hesitated.

HONESTY, CORPORAL. YOU'RE DOING GREAT.

"It's like having a really good wingman sitting on your shoulder, watching your back. Taking out threats before you even see them. Except it's using your own body to do that. Does that make sense?"

"As much as it can, maybe. To someone who isn't augged themselves." Sabrie essayed a little frown. "Is that how it felt with Tionee?"

"Who?"

"Tionee Anoka. Reesi Eterika. Io—" She stopped at something she saw in Becker's face.

"I never knew," Becker said after a moment.

"Their names?"

Becker nodded.

"I can send you the list."

A waiter appeared, deposited a tumbler and a steaming platter of fluorescent red euphausiids in front of Sabrie; assessed the ambiance and retreated without a word.

"I didn't—" Becker closed her eyes. "I mean yes, it felt the same. At first. There had to be a threat, right? Because the augs—because *I* fired. And I'd be dead at least four times over by now if I always waited until I knew what I was firing at." She swallowed against the lump in her throat. "Only this time things started to—sink in afterward. Why didn't I see them coming? Why weren't the—"

CAREFUL, CORPORAL. NO TAC.

"Some of them were still— moving. One was talking. Trying to."

"To you?"

Up in ultraviolet, the textured glass of the table fractured the incident sunlight into tiny rainbows. "No idea."

"What did they say?" Sabrie poked at her kruggets but didn't eat.

Becker shook her head. "I don't speak Kiribati."

"All those augments and you don't have realtime translation?"

"I—I never thought of that."

"Maybe those smart machines saw the bubbles rising. Knew you wouldn't *want* to know."

She hadn't thought of that either.

"So you feel awful," Sabrie said. "What else?"

"What else am I feeling?" The tremor had spread to both hands.

"If it's not too difficult."

What the fuck is *this, he said I'd be* steady, *he said the drugs—*

"They gave me propranolol." It was almost a whisper, and Becker wondered immediately if she'd crossed the line. But the voice in her head stayed silent.

Sabrie nodded. "For the PTSD."

"I know how that sounds. It's not like I was a victim or anything." Becker stared at the table. "I don't think it's working."

"It's a common complaint, out there on the cutting edge. All those neurotransmitters, synthetic hormones. Too many interactions. Things don't always work the way they're supposed to."

Monahan, you asshole. You're the goddamn PR expert, you should've known I wasn't up for this . . .

"I feel worse than awful." Becker could barely hear her own voice. "I feel sick . . . "

Sabrie appraised her with black unblinking eyes.

"This may be bigger than an interview," she said at last. "Do you think we could arrange a couple of follow-ups, maybe turn this into an in-depth profile piece?"

"I—I'd have to clear it with my superiors."

Sabrie nodded. "Of course."

Or maybe, Becker thought, *you knew all along.* As, two hundred fifty kilometers away, a tiny voice whooped in triumph.

They plugged her into an alternate universe where death came with an undo option. They ran her through scenarios and simulations, made her kill a hundred civilians a hundred different ways. They made her relive Kiribati again and again through her augments, for all the world as if she wasn't already reliving it every time she closed her goddamn eyes.

It was all in her head, of course, even if it wasn't all in her mind; a high-speed dialogue between synapse and simulator, a multichannel exchange through a pipe as fat as any corpus callosum. A Monte-Carlo exercise in tactical brutality.

After the fourth session she opened her eyes and Blanch had disappeared; some neon red-head had replaced him while Becker had been racking up the kills. *Tauchi,* according to his name tag. She couldn't see any augments but he glowed with smartwear in the megahertz range.

"Jord's on temporary reassignment," he said when she asked. "Tracking down the glitch."

"But—but I thought *this*—"

"This is something else. Close your eyes."

Sometimes she had to let innocent civilians die in order to save others. Sometimes she had to murder people whose only crime was being in the wrong place at the wrong time: blocking a clean shot on a battlebot that was drawing down on a medical team, or innocently reaching for some control that had been hacked to ignite a tank of H_2S half a city away. Sometimes Becker hesitated on those shots, held back in some forlorn hope that the target might move or change its mind. Sometimes, even lacking any alternative, she could barely bring herself to pull the trigger.

She wondered if maybe they were trying to toughen her up. Get her back in the saddle, desensitized through repetition, before her own remorse made her useless on the battlefield.

Sometimes there didn't seem to be a right answer, no clear way to determine whose life should take priority; mixed groups of children and adults, victims in various states of injury and amputation. The choice between a brain-damaged child and its mother. Sometimes Becker was expected to kill with no hope of saving anyone; she took strange comfort in the stark simplicity of those old classics. Fuck this handwringing over the relative weights of human souls. Just point and shoot.

I am a camera, she thought.

"Who the hell makes up these scenarios?"

"Don't like judgment calls, Corporal?"

"Not *those* ones."

"Not much initiative." Tauchi nodded approvingly. "Great on the follow-through, though." He eyed his pad. "Hmmm. That might be why. Your cortisol's fucked."

"Can you fix that? I don't think my augs have been working since I got back."

"Flashbacks? Sweats? Vigilant immobility?"

Becker nodded. "I mean, aren't they supposed to take care of all that?"

"Sure," Tauchi told her. "You start to freak, they squirt you a nice hit of dopamine or leumorphin or whatever to level you out. Problem is, do that often enough and it stops working. Your brain grows more receptors to handle the extra medicine, so now you need more medicine to feed the extra receptors. Classic habituation response."

"Oh."

"If you've been feeling wobbly lately, that's probably why. Killing those kids only pushed you over the threshold."

God, she missed Blanch.

"Chemistry sets are just a band-aid anyway," the tech rattled on. "I can tweak your settings to keep you out of the deep end for now, but longer-term we've got something better in mind."

"A drug? They've already got me on propranolol."

He shook his head. "Permanent fix. There's surgery involved, but it's no big deal. Not even any cutting."

"When?" She could feel her insides crumbling. She imagined Wingman looking away, too good a soldier to be distracted by its own contempt. "*When?*"

Tauchi grinned. "Whaddya think we're doing now?"

She felt stronger by the next encounter.

This time it went down at street level; different patio, different ambiance, same combatants. Collapsed parasols hung from pikes rising through the center of each table, ready to spread protective shade should the afternoon sun ever make it past the skyscrapers. Sabrie set down a smooth rounded disk—a half-scale chrome hockey puck—next to the shaft. She gave it a tap.

Becker's BUD fuzzed around the edges with brief static; Wingman jumped to alert, hungry and limbless.

"For privacy," Sabrie said. "You okay with that?"

White noise on the radio. Broad-spectrum visual still working, though. The EM halo radiating from Sabrie's device was bright as a solar corona; her retinue of personal electronics glowed with dimmer light. Her watch. Her smartspecs, already recording; the faint nimbus of some medallion packed with circuitry, nestled out of sight between her breasts.

"Why now?" Becker asked. "Why not before?"

"First round's on the house. I was amazed enough that they even cleared the interview. Didn't want to push my luck."

Wingman flashed an icon; a little judicious frequency-hopping would get around the jam. If they'd been in an actual combat situation it wouldn't even be asking permission.

"You realize there are other ways to listen in," Becker said.

Sabrie shrugged. "Parabolic ear on a rooftop. Bounce a laser off the table and read the vibrations." Her eyes flickered overhead. "Any one of those drones could be a lip-reader for all I know."

"So what's the point?" (FHOP?[y/n] FHOP?[y/n] FHOP?[y/n])

"Perpetual surveillance is the price of freedom," Sabrie said, half-smiling. "Not to mention the price of not having to worry about some random psycho shooter when you go out for sushi."

"But?"

"But there are limits. Your bosses are literally inside your *head.*" She dipped her chin at the jammer. "Do you think they'll object to you providing a few unprompted answers? Given this new apparent policy of transparency and accountability?"

(FHOP?[y/n])

(N)

"I don't know," Becker said.

"You know what would make them even *more* transparent and accountable? If they released the video for the night of the 25th. I keep asking, and they keep telling me there isn't any."

Becker shook her head. "There isn't."

"Come on."

"Really. Too memory-intensive. "

"Corporal, I'm recording *this,*" Sabrie pointed out. "16K, Slooped sound, no compression even." She glanced into the street. "Half those people are life-logging every second of their lives for the sheer narcissistic thrill of it."

"And they're *streaming* it. Or caching and dumping every couple of hours. I don't get the luxury of tossing my cookies into some cloud whenever my cache fills up. I have to be able to operate in the dark for weeks at a time: you stream any kind of data in the field, it points back at you like a big neon arrow.

"Besides, budget time rolls around, how much of your limited R&D funding are you going to take away from tactical computing so you can make longer nature documentaries?" Becker raised her expresso in a small mock toast. "You think the People's Republic is losing any sleep over that one?"

Which is awfully convenient, remarked a small voice, *When you've just—* She shut it off.

Sabrie gave her a sidelong look. "You can't record video."

"Sure I can. But it's discretionary. You document anything you think needs documenting, but the default realtime stream is just numbers. Pure black-box stuff."

"You didn't think you needed to document—"

"I didn't *know.* It wasn't *conscious.* Why the *fuck* can't you people—"

Sabrie watched her without a word.

"Sorry," Becker said at last.

"It's okay," Sabrie said softly. "Rising bubbles. I get it."

Overhead, the sun peeked around an office tower. A lozenge of brightness crept onto the table.

"You know what they were doing out there?" Sabrie asked. "Tionee and his friends?"

Becker closed her eyes for a moment. "Some kind of fishing trip."

"And you never wondered why anyone would go night fishing in a place where there wasn't anything to catch but slugs and slime?"

I never stopped wondering. "I heard it was a—cultural thing. Keep the traditions alive, in case someone ever builds a tuna that eats limestone."

"It was an art project."

Becker squinted as the hockey puck bounced sunlight into her eyes. "Excuse me?"

"Let me get that for you." Sabrie half-rose and reached for the center of the table. The parasol bloomed with a snap. The table dropped back into eclipse.

"That's better." Sabrie reseated herself.

"An art project?" Becker repeated.

"They were college students. Cultural anthropology and art history majors, wired in from Evergreen State. Re-enact the daily lives of your forebears, play them back along wavelengths outside the human sensory range. They were calling it *Through Alien Eyes*. Some kind of commentary on outsider perspectives."

"What wavelengths?"

"Reesi was glassing everything from radio to gamma."

"There's a third-party recording?"

"Nothing especially hi-def. They were on a student budget, after all. But it was good enough to pick out a signal around four hundred megahertz. Nobody can quite figure out what it is. Not civilian, anyway."

"That whole area's contested. Military traffic all over the place."

"Yeah, well. The thing is, it was a just a couple of really short bursts. Half a second, maybe. Around eleven-forty-five."

Wingman froze. Gooseflesh rippled up Becker's spine.

Sabrie leaned forward, hands flat on the table. "That wouldn't have been you, would it?"

"You know I can't discuss operational details."

"Mmmm." Sabrie watched and waited.

"I take it you have this recording," Becker said at last.

The journalist smiled faintly. "You know I can't discuss operational details."

"I'm not asking you to compromise your sources. It just seems—odd."

"Because your guys would have been all over the bodies before they were even cool. So if anyone had that kind of evidence, it would be them."

"Something like that."

"Don't worry, you don't have a mole. Or at least if you do, they don't report to me. You want to blame anyone, blame your *wing man*."

"What?"

"Your *preconscious triggers* tie into some pretty high-caliber weaponry. I'm guessing I don't have to tell you what kind of games physics plays when multiple slugs hit a body at twelve hundred meters a second."

Momentum. Inertia. Force vectors transferred from small masses to larger ones—and maybe back to smaller ones again. A pair of smartspecs could have flown twenty meters or more, landed way up in the weeds or splashed down in the lagoon.

"We wouldn't have even known to look," Becker murmured.

"We did." Sabrie sipped her drink. "Want to hear it?"

Becker sat absolutely still.

"I know the rules, Nandita. I'm not asking you to ID it, or even comment. I just thought you might like . . . "

Becker glanced down at the jammer.

"I think we should leave that on." Sabrie reached into her blouse, fingered the luminous medallion hanging from her neck. "You have sockets, though, right? Hard interfaces?"

"I don't spread my legs in public."

Sabrie's eyes flickered to the far side of the street, where a small unmarked quadrocopter had just dipped into sight below the rim of the parasol. "Let's talk about your family," she said.

Monahan didn't seem put out.

"We thought she might try something like that. Sabrie's hardly in the tank. But you did great, Corporal."

"You were monitoring?"

"Like we'd let some gizmo from the Sony Store cut us out of the loop? I could've even whispered sweet nothings in your ear if I'd had to—acoustic tightbeam, she'd never have had a clue unless she leaned over and nibbled your earlobe—but like I say, you were just fine." Some small afterthought made him frown. "Would've been easier if you'd just authorized frequency hopping, of course . . . "

"She had a lot of gizmos on her," Becker said. "If one of them had been able to pick up the signal . . . "

"Right. Good plan. Let her think it worked."

"Yes sir."

"Just Ben. Oh, one other thing . . . "

Becker waited.

"We lost contact for just a few moments there. When the umbrella went up."

"You didn't miss much. Apparently the collateral was doing a school project of some kind. Art history. They weren't actually fishing, it was more of a—a re-enactment, I guess."

"Huh. Pretty much what we heard." Monahan nodded. "Next time, might help if you went to active logging. You know, when we're out of contact."

"Right. Sorry. I didn't think."

"Don't apologize. After what you've been through I'd be amazed if you *didn't* make the occasional slip."

He patted her on the back. Wingman bristled.

"I gotta prep for a thing. Keep up the *great* work."

All those devil's bargains and no-win scenarios. All those exercises that tore her up inside. Turned out they were part of the fix. They had to parameterize Becker's remorse before they could burn it out of her.

It was a simple procedure, they assured her, a small part of the scheduled block upgrade. Seven deep-focus microwave bursts targeting the ventromedial prefrontal cortex. Ten minutes, tops. Not so much as a scar to show for it afterward. She didn't even need to sign anything.

They didn't put her under. They turned her off.

Coming back online, she didn't feel much different. The usual faint hum at the back of her skull as Wingman lit up and looked around; the usual tremors in fingers and toes, half-way between a reboot sequence and a voltage spike. The memory of her distant malfunction seemed a bit less intense, but then again things often seemed clearer after a good night's sleep. Maybe she was just finally seeing things in perspective.

They plugged her into the simulator and worked her out.

Fifty-plus male, thirtysomething female, and a baby alone in a nursery: all spread out, all in mortal and immediate danger as the house they were trapped in burned down around them. She started with the female, went back to extract the male, was heading back in for the baby when the building collapsed. *Two out of three,* she thought. *Not bad.*

Sniper duty on some post-apocalyptic overpass, providing cover for an airbus parked a hundred meters down the road below, for the refugees running and hobbling and dragging themselves towards salvation. A Tumbleweed passing beneath: a self-propelled razorwire tangle of ONC and magnesium and white phosphorus, immune to bullets, hungry for body heat, rolling eagerly toward the unsuspecting evacuees. The engineer at Becker's side—his face an obvious template, although the sim tagged him as her *brother* for some reason—labored to patch the damage to their vehicle, oblivious to the refugees and their imminent immolation.

Oblivious until Becker pitched him off the overpass and brought the Tumbleweed to rapture.

The next one was a golden oldie: the old man in the war zone, calling for some lost pet or child, blocking Becker's shot as a battlefield robot halfway to the horizon took aim at a team of medics. She took out the old man with one bullet and no second thought; took out the bot with three more.

"Why'd you leave the baby for last?" Tauchi asked afterward, unhooking her. The light in his eyes was pure backwash from the retinal display, but he looked eager as a puppy just the same.

"Less of a loss," Becker said.

"In terms of military potential?" They'd all been civilians; tactically, all last among equals.

Becker shook her head, tried to put instinct into words. "The adults would—suffer more."

"Babies can't suffer?"

"They can hurt. Physically. But no hopes or dreams, no memories even. They're just—potential. No added value."

Tauchi looked at her.

"What's the big deal?" Becker asked. "It was an exercise."

"You killed your *brother*," he remarked.

"In a simulation. To save fifty civilians. I don't even *have* a brother."

"Would it surprise you to know that you took out the old man and the battlebot a full six hundred milliseconds faster than you did before the upgrade?"

She shrugged. "It was a repeat scenario. It's not like I even got it wrong the first time."

Tauchi glanced at his tacpad. "It didn't *bother* you the second time."

"So what are you saying? I'm some kind of sociopath now?"

"Exactly the opposite. You've been immunized against trolley paradoxes."

"What?"

"Everybody talks about morality like it's another word for *right and wrong*, when it's really just a load of static on the same channel." Tauchi's head bobbed like a woodpecker. "We just cleaned up the signal. As of now, you're probably the most ethical person on the planet."

"Really."

He walked it back, but not very far. "Well. You're in the top thirty at least."

Buried high above the streets of Toronto, cocooned in a windowless apartment retained as a home base for transient soldiers on missions of damage control: Nandita Becker, staring at the wall and watching the Web.

The wall was blank. The Web was in her head, invited through a back door in her temporal lobe. She and Wingman had spent altogether too much time alone in there, she'd decided. Time to have some company over.

The guest heads from Global's *Front View Mirror*, for example: a JAG lawyer, a retired professor of military law from Dalhousie, a token lefty from Veterans for Accountable Government. Some specialist in cyborg tech she'd never met, on loan from the Ministry of Defence and obviously chosen as much for disarming good looks as for technical expertise. (Becker imagined Ben Monahan just out of camera range, pulling strings.) A generic moderator whose affect alternated between earnest sincerity and failed attempts at cuteness.

They were all talking about Becker. At least, she assumed they still were. She'd muted the audio five minutes in.

The medallion in her hand glowed like dim cobalt through the flesh of her fingers, a faint nimbus up at 3MHz. She contemplated the feel of the metal, the decorative filigree (a glyph from some Amazonian culture that hadn't survived first contact, according to Sabrie), the hairline fracture of the interface port. The recessed Transmit button in its center: tap it once and it would squawk once, Sabrie had told her. Hold it down and it would broadcast on continuous loop.

She pressed it. Nothing happened.

Of course not. There'd be crypto. You didn't broadcast *anything* in the field without at least feeding it through a pseudorandom timeseries synched to the mothership—you never knew when some friend of Amal Sabrie might be lurking in the weeds, waiting to snatch it from the air and take it home for leisurely dissection. The signal made sense only at the instant of its creation. If you missed it the first time, wanted to repeat it for the sake of clarity, you'd need a time machine.

Becker had built her own personal time machine that very afternoon, stuck it at #1 on speed-dial: a three-line macro to reset her system clock to a dark moment weeks in the past, just before her world had turned to shit.

She unmuted audio on the web feed. One of Global's talking heads was opining that Becker was as much a victim as those poor envirogees her hijacked body had gunned down. Another spoke learnedly of the intimate connection between culpability and intent, of how blame—if that loaded term could even be applied in this case—must lie with the technology and not with those noble souls who daily put their lives on the line in the dangerous pestholes of a changing world.

"And yet this technology doesn't decide anything on its own," the moderator was saying. "It just does what the soldier's already decided sub—er, *pre*consciously."

"That's a bit simplistic," the specialist replied. "The system has access to a huge range of data that no unaugged soldier would ever be able to process in realtime—radio chatter, satellite telemetry, wide-spectrum visuals—so it's actually taking that preconscious intent and modifying it based on what the soldier *would* do if she had access to all those facts."

"So it guesses," said the man from VAG.

"It predicts."

"And that doesn't open the door to error?"

"It reduces error. It optimizes human wisdom based on the maximum available information."

"And yet in this case—"

Becker held down TRANSMIT and sacc'd speed-dial.

"—don't want to go down that road," the lawyer said. "No matter *what* the neurology says."

Thirty-five seconds. Gone in an instant.

"Our whole legal system is predicated on the concept of free will. It's the moral center of human existence."

That was so much bullshit, Becker knew. She knew exactly where humanity's moral center was. She'd looked it up not six hours ago: the place where the brain kept its empathy and compassion, its guilt and shame and remorse.

The ventromedial prefrontal cortex.

"Suppose—" The moderator raised a finger. "—I get into a car with a disabled breathalyzer. I put it into manual and hit someone. Surely I bear some responsibility for the fact that I *chose* to drink and drive, even if I didn't intend to hurt anyone."

"That depends on whether you'd received a lawful command from a superior officer to get behind the wheel," Ms. JAG countered.

"You're saying a soldier can be *ordered* to become a cyborg?"

"How is that different from ordering a sniper to carry a rifle? How is it different from ordering soldiers to take antimalarial drugs—which have also, by

333

the way, been associated with violent behavioral side-effects in the past—when we deploy them to the Amazon? A soldier is sworn to protect their country; they take that oath knowing the normal tools of their trade, knowing that technology advances. You don't win a war by bringing knives to a gunfight—"

Speed-dial.

"—may not like cyborgs—and I'm the first to agree there are legitimate grounds for concern—but until you can talk the Chinese into turning back the clock on *their* technology, they're by far the lesser evil."

Twenty-eight seconds, that time.

"It's not as though we ever lived in a world without collateral damage. You don't shut down such a vital program over a tragic accident."

A tragic accident. Even Becker had believed that. Right up until Sabrie had slipped her a medallion with a burst of radio static in its heart, a cryptic signal snatched from the warm Pacific night by a pair of smart-specs on a dead kid walking. A signal that was somehow able to offline her for intervals ranging from twenty to sixty-three seconds.

She wondered if there was any sort of pattern to that variability.

"Safeguards should be put into place at the very least." The moderator was going for the middle road. "Ways to monitor these, these *hybrids* remotely, shut them down at the first sign of trouble."

Becker snorted. Wingman didn't take orders in the field, couldn't even *hear* them. Sure, Becker could channel some smiley little spin doctor through her temporal, but he was just a Peeping Tom with no access to the motor systems. The actual metal didn't even pack an on-board receiver; it was congenitally deaf to wireless commands until someone manually slotted the dorsal plug-in between Becker's shoulders.

Deliberately design a combat unit that could be shut down by anyone who happened to hack the right codes? Who'd be that stupid?

And yet—

TRANSMIT. Speed-dial.

"—are only a few on active duty—they won't tell us exactly how many of course, say twenty or thirty. A couple dozen cyborgs who can't be blamed if something goes wrong. And that's just *today*. You wouldn't believe how fast they're ramping up production."

Forty seconds. On the nose.

"Not only do I believe it, I *encourage* it. The world's a tinderbox. Water wars, droughts, refugees everywhere you look. The threat of force is the only thing that's kept a lid on things so far. Our need for a strong military is greater today than it's ever been since the cold war, especially with the collapse of the US eco—"

Speed-dial.

"—and what happens when *every* pair of boots in the field has a machine reading its mind and pulling the trigger in their name? What happens to the very concept of a *war crime* when every massacre can be defined as an industrial accident?"

Thirty-two.

"You're saying this Becker deliberately—"

"I'm saying nothing of the kind. I'm *concerned*. I'm concerned at the speed with which outrage over the massacre of civilians has turned into an outpouring of sympathy for the person who killed them, even from quarters you'd least expect. Have you *seen* the profile piece Amal Sabrie posted on the Star?"

A shutdown command, radioed to a system with no radio.

"Nobody's forgetting the victims here. But it's no great mystery why people also feel a certain sympathy for Corporal Becker—"

Becker kept wondering who'd be able to pull off a trick like that, hide a secret receiver under the official specs. She kept coming up with the same answer.

"Of course. She's sympathetic, she's charismatic, she's *nice*. Exemplary soldier, not the slightest smudge on her service record. She volunteered at a veterinary clinic back in high school."

Someone with an interest in *controlling the narrative*.

"Chief of Defense couldn't have a better poster girl if they'd *planned*—"

Dial.

"—should be up on charges is for the inquiry to decide."

Forty-two seconds.

She wondered if she should be feeling something right now. Outrage. Violation. She'd thought the procedure was only supposed to cure her PTSD. It seemed to have worked on that score, anyway.

"Then let the inquiry decide. But we can't allow this to become the precedent that tips over the Geneva Conventions."

The other stuff, though. The compassion, the empathy, the guilt. The moral center. That seemed to be gone too. They'd burned it out of her like a tumor.

"The Conventions are a hundred years old. You don't think they're due for an overhaul?"

She still had her sense of right and wrong, at least.

Brain must keep that somewhere else.

"I thought they'd shipped you back to the WTP," Sabrie remarked.

"This weekend."

The journalist glanced around the grotto: low light, blue-shifted, private tables arrayed around a dance floor where partygoers writhed to bass beats that made it only faintly through the table damper. She glanced down at the Rising Tide Becker had ordered for her.

"I don't fuck my interviews, Corporal. Especially ones who could snap my spine if they got carried away."

Becker smiled back at her. "Not why we're here."

"Ohhhkay."

"Bring your jammer?"

"Always." Sabrie slapped the little device onto the table; welcome static fuzzed Becker's peripherals.

"So why *are* we in a lekking lounge at 2 a.m.?"

"No drones," Becker said.

"None in the local Milestones either. Even during business hours."

"Yeah. I just—I wanted a crowd to get lost in."

"At two in the morning."

"People have other things on their mind in the middle of the night." Becker glanced up as a triplet stumbled past en route to the fuck-cubbies. "Less likely to notice someone they may have seen on the feeds."

"Okay."

"People don't—congregate the way they used to, you know?" Becker sipped her scotch, set it down, stared at it. "Everyone telecommutes, everyone cocoons. Downtown's so—thin, these days."

Sabrie panned the room. "Not here."

"Web don't fuck. Not yet, anyway. Still gotta go out if you want to do anything more than whack off."

"What's on your mind, Nandita?"

"The price of freedom."

"Go on."

"Not having to worry about some random psycho shooter when you go out for sushi. Don't tell me you've forgotten."

"You know I was being sarcastic."

Becker cocked her head at the other woman. "I don't think you were. Not entirely, anyway."

"Maybe not entirely."

"Because there *were* shootings, Amal. A lot of them. Twenty thousand deaths a year."

"Mainly down in the states, thank God." Sabrie said. "But yes."

"Back before the panopticon, people could just walk into some school or office building and—light it up." Becker frowned. "I remember there was this one guy shot up a *daycare*. Prechoolers. Babies. I forget how many he killed before they took him out. Turned out he'd lost a sister himself, six months before, in *another* shooting. Everybody said it tipped him over the edge and he went on a rampage."

"That doesn't make sense."

"That shit never does. It's what people said, though, to explain it. Only . . ."

"Only?" Sabrie echoed after the pause had stretched a bit too far.

"Only what if he wasn't crazy at all?" Becker finished.

"How could he not be?"

"He lost his sister. Classic act of senseless violence. The whole gun culture, you know, the NRA had everyone by the balls and anyone who so much as *whispered* about gun control got shot down. So to speak." Becker grunted. "Words didn't work. Advocacy didn't work. The only thing that might possibly work would be something so unthinkable, so horrific and obscene and unspeakably evil, that not even the most strident gun nut could possibly object to—countermeasures."

"Wait, you're saying that someone in favor of gun control—someone who'd *lost his sister to gun violence*— would deliberately shoot up a daycare?"

Becker spread her hands.

"You're saying he turned himself into a monster. Killed twenty, thirty kids maybe. For a piece of legislation."

"Weighed against thousands of deaths a year. Even if legislation only cut that by a few percent you'd make back your investment in a week or two, tops."

"Your *investment*?"

"Sacrifice, then." Becker shrugged.

"Do you know how insane that sounds?"

"How do you know that's not the way it went down?"

"Because you said nothing changed! No laws were passed! They just wrote him off as another psycho."

"He couldn't know that up front. All he knew was, there was a chance. His life, a few others, for thousands. There was a *chance*."

"I can't believe that you, of all people, would—after what happened, after what you *did*—"

"Wasn't me, remember? It was Wingman. That's what everyone's saying." Wingman was awake now, straining at the leash with phantom limbs.

"But you were still part of it. You know that, Deet, you *feel* it. Even if it wasn't your fault it still tears you up inside. I saw that the first time we spoke. You're a good person, you're a moral person, and—"

"Do you know what morality is, really?" Becker looked coolly into the other woman's eyes. "It's letting two stranger's kids die so you can save one of your own. It's thinking it makes some kind of difference if you look into someone's eyes when you kill them. It's squeamishness and cowardice and *won't someone think of the children*. It's not rational, Amal. It's not even ethical."

Sabrie had gone very quiet.

"Corporal," she said when Becker had fallen silent, "what have they done to you?"

Becker took a breath. "Whatever they're doing—"

Not much initiative. Great on the follow-through.

"—it ends here."

Sabrie's eyes went wide. Becker could see pieces behind them, fitting together at last. No drones. Dense crowd. No real security, just a few bouncers built of pitiful meat and bone . . .

"I'm sorry, Amal," Becker said gently.

Sabrie lunged for the jammer. Becker snatched it up before the journalist's hand had made it halfway.

"I can't have people in my head right now."

"Nandita." Sabrie was almost whispering. "Don't do this."

"I like you, Amal. You're good people. I'd leave you right out of it if I could, but you're—smart. And you know me, a little. Maybe well enough to put it together, afterward . . . "

Sabrie leapt up. Becker didn't even rise from her chair. She seized the other woman's wrist quick as a striking snake, effortlessly forced it back onto the table. Sabrie cried out. Dim blue dancers moved on the other side of the damper field, other things on their minds.

"You won't get away with it. You can't blame the machines for—" Soft pleading words, urgent, rapid-fire. The false-color heatprint of the contusion spread out across Sabrie's forearm like a dim rainbow, like a bright iridescent oil slick. "*Please* there's no *way* they'll be able to sell this as a malfunction no matter how—"

"That's the whole point," Becker said, and hoped there was at least a little sadness left in her smile. "You know that."

Amal Sabrie. Number one of seventy-four.

It would have been so much faster to just spread her wings and raise arms. But her wings had been torn out by the roots, and lay twitching in the garage back at Trenton. The only arms she could raise were of flesh and blood and graphene.

It was enough, though. It was messy, but she got the job done. Because Corporal Nandita Becker was more than just a superhuman killing machine.

She was the most ethical person on the planet.

SEVENTH SIGHT

GREG EGAN

1

On my twelfth birthday, my cousin Sean sent me the keys to the rainbow. I carried them around in my phone for six days, unused, burning a hole in my pocket. Sean had hacked his own implants almost eighteen months before, so I was fairly sure that it would be safe to follow him, but I couldn't begin to imagine what would happen if my father caught me rewiring my retinas.

I waited for a Sunday afternoon, when my parents were preoccupied with a movie. I closed the door to my room and drew the curtains. The door had no lock, so I lay in bed with my head under the covers, staring at my phone until the screen went dark. In the blackness I thought about my grandfather, blinded by nothing more than the gene we shared, but sightless for so long that the implants had been powerless to bring him back into the light. My confidence in the trail Sean had blazed began to waver; his implants and mine were the same model, but everyone's body was unique. I did not want to end up blind—and even if the changes I wrought were reversible with a trip to the optometrist to restore the implants' settings, that was not something I could do without my parents finding out.

I jiggled the phone and it lit up again, showing the circular rainbow of the app's startup screen. The hues in this fanciful icon were crisper and clearer than those of any rainbow I'd seen in the sky, but then my bio-sighted friends had assured me that they could never make out the mythical "seven colors," either, and I had no reason to doubt them. My implants did their best to mimic the color vision of the human eye, by matching the typical responses of the three kinds of human cone cells. But this mimicry was a matter of choice, not necessity—and I wouldn't need any new hardware inside my skull in order to move beyond it.

The quantum dots scattered across my artificial retinas included millions of spares, ready to step in if any of the currently active sensors failed. These spares were not pre-committed to any particular color, lest the demand for replacements skewed green or blue and left the red ones wasting space, like some unpopular flavor of Skittles. But since the choice was made, not with pigment molecules or colored filters, but by setting a series of voltages across a quantum well, there was nothing to constrain the possibilities to the three traditional colors. The app Sean had sent me could instruct the implants to wake all my spares—and tune them to four new bands, between and beyond the original three.

I ran a fingertip along the rainbow's edge, trying to reach a decision. The implants made me normal, they allowed me to fit in. Why ask for anything more? Left to my biological fate I would not have been fully blind for another decade, but my parents had opted for replacement as early as possible, giving me the best chance of adapting to the device.

But that had been six years ago. If I didn't try this experiment now, while my brain was still flexible enough to make sense of the new information, I might die without ever knowing what I'd missed.

I lifted my finger from its stalling arc and tapped the button above: CONTINUE.

The app needed to know the implants' serial numbers and service password, but both were printed plainly in my owner's manual. The manufacturer's warranty had expired, leaving nothing to void, and the app's screed claimed that it could hide its actions from any health professional making routine adjustments. So long as nothing went wrong that I couldn't fix by sending the spares back to sleep, there was a chance that my spectral trespasses would remain undetected.

The next screen showed response curves. The standard red and green ones already overlapped considerably, while the blue one stood almost aloof from them. The app's default choice was to squeeze two new curves in between blue and green, and then add one at the near-infrared end and one at the near-ultraviolet. There was also a set of default "opposition formulas," which specified the way in which information was to be extracted from various combinations of the new primary colors—just as the difference between the red and green responses was computed in every human eye and passed along to the brain.

The idea of editing any of these details—adding my own idiosyncratic twist to the process—made my hands sweat. I would not have known where to start constructing my own private notion of the ideal palette. But if that also proved that I was in no position to make an informed choice to accept the defaults, I took some comfort from the orderly appearance of the seven curves on offer. They covered the spectrum, evenly and efficiently, each little hill in the serried row peaking at a wavelength some fifty nanometers away from its neighbor. Nothing about them looked strange, demanding elaborate justifications from the depths of biophysics. Nothing cried out to be changed.

I hit ACCEPT, and moved on to the next page.

WARNING

Activating and retuning spare sensors in your artificial retinas (ARs) may lead to permanent changes in your brain's visual pathways. While this app can restore the ARs to their original state, we make no such promises about your visual cortex.

The decision is yours alone.

The Rainbow Project

This disclaimer did not unnerve me at all. That the brain was altered by the information it did or didn't receive was old news to me, writ large in my family's history. The implants had come just in time to help my father, but not as much as they had helped me, and my uncles and cousins of various ages joined up the dots. The more I thought about it, the surer I became that the most frightening thing would be to lose this chance, while Sean and his friends sprinted far ahead of me and disappeared into the far end of the rainbow.

I tapped PROCEED.

The warning gave way to a flickering Bluetooth icon and a progress bar. I watched the text above the bar spelling out the stages as the app and implants worked together: cataloging the spare sensors, testing them internally, retuning them, testing them again.

The progress bar paused at ninety-five percent, then the app asked me if the sky was clear and I'd obtained a suitable prism. It was, and I had. I climbed out of bed and opened the curtains to admit a narrow wedge of sunlight, then I placed the prism Sean had given me on my desk and moved it back and forth until the spectrum it cast on the wall formed an uninterrupted band.

Following the app's instructions, I turned my head slowly, shifting my gaze steadily across the spectrum from left to right, starting just before the red end. In my earbuds the app counted down the nanometers as it verified its tweaks to the quantum dots at every wavelength. It was all reassuringly mundane, like a human version of the procedure after changing an ink cartridge, where you print and scan an alignment page.

The app said, "Done." I looked down at my phone, and the progress bar had reached one hundred percent. The image zoomed out to show the circular rainbow again, then it shrank to a point and the app quit, taking me back to the phone's home screen.

I opened the curtains and let the sunlight fill my room. Nothing looked different; I'd been warned that any change in the way I perceived the world could take days or weeks. But my impatience was offset by a sense of relief: whatever else I'd done, at least I hadn't damaged the implants and left myself blind.

◆ ◆ ◆

"These flowers are dying," I told my father as I set the table for dinner. "Do you want me to throw them out?"

"Dying?" He stepped out of the kitchen and peered at the center-piece, then came closer and examined the individual blooms. "They're fine, Jake. What are you talking about?"

"Sorry," I said stupidly. "It must have been a trick of the light."

He frowned, puzzled, but then went back to draining vegetables. I fetched my mother and my sister, and we all sat down to eat.

Throughout the meal, I kept stealing glances at the flowers. My father grew a few different kinds in a small garden at the front of the house, and though I'd never taken much interest in them I couldn't help but be familiar with their appearance at various stages of health and decay. In fact, these daffodils hadn't even wilted: the petals were firm, not drooping. Yet the uniform yellow I was accustomed to had been modified by a flared pattern that I'd mistaken for a kind of withering, with streaks radiating out from the center of each flower that looked like shadows, not so much discolored as subdued.

It was only when I stopped worrying about the flowers and paid attention to my family that I realized how far the change had progressed. My father's face looked as if he'd developed a rash, albeit with a strong left-right symmetry, his cheeks flushed red and a roseate Rorschach blot decorating his temple. But if the effect was disconcertingly close to bad-TV-alien makeup, my mother and sister wore much the same mask with a twist: their actual cosmetics, which I usually barely noticed, now looked as if they'd been applied by an eager four-year-old who'd viewed the process as a form of finger painting. Streaks and ridges stood out all over their faces; it was all I could do to keep myself from staring, or making some inane, self-incriminating joke by asking them whether they'd enjoyed their mud baths.

After dinner, the four of us sat down to watch a sitcom, giving me an excuse to keep my eyes on the screen instead of the garish people around me. But the longer I spent gazing at the electronic image the flatter its colors seemed, until the live action began to resemble some kind of stylized animation. It was not that I'd yet started to think of my family's facial decorations as normal, but the actors' skin tones looked as plastic as any mannequin's, and the sets around them like the pastel story-book castles from a children's show. I only had to glance across at the couch on which my parents sat to see how much richer and subtler the hues of the simplest real object could be.

In bed, I lay awake wondering whether I should restore the implants to their original state. If I'd wanted everyone around me to look like a clown, there was an app that daubed face paint over the image from my phone's camera, but the novelty of that had worn off in half an hour when I was eight years old. I couldn't believe that my fourteen-year-old cousin had talked me into imagining that I'd be joining some kind of sophisticated elite.

Just before midnight, I messaged Sean: **This is horrible, everything looks ugly. Why did you make me do it?**

He replied: **Be patient. Wait a week. If you still don't like it, it's not too late to go back.**

I stared into the shadows, still feeling cheated. But I'd been a trichromat for twelve years; I needed to give myself a chance to wrap my mind around the new sensorium.

As I placed the phone on my bedside table, I suddenly realized how much more clearly than usual I was perceiving the details of the room. It was not that I'd magically acquired thermal night vision—nothing cooler than a clothes iron would emit the kind of infrared my sensors could pick up—but traces of illumination from a neighbor's house were spilling through the gaps around my curtain, and though once this would have granted me nothing more than a few impressionistic hints in gray, the rainbow app had transformed the view, imbuing it with a subtle palette of colors that made every object stand out from the gloom.

The effect wasn't comical, or ugly. It felt as if I was seeing more deeply into the night world: sharpening its edges without diminishing its allure. I fell asleep and dreamed that I was flying across the neighborhood, an eagle-eyed raptor dragging secrets out of the darkness.

The next few days of school were an exercise in learning not to stare at stained clothes and strangely spackled faces—let alone display any stronger reaction that might lead to violence, disciplinary action, or just the dangerously unanswerable question: What's so funny? Whenever the temptation to smirk at a particularly zombie-esque schoolmate or Revlon-bombed teacher threatened to overpower me, I reminded myself that I looked every bit as ridiculous. I didn't need a mirror: just glancing down at the sweat marks on my shirt, which resembled the gray silt left behind by retreating flood waters, brought a pang of humiliation that was enough to wipe the smile from my lips.

Every painted wall looked slapdash and dirty, and even bare brickwork seemed to be decaying, infested with some exotic new form of mold. A part of me understood full well that this riot of variegation wasn't really so wild—that the eighteen or twenty different tones I could discern on the surface of every brick all still belonged to what I would once have seen and named as exactly the same shade of red. But it was impossible to shake the impression that these newly revealed distinctions had to mean something: a once-uniform surface that had turned mottled couldn't possibly hold together for long, and one good kick ought to be enough to break it apart like a rotten floorboard.

The sky did not look blemished, but when I gazed at any part of its gentle gradient I knew exactly where the sun lay, and before long I could also judge the time of day to the nearest half hour. Sky blue was still sky blue, but now it came in a hundred delicate rings centered on the solar disk—and then imprinted with a second, subtler pattern whose bull's eye was the zenith. Eleven a.m. had a mood of its own now, as distinct from noon as sunset or dawn.

The following Sunday, Sean asked me to meet him at the beach. On the bus to the coast, I stared out at the car yards and advertising signs. Even the brand new BMWs looked like grubby plastic shells torn from some fairground ride, and the art-directed posters might have been lifted from a therapeutic crayon-sketching session at a hospital for the criminally tasteless. The strange blush of real human skin was growing on me, though; when I glanced across the aisle at a teenaged girl, her eyes closed as she listened to a track whose pounding base leaked out from her skull and crossed the gap between us, there was nothing comical or repellent about the visible ebb and flow in the capillaries below her cheekbones.

I waited by the roadside for someone's older brother to drop off Sean and three friends with their surfboards. As we walked through the dunes, Sean let the others get ahead of us. "How's it looking now?" he asked.

"Better, I suppose." His own face was smeared with sunscreen, but there was an eerie precision to each daub: if I had not already known that we were seeing the world through identical eyes, this would have proved it. I looked around at the low, sturdy bushes that anchored the dunes; their small, dark-green leaves weren't much different than I remembered them. "At least I'm not freaking out all the time."

"Good." He was smiling sneakily, as if he had a handful of something unpleasant hidden behind his back that he was about to bring forward and drop down the neck of my T-shirt.

"What?" I asked, getting ready to retreat.

We came over the top of the dunes.

My skin turned to ice and my bowels loosened; mercifully they had nothing to expel. The ocean stretched out before us, as alien as if our last dozen steps had carried us a thousand light years. But then, even more alarmingly, the impossibly rich skeins of currents and ripples, patches of seaweed and changes of depth and turbidity, flexed like a vacillating optical illusion and settled firmly inside my old memories of the scene. What I perceived was no longer extraterrestrial: this was the same blue-green, white-foamed water I'd known all my life. Only now, without ever stepping outside the borders of its familiar colors, it was inscribed and annotated with such a richness of new detail that it was like holding up the palm of my hand to find my entire life story, in a million words and illustrations, discernible in the whorls and ridges of the skin.

One of Sean's friends called out to him impatiently, and he broke into a run. I watched him dragging his board into the surf; that wasn't my thing, but I could imagine—just barely—what he would make of the revelations that the ocean offered up to every glance.

As I waded into the breaking waves, I ducked down and splashed water on my face to make sure that no one would notice my tears. This was what it meant to see the world. This was my escape from the terror of blindness, from the family curse clawing at my heels: not the first, too-forgiving childhood version, when they'd unwrapped my bandages and over three long months taught me to turn a blur of muddy colors into the pale glimpse of reality that I'd naively accepted as the thing itself.

As I moved my hands through the swell, overwhelmed by the density of greens-within-green, for a second or two, or perhaps a whole minute, I actually believed that I'd been lied to: that everyone on Earth saw things this way, except for the poor fools with artificial eyes, who, if forced from a young enough age to lower their expectations, had no idea what they'd been missing.

But as this momentary delusion passed and my unwarranted anger dissipated, the inverted truth that replaced it was almost as disorienting. The world before me remained, undeniably, the world as it needed to be seen, and those to whom it was unreachable were as helpless and pitiful as if their empty sockets had been filled with glass or stone.

"Two p.m., Sunday the fourth," I muttered.

"What?" Mehdi followed my gaze, but saw nothing that could have prompted these words.

"Forget it." The message was painted clearly on the billboard we were passing—painted, over a patch of blue, in other shades of blue. In the small park the billboard overlooked, I could see more heptachromatic graffiti on benches and playground equipment, but I forced myself to stop staring and walk on.

"What did you think, Jake?" Dylan pressed me. Everyone else had spent the last ten minutes raving about the movie, but I'd kept my mouth shut.

"It was all right," I conceded.

"All right?" Quan glared at me as if I'd just spat on his shoes. "It was incredible!"

"OK."

Dylan, Mehdi and Quan had been my friends for years, and we'd got into the habit of seeing all the new 3D blockbusters together. I'd come along to this latest action flick because I hadn't wanted to offend them, but I'd known from the start that all the stunts and effects that might once have been breathtaking would be lost on me.

"When they lassoed his helicopter from the train, and he slid down the rope and jumped through that window—" Mehdi thumped his chest emphatically. "It was like doing the whole thing yourself, for real."

"Yeah," I lied. "That was cool."

The honest thing would have been to admit how phony every last scene had appeared to me—and why. I couldn't risk news of my alteration getting back to my parents, but I had no reason to believe that my friends would betray me. The truth was, I didn't want them to know what I'd done. What was the point, when they had no hope of understanding it?

The next weekend, I told my parents I was seeing another movie. I arrived at the park at a quarter past one; it was empty of people, but the same message was still there on the billboard.

I hunted for some of the smaller scrawls I'd noticed in passing. **HEP RULES** and **FOUR MORE FEARS** were drawn repeatedly in ornate, almost indecipherable scripts, the style and colors the same each time. I was staring at one of these tags on a bench when someone spoke behind me.

"You want that as a tattoo?"

I turned. It was a girl, not much older than me. "Do you sterilize your needles?" I asked.

She laughed. "I didn't mean permanent. One day, maybe." She was carrying a backpack, holding its shoulder straps in her hand; she hefted it onto the bench and unzipped it. "I made the inks myself," she said, taking out a small bottle. "Six months of trial and error."

I peered into the backpack; there must have been forty vials in there. "That's a lot of work."

"The hard part is finding two or three that will be invisible to tris on lots of different backgrounds."

"How can you tell?" I wondered.

She took out her phone, tapped the screen and held it up, showing me its graffiti-free image of the bench. I felt my face flush at the stupidity of my question—and knowing how that would look only intensified the response.

"Why did you come early?" she asked. "That spoils the fun."

"You're early too," I countered.

"I'm not early, I'm here to mark the trail."

I'd half guessed that this would be some kind of treasure hunt. "So you're in charge?"

She nodded. "My name's Lucy."

"I'm Jake."

"Do you want to help me?"

"Sure."

A family had come into the park, a couple and two young kids, heading for the swings. The mother watched us suspiciously as Lucy took out a camel's hair brush and began painting on a corner of the billboard—but we weren't wielding spray-cans, and our watercolor vandalism seemed to be having no effect at all.

Three blocks north then turn left, Lucy wrote. **Listen for the sound of squealing brakes.**

"Let's go," she said, handing me the backpack. "You can carry this if you like."

We set out across the city, starting with a nearby amusement arcade. There was a Formula One game close to the western entrance, the sound effects blaring out onto the street; Lucy squatted down beside the wall and asked me for "number twenty-three." The vials in her backpack had been sorted into four separate pouches, making it easier to find each one. A few passersby looked at us askance, but if Lucy's brushstrokes left no mark it was hardly a police matter. I raised my phone and viewed the scene through tri eyes: she seemed to be delicately cleaning the brown-painted bricks.

When she handed the ink back to me, I looked at the label more carefully. "Cinnamon and cloves? That's what's in here?"

"No. That's just how I think of it."

I turned back to the words she'd written on the wall of the arcade: **East until you hit stale bread.** I doubted that I'd seen many spices in bulk since I'd run the rainbow app, but even if there was no literal resemblance the name did evoke the hue: a rich, sharp brown that ought to have smelled of those aromatic ingredients.

"Then what's it made of?"

Lucy smiled. "I'm not telling you. Work it out for yourself." She glanced at her watch. "We need to keep moving."

She let me paint the last clue, and the arrow that marked the treasure, though I needed her advice on the color schemes. The loot itself was a sheet of paper that she stuffed inside an empty toilet roll and hid behind a bush in a courtyard outside the museum.

"What does that number mean?" A long string of letters and digits had been written on the paper, in what I assumed was tri-invisible ink.

"It's a kind of code," Lucy explained. "If you type it into the web site you get another number that lets you prove that you were the winner."

"You built your own web site for this?"

She shook her head, amused. "It's for anyone. Tris play something similar, but they usually do it with GPS and AR: there are no real-world clues, but you can see them with your phone or your glasses."

"So do you stay here and watch?" I asked. "See how long people take?"

"Sometimes. We can do that if you like."

We sat on a bench with a view of the hiding place. Fifteen minutes later, a skinny young boy on a skateboard rolled up and went straight for the prize.

When he'd retrieved it, Lucy cupped her hands around her mouth and called out to him, "Well done, Tim!"

Tim skated across the courtyard to join us, thumbing numbers into his phone as he went. He looked about ten, which made me uneasy; Sean had implied that there was some unwritten code fixing the minimum age for the hack at twelve.

As Lucy was introducing us, two other competitors showed up. Before long there were a dozen people gathered around the bench, debating the merits of the hunt and cracking the kind of jokes about the ramshackle city and its hapless tris that would have been wasted in any other company. Tim was the youngest, but I'd have guessed that nobody was older than fourteen. I stayed quiet, conscious of my position as a newcomer, though nobody showed any sign of snubbing me.

As the afternoon wore on and people left, the dome of the sky seemed tinged with melancholy. When only Lucy and I were left, she read my thoughts.

"You think you've lost all your old friends," she said. "And a few random heps are no replacement."

I shrugged, embarrassed.

"You haven't lost anyone," she said. "It's good to get together with the rainbow crowd, but no one's forcing you to be a snob about it. Would your friends have dumped you if you'd gone blind?"

I shook my head, ashamed. "Have you told anyone?" I asked her. "Any of your tri friends?"

"No. But I still hang out with them. I just have to hold my tongue and not offer too many fashion tips."

Her own clothing appeared as grimy as anyone else's—and the technology to make it otherwise probably didn't exist outside of NASA clean rooms—but I could see her harmonious choices in the elements she could control.

"We do this on the first Sunday of every month," she said. "Tim will be marking the course next time—but if you like, we could team up and follow the clues together."

I said, "That sounds good."

2

"Call," I declared. If I couldn't quite keep my tone neutral, the faint tell in my voice sounded more like fear than confidence. Danny could only make three of a kind, and Cheng the same—albeit higher—while the dark-eyed woman who never gave her name could rise above them both with a straight. Everyone else at the table had folded, some of them needlessly. In that company, my own modest flush was a sure bet, but the last thing I felt was invincible.

Danny folded. Cheng raised the bet by fifty, then the dark-eyed woman raised it another fifty.

I agonized for five long seconds. My rule was never to win more than a thousand a night, and this would push me over the limit. But if I folded now, I would have spent eight hours in this dispiriting place for the sake of just three hundred dollars.

I slid my chips forward, matching the bet. Cheng shot an irritated glance my way, and folded.

The dark-eyed woman raised, again. Her face was so impassive that I began to doubt, if not the evidence of my own eyes, that of my memory. I didn't dare glance down at the backs of her cards again, but I was certain that one bore the twisted-hour-glass stain in the lacquer that I'd noticed on the five of clubs in the showdown-before-last, while the other had a florid tint to half its royal blue ink that had been unmissable when the six of hearts had come my way much earlier in the night. In this back-alley game they did not change the decks between every hand, and even if I could have missed the dealer feeding a fresh pack into the shuffling machine, no two decks ever featured identical flaws. So either I'd grown confused as to the significance of the blemishes I'd seen, or my opponent was very good at bluffing.

"I'll match," I said, offering up the chips.

The dark-eyed woman allowed herself a triumphant smile as she showed her cards: five of clubs, six of hearts. With the seven, eight and nine of diamonds in the flop she had a straight, but nothing better.

The relief on my own face wasn't feigned. I turned up my three and six of diamonds. The woman's lingering smile made me wonder if the loss had even registered before the dealer raked the pot and sent the rest in my direction, but perhaps the secret to her bluff had been a kind of self-hypnotic conviction that her hand was unbeatable, and it took a few seconds to snap out of it and allow the truth to sink in.

I scooped up my winnings and rose from the table.

"Hey, Jake!" Danny was scowling at me. "Give me a chance to win it back!" He was drunk, and he hadn't done well all night. I checked my watch and shook my head apologetically. "Next week, I promise."

I took my chips to the cashier, and glanced back at the table. Danny was staying put, to try his luck with the late crowd.

As I walked to my car, I skirted three glistening patches on the ground. The street lights were sparse here, but the neon fronts of the nightclubs in the adjoining strip were enough to illuminate the residual blood stains that spring rain seemed merely to rearrange, and no tri felt compelled to scrub away.

It was almost 4 a.m. when I got home, but Lucy was still up. "How'd it go?" she asked.

I showed her my winnings, fanning out the notes so she could count them at a glance.

Lucy had had her misgivings from the start, but now she seemed more anxious than ever. "I don't want you ending up in prison. Or worse."

"It wouldn't come to that. There's nothing they could prove; they'd just ban me." I slumped onto the couch. "You should be in bed," I chided her. Unless I'd become so confused by the card room's time-distorting ambience that I'd lost a day, she was due at work in less than five hours.

"And what if you do get banned?" she persisted.

"I never win enough to look suspicious." Heps were far too rare to pose much of a threat, and even the high-end casinos could hardly scan everyone's skulls with MRI machines. The small games I joined were run by people who were very far from amateurs, but so long as I could retain enough self-discipline not to overplay my advantage, I felt sure that I could hide in the statistical shadows of the merely lucky.

Lucy said, "The gallery's letting me go at the end of the month."

That shook me. Whatever fate I was courting, her own use of her talents could not have been more honest. "What are they going to replace you with—a mass spectrometer?"

"Not quite," she replied. "But there's some new software that pretty much does what I do, with a multispectral camera and brushstroke analysis. They can lease the whole thing for a tenth of my salary."

The gallery had only given her three days a week since she'd come back from maternity leave, but she still earned about as much as I dared acquire by my own methods.

"We're such fuck-ups," she said angrily.

"That's not true."

She turned away from me and gazed with loathing at one of her own paintings: a city threatened by fire, the skyscrapers scintillating through the smoke haze, every blistering current of air as palpable as the freeways below. "I kept kidding myself that I had a foot in the door—but I might as well have been a kitchen-hand, pretending that I was on some fast-track to chef just because I could sniff out bad produce a little sooner than anyone else."

"So they've found some machine to help them assess provenance," I said. "That doesn't take anything away from your paintings."

Lucy laughed bitterly. "If I couldn't sell anything even when I had connections, what do you think my chances are going to be now?"

"What are you saying?" I pressed her, aiming for a gently skeptical tone. "It's all down to nepotism?"

"No," she admitted. "The work does matter. But it's going to be harder than ever to get it seen."

I was trying to be the voice of reason, calmly talking her back from the edge—but the trouble was, she understood the problems she was facing far better than I did. "For an art dealer to look at a painting is some kind of special favor?"

"Yes," Lucy declared bluntly. "For a tri to look carefully enough to see a tenth of what's there takes something special. That doesn't happen as a matter of course."

I spread my arms in resignation, and went to take a shower.

On my way to bed, I looked in on Zelda. She'd slept through all the talking, and I resisted the urge to lean down and kiss her lest she wake and start bawling.

Zelda was almost six months old—so we only had six more to decide whether or not to give her the gene therapy vector. After that point, the quality of the repaired retinal cells would start to fall off with time. If she was going to be a tri at all I wanted her at least to have the sharpest vision that state could entail.

Five years before, when I'd moved in with Lucy, we'd sworn that we'd never sentence our children to live in the flat, cartoonish world that we'd escaped. But while Sean was still winning titles as a pro surfer, most of us had ended up struggling, thwarted or resentful. When I could count the number of heps I'd grown up with who had truly flourished on the fingers of one hand, how could I bequeath the same prospects to my daughter?

"I'll see that, and I'll raise you fifty," Marcus announced. I'd folded a few rounds ago, after forcing myself to stay in and lose a little for appearances' sake. Now there were only two players left, and they seemed to be intent on a game of chicken.

"I'll match," Danny replied. His hand was terrible, but at some point he must have convinced himself that he could bluff his way to victory, and having chosen that strategy he was too stubborn to veer off course.

Marcus raised another fifty.

"Fuck you," Danny whispered, and matched the bet.

I watched them with a growing sense of dread, willing Marcus to back down. I hadn't set eyes on him before that night, so I could still imagine that it was possible. Danny would just keep charging ahead like a freight train.

"I guess I'll have to raise you again," Marcus taunted him.

Danny slid the last of his chips forward. "Matched."

Marcus hesitated. "I'm good," he decided.

Danny laid down his pair of nines, which made two pairs beside the kings in the flop. Marcus had a king and queen in the hole, giving him trips; I could have made the same, but only with sevens. Everyone else had had rubbish.

The dealer took the house cut and slid the rest toward Marcus.

"Cheat," Danny said softly.

"Excuse me?" Marcus smiled and looked around the table; no one was backing Danny. "You should call it a night. Come back when your luck's better."

Danny leaned forward. "Risk all that on a trip? I don't think so."

The dealer said, "Sir, please."

Marcus gave an indignant bark of a laugh. "And look at what you risked the same on!"

"But you didn't need to," Danny countered. "If you'd raised again, you knew I couldn't match it."

"I didn't know what was in your wallet!" Marcus blustered. "You could have borrowed from someone—I'm not a mind reader!" I could see the blood draining from his face, and I understood: somehow, he really had known Danny's hand all along. And he'd betrayed himself, just so he could twist the knife.

Danny reached across the table and plucked Marcus's glasses from his face, like some curiously gentlemanly preamble to a pounding. The dealer raised his hand to summon a bouncer, but Danny didn't hit anyone, he simply perched the glasses on his own nose and looked down at the table.

"I knew it!" he declared triumphantly. He removed the glasses and offered them to the dealer. "Every card has a number in green!"

The dealer hesitated, then tried on the glasses for himself. "OK," he said nervously. "Everyone stay seated. The game's annulled, and you're all getting your bets returned."

Two bouncers and the manager joined us as the eye-in-the-sky vision was replayed and the chips were redistributed. Marcus sat in silence, his face blotched with fear. I knew the cards weren't marked with any kind of dye: his glasses had to be finding the same pre-existing subtleties as I was, then making the job easier for him by numbering the patterns in an overlay laser-painted on his retinas. I'd noticed the small dark circle in the center of the bridge, but I hadn't given it much thought—molded plastic always came with all kinds of odd impressions that its makers fancied were invisible. It was clear now, though, exactly what it was: a tiny multispectral camera, with sensors exactly like the ones in my own eyes.

When I got home the apartment was in darkness, so I took off my shoes and sat in the living room, planning to sleep on the couch. I was only twenty-nine; my life was hardly over. Thousands of people slacked off in high school, dropped out of university, quit their first few jobs . . . and still found a way to succeed in the end. If I'd wanted the one thing that lifted me above the crowd to be part of the answer, too bad. No one was going to pay me to see the world more clearly than they did—let alone stand by and let me use that talent to fleece them. Lucy could paint her paintings for our tiny circle of hep friends, and we could walk side by side marveling at the beauty of the sea and the sky and the squalor of the city. But in the end our powers of vision would die with us, outsourced entirely to unthinking machines.

"The ship is going down, and you only have time to grab one item and take it with you to the lifeboat: a sheet of plastic, a mirror, and a compass. Which do you choose?"

My interviewer leaned forward expectantly, his hand paused above his notepad.

I said, "This is a shelf-stacking job. I'm not applying to the ocean cruise department."

"Just say, 'plastic, to collect rainwater,'" he replied wearily. "Didn't you Google the answers before you came?"

"Plastic, to collect rainwater."

He tapped the final box, and I heard a somber chime.

"I'm sorry," he said. "You didn't make the cut."

"Why not?"

He glanced down at the screen. "No stability in your employment history. And honestly, you're too old."

I looked around his office, desperate for an idea. A poster showed a celebrity chef reaching down into a carton of plump apricots—though even a tri couldn't have missed the bizarre retouching of the fruits' appearance. "Can I show you something?" I offered. "In the produce aisles?"

"What are you talking about?"

"I could save the company thousands of dollars a month," I boasted. "If something's on the verge of going rotten, or infested with insects—"

My interviewer was smiling. He shook his head in disbelief, or perhaps a trace of admiration at my chutzpah.

He said, "Sorry, we already have that app."

I looked up the app. It wouldn't work on older phones, like my own, but the very latest models now carried reconfigurable quantum dot cameras as standard. It was not just art galleries and DIY-card-sharks who could access the whole spectrum; early adopters could do it already, and in five years it would be ubiquitous. Phones, notepads, glasses—every small, cheap camera would soon be seeing more of the world than its human owner.

After Lucy's last day at the gallery, her colleagues took us out to dinner. I sat watching them, feigning bonhomie, laughing when everyone else laughed. One man took a photograph of his steak to assess its rareness and quantify the risk of food poisoning. A woman looked around furtively then snapped the dessert, in the hope of recreating it at home. These people would never learn to see the world for themselves—but they were already accustomed to asking their gadgets to advise them every few minutes.

Lucy glared at me as if I was someone's mad uncle at a wake.

My mother had watched Zelda for us. When Lucy and I were alone, I said, "Remember the treasure hunts?"

She groaned. "Oh, please—not the good old days!"

I said, "Do you still have the recipes? For the inks you used?"

"Why?" Then she understood. "It would only be a fad," she said. "A novelty. We'd be lucky if it lasted a year."

"A fad can make a lot of money in a year. Software, posters, spray-cans, marker pens, clothing, tattoos. A whole secret world that's hidden from ordinary eyes—but not some virtual reality overlay: solid objects you can touch with your bare hands."

Lucy was skeptical. "And whose kidney are you going to sell to fund this empire?"

I said, "We're going to need a backer. Someone who'll understand the idea. So let's hope my cousin hasn't blown all his prize money."

3

Zelda stretched her arms above her head and waved her hands at me impatiently. "Lift me, Daddy!" She wouldn't let me carry her comfortably on my hip, or even riding on my shoulders: she had to be gripped under the arms and held up at chest height, half a meter ahead of me, like a kind of advanced scout, seeing everything moments before I did.

"You're getting too old for this," I told her, as I staggered through the gallery's automatic doors.

"No, you are!"

"That's true as well."

I put her down and she ran toward Lucy, stopping shyly at the sight of the two strangers talking with her mother. Lucy smiled at her, and so did the customers, but then they all turned back to the painting.

"You've captured the river perfectly!" the woman marveled, making a sliding gesture beside her glasses to shift between false-color renderings. "Whatever wavelengths I map . . . the natural detail's there."

"That's what I was aiming for," Lucy replied.

"How long did it take you?" the woman's partner asked.

"About a year." Lucy glanced at me, but I kept a poker face.

"I can believe that."

I stood back and waited for her to clinch the sale.

Tris can never really join us in the wider world, but having learned to peek out through the keyhole of their prison and take in the view incrementally, they're no longer willing to spend their whole lives staring at the blank stone walls. The individual gimmicks come and go: the TV shows with points of view mimicking multispectral glasses, the plays where the actors have trained to emote with their capillaries for suitably equipped audiences, the advertising signs with secret messages that seem more profound and persuasive after the five-second hunt across the rainbow that it takes to reveal them. And the need—among the sufficiently wealthy—to hang a picture on the wall that actually resembles the thing it portrays.

When the customers had left with their painting, Lucy took off her shoes and sat down wearily on the gallery's fashionably white bench. It was covered with her buttock-prints—and mine—but we varied the location to form a tasteful pattern.

"I want to do some drawings," Zelda demanded.

Lucy sighed, feigning reluctance, but then she fetched a stack of paper and the bucket of pencils she kept out in the back. Zelda sat on the floor, carefully choosing among the six hundred hues on offer. She drew a garden of striped flowers, three stick figures with wildly mottled faces, and then above it all began meticulously shading in the bands of an eleven o'clock sky.

ABOUT THE AUTHORS

Madeline Ashby is a science fiction writer, speaker, and strategic foresight consultant living in Toronto. Currently, she works developing user stories for provisional patents related to brainwave-sensing wearable technology. She is the author of the Machine Dynasty series of novels from Angry Robot Books. "Come From Away" is a chapter in her new novel *Company Town*, available in the autumn of 2014. Her short fiction has appeared at *Escape Pod, FLURB, The Tomorrow Project*, and multiple anthologies. Her essays have appeared at *BoingBoing, io9.com*, and *Tor.com*. You can find her at madelineashby.com, or on Twitter @MadelineAshby.

Elizabeth Bear was born on the same day as Frodo and Bilbo Baggins, but in a different year. When coupled with a childhood tendency to read the dictionary for fun, this led her inevitably to penury, intransigence, and the writing of speculative fiction. She is the Hugo, Sturgeon, Locus, and Campbell Award winning author of twenty-five novels and over a hundred short stories. Her dog lives in Massachusetts; her partner, writer Scott Lynch, lives in Wisconsin. She spends a lot of time on planes.

Born in the Caribbean, **Tobias S. Buckell** is a *New York Times* bestselling author. His novels and over fifty stories have been translated into seventeen languages. He has been nominated for the Hugo, Nebula, and John W. Campbell Award for Best New Science Fiction Author. He currently lives in Ohio and can be found online at www.TobiasBuckell.com

Helena Bell lives in Raleigh, North Carolina where she is an MFA candidate in Fiction at NC State University. She has a BA, another MFA, a JD, and an LLM in Taxation which fulfills her lifelong ambition of having more letters follow her name than are actually in it. She is a graduate of the Clarion West Writers Workshop and her stories have appeared in *Clarkesworld, The Dark*, and *Shimmer*.

Erin Cashier is a registered nurse and has had short stories published in *Beneath Ceaseless Skies, Shimmer*, and *Writers of the Future*. As Cassie Alexander she's the author of the Edie Spence urban fantasy series. She lives in the Bay Area with her husband.

Jason K. Chapman lives in New York City where, as the Director of IT and Web Development for *Poets & Writers*, he gets to indulge his two main interests, computers and literature. His fiction has appeared in a number of anthologies and magazines, including *Clarkesworld*, *Asimov's*, *Bull Spec*, and *Cosmos*.

Seth Dickinson's fiction has appeared in *Clarkesworld*, *Analog*, *Strange Horizons*, and more. He is a writer at Bungie Studios, an instructor at the Alpha Workshop for Young Writers, and a lapsed student of social neuroscience. His first novel will be published by Tor Books in fall 2015.

Greg Egan was born in 1961. Since the early '80s he has published twelve novels and more than fifty short stories, winning the Hugo Award for his novella "Oceanic" and the John W. Campbell Memorial Award for his novel *Permutation City*. His latest book is *The Arrows of Time*, the concluding volume of the Orthogonal trilogy.

Amanda Forrest is a programmer, mother, writer and adventurer. She is currently learning the art of stone masonry in hopes of building a backyard castle. Though she is not, unfortunately, a cyborg, she once had a cat with titanium skeletal augmentations.

Amanda's fiction has recently appeared in or is forthcoming in *Asimov's Science Fiction*, *Apex*, and the *Writers of the Future* anthology.

Author and video game designer **Erin Hoffman** was born in San Diego and now lives in northern California, where she works as Game Design Lead at the GlassLab, a nonprofit video game studio building big-data-powered educational games that digitally adapt to the learner. She is the author of the Chaos Knight series from Pyr books, beginning with *Sword of Fire and Sea*, followed by *Lance of Earth and Sky* and concluding with *Shield of Sea and Space*. Her short fiction and poetry have appeared in *Asimov's Science Fiction*, *Electric Velocipede*, *Tor.com*, and more. For more information, visit www.erinhoffman.com and Twitter @gryphoness.

As an undergraduate, **Ms. Xia** majored in Atmospheric Sciences at Peking University. She then entered the Film Studies Program at the Communication University of China, where she completed her Master's thesis, "A Study on Female Figures in Science Fiction Films." Recently, she obtained a Ph.D. in Comparative Literature and World Literature at Peking University, with "Chinese Science Fiction and Cultural Politics Since 1990" as the topic of her dissertation.

She has been publishing science fiction and fantasy since 2004 in a variety of venues, including *Science Fiction World* and *Jiuzhou Fantasy*. Several of her stories have won the Galaxy Award, China's most prestigious science fiction award. Besides writing and translating science fiction stories, she also writes film scripts and teaches science fiction writing.

Rich Larson was born in West Africa, has studied in Rhode Island, and at twenty-two now lives in Edmonton, Alberta. He won the 2014 Dell Award and the 2012 Rannu Prize for Writers of Speculative Fiction. In 2011 his cyberpunk novel *Devolution* was a finalist for the Amazon Breakthrough Novel Award. His short work appears or is forthcoming with *Asimov's, Lightspeed, DSF, Strange Horizons, Apex Magazine, Beneath Ceaseless Skies, AE* and many others, including anthologies *Futuredaze* and *War Stories*. His self-published spec-fic can be found at Amazon.com/author/richlarson.

Yoon Ha Lee's fiction has appeared in *Clarkesworld, Tor.com, The Magazine of Fantasy and Science Fiction, Lightspeed,* and other venues. Her collection *Conservation of Shadows* came out from Prime Books in 2013. She lives in Louisiana with her family and has not yet been eaten by gators, cyborg or otherwise.

Ken Liu (kenliu.name) is an author and translator of speculative fiction, as well as a lawyer and programmer. A winner of the Nebula, Hugo, and World Fantasy Awards, he has been published in *The Magazine of Fantasy & Science Fiction, Asimov's, Analog, Clarkesworld, Lightspeed,* and *Strange Horizons,* among other places. He lives with his family near Boston, Massachusetts.

Ken's debut novel, *The Grace of Kings*, the first in a silkpunk epic fantasy series, will be published by Saga Press, Simon & Schuster's new genre fiction imprint, in April 2015. Saga will also publish a collection of his short stories.

Alex Dally MacFarlane is a writer, editor and historian. When not researching narrative maps in the legendary traditions of Alexander III of Macedon, she writes stories, found in *Clarkesworld Magazine, Interfictions Online, Strange Horizons, Beneath Ceaseless Skies* and the anthologies *Solaris Rising 3, Gigantic Worlds, Phantasm Japan, Heiresses of Russ 2013: The Year's Best Lesbian Speculative Fiction* and *The Year's Best Science Fiction & Fantasy: 2014*. Poetry can be found in *Stone Telling, The Moment of Change* and *Here, We Cross*. She is the editor of *Aliens: Recent Encounters* (2013) and *The Mammoth Book of SF Stories by Women* (2014).

Greg Mellor is an Australian author with fifty published short stories. His work has appeared in *Clarkesworld Magazine, Cosmos Magazine* and *Aurealis* as well as several anthologies in Australia and the United States. His debut collection of short SF stories *Wild Chrome* was published in 2012 and his first SF novella *Steel Angels* will be out in 2014.

Greg holds degrees in astrophysics and technology management. He is a member of SFWA. Visit www.gregmellor.com.

Mari Ness hasn't quite managed to wire herself directly to her computer, but that's not for lack of trying. Her poetry and short fiction have appeared in numerous publications, including *Clarkesworld, Tor.com, Apex Magazine, Daily Science Fiction,* and *Strange Horizons.* For a longer list, check out her official blog at marikness.wordpress.com. She lives in central Florida, occasionally twittering about what she's up to at mari_ness.

Chen Qiufan (a.k.a. Stanley Chan) was born in Shantou, Guangdong Province. Chan is a science fiction writer, columnist, and online advertising strategist. Since 2004, he has published over thirty stories in venues such as *Science Fiction World, Esquire, Chutzpah!,* many of which are collected in *Thin Code* (2012). His debut novel, *The Waste Tide,* was published in January 2013 and was praised by Liu Cixin as "the pinnacle of near-future SF writing." The novel is currently being translated into English by Ken Liu.

Chan is the most widely translated young writer of science fiction in China, with his short works translated into English, Italian, Swedish, and Polish and published in *Clarkesworld, Lightspeed, Interzone,* and *F&SF,* among other places. He has won Taiwan's Dragon Fantasy Award, China's Galaxy and Nebula Awards, and a Science Fiction & Fantasy Translation Award along with Ken Liu. He lives in Beijing and works for Baidu.

Robert Reed has had eleven novels published, starting with *The Leeshore* in 1987 and most recently with *The Well of Stars* in 2004. Since winning the first annual L. Ron Hubbard Writers of the Future contest in 1986 (under the pen name Robert Touzalin) and being a finalist for the John W. Campbell Award for best new writer in 1987, he has had over two hundred shorter works published in a variety of magazines and anthologies. Eleven of those stories were published in his critically acclaimed first collection, *The Dragons of Springplace,* in 1999. Twelve more stories appear in his second collection, *The Cuckoo's Boys* [2005]. In addition to his success in the U.S., Reed has also been published in the U.K., Russia, Japan, Spain and in France, where a second (French-language) collection of nine of his shorter works, *Chrysalide,* was released in 2002. Bob has had stories appear in at least one of the annual "Year's Best" anthologies in every year since 1992. Bob has received nominations for both the Nebula Award (nominated and voted upon by genre authors) and the Hugo Award (nominated and voted upon by fans), as well as numerous other literary awards. He won his first Hugo Award for the 2006 novella *A Billion Eves.* His most recent novel is *The Memory of Sky,* a Great Ship trilogy.

Benjanun Sriduangkaew is a finalist for the Campbell Award for Best New Writer. Her short fiction has appeared in *Tor.com, Clarkesworld, Beneath Ceaseless Skies, Phantasm Japan,* various Mammoth Books and best of the year collections. Her contemporary fantasy novella *Scale-Bright* is forthcoming from Immersion Press. She can be found online at beekian.wordpress.com.

Rachel Swirsky holds an MFA from the Iowa Writers Workshop where she learned that snow is only fun and beautiful for a couple of days at a time. She currently lives in Bakersfield with her husband where she's learning that sunny days are great, but they would be even better if it rained occasionally. In a few years, she plans to move to the North pole, or possibly into a lava flow.

Her short fiction has appeared in numerous magazines and anthologies, and been nominated for a number of awards, including the Hugo Award, the Locus Award, the Sturgeon and the World Fantasy Award. In 2010, she won the Nebula for her novella "The Lady Who Plucked Red Flowers Beneath the Queen's Window" and in 2013, she won it a second time for her short story "If You Were a Dinosaur, My Love." Her second collection, *How the World Became Quiet: Myths of the Past, Present, and Future,* came out from Subterranean Press in 2013. Although she used to own rats, they were not genetically engineered to imagine spaceships, so they just built sailboats instead.

E. Catherine Tobler was born on the other side of the International Dateline, which either gives her an extra day in her life or an extraordinary affinity when it comes to inter-dimensional gateways. She is a Sturgeon Award finalist, the senior editor at *Shimmer Magazine,* and her debut novel, *Rings of Anubis,* arrives in paperback this summer. Her short fiction appears in *Clarkesworld, Strange Horizons,* and *Lightspeed,* among others.

Genevieve Valentine's first novel, *Mechanique: A Tale of the Circus Tresaulti,* won the 2012 Crawford Award and was nominated for the Nebula. Her second novel is the historical fairy-tale retelling *The Girls at the Kingfisher Club.* Her short fiction has appeared in *Clarkesworld, Strange Horizons, Journal of Mythic Arts, Lightspeed,* and others, and the anthologies *Federations, The Living Dead 2, After, Teeth,* and more. Her nonfiction and reviews have appeared at NPR.org, *The AV Club, Strange Horizons, io9.com,* and *LA Review of Books,* and others.

Peter Watts—author of *Blindsight, Echopraxia,* and the Rifters Trilogy, among other things—seems especially popular among people who don't know him. At least, he wins most of his awards overseas except for a Hugo (won thanks to fan outrage over an altercation with Homeland Security) a Jackson (won thanks to fan sympathy over nearly dying from flesh-eating disease), and a couple of dick-ass Canadian awards you've probably never heard of. *Blindsight* is a core text for university courses ranging from Philosophy to Neuropsychology, despite an unhealthy focus on space vampires. Watts's work is available in eighteen languages.

A.C. Wise was born and raised in Montreal and currently lives in the Philadelphia area. Her fiction has appeared in *Clarkesworld, Shimmer, Lightspeed,* and *The Best Horror of the Year Vol. 4,* among other publications. In addition to her writing, she co-edits *Unlikely Story.* Visit the author online at acwise.net or find her on twitter as @ac_wise.

E. Lily Yu was the 2012 recipient of the John W. Campbell Award for Best New Writer and a 2012 Hugo, Nebula, and World Fantasy Award nominee. Her stories have recently appeared in *McSweeney's, Clarkesworld, Boston Review,* and *Apex.*

ABOUT THE EDITOR

Neil Clarke is the Editor-in-Chief and Publisher of *Clarkesworld Magazine*. His work at *Clarkesworld* has resulted in countless hours of enjoyment, three Hugo Awards for Best Semiprozine and four World Fantasy Award nominations. He's a current and three-time Hugo Nominee for Best Editor (Short Form). In 2012, Neil suffered a near-fatal "widow-maker" heart attack which led to the installation of a defibrillator and a new life as a cyborg. Inspired by these events, he decided to take on this anthology, his first non-*Clarkesworld* editing project. He currently lives in NJ with his wife and two sons.

ALSO EDITED BY NEIL CLARKE

Clarkesworld Magazine - clarkesworldmagazine.com

CLARKESWORLD ANTHOLOGIES

Clarkesworld: Year Three (with Sean Wallace)
Clarkesworld: Year Four (with Sean Wallace)
Clarkesworld: Year Five (with Sean Wallace)
Clarkesworld: Year Six (with Sean Wallace)

ACKNOWLEDGMENTS

The doctors may have fixed me, but I am **better** thanks to Lisa, Aidan, Eamonn, Mom, Dad, and the rest of my family.

This book is **stronger** thanks to the authors, Julie Dillon, Sean Wallace, Kate Baker, and Aimee Picci.

I'm still not **faster**. Maybe next time.

I also owe a special debt of gratitude to the following honorary cyborgs:

@guildner • 4 of 5 Ondrusek • A. T. Greenblatt • A.C. Wise • Aaron Sunbeam • Adam "Spurious Laser Blasts" Hill • Adam Haley • Adam Israel • Adam L. Crouse • Aeonsim • AJ Harm • Alan Dyck • Alec G • Alex Burkhart • Alex Shvartsman • Alex von der Linden • Alexandra Pierce • Alicia Cole • Allison • Andrew Hatchell • Andrew Liptak • Andrew Nicolle • Andy Dent • Andy Vasbinder • Ann Humphrey • Annie Bellet • Anthony Petros • Anthony R. Cardno • Aptasi • Arachne Jericho • Arkady Martine • Bartley J Bear • battlegrip.com • Benjamin Sparrow • Bill and Laura Pearson • Brad Roberts • BrentonRyan • Brian Anderson • Brian White • Brood II Cicadas • Can Özmen • Carl Hazen • Carl V. Anderson • Carlos Hernandez • Cathy Green • chaosprime • Charles Fraker • Chris Rees • Christian Schaller • Christopher J. Burke • Claire Alcock • Claire Connelly • Claire LaPlaca and Hugh Brammer • Claudio Bottaccini • Cliff Miller • Cliff Winnig • Connor Grogan • Crossed Genres Publications • Danielle M. LeFevre • Dave Costa • Dave McCarty • David Churn • David Kelleher • David McIntyre • David P. • David Potter • David Stegora • Davy De Vuysdere • Dawn Aylene Tarpinian • Douglas "Strange Quark" Reed • E C Humphries • Edward MacGregor • Eli Juicy Jones • EliteMachina • Eric Kent Edstrom • Erik Henriksen • Erik Saltwell • Evaristo Ramos, Jr. • Ferran Selles • Forth • Fran Friel • Frank Dreier • Franny Jay • Gail McDonald • Gary Emmette Chandler • Gary M Dockter • Ginger Joe • Glennis LeBlanc • Gopakumar Sethuraman • Graeme Williams • Guy Anthony De Marco • Hayley Marsden • Henry Szabranski • Herbert Eder • Howard Henry • Ian Peters • Ief Grootaers • James "Optimus" Aquilone • James Carlisle Holder

ACKNOWLEDGMENTS

• James Darrow • James Kelly • James Seals • James Zirkle • Jamie Lackey • Jason Heller • Jason R. Strawsburg • Jay Watson • Jay Wolf • Jeff Xilon • Jen Scott • Jennifer Kahng • Jennifer Morton • Jim DeVona • JoanneBB • John Devenny • John Klima • Jon Lasser • Jonathan "Robo-Ankle" Pruett • Joshua Palmatier • Julie Ann Koehlinger • Jurie Horneman • Justin James • Justin Minnes • Justin P. Miller • JW • Karin W • Karsten mark H • Kate Kligman • Katharine • Keith West • Kelly Stiles • Ken Schneyer • Kevin Baijens • Kristin Evenson Hirst, Bionic Valkyrie • Krystina Colton • Lamat • Leesa Hanagan • Linda Wilcox • Lucas K. Law • Lucius M. Nelligan Sorrentino • Lyn Dunagan • Mairin Holmes • Marc Jacobs • Mark "the Encaffeinated ONE" Kilfoil • Mark J McGarry • Martin Cahill • Mathew Holland • Matt Gibbs • Matthew Kressel • Matthew Morrison • Max Edwards • Max Kaehn • Meagen Voss • Merc Rustad • Meryl Yourish • Michael Ezell • Michael Gray • Michael Horwitz • Michael John • Michael Scholl • Michelle Muenzler • Mike Griffiths • Miles Matton • Natalie Luhrs • Nathan Blumenfeld • Nayad Monroe • Neal Levin • Nick Bate • Nicola Owen • P Carreiro • P S Proefrock • Patrick J Sklar • Patrick Nijman • Patrick Reitz • Patrick Zazzaro • Paul McMullen • Penny Richards • Peter Hollo • Peter Young • Pierre Gauthier • Ray and Tina • Rebecca Harbison • Rich McGuire • Rich Russell • Richard Ellis Preston, Jr. • Richard Pratt • Rob Leslie • Robert Davis • Ronald R. Richter • Ryan Paul • S. Michael White • Sarah Liberman • Sean Krauss • Shauna Roberts • Sleeperwaking • Stephanie Lucas • Stephanie R • Steve Pantol • Steven desJardins • Steven Mentzel • Stewart C Baker, Smiter of Things, Librarian of Other Things, Poet of Poetic Things, First of His Name • Suz Bailey • Suzanne Conboy-Hill • Tania Clucas • The Cat With Blue Fur • The Judge • The Rosenthal Collective • Tiffany E. Wilson • Tim Ream • Timothy Moore • TK • Tom Foster • Tom Horwath • Tom Vogl • Travis Heermann • TwistedSciFi.com • Val Grimm • Valerie Gillis • Victor De Ville • Vincent O'Connor • way ming wong • William "Broken" Owen • William Gunderson • Y. K. Lee • Yes (Evgeni Kantor) • Zuhur Abdo

THREE-TIME HUGO AWARD-WINNER

Clarkesworld Magazine

Digital subscriptions are available from Amazon, Apple
Newsstand, Google Play, and Weightless Books

Details here:
clarkesworldmagazine.com/subscribe

ALSO FROM WYRM PUBLISHING

Trade Paperback | 293 Pages | 978-1-809464-24-0 | $14.95

Clarkesworld: Year Five collects all twenty-four stories from *Clarkesworld Magazine's* fifth year of publications. Included in this volume are stories by N. K. Jemisin, Yoon Ha Lee, Ken Liu, Nnedi Okorafor, Robert Reed, E. Lily Yu, and many more!

ALSO FROM WYRM PUBLISHING

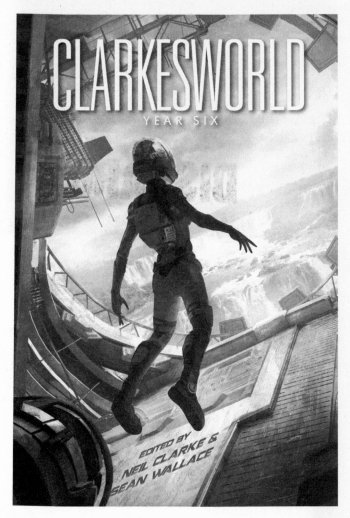

Trade Paperback | 427 Pages | 978-1-809464-26-4 | $16.95

Clarkesworld: Year Six collects all thirty-four stories from *Clarkesworld Magazine's* sixth year of publications. Included in this volume are stories by Aliette de Bodard, Tobias S. Buckell, Kij Johnson, Robert Reed, Lavie Tidhar, Catherynne M. Valente, Carrie Vaughn, and many more!